Space Rabbits!

Tooky as a baby bunny. Tooky appears on our Front Cover as a fully-grown young Space-Rabbit. He is the forerunner of a new tribe of gifted super-rabbits with unique abilities.

Space Rabbits!

A Cosmic Adventure!

DEREK V. EVERARD

Order this book online at www.trafford.com
or email orders@trafford.com

Most Trafford titles are also available at major online book retailers.

Printed in the United States of America.

ISBN: 978-1-4907-4304-2 (sc)
ISBN: 978-1-4907-4305-9 (hc)
ISBN: 978-1-4907-4306-6 (e)

Library of Congress Control Number: 2014914121

Trafford rev. 08/07/2014

www.trafford.com

North America & international
toll-free: 1 888 232 4444 (USA & Canada)
fax: 812 355 4082

A young Hill-Clan bunny.

Other books by author

Little Boy Wild — 2006.

www.littleboywild.com

The Wiser-Mouse Legacy. 2012. 2014.

www.wiser-mouse.com

Table of Contents

Acknowledgements

Throughout this intriguing journey I need to express my gratitude to the Hill-Clan Tribe of Rabbits for accepting me as one of their own. It enabled me to be privy to the more advanced rabbits' cosmic aspirations. This type of active collaboration can only be achieved through endowed universal wisdom. Having long lived in the space-time of the natural wilderness—sharing life with creatures at every level of cosmic unity—I felt honored and humble to act as an observer with the Rabbits.

My heartfelt thanks go to the excellent photographers I met through Shutterstock Photo and Thinkstock photo. Their dedicated efforts bridged continents as we came together to capture many images of the Space-Rabbits. A mere few bunnies were selected to give the reader the core-feeling of living among the key characters in our unusual adventures. As a life-long wild-life photographer myself, I see through the same eyes as our professional contributors—each instant of time, light and image, just as it was taken—with love and great care!

It was not possible to acquire photos of our Rat-Star participants. We discovered that the golden-furred flying space-rats were not always as solid and molecular as they appeared—but were in reality—advanced types of Beings—beyond that which we might describe conceptually as holographic in nature. Based on oscillatory and frequency factors—although their bodies were elementally 'normal'—they were not backwards-compatible so as to be recorded with our current equipment known as 'photographic'. However, the way I have described them may suffice in place of images.

We were fortunate in discovering Zack—the wilding—appear among the rabbits and wild strawberries when we did. Zack was and is—a 'work in progress'. He is a 'Phoenix-Boy', whom we trust, in time, will overcome his disastrous experiences with the Humans which spanned his young life. I'm also grateful that Zack felt free to briefly mention his 'dissociation'; wherein he opts-out of reality when his psychic pain levels become too high to handle. Interestingly, in all innocence—he assumes this is a normal behavioral response for everyone!

Finally, our thanks to Shendra Hanney for her critique of the manuscript. Shendra's invaluable insight into matters of continuity—born out of her experience with film and video productions added a significant contribution to our textual flow.

Timken — the bunny who 'appeared' and claimed he could fly!

Chapter One

It was another warm blue-sky day. Buttercups and daisies carpeted their early summer colors across the meadows and hills almost as far as the eye could see. Dawn as always had gifted the day with limitless possibilities, each of them a creation awaiting unfoldment into reality. In fact, their very discovery brought them into 'being' so naturally, it seemed they always 'were'. In Rabbit Land it all started out like things usually do, they sort of 'just are'. Today, it was *HE* who was an exciting surprise! Right out of nowhere, the strange rabbit had appeared. First he was *'not'*, and then he *'was'*.

The new rabbit was very small and extremely timid; and for some reason his nose twitched at about half the rate of normal rabbit noses. Close by under the ancient Oak tree, two Hill-Clan rabbits, Kotar and Tooky, were curious as to where the stranger had come from. Approaching him with caution, Kotar asked him who he was, and why he had a yellow tag peeking from his left ear.

They discovered his name was Timken—not that this had any real bearing on the matter. Kotar thought of him as 'Waify', because his face expressed the hurt and sadness that little lost orphan bunnies have on finding themselves alone. Timken was a little hesitant in answering their questions, and his replies certainly created more questions than answers. He lay quietly in a patch of white clover where he settled in with a small sigh. He met Tooky's eyes and began his story.

"One day, far away," Timken started to explain, "I was picked up by the ears, stuffed into a bag—and then I felt myself flying. I flew for a long, long time. Even though I had no wings like birds do, I somehow became a magic kind of flying rabbit! I lost track of time because it was so dark, and I was so scared!" Upon hearing this, Tooky gave a small surprised squeak, and chortling with delight he exclaimed, "A flying rabbit!" Laughing softly, his uncle Kotar encouraged the new rabbit to continue.

"You'll understand why I was somewhat terrified," said Timken. "I began to think of the strange tales where it was rumoured that at Easter time, some of the two-legged creatures always bite the ears off their chocolate rabbits first—so they can't hear themselves squeaking while they are being eaten! Although I'm a real rabbit, I was petrified with fright. My little heart was pounding. I wanted to squeak, but it seems my squeaks were frozen too, and wouldn't come out! I guess they were scared also!" Timken trembled at the memory.

He was also surprised that Kotar and Tooky had difficulty in believing him—even though it was the whole truth. Rabbits never lie!

In fact it was all too much for Tooky and Kotar, who, shaking their heads, burst out laughing, and slapping their sides with fuzzy paws, rolled down the hill to the creek below.

Truly, Timken didn't belong with any local rabbit family. He was alone and didn't know why. He didn't ask *how* it came about, because he hadn't learnt to ask 'how' types of questions as yet. To complicate things was the fact that sometimes rabbits appear—and sometimes they don't! Timken stared down at a ladybug. It looked friendly. He allowed the little orange creature to crawl onto his front paws, but when he sniffed at it, it spread its black-spotted wings and flew away. He was alone once more. He hoped he would be welcomed into this new rabbit-clan because they were such a happy bunch.

Meantime, down by the creek Kotar and Tooky sobered up from their hilarity, and quite suddenly the eyes of both rabbits become wide with wariness as they looked, listened and sniffed the cool air around them. Kotar outlined their situation to Tooky, and explained the high probability of a bad 'reality' coming upon the scene.

They both knew that careless rabbits sort of disappear. In the blink of an eye, in the flick of a whisker—they vanish. In his own wise way, Kotar declared to Tooky that the world of rabbits always *'IS'*. It carries on, except for the ones that vanish. However wary a rabbit may be, there are times when an evil 'reality' may suddenly appear, and rabbits that *'are'*, become rabbits that *'are not'*.

"What's a reality?" Tooky asked, wrinkling his furry forehead.

Kotar thought for a few moments and said, "A *'reality'* is something that happens that rabbits have no control over. There are good realities and bad ones. A good one is like finding a fresh juicy carrot; while a truly bad one causes rabbits to disappear. No one knows where they go, and no one can follow them. That's because you can't follow a rabbit into a *'reality'* that is no longer there! Nor can you borrow a reality, or lend one, and certainly no rabbit wants to own one that can make him disappear. So the truth or *reality* is—that we rabbits just *'are'*, or we *'are not'*!

Tooky's eyes were filled with questions about 'realities', but Kotar assured him that they would have a good discussion about them in a different place at another time.

Before going back up to their little look-out hill, both rabbits lay quietly side by side listening to the creek 'music'. The fast-flowing water burbled over and around the rocks with wishy-washy rushing sounds. Kotar said the creek told tales from other worlds beyond Time. But Tooky, being so much younger, could not capture an inside vision of other worlds, or what they were, where they were, or why they were there; and he certainly could not see himself exploring one. It was also a little terrifying to realize that perhaps bad 'realities' lived there too.

"Tell me! Tell me!" exclaimed Tooky, "what are the creek songs all about?"

"Not right now Tooky, let's go back up and see Timken. It was rude of us to just laugh at him, although it is funny to imagine him as a flying rabbit that just fell out of the sky! I don't quite know what to make of that. Let's find out what he's all about. He seems like a nice little guy, except he's far too sad".

So the two rabbits quickly scampered back up the slope to their look-out post. It was a special place from where they could see enemies like a fox or weasel if one were to approach. All was clear—or was it? No predators were in sight, and there was no long grass in which they could hide, nor were there any hawks in the sky or in the trees. Even the smoky two-legged creatures were silent at this time of morning. But Kotar in particular had a distinct feeling they were being watched—from somewhere.

"What is it Kotar—what is watching us?" asked Tooky anxiously. Both of them experienced the approach of fear;

but as yet, no advance warning had occurred, like the rapid thump of rabbits' feet, or the flashing of white tails. As Kotar surveyed the scene, his intuition called for obedience and immediate action.

"I'm not sure Tooky, but for safety, we need to go underground—right now! If in doubt—hide!" Even as he spoke, a nearby rabbit loudly squeaked, "Dogs!" Two wild dogs appeared as if from nowhere. They charged among the escaping rabbits with deadly intent. Amid much thumping and squeaks of terror, the Clan scattered into their burrows. They all managed to get safely into the cool dark underground passageways, including Timken.

"Wow!" said Tooky, "We made it. I actually felt the hot air-blast from the mouth of that big black one." The whole Clan agreed it was a close call and that extra care was needed. Tooky planned to ask Kotar about 'how', and 'when' he knew it was time to dive for safety.

Later, when all was clear, Kotar and Tooky found the 'new' rabbit had survived the ordeal and was now again crouched low in the clover-patch. He looked pleased at their appearance; and they both apologized for having ridiculed his story. Timken looked up with a faint smile of forgiveness. These friendly rabbits made him feel good all over! Timken flipped his ears into the upright position. Truly he was 'all ears' as they say in the Hill-Clan rabbit world, and he was anxious to learn all about this new colony.

Kotar and Timken quietly began to share the history and news of their respective clans. Tooky listened intently. He liked Timken's deep understanding eyes, and wondered why his whiskers were so long. He wanted to ask a lot of questions—some of which might be too personal and against rabbit-rules to ask. In any case, Kotar was giving him a real going-over as only a senior rabbit can.

Just then, Tooky's best friends Boofy and Bifflets joined them along with an odd-colored rabbit named Snickets. He was brown all over, except for his extra big powder puff tail—which was all black! In the whole wild-rabbit world, black tails are unheard of, except for far, far away, where it was rumoured there were big black-tailed Jack Rabbits. In comparison, Snickets, black tail and all, would be a relatively small field rabbit. For this reason, although he was a Hill-Clan member, some of the rabbits looked upon him with distrust. His black tail was just too different!

Snickets sat and listened to Timken and Kotar, but first he wriggled his black tail into a dandelion clump. He need not have worried, because the other rabbits were sort of spell-bound with the strange things they were hearing. Timken was saying that every rabbit has some knowledge of all rabbits, but each has his own very special insight and thinking. He also said he was concerned about his home-town rabbits because in the dark of night, they often had real scary kinds of thoughts that came to them from unknown places; and this caused them to squeak and flip around in their sleep.

"Squeaking flipping rabbits!" exclaimed Tooky, soaking up every bit of news.

When Timken asked Kotar about the alien thoughts, that wise rabbit said they were nothing new to him, and without a doubt, the whole Hill-Clan had the same problem.

It was well known that sometimes the flipping and squeaking at about 2.00 a.m. was so loud, it even woke up the very baby bunnies, which in turn disturbed all the female rabbits. When the young mothers didn't get enough rest, the whole colony became disturbed. Kotar said this was an issue that demanded the attention of the entire tribe. It had gotten out of hand to the point of being a serious matter, and that he and the elder rabbits would find solutions to the problem.

Timken nodded in agreement. "Let's do everything we can to help the mothers. I wouldn't want to be awakened every night with baby bunnies crying. I like to sleep peacefully!"

"Me too Timken," exclaimed Kotar, "it's the bigger rabbits who create the most disturbance. They kick up quite a ruckus! You know Timken, it's the female rabbits who do most of the real family work, and they need their sleep. We male rabbits tend to make light of what they do for us; and usually make out that we're fully occupied with handling important, 'affairs of state'. But, we can never forget that it was our mothers who raised us, loved us, cleaned us, fed us, and protected us with their very lives! It's they who kept us snuggly-warm and safe from rabbit enemies, and taught us when and how to flee from danger. Timken, that's the sole reason that many of us are still alive today!"

Both rabbits stopped talking as Simbala hopped by. She was the most senior and wisest of all the female rabbits. Kotar pretended he was examining the yellow tag in Timken's ear. When the coast was clear again, Kotar said, "Timken, when Simbala comes up with an idea, we all listen, and most of us obey. She sees things before the others do. I mean in her mind, she's a very wise rabbit!"

Timken said, "I'm new here Kotar, and I welcome any help you can give me. Already, I really like Simbala. You're right, she sort of looks right through you. There's little she misses."

"You're 'on-track' Timken. I know of at least five rabbits who didn't follow her updated survival instructions, and sad to say, they are no longer with us."

"Yes, that is sad," commiserated Timken, "but Tooky told me that you and Simbala may have some special thoughts on how we can learn to overcome our fears."

"Yes Timken. There are big changes coming up—and," Kotar chuckled, "can you believe it? They originated with a big, fuzzy Bumblebee!"

The loud cawing of crows prevented them from talking further, and even before they could look up, Snickets shouted, "Fox! Fox!", and they saw their enemy's bushy red tail melt among the woodland trees nearest them. The fox knew he'd been seen, and the chance of a fresh rabbit breakfast had escaped him.

When the feeding-meadow was once again safe, others began joining the small group to listen to Kotar and Timken. So in addition to Boofy, Bifflets, Tooky and Snickets, there were now Squibby, KeKe, Tyko, Derky, Marky and Teslakin whom they called Tesla. This last rabbit was most peculiar in a way that rabbits have no way to describe. Tesla was Tesla. He was quiet, confident and quite handsome, with very dark fur and black ears. On the rare occasions that he did speak, it was about some pretty weird things called 'oscillations'—whatever they were. He also spoke of 'frequencies'. Most of the rabbits listened politely, but only Kotar's eyes lit up once in a while with any real understanding.

"As I was saying," said Kotar raising his voice so all the rabbits could hear, "the disturbing thoughts that invade our Hill-Clan colony at night are evil intruders, and although we might track them to their source, the attacks cannot be stopped! They are like the hawks we see flying around in the daytime. No one has control over them; they can land anywhere. In fact our night-thoughts seem to have as much power to terrify us as do real hawks and owls do by day."

Timken shivered at the thought of owls. He stretched himself, flipped his ears and settled down again. His eyes kept wandering back to Tesla. Not only did this rabbit sort of create and carry his own world with him, but he *WAS* his world. All the rabbits could feel it. It was different, a special kind of *'IS'*, from which Tesla peeked into *their* world.

Kotar now spoke in a newer more powerful tone of voice than he had ever used before. "I know how each member of the Colony can make these disturbing thoughts disappear, so all of us can sleep peacefully. It would be quite a project, but we can do it!" Timken and most of the rabbits were much impressed.

But suddenly at that point in their discussion something very strange happened. One of rabbits began squeaking and flipping! He was not asleep or dreaming. It was broad daylight! The rabbits had heard of nightmares; but nightmares in the daytime—never! Their eyes became wide with fear in case they all suffered the same fate. They checked out the rabbit thrashing around in the grass. To their surprise—it was Snickets!

Kotar's talk of alien thoughts and nightmares had become too much for poor Snickets who exclaimed, "I'm sick of being scared and running away in my dreams! There's this big black thing that keeps chasing me. I don't know whether *'it'* catches *me,* or I catch *'it'*. Then of all things, I wake up in a panic, and find I'm holding my own tail." He sniffed and shed a tear in self-pity.

Timken and the other rabbits gathered around him including Simbala who had quietly joined the group. Simbala was quite a senior rabbit, and it was said that she was wiser than Kotar because compared to him, she never allowed herself to get 'spaced out'. She disapproved of the whole subject of 'Space-Rabbits', so the topic had largely become taboo in the colony. Certainly it was a topic to be avoided when Simbala was present.

Simbala now spoke to Snickets in a low voice that gave all of them confidence. With a half-smile she calmly said, "Snickets, you can let go of your tail now", and then she gave him a full smile! Simbala seemed to exude wisdom, and Snickets relaxed. Determined to get to the bottom of his black-tail nightmares, in simple terms she explained the reason *why* rabbits have white tails. Most of them did not understand *'why'* types of questions, because they based their lives simply on, 'it's the way things are'. But as Simbala explained, "White flashing tails can be seen from any direction when rabbits have to dive down their burrows. It's a special fast-warning signal to any rabbit nearby that danger is approaching."

Quickly—all eyes were on Snickets. He didn't have a 'warning' white tail. His tail was jet black! It was like he was a traitor to his own tribe. Suddenly Snickets felt guilty. He was surrounded by accusing eyes that seemed to bore into him. Snickets closed his eyes and tried to make himself disappear, but when he opened them—he was still there. There was no escape!

But suddenly Kotar came boldly to his rescue just as Snickets was about to dissolve into a puddle of tears. "Wait!" called out Kotar, "Black tail or not, how could you all forget for one moment that Snickets has the sharpest eyes of any rabbit here? Remember the weasel and the wild dog incident? Oh! And also the golden eagle warning—it was Snickets who saved us—Snickets with the black tail! It was also he who gave the first fox alert only a few minutes ago!"

At this point Boofy and Bifflets suddenly jumped up and patted Snickets with their soft paws, and despite their shamed faces, other rabbits joined in. But it was Timken who shook with painful sobs as he cried in spite of himself. He just could not help but shed tears of happiness at having such caring, loving friends.

Simbala assured Timken that he could carry on being happy, because she was going to adopt him into her branch of the Hill-Clan family. Timken's eyes glowed with love for this very motherly senior rabbit. "Yes!" he murmured, "that's it. She makes me feel loved. I feel warm all over—just like when I was a baby bunny."

Meanwhile, mainly for the benefit of Timken, Kotar highlighted certain facts about rabbits and what makes them 'tick'. He just wanted to make sure that Timken, he, and the Clan, were on the same wavelength. Tooky frowned. He'd never heard of 'ticking rabbits' before, but from now on he was determined to listen very carefully.

Kotar enjoyed having the full attention of the group. The expression on the faces of the younger bunnies could only be described as 'worshipful'. Kotar explained to the little rabbits that at one time, all the wild Clan rabbits including his ancestors were greyish-brown in color. But that had all changed when a group of tame rabbits from the farm below had escaped and come to live with them. Kotar's light fur was as unique and attractive as were all of the multi-color Hill-Clan members. Anyone seeing them feeding together could rightly say they were now quite a 'motley' crew! However, no white ones remained.

Kotar explained that rabbits are snuggly little animals with beautiful eyes, long silky ears, and little noses that are always twitching, and that everyone loves them. Then he added in somewhat ominous tones, "But for very different reasons!"

"We rabbits," he exclaimed, "have a lot to learn before we become wise, and wise rabbits are few and far between. When we hear things, we rotate our ears and turn the sounds we hear into pictures in our minds. This lets us decide what to do. All day long and far into the night, all rabbits need to make the right decisions from the messages that come into their ears. Fortunately for rabbits and all the creatures on Earth, there are natural *laws* that often have to make decisions for them."

"Where do they come from?" asked Tooky.

"Nobody really knows," said Kotar thoughtfully. "It's believed they sort of fall silently from the stars at night. But I believe they just *are*—something like rabbits, and the very air we breathe." Timken flipped his ears and nibbled on a clover flower.

"Some of you will remember that baby squirrel last week," continued Kotar, "he was high in the Oak tree when he lost his balance, and for the briefest of moments he was suspended in mid-air. Then in a flash of a second, the Star Laws said, 'You can't be *up* and *down* at the same time!' So down went that little squirrel. He had to obey the law, even though he didn't know about it, and had yet to learn from his mother about obedience. Luckily he fell into some soft leaves, and before he could even recover his thinking, his mother had rescued him and scurried back up the tree to their nest." Kotar paused. It was evident that some of the rabbit group were overcome with hunger and were already nibbling on cowslips. Others had begun feeding on the lush clover leaves.

Undeterred however, Kotar continued with his thoughts, "At some point we all discover that it is we who allow ourselves to '*be*' or '*not to be*'. Every rabbit wants to '*be*'. It's the thrilling experience of hopping around in '*now*'. Of course we all live in '*now*', which is a tiny fragment of Time. It is here where rabbits sniff the early morning air, the scent of purple clover, and yellow cowslips. They also see and smell the whole world of *realities*, some of which have four legs and fur, while other strange smoky animals have only two legs and no fur. But the most wonderful feeling for all of us is to be alive, feeding, and frisking around in the warm sun with our friends."

Kotar's discourse caused some of the rabbits to fall into a dazed state as they tried to pay attention from a sense of duty. It was said to be rude to fall asleep when a senior rabbit was speaking; but in the end it was the Star-Laws that took over.

Tooky didn't sleep, but pondered through half-open eyes one of the saddest mysteries of rabbit life. Tooky wanted to know what actually happens at a special point in time when a rabbit no longer '*IS*', because he becomes a rabbit that '*was*'. Tooky was determined to ask Kotar all about it sometime, because Kotar always had that unspoken air of mystery about him. It quietly hinted that he knew more about the invisible worlds than all the other rabbits put together.

This was true. He claimed they were all immersed in non-molecular realities, of which they were mostly unaware. Just the mention of such strange things caused most Clan members to avoid discussions with him. Some even looked over their shoulders in fear that some unseen element might suddenly make them disappear. Kotar's concepts made them dizzy. Tesla's ideas had the same effect, but he had isolated his thinking from theirs. He kept to himself. Kotar told Tooky and his friends that when a rabbit finally knows all about the what, who, when, where, why and the how of things, a rabbit is at the root of all *'realities'*.

However, when Bifflets asked him to explain what he had said, Kotar gave a sigh of resignation, because he knew he could not escape Bifflet's questions. He also knew that each fragment of wisdom that escaped through his whiskers would create even more questions. And those questions would create many other questions; so that ignorance expands so quickly—that it grows way faster than rabbits can multiply! He was going to say that each question that is answered gives rise to ignorance which expands 'exponentially', but that was too big a word for Tooky and some of the others.

Finally, Kotar decided to close the whole matter with a short statement before they all became dizzy, because when rabbits get dizzy, bad things happen!

"What you are asking of me is difficult to put into Rabbit language," said Kotar. "But for the time being, let's just say that all 'realities' live in the world of *'now';* which is always in the *'present'*, except when it is *'not'*, because it has become your *'past'*. In fact *'present'* and *'past'* are so sequentially instant, it's as though the Time-point of *'now'* does not exist, and that is difficult to grasp. It could be said that this makes us believe we are *'here'*—when maybe we are not!"

At this, all the rabbits, except for Tooky, rolled their eyes in the peculiar way that rabbits do when trying to face mysteries that make their heads spin. It really said to Kotar, "Eeeeeeek! We've had enough!"

Now, before we rejoin Timken and the Crew, I have to digress to tell you several rather personal things about Kotar. If he were here he would blush under his fur, flap his ears and look sort of embarrassed! But truth is that Kotar was a special rabbit right from his baby-days. His mother had often said of him almost in despair, "He's just plain weird. I don't know where his thoughts come from. Our ancestors were all sensible rabbits."

Kotar's mother had told him time and time again to turn over a new leaf, or he would be a failure. Kotar could not image how a failure looked. Maybe it had a long tail and short ears! All he really wanted was to be a super-special rabbit, and to be that, he sensed he had to think differently from other rabbits.

As for 'turning over a new leaf', he'd found this was very hard to do, because the new leaves he turned over, always turned back again to the way they were before he turned them. It was much easier to turn over old dead leaves, because they stay turned after you turned them. Also, Kotar experienced the excitement of discovering things that hide under old leaves. Once he exposed a strange, heavy thing that 'ticked', with hands that moved. He told no one of what he had found, and secretly hid it away deep inside an old hollow tree stump.

It is possible that Kotar was born as an 'idiopathic' rabbit, which means that he 'became' from an unknown cause peculiar to that particular rabbit. Of course idiopathic rabbits ask questions like, "Why is a mouse?" or "Why is a bee?" because these questions come naturally. However, it is assuring to know that even an idiopathic rabbit would never dream of asking anyone, "Why is a rabbit?" because as everyone knows—rabbits just '*are*', and '*why*' has nothing to do with it at all!

It seemed that Kotar acquired knowledge of other worlds and strange places he called '*now*' dimensions. Whenever he tried to explain what they were, he became so lost that he almost disappeared inside himself! Kotar had become a unique rabbit with far-out thoughts. It was the one and only reason that Tesla accepted him as such a close friend. Tesla explained many new ideas to him; but Kotar's problem was that he had only to blink but once—and a big 'delete' wiped out everything he thought he had understood. On Tesla's part, he hid his most original and exciting ideas deep inside himself; because right from the start, most inhabitants of Rabbit Land had 'deleted' both him and his ideas without knowing why. Tesla often asked '*why*', and that made him different. Kotar really liked Tesla, and viewed him as a friendly black-eared potential 'Space-Rabbit' of many unusual talents.

Kotar's failure to explain to the other rabbits what he saw in his mind did not deter him. What Kotar had already achieved in his '*now-dimension*' travel, no rabbit could take from him. It was his. His eyes lit up with a special brightness when he recalled a conversation he had one day with a really big fuzzy bumblebee. She was a kind of 'freighter' bee, designed to haul big loads of pollen back to the hive.

The huge bumblebee was glad to rest for a moment or two to chat with Kotar, who asked her, "How're things Bumby?" She cleaned the yellow pollen off her face. "Well," she said, "I get tired at times. It's heavy-going in the dew of early morning."

"I think you do amazingly well for your size," said Kotar as he looked admiringly at her beautiful body. It was banded with fuzzy black and yellow stripes, and her huge pollen bags were full almost to overflowing.

"Did you know?" asked Bumby, "that there is a rumor that we bees are not supposed to be able to fly? At least that's what the two-legged animals say. But, as you can see Kotar—we fly anyway! Why? Because we didn't know that we could not! What do you think about that?"

Kotar squeaked and almost alarmed Bumby, when he quite suddenly flipped into the air and landed with a delighted rabbit-shout of, "Eureka! Bumby! Bumby!" he exclaimed. "That's it! That's it! Often the whole key to solving problems and making progress is to simply '*do*' that which you and others '*knew*' could *not* be done. It's a lot like creating an '*IS*' reality! You just *do it!* Often it is scary, but you do the thing you perhaps fear most, and in doing so, you overcome yourself and become a different Being!" Kotar smiled in self-satisfaction. His internal 'delete-key' had not been activated. He understood!

"Of course," said Bumby with caution, "one should handle these thoughts wisely. Some things *are* impossible; and sheer foolishness can kill the explorer and his idea!"

"Thanks Bumby!" said Kotar gratefully, "you're a fuzzy flying inspiration to all of us."

She smiled, and revving up her bee-engine, took off with a low hum to unload her precious cargo. Kotar waved back, "Bye Bumby," he murmured.

Kotar often talked with himself. He confirmed in his mind that frequencies involving other dimensions of space, according to Tesla, offered him a unique way to travel to unknown places. Only recently had it occurred to Kotar that Tesla had yet to ask '*why*' he wanted to go where no rabbit had ever gone before. After all, was he not already living in a 'dimension', which is actually a rather beautiful self-contained world in itself?

Kotar was determined that neither he nor the other rabbits should get dizzy while he explained the abstract visions in his mind. It would have to be in the crystal clear language of Space-Rabbits. For a start he realized that Tooky and Tiska would ask, "What's an abstract vision?" He in turn would reply, "It means difficult to understand." Then Tooky or Tiska would ask, "Then why don't you make it simple and say what you mean?" For one brief moment Kotar envisioned the futility of the whole idea. It was high time that he gave this matter some real thought.

Kotar did his private thinking under a beautiful Silver Birch tree. He could also talk with this Birch for she was wise far beyond his years, and he had often benefited from her advice. Kotar also felt extra safe in his visits because she had shown him a deep burrow hidden at her base. The Silver Birch greeted him breezily with a million whispering green leaves. Kotar lay back watching her flutter against an azure blue sky. The never-ending trilling songs of sky-larks relaxed him. Close by, Chickadees called one to another. Kotar was at peace.

Tesla had told Kotar quite a while ago that in approaching a problem he was really solving an equation. That is, he had to study, 'a complex of variable factors'. "Wow! That's it I guess," he stated out loud as he repeated the phrase again. It had a nice sound to it that made him feel more intelligent than he really was. Suddenly, the voice of Snickets piped up, "A complex of variable factors! What's that?" Kotar sprang up with surprise.

He had not realized that Snickets and KeKe had followed him to the Birch tree. It also told him, much to his chagrin, that he'd become careless by feeling too relaxed under the Birch. Supposing a stoat or a weasel had turned up?

"Snickets!" exclaimed Kotar, "what are you two doing here?" He eyed KeKe with curiosity. The intruders said they wanted to be as wise as Kotar and had joined him to learn whatever he might learn under the 'talking' Birch tree. Kotar was satisfied and lay down again with a big sigh.

"This may be beyond your understanding," he said, "but I'm trying to solve a Star-travel problem that may involve the entire Hill-Clan. They need to understand certain Space-Rabbit language, because what we say, and do, will in many ways affect the whole Colony. But I need Tesla's help to achieve this because I'm not yet sure of what I'm trying to say!"

"Wow," breathed Snickets. "That is so cool! It's even cooler than having a jet black tail!"

"Why not keep it simple," suggested KeKe. "All I really hear you saying is that you have some ideas that the Colony should consider and probably adopt. So why use complicated terms? After all, if you can't understand it, how can they?"

"KeKe, you're absolutely right!" Kotar exclaimed, "When the time comes, I'll just keep it simple." He then visibly brightened. "Hey! What say you we sneak out to the farmer's garden tonight for a rich feed of carrots? The moon is only in its first quarter, and that will make it difficult for most evil realities to see us, although they might scent us."

"Sounds good to me," said KeKe, "can we have Tooky along?"

"I don't see why not," said Kotar, "he's always game for a raid on the carrot-patch." Then he added thoughtfully, "You know, although Tooky may be quite small, I think he may be developing into a type of Super-Rabbit. He not only thinks well, but he picks up 'thought images' from both the good and the bad realities in his vicinity. That could make him pretty useful on a carrot-raid."

When Kotar, Snickets and KeKe arrived back at the Hill-Clan burrows to plan the carrot expedition—Tooky was nowhere to be seen. Several of the Clan joined KeKe to look for him. But it was close to sun-down before Tooky finally showed up, looking tired but rather pleased. Apparently he'd 'seen' a red fox in his mind, and could not determine where it was. So he'd dived for safety into an older disused burrow. The patient fox had stayed close by for a long while. There was no way it could know that its image continually streamed into Tooky's awareness. In the the end, it abandoned its wait and gave up in defeat. Tooky had watched for his mind-screen to go blank, and then quickly scampered home. He looked at his friends and heaved a big sigh of relief. "It's sure good to be safely home," he declared, "foxes give me cold shivers!"

Kotar, Snickets and KeKe looked knowingly at each other. KeKe said, "I don't believe for one moment that Tooky is aware that he's been gifted in a special way. He just innocently assumes that all rabbits have his remarkable ability of 'picking up images'." They invited Tooky to the upcoming night-raid, whereupon that wise little rabbit met their gaze with a far-away look in his eyes. "Yes," he said, "the star-music says that all is well. We'll have a real feast!"

Kotar — A wise senior rabbit who has already experienced a different type of Space-travel.

Chapter Two

Kotar's crowning glory of insight was his realization that he was not his body. He lived in his body—but he was not his body! He often felt that deep inside him he was a rabbit that alternated half-way between *'is'* and *'is not'*. Sometimes it seemed that he and his body were as one, yet at other times they were quite separate! The other rabbits had extreme difficulty in comprehending anything to do with it! Of course his body was not able to travel with him when he took off to explore other dimensions; which meant that in the simplest of terms he travelled as a package of 'thought-energy'. He, being the real Kotar who had temporarily left his body behind.

A rabbit needs to be in a very safe, quiet place in order to leave and explore a distant star or another dimension. If he were careless, he would have no place to which to return. What happens to a rabbit who *'IS'*, who comes back to find that his body *'is not?'* Kotar could not figure that one out and he didn't want to tackle such mind-boggling questions without Tesla. If he thought too deeply about them, he became a dangerously dizzy rabbit!

Then one day when Kotar had sneaked into the carrot-patch alone—a dangerous venture at any time—a different kind of thought came to him. It all started when he came across some young two-legged creatures with a noisy kind of box. They blew strange smelling smoke from their mouths like they were on fire. Peeking out from under a large cabbage leaf, Kotar watched them gyrate their tall bodies as the box made queer thumping sounds which vibrated the very ground on which he was crouched. There were other raucous noises too, accompanied by strange rhythmic chanting. The creatures contorted themselves in reckless abandon to this 'music'. They danced around or jumped up and down like they were puppets attached to the box. The sheer volume of sound disturbed Kotar and hurt his ears. He decided to escape the situation as soon as he could safely leave without being seen.

Both males and females swayed, whirled and twirled with raised arms. Their faces held rapt, vacant expressions, while in their strange language they gasped, "Rock me baby". They all possessed a dreamy, trance-like, ecstatic look; much like Kotar imagined space-rabbits would have on their return from living in other dimensions. He wondered what they thought about as they didn't appear to have any enemies.

Then again, the idea came to him that perhaps they were their own worst enemies, if they allowed the noisy box to control them. It was hard to understand. Kotar pushed himself further underneath the big cabbage leaf to keep out of sight. It was not yet safe to leave.

But what captured Kotar was that when the creatures had enough of keeping pace with the weird rhythms, one of them touched the boxy noise-maker, and it made different noises. He saw they did this by turning a little knob one way or the other. Ever curious, this was nothing new to Kotar, and he knew from experience all about *'turning'* things. He recalled that in the orchard he had to keep turning the wind-fall apples as he nibbled. In this way he was able to avoid the hungry and dangerous hornets that were also sucking up the apple juices. The thought struck

Kotar; 'the whole world changes when something gets turned'. As the world turns, things happen!

You will appreciate that all this is quite confidential data on Kotar. He would be horrified if he learned that I had told you. Another juicy bit of news that is much more than mere rabbit-gossip, is that Kotar's female, Aleska, is pregnant, and already I know the name of one member of the new family. Kotar always said he was a questing rabbit in search of 'truth'; and that if he ever had baby bunnies, one of them would be called Questy!

Anyway, the more Kotar investigated 'new dimensions', the more of them he discovered, at least in theory. He said that every dimension of space-thought created bands of colored light, like the most brilliant rainbows he'd ever seen. All he had to do in order escape and travel was to 'turn' them in his mind and new ones appeared. However, sometimes he became very frightened. On several occasions he'd almost forgotten the coding of the frequency he was exploring, and in which dimension of color in the light-spectrum on which he was travelling. In actual fact, once he became so lost he panicked! He discovered that he couldn't even return to himself! Now that is really being lost!

It became all the more difficult because his actual location in Time and Space had become so variable. Time-wise, '*now*', is where a rabbit's consciousness currently '*is*', but does not reveal '*where*' a rabbits' body may be located. Rabbits are a little slow in linking things up in their minds and Kotar was no exception.

He was also totally unaware that a Space-Rabbit could get lost by falling into any one of the 'gaps' between his own thoughts, whether he was in 'space' or on Earth. Kotar didn't know that this lack of knowledge presented hidden dangers. In all innocence, he was a prime expression of the illusion known as, 'ignorance is bliss'.

Interestingly, it was while Kotar was trapped in a freaky dimension that he met a strange *'Being'*. A creature so far beyond his understanding, that he felt keen disappointment to learn that he, Kotar, a relatively brilliant animal, was seen by this creature as a mere inconsequential Space-Rabbit! This Being walked right through him while it scanned his consciousness, past and present. Kotar's impression was that '*IT*' tolerated him, and that's about all! Then, in absolute silence, it projected him on a beam that zapped him directly to his home base. Despite himself, Kotar was more than just grateful for the assistance.

It was while this was happening that Kotar had lost his dignity, and no matter how diligently he searched his mind, whether here, there, or anywhere, it simply could not be found. He felt humiliated. This bothered him, because he'd always considered himself to be a humble animal. He paused and looked around inside himself. Then the truth hit him! Far from being filled with humility, he was really a very proud ego-driven rabbit. Kotar realized this rabbit pride problem was common to the whole Colony, but now it also included him! It caused him to drop his ears in shame. In fact, when he tried to deny it and regain face, it started a sort of tug-of-war inside of him!

From long habit Kotar solved his dilemmas in solitude, and now, ensuring he was alone, he trailed to the Silver Birch tree to relax under her shelter in silence among the buttercups. It seemed that his memory was playing back words from Tesla. "Kotar, few rabbits know the difference between 'self importance' and 'self-esteem'", the voice said. "Self-important ego-driven rabbits are a power unto themselves. They sit as though they are stuck with 'Crazy-Glue' on a throne of 'self', which they are loath to give up!

It's an attitude problem that proclaims no rabbit knows more than they! However, if challenged on this point, in denial, they throw up a façade of humility and claim to be always open to suggestion; but woe unto any rabbit that challenges their status quo!"

"That is really false humility," Kotar exclaimed. His voice charged with insight and discovery.

"Exactly," fluttered the Silver Birch. "Kotar," she said, "these changes are quite critical, because when you switch from a foundation of self-importance—to zero self-importancet—and replace it with high self-worth with no self-conceit—one has humility. You not only change yourself, but you change the world around you. Tesla says that self-esteem is high self-worth without any pride or conceit. That is humility in action. Humility increases exponentially with accountability."

"Thanks Birchy! In actual practice I find I have to guard against my 'ego-self', because most of us deny that we have any self-importance. But I'm learning, slowly." At that point Kotar scampered from the edge of the woodland across to the Colony burrows for an overdue nap.

There are still certain things that you should know about Kotar. He may tell you more himself, but I can't, because he swore me to secrecy. But, what I can tell you, I will!

An important thing to understand is that although Kotar knows much about space, time, dimensions and different realities, there are many critical things of which he is not yet aware which could well endanger the lives of the Hill-Clan.

There is one astounding fact that only Simbala knows, and she too is sworn to secrecy. It has to do with Kotar's eyes. In certain situations, when Kotar's left ear becomes floppy and appears to be at a strange angle, no rabbit or any other creature should catch his eye with theirs. When Kotar's left ear goes down at that special angle—it's weird—his eyes light up—like blue death-rays! It's shocking to see! His eyes glow like no earthly rabbits' eyes ever should. In fact, just thinking about it chills me. He told me he can capture and immobilize any living creature and make it disappear—just by thought processes!

Kotar claims he has mastered the rarest of all the rabbit arts; that is, he can turn an '*is*' into an '*is not*'. Kotar has moved many a bad '*is*' into the '*now*' of another dimension. An '*IS*' is really just another form of 'reality'. One day however, Kotar finally realized that although projected realities may be so far away they may never be seen again, nevertheless, they are still alive, intelligent, and possibly obeying some Star-Laws that may have yet to be discovered in this section of the Universe. Energy always '*IS*' in some form or another. It's scary!

Confidentially, I believe Kotar is a little 'off-track' in this whole matter and it gives me the 'creeps'! What Kotar is calling '*is*' and 'is not', are really '*here*' and '*not here*', which is an entirely different matter!

He doesn't know what to do with this problem. I call it 'cosmic corruption', and as surely as Kotar has sown this interstellar-aberration, so will he also reap the terrible consequences of his acts. Some day he may no longer be a Hill-Clan elder of superior intellect.

You'll appreciate that Kotar means well, he's always working for what is best for the Clan. But I suspect he's too close to this problem to bring it into focus and take action. I believe someone has to help him, before it's too late for all of us!

This indeed was the very thing that kept bothering Kotar. He knew he had not paid enough attention as to *where* he had projected the '*living*' bad '*is*' realities. The thought came to him that supposing while he was away exploring, he might accidentally meet up with them on the same frequency on which he too was traveling. This was almost too scary for him to contemplate!

Kotar was sure was that they were all more or less in the same place, because he had used the same amount of projection energy on each of them. He dared not think of what might happen if some Star-Creature turned 'Time' backwards. The writings of one ancient rabbit-scribe said this had happened before. At that time the sun went backwards by ten degrees! Kotar's head began to ache, and he was almost annoyed when a familiar dizzy-spell descended. A little voice said to him, "If *you* don't handle the problem, *it* will handle *you*". Another not so little voice said, "*Yikes!*"

The little group of rabbits, those who were still awake that is, observed that Kotar had fallen into some kind of space-trance, and they were fearful that his left ear might lean over, and maybe disaster would strike them all. Boofy and Bifflets who always had their wits about them, yelled to the group, "Run! Run down to the creek. Now! Go wash your faces in cold water and take a drink!"

The alarmed rabbits fled down the hill to the creek, so fast, that three of the smaller bunnies simply turned into fur-balls and rolled all the way down. One splashed right into the water, but was quickly dragged ashore by Snickets. It was mutually agreed that all is well that ends well. But it was Boofy who exclaimed, "It's not over yet! We have to check out Kotar. He looks dangerous! Maybe we can roll him down the hill to the creek, and then he would come to himself pretty quickly."

When they came back up the hill, Kotar was still lying in the same place. But rather than roll him down to the water, they just jumped all over him until his fur was also cold and soaking wet. Kotar came around fast, and far from being angry, he was very pleased. In just a few minutes he became his normal earth-bound happy self, full of wisdom. Once again, he'd become a rabbit to be admired. However, there were many rabbits who did not admire him, because Kotar often attempted to expand their levels of consciousness. He would target those rabbits who might be on the verge of exploring whatever lay beyond mere eating, sleeping, raising families and survival. A challenge in itself!

On these occasions Kotar persisted in telling the other rabbits about his 'space-type' adventures. These included his visions of different worlds. Some were unexplored dimensions of thought, and still others were tales of intriguing and beautiful places he'd discovered. But more often than not, he was rewarded only with blank stares. Although Kotar was a senior rabbit, when he spoke about his abstract adventures, it caused many rabbits to have reservations and to question his authority in the Hill-Clan.

Even further confusion fell upon his former friends when he stated that he had discovered that rabbits create and control their own realities. That was accepted to be within the realm of possibility; but, when he claimed that he and most of the Hill-Clan would be travelling into outer-space, and soon, they drew the line. Tooky said, "Kotar, that sounds exciting, but I'm not sure why I would want to go!" KeKe then exclaimed that Kotar's thoughts went way beyond being 'other-worldly'. He called them 'infinity thoughts', because he sensed they went right out of sight into the Galaxy and beyond!

Boofy and Bifflets were always thrilled with Kotar's stories, especially when he became all serious and his eyes got bigger and bigger as he tried to explain what he called his 'special' worlds. For Kotar they were filled with intrigue and were more real than the regular rabbit-world. However, the main Hill-Clan tribe of rabbits almost bordered on being nasty when abstract concepts came to the forefront. They gave the aspiring Star-Travelers among them a rude, insulting ear-flip and called them a bunch of 'weirdo rabbits'. It was all very mysterious because every rabbit knows his 'real world' also includes the 'IS' world of every other rabbit.

The whole secret of long life is to be an *'IS'* rabbit inside of 'now', and not turn into a 'was' rabbit inside of 'then'.

"Kotar!" exclaimed Tooky, "what do *'is'* and *'was'* look like? How and why do they make *realities?* And where are they? Suppose I meet them, how will I know which is which?"

Kotar sighed due to the enormity of the question. "Tooky, one of them is well known to you, the other may elude you for a long, long time. They are both in 'Time'. The Chief of the learned rabbits says that Time, 'Has a tendency to exist'. I think he means that Time can simultaneously *be*—or *not be*. We can't go into it right now Tooky as we all have things to do. Let's just be happy with the *'now'* in which we currently exist."

"Kotar!" said Tooky, "you make my head spin. When I try to think, I get dizzy!" And with that he dashed up to the 'flying rabbit', alias Timken, and kissed him on the ears. "Timken! Timken!" he cried, "tell us more about you."

Kotar sat down beside them, pulling his silky ears down one by one to clean them; while Timken tried to explain his sudden appearance in Rabbit Land. "Back home, wherever that is now, they called me Twinky, because I became a star-gazer."

"What's a 'star-gazer?" asked Tooky.

"Well, I'll tell you," said Timken, his nose twitching at a faster rate. "Maybe you'll try it sometime, although it is a very dangerous thing to do. At night I'd sneak out of the burrow to watch the night-lights in the sky. You know, the stars, as they twinkle and talk to you."

"Stars talk with you?" exclaimed Tooky.

"Why, of course, and once you have one star connection, others just happen. Lying under the maple tree I would dream myself right into distant star galaxies, and then come back again in an instant!"

"Wow!" exclaimed Tooky. "That is the coolest thought I ever heard!"

It became immediately apparent to Kotar that he and Timken were kindred spirits. Kotar had long known that where there are two or more star-rabbits working on a project, things happened that were not possible when one worked alone. A warm feeling surged up within him.

"Back where I came from," Timken explained, "I was not scared of the strange sounds and the even stranger creatures that went by the burrow each night." This was hard for Tooky to understand, because anything unusual would send him thumping back down into his burrow.

In Rabbit Land things are never as they really appear to be, until they '*are*'. Tooky could never quite understand how that could be, because it meant many different scenarios simultaneously occupied the same space in Time.

He questioned why and what caused them to come into 'being'. Although Tooky tried, he was never able to pin-point the exact instant that a 'Time-Frame' came into being as '*now*', or where it came from, or where it went.

But, as Timken continued with his story, he told them that one day things really were not as they just seemed to be. In an instant those busy elements of Time, '*is*' and '*was*', took Timken's daddy away in the sharp talons of a Red Tailed Hawk without even a single farewell squeak. Just a week later his mother was killed and dragged away among the cowslips by a weasel. '*Is*' and '*was*' were always hard at work inside of Time.

Timken was thrilled to no longer be an unclaimed waif, an orphaned rabbit with no family, because now he belonged to Simbala's clan. She had adopted him and he had lost his sadness. Timken's bearing and his whole appearance seemed to be different inside and out. He was overcome with beautiful warm feelings that told him he was loved.

*Inde*ed, Timken was welcomed into the tribe just as he was, true, innocent and vulnerable. No one told jokes about flying rabbits ever again. But once in a while, just for fun, a very young bunny would pull at the yellow tag in Timken's left ear, and run away giggling with delight.

In a moment of pure joy, for he had never really felt loved before, Timken spontaneously flipped into the air with a mighty leap, surprising even himself, and then ran round and round making curious little squeaking sounds. Then all the rabbits frisked and leapt into the air. It was a free-for-all celebration. Simbala was happy, but she warned Timken to stay clear of the Space-Rabbit Crew.

Some weeks went by and the Clan settled into a normal rabbit routine. They accepted Timken and invited him to feed in the best cowslip patches. But something was brewing. There were secret meetings and discussions between those who wanted to be part of a proposed Star-Mission crew. They were Kotar, Tesla, Timken, Boofy and Bifflets, Squibby, Tooky, Derky, KeKe and Snickets.

Eventually after much talk, they decided that under the leadership of Kotar and Tesla, they would do some star-gazing. Even more exciting, with furtive eye contacts and hushed whispers they hinted at actual star-travel. Of course they invited Timken to share his secret experience of star exploration with them, as well as be part of the crew. This whole scenario was charged with excitement. It made every rabbit's heart beat faster, just to think of living on the edge of undiscovered cosmic realities.

The space-crew advised Timken not to consult with Simbala, his adopted mother. She had pretty much forbidden Timken to even talk with members of the Star-Mission crew.

This created conflicts and sadness within Timken. His loyalties were torn between his love for Simbala, and his love for each of his close friends on the Star-Crew. He also knew beyond a shadow of doubt that he was not willing to drop out of his commitment to the space-project. Kotar had already asked for volunteers from the rest of the Hill-Clan rabbits, but they had shaken their heads and refused to be a part of such a dangerous adventure. In fact Katrix and Tika, two young female rabbits, had poked fun at Kotar by rolling in the grass and laughing, "Ridiculous, ridiculous! Whoever heard of Star travel" Timken disposed of his conflicts by placing each of his loyalties into correct perspective. He would honour and receive Simbala's love as an adopted son; but he would also be true to himself as an independent entity—with definite commitments to his new friends.

In the end it was Tesla who had to restore order. He somewhat cooled the Star-Rabbit excitement down and explained they'd have to adopt an altogether slower pace. He simply warned them that a lot of special learning was involved before they could do anything, or they would all meet a quite untimely death. Tesla's words possessed the power of finality. He had created an *'IS'*, and his concept became theirs. Tesla had dropped a 'reality' on them, and it was accepted.

As usual, Tooky almost on cue as it were, interrupted with a question, "What is death?" he asked with his air of young untainted innocence. It brought tears to the eyes of most of those rabbits present, and a hush fell upon the gathering. Kotar took over. He spoke almost gruffly. "Tooky, death is when *'IS'* becomes *'IS NOT'*. We'll talk about it later." The sadness brought on by Tooky's question broke up the meeting and they all went home. For several days Tooky was remarkably subdued. He had finally gotten an answer to the question that had plagued him for some time. But other questions still left him sort of in-between, neither *'up'* nor *'down'*, neither *'in'* nor *'out'*. They left Tooky *'on'* and *'off'* in his whole comprehension. He felt like a big bunch of questions with long ears, and wondered whether the 'Star-Laws' would take over with answers and make decisions for him.

Tooky gazed out across the familiar Hill-Clan territory, the meadows, the woodland beyond, and all the colors of the beautiful countryside, and thought out loud. "What would there be if there were *nothing?* Supposing I were not here! But, everything just *'is'*! Where did *'it'* all start? How can nothing be *something*? In fact, if I were not here and did not see *'IT'*, for me, nothing would exist! When I first became conscious of '*it*', I sort of looked in on '*it*', and then one day I became a part of '*It*'. '*It*' was here before I came, and '*It*' will be here after I am gone—you know, when I become an 'is not' rabbit!"

Tooky's mind alternated between pictures of the black emptiness of 'nothing', and the whole Rabbit Land of '*now*' as it '*is*'. He decided it was time to nibble, and he did just that. It was a wise decision, because careless rabbits who explore in detail why they exist, usually get so dizzy—that some are 'weaselized' and disappear.

That evening as Tooky scented the night breeze, his eyes caught the planet Venus, brightly shimmering low in the western sky. "Other worlds," he murmured to himself. He laid back in the dry grass, alone, just him and the early stars. He relaxed completely without a single thought on his mind while several 'Timeless' minutes passed. Tooky was inside of Time.

He saw his '*Now*' become his '*Past*' and realized that when a slice of Time went by, it became '*is not*', but it left Tooky as an '*is*' rabbit, which is all he wanted to be.

Then, sudden as a shooting star spilling across the night sky, he voiced a reality that became *him*. "The most important truth in life is to know that '*I am*', because everything that ever was, is, or will be, is somehow connected to '*I Am*'." He smiled and hugged himself.

At their next scheduled meeting, ten of the Hill-Clan rabbits formed a group which became officially known as the Star-Crew. The motto for the Space-Rabbits was far from being original, but it fitted their situation! It was Tesla who spoke up in his quiet, powerful, and understated way, "per ardua ad astra," he articulated in typical Tesla tones. "Yes! That is it, 'per ardua ad astra'. In the official

Rabbit Latin-Book it means, 'Through adversity to the stars'!"

Tooky, who had almost recovered from failing to come to grips with the concept of death, had that innocent questing look on his cute furry face when he asked, "What's an 'adversity'? Do we have to go through it to get to the stars? Why can't we go around it, whatever it is?"

It was Boofy who stepped in and replied, "It means we might have misfortunes and that we may have to suffer through some disastrous conditions. Tooky, you have some growing up to do. That flippin' and squeakin' you've been doing is nothing compared to what you are about to experience. You might even decide not to stay with the Star Group." To the amazement of them all, Tooky suddenly flipped his ears down and slowly left the meeting without a further word.

Kotar said, "That squeaking and flipping has to be taken care of. In fact I'll handle it right now," and he too left the meeting which was breaking up anyway, because everyone was hungry—again.

Kotar quickly hopped over to Simbala's burrow. She greeted him with a lovely smile, "Kotar, I was just coming over to speak with you about the nightmare rabbits!"

"Me too!" exclaimed Kotar. "I've been working on an idea for quite a while now, that might catch on, but it involves you!" Simbala placed a couple of fresh carrots on the table and looked at him expectantly. "Well", thought Kotar, "is she trying to tell me she is not going to be part of any plan I may have? After all, everyone knows a rabbit simply cannot munch carrots and talk at the same time!" So he ignored the carrots, and pushed the chair back. "Simbala, you are the wise one, and all the rabbits believe in you.

They see you as a 'Super-Rabbit'. They love you and trust you. Between us, we need to get across to all the rabbits, that when any negative, dark, upsetting thought comes to them at night, or any time for that matter, they can '*capture' it*—and bring it into *'obedience* to the laws of light!" Kotar's eyes lit up with enthusiasm.

"Capture it?" questioned Simbala in rapt attention.

"Yes! In one's mind. You seize it! Get hold of it! It would be like throwing a net over a phantom weasel, and then disposing of it! All rabbits have the power to bring any negative thoughts under control; but, it is a power that has to be awakened, recognized, and then acted upon in faith. It is a *law of light.*

"Kotar! Kotar! This is becoming almost too much for me! Just what *does* a rabbit do when he is attacked by disturbing thoughts? We all need this type of protection!"

Kotar looked thoughtful, and taking a deep breath he said, "Firstly, a rabbit need not—and *must not* give in to negativity. Because when a rabbit yields to such thinking, it overpowers him! So from now on, we propose that it is '*he*' who does *not allow* this!

His power comes from knowing that intelligently directed *light*—kills any form of darkness. He is a rabbit of light! His light is powered by 'Faith'. He does *not* give recognition to any fearful thought, because any act of acknowledgement, becomes an act of acceptance—whereby he unwittingly agrees to play host to this negative element. Finally it overcomes him! He creates it—and then empowers it!" Kotar paused briefly.

"Simbala! Do you realize that it is we who unwittingly keep focusing on our problem thoughts, and the longer we do this, the more power we give them? Even the mature rabbits are overcome by worry and stress.

Darkness of any type cannot survive exposure to light! To prove our point, we'll tell the rabbits to watch the sun come up! Immutably, the King of Darkness disappears before the King of Light!"

"I'm not so sure about that," said Simbala, "suppose the rabbits see it the other way round, and ask us to watch the sunset—when darkness overcomes light?

They might retort, 'watch the light run away from darkness!' What do we do then?"

Kotar chuckled, "Good thinking Simbala. We'll have a lot of work to do to get this off the ground. We must bear in mind though, that it is light, intelligently-directed by a 'Faith-filled' rabbit that achieves this. We'll sort it out!"

"Anyway!" exclaimed Simbala, "you know, it has never occurred to me or to them, to focus control over a situation. Let's face it, from sheer habit it seems we just follow the paw-trails of non-thinking rabbits. Why, if even some of the rabbits put this into practice, the idea would grow! I hope that all the rabbits will develop enough courage to recognize they have this power—and use it!"

"Simbala, do you remember when I told you about that chat I had with the big fuzzy Bumblebee? She said to me, 'Kotar, rumor has it that bees should not be able to fly, something about aeronautical laws, power and weight ratios. But, bees don't know they cannot fly, so they just fly anyway!' That big Bumblebee was highly amused! It's the same with rabbits. Some tribes just routinely reject powers that threaten to overtake them. All the time, *those rabbits simply do things that are not normally done.* Why? *Because they didn't know it could not be done!"*

"Just imagine," said Simbala, "No more flipping and squeaking at night. We'll all get a good night's sleep!" Kotar reached for a carrot, he'd got his point across. Now he could crackle, crunch and munch carrots to his heart's content. Simbala interrupted Kotar's voracious nibbling to say, "Your law-word is equally as powerful as mine Kotar. When we start to expose the Hill-Clan to these ideas, they need to place their trust in both of us!" Thus the plan was laid.

Suddenly, from down by the creek came a long, terrified rabbit-squeak. Simbala, who was about to return to her burrow, stopped, freezing in her tracks whilst terror spread amongst the Clan.

Before fleeing down their burrows, the rabbits looked toward the creek below and were shocked to see it was Timken who was shrilly squeaking in terror. They also saw that he was being held fast by some kind of fearsome creature who was taller than any of them. The existence of such an animal they could not have imagined in their worst types of nightmares. It had to be from another world.

Kotar exclaimed, "Hold on! Maybe we can help him, let's not go underground yet!" Kotar forced himself to hop cautiously about two thirds of the way down the hill before stopping to observe Timken, who was now emitting pitiful squeaks of resigned terror. His eyes were large with deadly fear. One ear had collapsed, and his fur was badly ruffed up from the skirmish in which he had become involved.

Kotar approached Timken and the 'horror-creature' within a few yards. Never had he been so weak with fright. He really wanted to run and hide. Then, surprisingly he was quietly joined by Tesla, who, if he were frightened, showed no fear at all. This was beyond Kotar's comprehension. He looked back and forth between Tesla and the weird animal. It glared dangerously at both of them from the depths of its flashing purple eyes. The creature stood upright like other two-legged creatures and was covered mainly in short plush yellow fur. The eyes seemed to be set in the head of what looked like a large rat. Its ears were short and sharply pointed, and it had a short furry yellow tail.

The unusual feature was a pair of yellow wings closed smoothly to its body. But it was the hands that drew attention; they were pink, naked, and looked extremely powerful. One of them was gripping the stricken Timken who had ceased to struggle. Kotar thought he was already dead. None of the other rabbits came down the hill. Some had already gone to hide in the depths of their burrows.

Then, to Kotar's surprise Tesla began to smile at the 'rat-thing' which remained silent. Kotar looked at both of them in fear and wonderment. Then Tesla raised a paw, and met the creature's flashing purple eyes with a typical Tesla-like look of understanding. It was quite a sight! Tesla with his sharply erect jet black ears and dark fur, standing in an assured manner before this apparition, which had begun to vibrate its wings like it might take off with Timken. Kotar was sweating with fear.

"Kotar," said Tesla quietly, "I'm going to talk aloud so that you will know what's going on, but I want you to remain silent. Did you see the way it rotates its ears? I'll refer to it as 'Ratto', and I'm going to project images to it from my mind if I can. It's probably as scared as we are, at least I hope so." Tesla closed his eyes for several moments.

It was then that something almost magical happened. Ratto let go of Timken, who collapsed into a furry ball of unconsciousness. At the same time, Ratto's purple eyes changed into flashing golden orbs. They were so bright they gave his whole head a golden glow. His wings ceased to vibrate, and in one liquid flow of motion he was directly in front of Tesla. The movement was so instantaneous, so fast, that it had Tesla rattled for a moment. But what really shook Kotar was when Ratto took Tesla's paw into his own powerful pink hand with a gentleness that was hard to believe. Kotar was amazed at the change in Ratto. He struggled to understand why Ratto had become so friendly. Then, just moments later, Tesla relaxed and was laughing with relief as he began receiving Ratto's mental images.

"Kotar! Ratto and I met some time ago in a parallel-dimension. At that time I was new to space exploration, and had accidentally dropped in on a rather beautiful planet known as Rat-Star. It was a scary encounter—because we both came face to face so unexpectedly. We were both equally terrified! I escaped immediately into the space vertical to Time. I don't know what Ratto did! Can you believe that?"

Ratto stepped back a few paces to survey the scene, his eyes glowed with a soft golden light. He also emitted some peculiarly beautiful musical sounds that may have been laughter. Kotar slowly shook his head in wonderment.

Just then Timken stirred and uttered faint squeaks of recovery. He opened his eyes and flipped up his ears. Tesla moved to comfort him, but it was at this point that Simbala who had quietly joined them, stepped in and hustled Timken off to their home burrow. Ratto and Tesla continued with their unique communications via mental images.

Now that peace and good will had been established, other rabbits were slowly appearing from their burrows; and, seeing Kotar, Tesla and Ratto coming up the hill, followed them to the old Oak tree. Still others hopped along to join the assembly at short intervals. Most of the rabbits sat expectantly around Ratto and Tesla in excited anticipation. Snickets wanted to see Ratto fly, and some of them wanted to hear him talk. More than anything else, most of the gang wanted to stroke Ratto's plush yellow fur. Tooky was the first do so and others quickly followed suit. This they did one and two at a time, while he in turn felt their tall silky ears and fur with considerable pleasure. Ratto's golden eyes flashed and he seemed to glow all over. He didn't mind their curiosity because he could read their minds from the images he received from them.

None of the rabbits could quite understand why Ratto had wings and didn't seem to use them. They assumed that Rattos are just that way! They received streams of beautiful pictures from Ratto in exquisite color, but there was no sound-track. With no sound, the rabbits felt lost. They wondered what he might sound like when he spoke, regardless of whether they understood him or not. They well knew the music and magic of creek songs, the wind in the trees, bird songs, bats squeaking, thunder storms and the patter of falling rain, but they wanted to hear Ratto. Ratto on the other hand had adapted to the fact that the rabbit clan could receive images, but not consciously send them, and he had not spoken, knowing already they would not understand him. The rabbits looked upon him as some strange kind of flying cosmic-rat.

Ratto then amazed them all when his eyes changed to a flashing green color, and for the first time he spoke. His voice was softly melodious, and his words sounded like dancing wind-chimes in a strong breeze. Although mystified, the rabbits were so enthralled by his voice that they flipped their ears and looked at each other in wonderment. However, Tesla's brilliance enabled him to match up Ratto's words with the thought images he was receiving; and being sufficiently clear on what Ratto was saying, he became the Clan's interpreter. On Ratto's part, he was anxious to address whatever was on the rabbits' minds.

The Hill-Clan's primary question was as to whether he was hungry. Ratto's eyes now alternated between being gold and turquoise blue; it appeared that these changes always occurred when he was thinking. Ratto had said to Tesla, "Keep it simple, tell them I'm not hungry; I feed on star-dust." Technically, he had explained that his food was not molecular in nature. He was fed star-energy from his base via mega-images on assigned frequencies, and therefore was always energized and never hungry. The Hill-Clan was quite relieved to hear that he sort of fed on space-energy and not rabbits!

Then the rabbits asked to see him fly. It was probably the most exciting thing any of them had ever seen. First Ratto vibrated his yellow wings at very high speed. Then he spread them, and taking flight, displayed their scarlet tips which had previously been hidden. It was a dazzling sight as he flew around their meadow. He could also hover like a hummingbird by simply vibrating his wings at high speed anytime and anywhere he wished. Ratto landed in their midst. Tooky envisioned a ride on his back, and instantly Ratto's response was for him to climb on!

Tooky saw Timken had joined the group and squeaked at him, "I'm a flying rabbit too!" After a short flight to the creek and back, Tooky was speechless with delight when Ratto dropped him off. It was the last of all the merriment for the day. Ratto was no longer a dangerous nightmare, but a strangely good friend.

As the Hill-Clan rabbits accompanied Ratto during the day, he spoke of his home planet Rat-Star and of many strange things beyond their comprehension. However, this did not disturb the rabbits; they were just delighted to be part of his entourage while he explored their home territory. Safety from predators was the least of their concerns—it was almost a dangerous precedent.

Ratto had indicated to Tesla and Kotar that he'd like to stay for a couple or so days to get to know the Rabbit Clan, so they had the pleasure of showing him some roomy accommodation underneath the ancient Oak tree. Long ago it had been vacated by a badger family—now it appeared to be a good home-base for Ratto. "This is perfect!" he imaged. "Absolutely perfect, I'll just re-arrange a few things and set up communications with Rat-Star."

Simbala — the wise and matronly over-seer of the Hill-Clan Rabbit Tribe.

Chapter Three

Next day, the Clan having agreed to a short morning meeting, showed up with a display of visible excitement. Ears went up and down; whiskers twitched, and most looked at each other wondering what the day would bring forth. As Kotar joined them he greeted Simbala with a smile and said, "Well, what next?" To which Simbala replied, "Where did that fascinating 'space-rat' creature come from? I love the feel of his plushy fur—and what a lovely yellow—it's almost gold."

Kotar then brought all the rabbits up to date on what he knew about their strange visitor. Whereupon Simbala said, "Well, he almost killed my Timken. How could Ratto or any other life-form so suddenly appear in Rabbit Land?" At this point, Timken explained that he was innocently star-gazing like he had always done, when suddenly this Ratto animal had appeared beside him.

Almost instantly it had gripped him in a very painful hold. Most of the rabbits looked up in alarm; others shook their heads in disgust. They greatly feared that Ratto was one of many 'realities' that might drop in from nowhere, and if this Ratto incident was an example of space-rabbit travel, they wanted no part of it.

Indeed, Boofy, Bifflets, Derky, Tiska and Aleska agreed that they already had enough enemies without unexpected arrivals from outer-space. There were weasels, hawks, owls, ferrets, dogs, man and his snares, why would they want to import weird killer creatures from other dimensions, accidentally or otherwise? While they discussed this, each rabbit was at one time or another thinking of Ratto. Little did they know they were instantly transmitting their thoughts and fears to him.

Other topics of no real consequence followed, as Ratto was the star attraction. The meeting quickly came to a close with Kotar concluding, "Tomorrow, we'll discuss Ratto's Earth plans, and find out when he might elect to return to his own planet. We also have to organize a series of meetings to introduce some exciting new ideas that well may change our entire lives. However, in addition to this, I understand from Tesla that Ratto will speak to us on a matter of importance. It involves the manner in which our Clan is apparently involved in the dangerous misuse of certain cosmic powers—so it is mandatory for every Clan member to be present when Ratto speaks to us tomorrow." All the rabbits went to their feeding places except for Tesla and Kotar who planned to show Ratto their entire domain, including some of the smoky two-legged animals.

The next morning arrived with warm sunrays falling on the ancient Oak. Ratto emerged and was greeted by a dawn wet with heavy dew. He scanned the clear blue sky. The air was filled with the early melodies of song-birds with which he was delighted. Thinking of the morning meeting—he decided that he really liked the rabbits. They were an innocent, furry, truthful bunch of creatures he felt he could trust. He relaxed in the sunlight and scented wild roses on the soft breezes.

By checking the images he was receiving, he knew that Kotar and Tesla were on their way to see him. So he lay back and relaxed. But only moments had passed when suddenly—new alarming pictures flooded his mind. He saw that Kotar and Tesla were stricken with terror and were being waylaid by two slim brown animals. Ratto didn't know they were weasels, or what weasels were all about; until he picked up the images they were projecting. These lithe, fierce animals were hunting down breakfast for themselves and their young. Ratto saw their white teeth flashing.

With no time to lose, he spread his powerful wings and flew directly to the scene as it unfolded before him. Both Tesla and Kotar seemed to have fallen into a 'weasel-trance' and were frozen in their tracks. One weasel had already fastened onto Tesla's head behind his right ear, and the other was just about to strike Kotar. It was impossible for Kotar to use his special power of eliminating bad 'realities', because the weasels already had them in a trance.

Ratto briefly hovered. Then he descended on the two weasels with the stoop and speed of a Peregrine Falcon. In a split second, each of his crushingly strong hands encircled the creatures.

The weasel that was gripping Tesla behind the ear, opened his mouth wide to shriek, but no sound came out—Tesla was free. Both of the weasels were stunned and at a loss to understand what was happening to them at such lightning speed. With the weasels in a death-grip, Ratto immediately flew high above the trees, and headed to the lake close by. From a great height and far from shore, he dropped them into the water. After splash-down the weasels struggled and tried to swim, but the excruciating pain of crushed ribs and torn bellies caused them to sink into the cold depths. Moments later bubbles surfaced, followed by more bubbles—and then nothing more. Only early morning-magic remained.

Ratto soared back to where he had left Tesla and Kotar. Tesla was bleeding slightly, but Kotar was fine. Both of them were utterly dejected and still shivering from shock and fright. Landing beside them, Ratto gently laid his hands on them. His eyes changed color, and he shot brilliant green beams of light at the frightened rabbits with such power, that it not only illuminated them, but wholly penetrated their bodies. Within a matter of about two minutes both rabbits were filled with boundless energy, and, amazingly, there was not the the slightest trace of damage to Tesla's ear.

"Well", said Ratto smiling, "seems I showed up in the nick of time!" Tesla and Kotar kept looking at each other in amazement; they could hardly believe the strength and good feelings that coursed through them. They instantly expressed to Ratto the depth of their gratitude and thanks.

When they arrived at the meeting by the ancient Oak a little late and none the worse for wear, both the 'weaselized' rabbits had a gripping story to tell. Derky and Squiblets were curious as to how, in the first place, a weasel was able to fasten itself to Tesla. Tesla then explained his plight in such graphic detail that Derky fainted with horror, and two other rabbits became petrified with fright. Ratto stepped in to restore normalcy. Clearly he had saved the lives of Tesla and Kotar. Thusly he became a golden-eyed hero, and a different relationship sprang up between him and all the rabbits. It was then that Ratto announced he had to return to his base for cosmic reasons.

He proposed what he called a Star-Alliance. He had the means of collaborating with the Hill-Clan space-rabbit crew in the event they attempted space-travel, and he made a commitment to help them. Ratto then stood at his full height. He he seemed to tower over the rabbits as he came to his feet.

He instructed the furry group before him that under no circumstance should a space-rabbit crew venture beyond its present reality. It was essential they first become proficient in the control-process of accessing other space-dimensions. The penalty for disobedience would be entirely beyond their control. It would be automatic and self-imposed, namely, the entire Colony would disappear.

Despite their best efforts they would become *'are not'* realities. "Dimensions are frequency related", Ratto stated, "and there are probably only five rabbits in the entire Hill-Clan that can approach this level of comprehension. These are simple cosmic facts."

Ratto's golden eyes flashed in fascinating ways as he explained what he wanted the rabbits to know. He held all of their eyes to his in an unbreakable linkage. It was not unpleasant; they just had to view the colorful images that entered their minds, which somehow enabled instant understanding. When Ratto spoke, the rabbits didn't twitch a single whisker.

Kotar looked first at Ratto, and then at Tesla—but Ratto interrupted what Kotar was about to image. "Kotar, I know of that special power you have developed, you know, turning what you call bad 'realities' into *'are not'* realities. You're on very dangerous ground with this practice. Kotar—you have yet to understand that your, *'is'* and *'is not'*, by which your intent of meaning is, *'live'* and *'dead'*, is in gross error! In reality you have only *removed* them from *'here'*, and transferred them to another place you call *'not here'*. These are entirely different concepts. Although you made the bad realities vanish, you need to know they are very much alive elsewhere!" Ratto spoke with such intentness and authority, that Tesla's interpretation caused two rabbits to faint in fear. Others dropped pellets where they stood, and Kotar, shocked, was left shaking with apprehension.

"I also know that you're aware of this Kotar", Ratto continued, "and are seeking a solution. What you are now doing is being performed out of ignorance. It's what is known in the inter-stellar world as 'cosmic-atrocity', and is attached to its own cosmic penalties. You must stop. Now! And I can help you."

Kotar looked dumbfounded and guilty. He agreed to implicitly obey any instructions that Ratto might issue at any time. He was overcome at the depth of Ratto's understanding. He recognized that there was nothing that Ratto didn't know about every individual rabbit in the entire Colony, including confidential matters between rabbits. This realization made Kotar weak with apprehension. He felt naked and exposed. But, he had the rabbit-maturity to realize and accept that his self-image and ego had taken a terrific beating—and it hurt. For the first time Kotar was was experiencing the full force of genuine humility.

"Incidentally, while I think of it", continued Ratto, "just so you all don't keep wondering; it was not entirely Timken's fault that I appeared here. It was a mix-up. I was involved with a creature that was out of his place, cosmically speaking. As I was about to apprehend him, he illegally switched dimensions and encroached on Timken's space. So I landed up here gripping your poor Timken instead of the wayward being! I've already made this clear to him and explained the risks incurred by 'star-gazing'. He learns fast, and he'll be a great asset to the Clan in future ventures."

Ratto handled himself with such authority that Tesla sensed that he was not just an ordinary 'space-rat'. He must hold some position of note 'somewhere'. Tesla also wondered what Ratto's real name was, inasmuch that the term 'space-rat' and his nickname 'Ratto' seemed to have stuck! Ratto picked up Tesla's thought-images.

"Tesla," stated Ratto, "my real name is Kirata. You'll note there is a 'rat' in it! But I would prefer if you would continue to call me 'Ratto', I like it, and yes! I suppose to you I am some kind of space-rat!" Suddenly Ratto made sounds as though he were laughing out loud. It, like his speech was extraordinarily similar to the loud tinkling of wind-chimes—delightfully relaxing, musical and friendly. Kotar and Tesla looked at him with new appreciation, even though laughing wind-chimes didn't match-up with their images of 'rats'.

"Tesla," continued Ratto, "on that other matter regarding my cosmic position and authority, you may not be able to understand this for quite some time. You'll have questions, the answers to which, even your mind is not yet sufficiently developed to understand. I agree with you that Rabbits just '*are*'; but rabbits also have limitations and cannot go beyond certain boundaries. These factors are pre-set in the design of most species at their time of creation!" Both Kotar and Tesla again heard Ratto's delightful, almost other-worldly wind-chime laughter. It thrilled them in an ethereal way that rabbits have no way of describing.

"I believe that as most of the Hill-Clan Colony are now here at this meeting", said Ratto, "this would be an ideal time for my departure. Kotar, I'll get back to you on that '*is not*' reality problem, but not in person. I can contact you from any place in our local Universe without difficulty. For the time being Kotar, in your lingo—cool it! Now! As I take off for Rat-Star under no circumstances are you to attempt to follow the brilliant flash with your eyes, it could blind you. I'll image to you the moment that you have to look away. Be assured that I have accepted your Colony into a Star-Alliance of which there are many."

He flashed his golden eyes at them. "Good bye for now friends. I'll be in touch!"

Ratto vibrated his yellow wings at an extremely high rate, but didn't spread them to fly. There was a brilliant flash of light as he imaged "*NOW*!" The whole Colony looked away and shaded their eyes. Split seconds later Ratto was just a receding speck that simply vanished. All the rabbits looked at each other as if to question that anything in connection with Ratto had ever existed!

"He's gone," said Tooky sadly. "We'll miss him," exclaimed two young females, Tiska and Tika. Tesla just looked extraordinarily pleased in comparison to Kotar who appeared to be quite crestfallen. Generally there was a feeling of 'Did any of this ever really happen?' and 'What do we do now?' It was quite a let-down.

It was Simbala who came up with the right answer. "You know what we need right now?" she asked. "We all need a good feeding session. It's the only way we'll get back to the reality we once had. Everyone watch out for weasels and other bad situations. Away we go!" Whereupon all the rabbits split up and went different ways to their favorite feeding places.

Squibby and Snickets stayed for a short while to watch five little Black-Capped Chickadees attempt their first flight. From close-by their parents called, "Chickadee-dee-dee Chickadee-dee-dee." After a while three of the babies plucked up enough courage to actually fly to a different bush, and at that point hunger overtook the two young rabbits and they scampered to a cowslip patch. As they nibbled the hours away, Squibby and Snickets kept thinking of golden-eyed Ratto. Was it just in their imagination that they heard wind-chimes on the breeze? The heat of the sun, the calls of the song-birds, and the wild flowers nodding their early summer colors restored a form of normalcy to the Clan, but, they would never again be quite the same.

The next day when the Clan held their regular morning meeting, Kotar and Simbala presented in detail the concept of dealing with, or even eliminating fears and negative thoughts. Everyone agreed that living in varying states of fear was unacceptable; and they agreed to experiment with ideas for change.

Kotar explained with much enthusiasm that bad 'realities' can be rejected! "All of us have this latent power to dismiss negative thoughts", he exclaimed. "We established long ago that we are all, 'rabbits of light'. We know that fears and darkness must flee from us. Light destroys darkness!" Simbala and Kotar then divided the rabbits up into groups of five for instruction sessions, which were to be put into operation over the next two weeks. The foundation of the early lessons would explore what a, 'Rabbit of Light' really is, and how he controls his own 'realities'. Neither Simbala nor Kotar had difficulty in asking for the rabbits' co-operation. They were only too eager to learn how to control their fears!

Tooky quickly immersed himself in his early lessons and learned well. Instead of flipping and squeaking, he now laughed loudly, giggled and tittered over the success he was achieving in dismissing the fear-forces. The problem was that the noises he now made, although different, still woke up the baby bunnies. Simbala didn't admonish him, but solved the problem by having him share a burrow farther away with Timken. Peace descended on all.

Then a few days later KeKe asked Tooky, "How do you get into the practice of this new program? I need a sequence I can follow. I'm still having problems. I was flipping and squeaking last night, and so were a lot of the others. Tooky, it's just a habit that seems to overcome us. We don't sleep peacefully."

"I'll try to help you KeKe. I call it the 'No Fear' program!" said Tooky, settling himself into a dry grassy hollow. "First, we need, 'conscious awareness', to run our lives, not fear! Now, when we're feeding in the meadow, we're extremely *wary.* This wariness keeps us alert—not fear. However, it's in the darkness of night that we're most vulnerable. As we relax our minds, *fears,* which are uninvited enemies, try to enter us and take control. But note this KeKe, it's *WE* who *'allow'* them to take over! We *accept* fears without question! We focus on them! We even '*nurture'* them! We dwell on them, and all of this '*empowers'* them!

In other words we need to realize that fears are subject to *'our'* control!" said Tooky with great emphasis. "We can allow them to stay—or we can '*kill'* them! KeKe, have you noticed how often we call them '*our'* fears? When and how did we claim ownership of them? Or was it the other way round, and they claimed ownership of *us?"* KeKe nodded in enthusiastic approval. "So, like me KeKe, you'll have to take this fear-thing one step at a time!

Right now, we allow fears to control *US*! But you're going to reverse that KeKe, and control *them!* The truth is that we become the servants of anything to which we yield. By yield, I mean things we give in to, be it fear or anything else." Tooky almost ran out of breath. He was as amazed at his explanation as was KeKe.

Tooky flipped his long ears and looked at KeKe who was squirming around in the grass. "Tooky, how come you know so much?" said KeKe, "you're far too young to be wise!" He smiled and gave Tooky an affectionate tickle in the ribs, which made him writhe and giggle in delight. But he became serious almost immediately. "I learned the hard way KeKe; I was just plain tired of being scared all the time. This all happened in the past few days, and that's why I'm so excited.

As you know, most of us can list dozens of fears, food shortages, bad weather, extreme cold, falling sick, you name it. Kotar and Simbala said we've always had this ability to control fear, but we never gave it any thought! We're our own worst enemies!" Tooky stretched and yawned. "On top of all that KeKe", he said, "most rabbits just 'knew' it couldn't be done, so they didn't do it. But Kotar knows of some colonies that despite 'knowing' it couldn't be done—just did it anyway!"

"Tooky! You really are amazing," said KeKe looking fondly at him.

Tooky suddenly responded as though a great thought in his mind had just connected. His eyes were shining with excitement when he said, "I was listening to Kotar one day, and he was speaking of an ancient rabbit-scribe from long ago who wrote down a great truth that we rabbits should never forget.

It was this KeKe, listen carefully! 'For the fear that I greatly feared is come upon me, and that which I was afraid of is come upon me.' Kotar explained that this was said by a rabbit who was in a lot of trouble. I can now see why. That rabbit gave life to his fears! He kept thinking of the things he was afraid of, and eventually a whole lot of bad realities descended upon him and almost killed him!"

"Wow! Wow! And Wow!" exclaimed KeKe. "I'm going to work on it Tooky. I have to dash off now. I'm meeting with Marky, Boofy, Bifflets and Tiska. Thanks a lot. I'll let you know how 'No Fear' works out." He was about to disappear with a flash of his white tail when Tooky shouted, "Hold on there KeKe, there is one more important thing you need to know!"

KeKe skidded to a stop on the green turf. "What's that Tooky?"

"I'm sorry KeKe, but it's maybe the most important part of all. It's about *how* to do it. We know it *can* be done—but *how?*" Tooky was a little taken aback that he had missed this vital part of the procedure, but he brightened up when KeKe sat down again to listen.

"I'll explain it as briefly as I can. Here's the scenario KeKe. You feel afraid of hunger, cold, weasels or whatever. When fear comes into focus *you* kill it without a second thought. You dismiss it from your mind! *You* are in control—not *'It'*; and here's *how* and *why* you can do it!

We already know we're 'rabbits of light'. As such, our *power* is in the recognition that light always overcomes darkness! So when a fear image approaches, we beam our 'control-light' on that fear. It's all in your mind KeKe! You'll see that fear vanish, instantly! It's gone—so don't image it back to see if it's still there; that's what Kotar calls 'lack of faith'. Try it KeKe, you'll be amazed. It works! Then you go back to sleep, or whatever! When you have 'faith' you can't fail. Kotar says it's an immutable sequence of events! Meaning, it's not capable of change!" Tooky chuckled.

"You know Tooky, I believe I can do that. I don't just think it, I believe it!" said KeKe.

"If you're ever in doubt, ask Kotar where the 'light' source comes from", replied Tooky. "You may find his talk on what he calls 'Faith-Power', boring as all get out, but he really knows his stuff, and he's still around to prove it!" Whereupon, Tooky yawned widely and concluded, "KeKe, I'm tired of all this thinking-stuff. Go to your meeting. I'm taking a nap." He smiled. KeKe kissed him on both of his silky ears and dashed off in jubilation.

Meantime on the cosmic scene, unknown to the inhabitants of Rabbit Land, golden-eyed Ratto had placed the entire Hill-Clan Colony under a Star-Alliance surveillance cover. Ratto did this as part of their mutual agreement, but more so from his cosmic viewpoint of saving the rabbits from themselves. He'd seen some dangerous experimentation, and was acutely aware of the deadly terrors that frequented certain space-dimensions. Ratto knew that Kotar may unwittingly enable insidious alien life-forms to land on Earth; where they could upset the natural 'world-order' established at the beginning of Time.

Ratto turned over in his mind the problem of Kotar's strange powers; that of changing what he called 'bad realities', or '*are*' creatures—into creatures that '*are not*'. He'd been recklessly transmitting them to an unidentified space-frequency, the location of which—was unknown even to him!

The really critical situation was that too many unstable negative elements may have become concentrated in one space-dimension. The possibility existed that at some point they might propagate and invade other cosmic places, an altogether dangerous form of contamination.

Ratto perceived this to be an upcoming disaster of the first magnitude. Even more amazing, was the fact that the whole affair originated with a bunch of unknown rabbits living on a small blue planet revolving on the edge of the galaxy!

Ratto was actually a top echelon Star-Alliance being. From a galactic viewpoint his official title and the scope of his powers would have no meaning on Earth. In matters of communication, he decided to project the image of himself as Captain Ratto; which designation was friendly and in terms the rabbits could understand.

It was as 'Captain Ratto' that he decided to contact Kotar to get an idea of the energy he had expended to transmit the '*are not*' beings. Kotar had said that he estimated that they would all be more or less in the same space-dimension. It had always been the 'more or less', that had bothered him so much. Just where did they go?

Kotar was nibbling some clover when Ratto's images lit up his mind. Instantly alert, he stopped to scan the pictures he was receiving. "Oh!" he imaged as he smiled, "Ratto—you're a captain! How are you?"

Ratto smiled. "Never better," he imaged. He then asked Kotar if he could estimate where the 'bad realities' now were. Kotar did a great deal of thinking. Finally he suggested that he would rev-up his transmission power to the level he had previously used; so that Ratto could measure space-time data and locate the creatures. He assumed correctly, that Ratto's instrumention had the ability to achieve this.

First assuring that he was safe, Kotar pretended to dispose of 'bad realities' by dropping his left ear to the 'weird angle'. He then cranked up his mind-power to its blue death-ray level. Ratto was both delighted and apprehensive. He suspected that most of the 'realities' would be in one 'place', but some might be scattered over several levels of 'space'. He thanked Kotar for the live data, and also issued him a firm, final warning not to repeat what he called, 'space-atrocities'.

For Kotar's well-being, Ratto softened his commands with a light touch of his wind-chime laughter. All the rabbits had found his musical sounds to be soothing and delightful. "Good luck Captain Ratto!" imaged Kotar. He then returned to his wary nibbling.

Ratto then performed some highly unusual cosmic calculations, and in a short while he was able to locate where Kotar had sent the creatures. Wherever they had been, they left tracks that could be traced. Most of them were in one place which contained a wide range of 'Time' elements. Others that Kotar had inaccurately beamed to close-by dimensions had simply switched themselves so they all landed up together. Ratto scanned their movements and location. He was both surprised and pleased to learn that certain immutable factors existed, of which the 'realities', and certainly Kotar, were not aware.

The particular 'space' to which Kotar had unwittingly transmitted the 'realities' was a 'one-way dimension'. Anything that had entered could not exit. This meant the 'bad-realities' still thought they could go elsewhere at any time they chose. None of them had as yet tried to travel elsewhere, so were completely ignorant of the fact that they might as well be in some type of cosmic jail! Ratto then recalled from his training that this space feature had been specifically designed to handle the very dilemmas with which they were now confronted. He was also aware that beyond time, the past, present and future had already been created, and was known to 'higher powers' than he. The message came to Ratto that he was to leave the 'realities' where they were. He obeyed. He was relieved.

Another problem had been solved. He had a definite feeling that Kotar would never again use his 'special powers'.

That evening Kotar brought Tesla up to date on what had transpired since they had last met. Tesla had suspected that Ratto was not a common type of space-rat, and was delighted that it was okay to address him as Captain Ratto!

Already he felt the structure of the Star-Alliance coming into force, and was happy that the Hill-Clan Colony had safe cosmic direction and control.

Tesla's intuition told him that Captain Ratto's appearance with the rabbit Colony was not just an accidental 'mix-up' as he had imaged, but rather, powers higher than any key Star-Alliance had directed Ratto to them for a specific purpose.

That evening, the Hill-Clan burrows and the whole countryside was bathed in soft moonlight. It was a magical night. A silvery half-moon sailed on high; stars twinkled brightly, and bats flitted, squeaking into the night. From their hill the rabbits could see almost anything that moved. The creek made faint rushing sounds. Owls hooted deep within the woodland. The rabbits were out feeding on the vegetation, still lush, as the really dry days of summer had not yet arrived.

It was quiet, almost too quiet. Even the tree swallow babies were fully asleep in their nest in the old Sycamore tree. Timken often heard them murmuring as they settled down for the night. So, if things were so incredibly quiet and the night so beautiful, why did some rabbits feel that special sense of something not being quite right? "Nonsense", said Katrix, a mother of three extra cute babies with very black ears. "Our new training program and our own logic tell us we are not to give into fear, so carry on feeding!" All was well—or was it?

Tragedy glides on silent wings. From the shadows of the ancient Oak, a Great-Horned Owl took flight ensuring that she did not cast a shadow. Within seconds her steely talons penetrated Katrix. Gripping her with non-stop in-flight motion, she simultaneously struck her rabbit victim a powerful blow to the base of her skull. Katrix did not utter a single sound. She was no longer an *'is'* rabbit. She had entered the realm of a rabbit that *'is not'*. Softly the warm night breezes rustled among the trees—almost as if they were whispering farewell to Katrix' memory. Her babies fled in three different directions, until several mothers came out of their burrows to usher the bewildered little ones underground to safety.

Simbala stepped in later that night and assigned all three baby bunnies to mothers who had only one or two little ones of their own. That fateful night, the whole Clan was confronted with deadly fears. Each rabbit was forced to make a choice; to wrestle with fear, or sleep. Some relinquished control to fear, others opted to run the 'No-Fear' program and slept soundly!

At dawn, Kotar met with Simbala and discussed the effects of Katrix' untimely death. The whole Clan were saddened by the news. Tesla was especially distraught as Katrix had mothered his three sons. After breakfast at the morning meeting, it was evident that many of the rabbits were preoccupied with their memories of Katrix. Kotar wisely thought that something should be done to get the Clan to, 'snap out of it', before fear and careless actions created another casualty.

Kotar held up a paw to get their attention. "There's no harm in remembering Katrix as a fine mother and friend, we shall all miss her; but right now we need to dismiss any lingering fear, whether it be of owls or anything else." It was quite evident from the frightened looks in the eyes of the younger rabbits that they had very real problems in this regard.

It was Tooky who stood, with his tall ears very erect, and said, "This is precisely where our 'No-Fear' program takes over. Let's practice!" He scanned the whole Clan until he had their attention. "Okay!" he squeaked, "We're rabbits of light. Let's kill the fears! Are you ready?" He paused to signal with his paw. "Now!" he exclaimed. There was some flipping of ears—then, Tooky witnessed wave after wave of frowns and whites of eyes disappear, until the last vestige of fear had vanished. It was similar to seeing a summer breeze chase a ripple of shadows through the tall grass. Eyes now sparkled, and happy faces beamed with pleasure and relief. Tooky smiled and looked across at Simbala, who, glancing around the group, said, "Well done! But we still need a lot more practice."

Tesla, who'd watched from the sidelines, was surprised at what Tooky's little exercise had achieved. In further discussion, the Clan decided to practice the 'No Fear' program until it became an habitual reaction in the face of imaginary threats. Indeed, their brave efforts would rise like a monument to the memory of Katrix. Kotar assured the Clan that each of them would become a powerful force-field of light.

"Skill to do—comes in doing", squeaked Tooky.

"Yes! It's a no-brainer," exclaimed Timken. "I love the 'No Fear' program!"

By this time many of the rabbits were fidgeting and some of the little ones complained of being hungry; so a break was called and they were to convene one hour later.

The rabbit-clock only worked when the sun was out, and Tesla marked where the time-tree sun-dial would be in one hour. Derky and Marky headed out, reminding the rabbits to feed in twos, side by side, facing opposite ways. It was a sort of 'buddy-system' for safety they had pioneered; and already it had saved several lives.

That hour passed swiftly, and the Clan reconvened with enthusiasm. In this session they would come to grips with the crux of Katrix' demise.

It was Boofy who shed light on her tragedy, and he opened his little talk in a manner that was rather 'Tesla-like'. Smiling, he explained, "We all know we primarily run our lives on instinctive logic. It's automatic. If it rains, we find a dry place. If we're hungry we eat, and so forth. That's simple. But we've never really focused our attention on intuition."

"What's intuition?" piped up Timken.

"I'm coming to that Timken," replied Boofy. "Intuition is often thought of as our 'sixth sense'. Say you have some good eating by the hedgerow, and from a logical viewpoint there's no danger. You can't see a weasel or a fox, or a hawk, or even a smoky two-legged animal. You settle in to eat, based on the logic of your 'safe' situation. Try to bear in mind that at that moment, you are trusting to logic, and by doing so—you're only using half your brain!" Some of the rabbits shifted uneasily. Others looked perplexed; they flipped their ears and looked at each other for some glimmer of understanding.

"However," continued Boofy, "we experience intuition as a special feeling. It's a specific kind of *'knowing'*. It can occur in many different situations. We're going to focus on—*knowing when something is wrong!* These sudden flashes of 'knowing' are *'insight'*. They are what we call, *'intuition'*. They occur in a fraction of a second! When we get a message like that, it flits through our minds so quickly we almost miss it! So, at all times we need to be aware and *anticipate* sudden inputs of intuition! Upon recognition—we need to obey them instantly. Those rabbits who were disobedient, or took time to run it through their logic system are no longer with us. It seems that Katrix mistook her intuitive messages for fears at the cost of her life. However, as we shall see, her sacrifice was not in vain.

"So what *IS* the difference between 'fear' and 'intuition?" asked Snickets.

"Yes!" exclaimed KeKe, "we all need to be very clear on this—it's truly a matter of life and death!"

"All in good time KeKe. Snickets, to answer your question, *we're* all familiar with fear," continued Boofy, "it's a bad type of thought that enters your mind and tries to control you. Intuition is different. It's like a sudden flash of lightning—but it's really a flash of insight focused on your exact situation in Time. It calls for instant obedience without question! Don't ever refer it to logic. If you do, *IT* will not only vanish—but you too may disappear!"

Kotar could hold back no longer. His eyes were shining with what he had to express. "Here is wisdom," he stated with intensity. "I'm only alive today because I learnt that I must never allow *'logic'* to override *'intuition'*. The power of intuition enables us to *'know'*, and that *'knowing'*, is the difference between life and death." Kotar glowed at the impression he'd made on the Clan.

Most of them were smiling, and many of their furry faces were alight with intent and understanding. The rabbits looked at each other in amazement. They had discovered they had more control over their lives than they ever thought was possible.

"Before we close our meeting," Boofy announced, "I feel there're a couple of highlights that need repeating. One—be aware that the message of logic is always to, 'get the facts'; and two—let's be wary of the phrase, 'It's the logical thing to do!'" he smiled. "The fact is, that in the face of intuition, logical inputs don't add up, nor do they have to—nor is there any possibility that they might! That should never concern you!" One glance told Boofy he'd made his point.

"Just before we leave," interjected Tesla, "I have a reality you need to etch into your minds." He flipped his jet black ears to their vertical position. "In one of my travel adventures, I overheard two young male Humans comment on the 'uneasy feelings' they were experiencing after paddling their kayaks into a beautiful and isolated wilderness location. They were tired and hungry. It was early evening and high time to set up camp for the night.

As they unloaded their gear and attended chores, both boys sensed shadows of lingering apprehension. It raised unspoken questions that neither of them were willing to talk about. It was intuition—unrecognized—calling for them to immediately relocate their campsite elsewhere. Although they did briefly acknowledge their misgivings; their resolve weakened in the face of logic, and the welcome scent of freshly brewed coffee as it wafted across the clearing. The gift of 'knowing and obeying' was left suspended in isolation—a mere niche element among the multiple choices in the fabric of time.

Tesla heaved a sigh. He looked first at the furry faces surrounding him, and then across the valley. He continued; "At dawn, both young men struggled fiercely as two Grizzlies dragged them screaming from their tent. I shall never forget the destructive horror of the killing scene. It will affect me forever. It was an orchestration of desparate trauma, cries of terror and futile struggles. Never had I seen so much blood at any one time. It was of course as normal and natural for the bears to take the boys as prey—in the same way as they fed on the Elk calves of early summer. Yes. I fled that scene."

As Teslas's last words fell on the host of furry ears, several rabbits dropped piles of pellets. It was an imaged reality too close to weasels' teeth. As Tesla left for his conference with Kotar—he flashed just one quick smile at the frightened group. "We need to obey intuition!" he said.

Boofy and Bifflets then suggested they all go out to feed, and this started much jumping, leaping and general frisking as they gave vent to their happy feelings. They scattered to their favorite feeding places. Timken and KeKe went to the cowslip patch where they joined Tooky, who said, "Let's remember every incident where intuition saved the day, and report it at our morning meetings." With a mouthful of yellow flowers, KeKe said, "I'm all for that—I want to live!"

Boofy — Older brother of Bifflets. He is confident, effective and highly intelligent.

Chapter Four

The entire valley including Rabbit Land had fallen under the spell of June sunshine with vibrant anticipation of things about to happen. Cherry and apple orchards had blossomed down in the valley, and the farmland meadows were dotted with Black Angus cattle. Many lay in the cool shade under a huge Beech tree; and all of them shook their heads or flicked their tails at the annoying flies of summer.

Kotar, Tesla, Boofy and Snickets were on a morning carrot raid at the local farmstead. They had envisioned the taste of carrots and young cabbages for almost three days. After they had satiated themselves, Tesla was planning to tell them of some exciting news that Captain Ratto had just transmitted.

Their thoughts were momentarily interrupted by the clatter of the loud mechanical monster that would occasionally growl and rythmically click along the shiny tracks between the woodland and the farms. Sometimes it would emit screaming sounds that disturbed the rabbits. Today, far off, they heard the metallic monster wailing a prolonged danger signal.

However, not all the creatures were affected by the noise. A couple of young two-legged male animals walked along the tracks. Their ears were plugged into the 'beat' that insulated them against all other sounds in the world. Their faces were alight with vacant ecstasy, while their agile thumbs 'twiggled' and flicked at the small black objects in their hands. The deepest and most profound thoughts of which the two-legged creatures were capable, displayed themselves as inane messages to each other while they walked only a few feet apart. As immutably as night follows day, the clamoring steel monster—a dual diesel rail-road engine unit, appeared to gobble them up. A further long screech of brakes rent the air. Time did not stop—but the two-legged creatures did. In split seconds they changed dimensions from '*are*' to '*are not*'!

Timken who was sneakily following the Tesla group to the cabbage patch, saw the whole terrible scene unfold. Hopping close by, he was somewhat shocked to see the blood-drenched tracks and torn clothing. He closed his eyes on seeing the almost naked mangled flesh of the inert lumps squished between the rails. Timken appraised his world. The sun still shone brightly, the rabbits feasted on fresh garden vegetables, and the world continued to turn. "Wow!" breathed Timken, "It's the way things *are*—except for the pathetic creatures that *were*."

A short while later there was a huge commotion at the farm, with people, dogs and trucks heading in all directions. The invading rabbits settled in for a sustained luxurious feast.

Back at the Hill-Clan home base, Tesla, Kotar, Simbala and a bunch of other rabbits listened to Tesla. His whiskers were even, his very black ears had a glossy, silky look to them, and his voice carried a tone of suppressed excitement. Captain Ratto had imaged to Tesla that he was monitoring the Clan as part of the Star-Alliance plan, and expressed sadness at the loss of Katrix.

To assist the Hill-Clan in their development he said he was sending his two sons and a few surprises on which he did not elaborate. His offspring bore the names Ratfink and Rudy. Captain Ratto had carefully explained that whereas Ratfink had a negative meaning on Earth, at the cosmic level it had 'elite connotations'.

None of the rabbits knew what an 'elite connotation' was, any more than Tesla. All they wanted to know was when these two young space-rats would arrive. Simbala said they could stay together in the Silver Birch tree burrow. They did not have to be fed, as they, like Ratto, were energized via image-relay.

The rabbits had to wait for quite a while; some almost lost interest. In fact three Earth days had passed before Captain Ratto's kids arrived in a brilliant white flash of light—blinding in its intensity. When the rabbits finished rubbing their eyes, there stood before them, Ratfink and Rudy. They had the same shape and features of Ratto, but scaled down somewhat because they were not yet fully grown. The young space-rats were clad in golden fur, and possessed the same type of yellow wings with scarlet tips as Ratto. Ratfink was the taller of the two. The big difference was in their eyes. Both were a dazzling turquoise blue, and flashed with suppressed devilment which matched their smiles.

"So you're Rabbits!" exclaimed Ratfink. His voice was as clear and fascinating as Ratto's. Its cadence too, flowed with wind-chime notes that almost made the rabbits want to sing. It was incredibly beautiful. All of them crowded round the two handsome young space-rats. Rudy said, "We are not able to give rides to any of you as our wings can't carry extra weight till we are fully grown." He had been warned of this demand and was prepared to head it off early. The air was charged with excitement that could hardly be contained. A number of rabbits wanted to feel the space-rat's plushy fur; and this they permitted without reservation.

"Okay you young space-rats," said Tesla, "Let's show you where you'll be staying while you're with us." They all trooped across to the Birch tree. She was as impressed with the Space-Rats as much as they. Ratfink and Rudy checked things out and settled in. For the first two days the golden-furred rats flew around exploring the whole area including the farmstead, where the rabbits regularly raided the vegetable garden. They were a pleasant addition to the Clan, but rather secretive, and when they spoke to each other privately, it was in a language no one could understand.

Timken sort of spied on them when he could, and the last time he saw them from his hiding place in the ferns, the space-rats were doing something rather weird.

In a small woodland clearing he saw that Rudy was holding what appeared to be a strange rabbit not known to Timken, and Ratfink was adjusting something on him. Then they let the rabbit go. It moved in a slightly unnatural manner, although its ears and head moved quite normally. Ratfink and Rudy hid deep in the bushes and waited. Timken lay even lower in the ferns.

From out of the blue, a Red Tailed Hawk swooped in to capture the apparently unwary rabbit. Hardly had its talons touched the fur of its intended victim, when a blindingly high voltage bolt of blue light flashed up at the hawk. It fell and flapped its wings disjointedly. Then after some further thrashing around among the ferns, with some difficulty it recovered and flew up and away with a loud cry.

Peals of melodic laughter burst from the two space-rats. "It works," exclaimed Ratfink. "And how!" shouted

Rudy. Again they exploded with their wonderful wind-chime laughter, and picking up what now Timken perceived to be a weird 'fake rabbit', the Rats went back to their home. Timken scampered over to Tesla's place to tell him what he had seen. Kotar and Simbala were there too, and none of them seemed to understand what Timken was talking about. Kotar said, "Let's wait and see what those two scamps tell us! This should be more than just interesting."

Later when they met Ratfink, he asked Kotar to assemble the Hill-Clan in the morning so he could show them some astounding ideas he had developed. The meeting was set up with no delay. Timken discussed with Boofy the amazing flight-ability of the golden space-rats, and wondered if the principles could be applied to rabbits.

"Flying rabbits!" exclaimed Boofy, "I don't think so—to where—and why would a rabbit want to fly?" Timken just looked thoughtful and started to feed in the cowslip patch.

It was a very peaceful night. Many of the rabbits were now using the 'No Fear' techniques; and having once achieved success, they repeated the experience night after night. They slept silently and well. These rabbits then helped their friends, and the 'No Fear' program really caught on. Kotar and Simbala were extremely pleased.

Even though the morning was wet and cold, Ratfink and Rudy showed up for the meeting looking very well-groomed and rested. It was Rudy who outlined the plan they'd conceived, while Ratfink managed the 'electric rabbit'. The whole idea was to set up a number of electronic rabbits around the area, and let the hawks, owls, weasels and other enemies feel free to attack them. The enemies would be almost electrocuted on contact, and the number of attacks on the rabbits would diminish. Ratfink declared the scheme would develop a 'conditioned response', and their enemies would realize the foolishness of attacking rabbits! They proudly revealed their research was based on some kind of Russian, 'slobbering Pavlovian dog' theory. Ratfink vibrated his golden wings, and Rudy's turquoise eyes flashed in anticipation of the Clan's approval.

But although the rabbits loudly applauded, both Kotar and Tesla disagreed with the plan. They took the two overly enthusiastic space-rats aside and explained their position. Kotar said they foresaw problems arising that could not be handled in the day to day scheme of earthly rabbit reality. The primary one being that all the rabbits would assume they were safe, when in reality, the particular enemy about to attack them—may not have experienced the 'zapping-procedure'. Neither Ratfink nor Rudy were offended at the decision, and flew back to the Birch. They had experienced a lot of creative fun and were generally enjoying themselves.

Meanwhile, some of the Star-Crew space-rabbits felt they were ready for some type of 'local' space exploration. Snickets and Squibby were becoming impatient, and secretly felt superior, older and wiser than the visiting space-rats.

Tesla however, told them they were grossly underestimating Ratfink's and Rudy's cosmic level of creation and birth. He explained that in the same way that 'rabbits just are', so also golden space-rats 'just are' by their other-worldly design. Tesla suspected that Ratfink's and Rudy's brains functioned in many dimensions of space and time.

At their level of cosmic-intuition, for them, even to 'think' would be to 'know'. Their instant cognitive ability gave them a stunning advantage over Earth beings. Their logic-circuits had parallel automatic intuition-override, requiring no additional thought processes. Tesla glanced at Squibby and Snickets; he could readily see they were not convinced. Their attitude was an ultimate display of youthful ignorance and arrogance, both of which, if not held in close check were a recipe for some form of untimely death.

The activity of the flying space-rats did not go unnoticed in the human village below. Several of the smoky two-legged animals had sworn over a number of beers, that they had seen two large 'rats' flying around up in the hills. It caused a lot of dissent and rowdiness. Feelings ran high, and in derision, those who had seen the flying rats were told they would soon see flying pigs next! In fact, the space-rats were reduced to mere figments of imagination, and the high quality of the beer!

However, as the inseparable beings with the flashing turquoise eyes discovered, not all 'men-creatures' were the same. In a small hollow between the Hill-Clan burrows and the woodland, they found a smaller version of the two-legged Beings. He was a slight, fourteen year old boy. His head was crowned with a mop of unruly golden hair, and his very blue eyes were set in a tanned face of innocence. His eyes held a distant-look, and held a sadness that told a story of its own. He wore a scruffy shirt that once was white, blue shorts, and dirty white socks. Frayed runners contained his feet. He was crawling among the wild strawberries eating them so quickly that he ate some stalks and leaves too. Ratfink and Rudy slowly approached him. The boy looked up. His name was Zack.

His eyes lit with wonderment and curiosity at seeing the golden space-rats. He, being taller than they, just crawled toward them. "Hello," he exclaimed in a low clear voice, "where did you come from?" He smiled at them and sat back hugging his knees. His disarming reaction to them came as quite a surprise. Then Zack stood, and leaning down, tentatively at first, touched, and then ruffled Rudy's golden fur, and then Ratfink's, drawing back each time. Next he gently felt their scarlet-tipped wings, and laughed delightedly as he fearlessly met their flashing eyes.

They in turn smoothed his silky hair, caressed his tanned cheeks, and held his hands. As they explored each other, it was evident that this was a meeting that opened the doors of intimate friendship.

Zack's face became 'alive' when he touched the two rat-creatures. Warm feelings so enveloped his entire body, that he became somewhat light-headed. It was so pleasurable and new, it was beyond his ability to understand. He surged with joy. Neither of the space-rats told him it was love.

It was Rudy who spoke first. "Hello Zack!" he said. "We won't hurt you in any way. We met the rabbits, and we wanted to meet you too!" Zack's eyes opened wide with surprise; never had he heard such fascinating musical voice sounds issue from any creature. He laughed, "Your voices are really strange! Sort of like wind-chimes!" he exclaimed. "Hey! How do you know my name; and how am I able to understand you?" Ratfink and Rudy sat in the deep grass beside him to explain their mission. They also gave him insight on their cosmic abilities to 'see and know', which also included methods of language and communication.

Zack just listened. He was entranced. He examined every inch of these new friends in detail. Although he was both stunned and a little apprehensive, he felt in no danger. Only once did he interrupt them to exclaim that he hoped the rabbits were his friends too; as he wanted to meet with them and explore the possibilities of living nearby. He offered no explanation of his intent.

Every moment that Zack spent with the Star-Rats caused his usual loneliness to vanish. He just could not help smiling, and his blue eyes flashed with suppressed excitement. Just being with these friendly creatures was as relaxing for him—as idly watching fleecy white clouds move slowly across the summer-sun. The trauma of his village origin, and these new warm feelings that coursed through him, ensured that if it were possible, he would never again return to what he had known as 'home'. The trio sat in the warm grass—just looking at each other.

As Ratfink and Rudy sat with him, they routinely scanned Zack's memory banks. They were both shocked at what they discovered. Zack had experienced extreme physical pain, rejection, hatred, and other more tragic forms of abuse; including attempts to kill him. Although these memories had been retained in isoloation—they were still directly linked to his everyday behavior. Often they influenced and controlled him beyond his conscious intent.

They also observed that when Zack's psychic or physical pain levels exceeded his tolerance levels that he disappeared inside himself. In reality he opted-out for varying periods of time, and 'came back' later to check on the damage. Love was conspicuously absent. Brutality reigned. This gave the golden space-rats the whole picture of the fourteen year life-span of the wilding known as 'Zack'.

Momentarily, Zack interpreted what he read in their faces as rejection; but Ratfink and Rudy picked up on this instantly. They reached out and both gently hugged him. Zack felt their plushy fur, and seeing their smiles of assurance, his whole being seemed to merge with theirs. Behind them, honeysuckle blossoms yielded their unique scent, and turning toward the flowers—Zack closed his eyes in ecstasy to inhale their precious fragrance. It relaxed him completely.

Ratfink caught Rudy's eye, "Remember that study we did on Earth knowledge at that Interstellar Centre—this kid's like that Phoenix mythology stuff we took. I see Zack not as a bird, but as a Phoenix Boy—rising from the ashes of destruction to take wing. With his background, that's exactly what he is—a Phoenix Boy!" He laughed. Rudy said, "I believe you're right on." They both chuckled.

Ratfink and Rudy noted that Zack's brain and comprehension abilities were of an entirely different design, and a far higher level to that of the rabbits. They agreed between them, that if Zack stayed with the Hill-Clan, he would be their liaison contact.

Suddenly Zack took Rudy's hands and pulled at him with a delightful peal of laughter. Rudy knew that Zack wanted some sort of game, and in the next moment they struggled, rolled and twisted among the grass in a wonderful wrestling match. Zack was stronger. The point of the game for him was not to win or to lose, he just needed to touch and be touched—it was the most different 'touching' he had ever experienced. It seemed to heal him in some way that released his inner-strength. Above all, he was thrilled when he smoothed Rudy's golden fur and looked into his flashing turquoise eyes. It was the way of best friends.

Ratfink watched them both, and despite his greater maturity, he could not help but shed a tear or two. He smiled and envisioned the future, deciding that Zack and the Hill-Clan rabbits should meet!

When Zack and Rudy at last desisted, Zack asked the space-rats about their wings and said he'd like to see them fly. To this they readily agreed and put on quite a dazzling aerial display. Their yellow scarlet-tipped wings painted 'flying rat' pictures in the sky around the woodland. Zack was elated and satisfied.

Timken, who had been on a spying mission revealed himself, and was introduced to Zack, and all four of them walked up the slope to the Hill-Clan burrows. Timken would have felt quite deflated to know that his whereabouts was always known to Ratfink and Rudy; they just didn't have the heart to tell him because he was such a cute little super-rabbit.

Suddenly they were surrounded by a mass of frisking fur with tall ears pointing in all directions. Kotar and Tesla were at first apprehensive because Zack was the tallest among them. But when the young space-rats explained things, it all became clear and the whole affair turned into a Hill-Clan celebration.

However, there was a problem. In the midst of all the furry jubilation, Zack had fainted—either from hunger, weakness or excitement, perhaps all three. The curious rabbits gathered round him. Tooky hopped onto him and sniffed at his face. The tickle of Tooky's whiskers stirred Zack, and he opened his piercing blue eyes to see he was surrounded by ears mounted on fur. He raised his arms, and was busy stroking the rabbits when Ratfink and Rudy approached.

Ratfink quickly produced a 'Cosmic-Creature-Scanner'. He instantly confirmed that Zack had eaten nothing but wild strawberries for three days, and physically was failing due to inadequate and incorrect food intake. Rudy had a constructive idea. He asked Ratfink if it were possible, due to Zack's unique brain structure, that maybe he too could be fed 'star-energy'. It could also be beamed from their base by 'mega-frequency'.

Zack, frowning slightly, asked, "What's that?" Ratfink said, "In simple terms, it's real food that can be changed into a formula to suit the creature that needs it. Its molecules are changed, then transmitted and reconstituted from the image within the creature receiving it. Rudy and I thrive on it all the time! Let's go up to the Silver Birch tree and sort things out. That's our base while we're here on assignment." So the trio left, while the Clan did whatever rabbits have to do at 2:00 p.m. on a sunny afternoon.

When they arrived on the edge of the woodland, Zack saw the Silver Birch and lay under the shadow of its fluttering leaves. Ratfink instructed him to be very still, close his eyes, and envision any substantial meal that would make him feel really good! He must not talk, just relax and image his meal. Zack was ordered not to be disturbed by minor oscillations he would experience. "Now," said Ratfink, "relax and eat until you feel full! Okay?" "Yes!" replied Zack. There was a slight low-pitched humming sound. His eyes closed. All he heard was the breeze whispering through the Birch boughs. In reality, he'd fallen asleep and didn't know it. Ratfink did know and was happy. The conditions could not be more ideal. Rudy and Ratfink sat by the wilding and watched him sleep and eat! They studied his boyish form and good looks; and became entranced with Zack's latent cosmic possibilities. He was a prime Rat-Star discovery.

Thirty minutes passed before Zack stirred, slowly at first, and then leapt to his feet. "Ratfink, Rudy!" he exclaimed, "You're here! And I feel so good! Can I eat like this every day?" "I see no reason why not," Ratfink replied in great satisfaction.

"Now," said Zack, "I'm going skinny-dipping in the creek, I feel sticky and yucky!" Without looking behind him he lightly skipped down to the creek where it burbled over the smooth shiny rocks. Upon arrival he heard Chickadees calling from the bushes, and scented wild roses from across the clearing. Zack peeled off his shirt and threw it in the grass, but before releasing his belt he carefully laid his sheath knife with the seven inch blade to one side, it being his only possession. Lastly he shed his shorts, socks and runners. Stepping into the fast water, Zack washed up and submerged only briefly before coming up the creek bank. He lay naked in the soft grass to dry off and warm up in the hot afternoon sun.

Surounded by bird songs, buttercups and all the living scents of summer, he allowed himself to dream a different reality. The Golden Rats along with Kotar, Tesla, Timken, Snickets and others came down to join him. Zack was elated at feeling so clean and strong. A strange and beautiful joy descended upon him at being surrounded by his furry rabbit friends. He especially loved the almost magical plushy space-rats. Every time their eyes met his, he felt warm all over in a way he could not explain.

Ratfink decided there was something not quite right with the appearance of Zack's body. He looked a lot thinner without clothes, and his back, chest and stomach bore scars of different sizes and shapes. Recent red welts on his back were still evident, as were multi-colored bruises that covered his upper arms. Despite this, one's eyes were drawn more to his tanned but shadowed young face and his arresting blue eyes, than his scars and discoloration. His shock of blond hair lay wet and plastered down slightly over his ears. Ratfink decided then and there that Zack must never again return to the village where he had experienced such trauma.

The warm sun drifted Zack into a sleepy state, and finally he snuggled down in dreamy surrender. His face in repose shed every care and became a mask of almost angelic beauty and innocence. Only Tooky checked up on him from time to time by peeking at him, and softly hopping away.

Rudy, Ratfink and Tesla in the meantime, went to check out the small clean den under the ancient Oak tree. Captain Ratto had used this prior to his departure. They decided it would make an ideal lair for Zack.

Red squirrels already made their home higher up in the Oak, and they noisily chased each other in a steady flow of bushy red tails up the trunk and across the branches. Zack would of course need to gather up soft bedding materials for comfort.

When He awoke, it was close to early evening. Quickly he rounded up his clothes and fastened the knife to his belt. He felt rested and strong. When Rudy and Tesla showed him his proposed new home, he was surprised and pleased. His tension dropped and a secure feeling overcame him. He would be missed, and he knew that one or two village people might search for him the next day. Recalling a hay meadow not too far away, he decided that one small bale of hay would suffice to make an ideal bed. Dusk was already falling when Zack returned to the Oak. With difficulty he pushed the hay bale into the hole, and heard it softly roll over further down. The entrance turned to the right upon entry, and Zack found that once he had crawled in, he could move around quite well even with his head raised. He cut the bale open, whereupon, with a rush of dry hay-scent it spread out to form his bed. He then carved a little shelf on which to place his knife.

Zack felt safe in his new home. He peeled off his shirt and draped it over a thick root. Then, pulling an armful or so of the hay over him, he relaxed and almost immediately fell into a deep slumber.

He awakened when Kotar and Simbala along with Rudy-Rat dropped in. They found him to be quite comfortable. "Hi," he greeted them. "I have to get a drink, I'll be right back." Sniffing the night breeze, Zack surged with elation at scenting the not so distant sea. He skipped down to the creek to quench his thirst and drank deeply. He knew he'd have to locate a water container on the morrow.

After his visitors had left, Zack lay relaxed and happy. The absence of foreboding trauma added a separate peace all its own. He remembered his older brother Brett and their parting before he was transferred to another foster home. Zack could still feel the wrench of their parting. It still hurt. Shafts of pale moonlight cast illumination through the entrance to his lair. An owl hooted from high above in the Oak branches, and he hoped his rabbit friends were safe in their burrows. He was thinking of their soft fur and silky ears when Timken suddenly showed up with Snickets, Tooky, Boofy and Bifflets.

After a typical session of rabbit-type chit-chat, much to Zack's surprise, all five of them snuggled around him in a nice warm heap of fur for the night. He hoped they would make their home with him permanently. He fell asleep again.

Zack awoke to the bird-chorus of dawn. He was already alone as the rabbits had left him for an early morning feed. Zack strapped on his knife and crawled up into the dewy morning where he stretched luxuriously before heading down to the creek to drink and wash up. He returned to the Clan burrows where he found Kotar and Tesla feeding. He expressed his concerns that he'd left a trail of hay strands behind him last evening when he had acquired the hay bale, and that it could be dangerous to all of them. Kotar agreed and immediately dispatched a whole troop of rabbits, who went out to obliterate any trace of hay leaving the meadow. It took them a lot longer than they thought, but when Tesla went to inspect their work, he was very pleased.

Ratfink and Rudy appeared in the morning sunlight. No one visited them at their Silver Birch base as they were very different creatures. They had also stated that this location was their private home and operational headquarters. This was where they communicated with Rat-Star and no doubt reported to Captain Ratto.

On meeting them again, Zack became awash with delight. He just couldn't take his eyes off their plushy yellow fur and scarlet-tipped wings, nor their flashing turquoise eyes. He loved them and the rabbits. They did not reject him, and their acceptance touched him with special warmth. Zack had yet to link that which he felt with the meaning of 'love'. Tooky explained to him that he'd been welcomed by the Clan because—a Zack just *'IS'!* Zack in turn, had wondered why the whole world was not populated by snugly rabbits and golden rats! He was smiling at this thought, when Ratfink asked him to join them for breakfast up at the Birch, which Zack had renamed the 'Birch Tree Inn'. Ratfink and Rudy said that Zack's presence was more than welcome by the Hill-Clan, because their various predators would be repelled by the sight, and smell of a two-legged creature living in the area. Kotar said that he was sure that this would drop their fatality rate, as most creatures associated the scent of Humans with death,

As to what they might breakfast on, Rudy said, "You don't have to lie down to image a meal. Just relax where you are! And, there are no sounds to listen for. Ratfink and I just supplied those yesterday to help you overcome your disbelief. It's a silent process, and you do not need us to activate it. You will possess this feeding-power' for as long as you require it, wherever you are. We have assigned a frequency specifically for you. The key-word here is 'require'. When you no longer need to feed this way, the frequency will deactivate—or to use your term, 'self-destruct'. It won't really be destroyed. It'll just auto-flip to another assignment.

Zack slowly shook his head from side to side almost in disbelief. He blushed, thanked the space-rats and imaged his breakfast. A short while later he felt satisfied. Although he did not chew or ingest in a normal manner, he discovered that as he imaged, the tastes were coordinated from his memory banks. Zack was very thankful and felt his normal high energy level returning. After his meal, he bid the space-rats 'Good By', and headed out toward the creek. He needed time to think and to be alone. Zack surged with joy, which gave rise to him whistling a favorite classic. He loved to whistle. This lilting tune in particular, gave him images of little streams wandering serenely through the woodland. It filled him with peace. He accompanied it with the full descants as though he were performing as the guest of some famous symphony orchestra.

Rabbits looked up from their feeding. Whistling was new them. Ears flicked and and noses twitched in the breeze, until they saw it was Zack. He cascaded his melodic whistling exactly as if he were following a conductor. He smiled and was quite elated. Scanning the copse ahead, he perceived a red fox just leaving, but on seeing him it melted into the trees again. Then suddenly, Zack's music-making came to an abrupt stop. Something clearly warned him with a sudden stab of fear, that humans in the farmland below might hear him. From then on he just whistled quietly to himself.

Back at their Birch tree base, Rudy and Ratfink were discussing Zack's learning abilities, especially his lack of ego. He'd not been pre-programmed by Man; nor did he possess any self-imposed barriers. Indeed, Zack was an innocent, highly intelligent cosmic-animal—with no crippling concepts of limitation. This meant he would be open to acquiring certain Rat-Star modes of thinking. The Rats were also aware that they would eventually need to go beyond any form of oral communication with Zack; possibly operating at some level of almost pure intuition. But, first they had to let the Clan down gently from their high expectations of being involved with space-travel; and just before lunch, Zack also joined the Clan to hear Ratfink's comments.

The golden space-rats smiled at the sea of furry faces. They had to address the matter of maturity and a host of other factors required for any rabbit to be eligible for space-ventures. After a short while they progressed to a period for answering questions. Meantime, Zack had been wriggling around and peeking at something he held in his cupped hands. Whatever it was, it caused him to exclaim, "Ouch!".

Rudy had seen that Zack was somewhat preoccupied, and asked, "What's up Zack? What do you have there?"

Zack stood and displayed his newest friend. "It's a baby hedgehog!" he announced proudly. "He's already prickly—but he's such a neat little guy. He started to follow me back from the creek, so I picked him up! I named him Snuffy!" Rudy and Ratfink met Snuffy and attempted to examine him; whereupon that little creature curled into a tight ball that hid his cute face and little pink tummy. Zack placed him a pocket. Many of the Clan were smiling at Zack and Snuffy—but, being quite familiar with hedgehogs, they wanted to refocus on Ratfink's space-travel comments.

Rudy often came up with bright, if not strange ideas, which was all to the good. In this case he suggested that the five overly eager Space-Crew rabbits be first exposed to an experiment with Time, which would be safe and small-scale compared to actual star-travel. Zack trembled with a sense of excitement that is only known to those who explore new frontiers of consciousness. For a few moments he was able to divert his mind from Snuffy.

"Before we proceed, we have one small problem," said Rudy, "we need a watch to enable our experiment."

"What's a watch?" asked Tooky curiously. Rudy was briefly describing what they looked like, when Kotar's ears flipped up and he said, "I think I know what you mean! Is that what it is? I found a watch one day under the leaves!"

"Where is it?" questioned Rudy. "Well," said Kotar, "I hid it in a tree stump in the woodland. It's not very far away!"

"Okay, let's go find it and pick it up," said Ratfink. It was elected that Zack, the golden-rats, Kotar and Tesla, Timken and Tooky would all go on the retrieval mission.

It was an exciting trip, and they kept a low, wary profile as they edged along the Hawthorn bushes to the woodland. So far, so good, but it took Kotar half an hour of scampering around to find the stump, because the vegetation had grown so high. It was almost hidden by fireweed, and everywhere the buzzing of bees gathering pollen added to the activity of the day.

"Here it is," exclaimed Kotar, as they all gathered around the stump. It was Zack who found the hole almost hidden and surrounded by moss. He reached deep inside and after scrabbling around, said with sudden excitement, "I have it!" and lifted the watch out.

Zack pulled it through the fireweed, pressed it to his ear and exclaimed, "It's still ticking!" and passed it to Ratfink. The Rolex Submariner was heavy. Unwittingly Kotar had hidden it in the middle of a pack rat's nest, and that happy pack-rat had pulled it around almost every day in fascination. He loved the way it talked to him, though it always said the same thing. But its ticking was magical, and he coud hardly wait for night-fall to see its luminous face light up the darkness of his treasure chest!

The little troop returned to the Clan headquarters with the Rolex, as warily and as carefully as they had set out. A whole bunch of rabbits gathered to look at the strange thing they called a 'watch' and to listen to it 'tick'. Rudy passed the watch to Zack and instructed him to keep it, and take care of it. Zack would be the new owner, as he was the only one apart from the Space-Rats that could understand it. He proudly strapped it on, after making several ajustments due to the slimness of his wrist. Zack's heart gave a little skip of joy in anticipation of the morrow's experiment. He had difficulty in realizing that he now owned this great gift from the woodland. Every time he and the face of his Rolex met, his heart pounded with excitement.

"So—now I know what makes rabbits 'tick'," said Tooky. "No", said Ratfink, "it's not the rabbits that are ticking, it's the watch." "Oh," said Tooky, now that the problem had become more complex.

The experiment was to be held the next day at about mid-morning at the Birch Tree Inn. Rudy invited the Space-Crew rabbits as well as Zack, Kotar and Tesla.

During the day Zack had discovered a tall 'Coke' bottle in the woodland and had washed it up. It was now on the shelf in his lair filled with crystal-clear water from the creek.

Evening allowed the first stars to appear as Zack prepared to turn in for the night. First he wriggled backwards down into his home, being extra careful not to squish Snuffy. He showed the little hedgehog around his lair before releasing him to do his night feeding. Snuffy gave a tiny squeak as he disappeared into the darkness. Zack settled into the hay and listened to the friendly personal tick of his watch. As the darkness deepened, his Rolex' green face seemed to smile at his illuminated wonder. A few minutes later he was again joined by Timken, Snickets, Tooky, Boofy and Bifflets. His lair was their burrow too. Then more rabbits joined them. He hungered for their warmth and company, and yet these feelings of treasured need—were beyond his understanding.

In the darkness, Zack felt tears trickling down his cheeks at the memory of losing his only true friend—a plushy little gold teddy bear named Binky. At seven he'd been scolded to 'Grow up', and helplessly watched poor little Binky wave a last paw as he vanished among the flames in the fireplace. Zack's screams of outrage translated into red welts of fiery pain. He tried to banish the tragedy from his mind.

Tonight he was grateful for the rabbits' company and released a huge sigh of satisfaction. What could be cozier he thought, than a snug home, a full tummy, a Rolex watch, a knife with a seven inch blade, a bed of warm hay, and a bunch of warm furry snuggly rabbits heaped around him. He loved the unique intimacy of touching noses with them, of caressing their silky ears, and the sheer joy of snuggling. In blissful relaxation, he watched the shafts of moonlight slowly disappear. Tooky's long silky ears lay across Zack's cheek; and along with the tickle of rabbit whiskers, it led him to the pathway of dreams. Time now 'ticked' by.

In the early hours of morning, Snuffy returned and sort of tumbled into Zack's lair. In doing so, he landed with his quills fully braced to break his fall, right onto KeKe's back—who in turn gave a loud squeak—which awoke the others. Being so young, Snuffy's quills were as yet quite soft, so no one was hurt. He shouldered his way through the rabbits to where Zack lay, snuffled in his ear, and emitting a tiny squeak, he fell asleep.

Mornings come as they always do. The rabbits say that morning just *'IS'*. Zack was feeling refreshed. He gently removed Snuffy from his shoulder placing him directly into the hay. Snuffy slept on. Zack peeked from his lair to breathe deeply of the cool fresh air. His furry friends had preceded him into their dawn feeding, and he recalled that this morning Ratfink and Rudy were conducting an experiment with Time.

Zack felt good. With an incredible burst of energy he raced across the purple clover meadow to where Simbala, Tika, Tiska, Squibby, Tooky and few other rabbits were feeding. They, seeing him frisking, got caught up in the excitement and joined him. In a ragged circle they all leapt and bounded, jumped, hopped and frisked in circles, eventually, collapsing into a happy heap among Zack's laughter.

Zack had become a vulnerable boy of raw sensitivity. He sensed a strong need to be held and touched differently—like when he played among the rabbits. It was an insatiable hunger that never left him. He was convinced that the rare feeling for which he so much yearned, did not exist with his own kind.

The elusive feelings that Zack sought were expressed in the caring touch of his brother Brett when he hugged him. It was also in the touch of the yellow-furred space-rats and in the warmth of the rabbits, and now Snuffy, as they snuggled up to him at night. None of the wild creatures rejected him, and he involuntarily returned their unconditional love. They needed to be loved as much as he. Switching his thoughts from himself, he returned to his den to dress. Snuffy was still sleeping, curled in a tight ball; and glancing at his watch, Zack saw it was almost time for the experiment.

All those rabbits who were to participate showed at the Silver Birch Inn on time. They included Squibby, Snickets, Tooky, Derky, KeKe, Timken and of course Zack, Tesla and Kotar. Other rabbits showed up just so as not to be left out of anything. Ratfink accepted this, because it was evident from their furry facial expressions that they were entirely clueless—through no fault of their own. They assembled in what looked like a meeting room. Ratfink and Rudy had set up everything at their base exactly the way they wanted. Two or three members of the proposed Space-Crew had a slightly superior air, almost as if they were challenging Ratfink and Rudy with greater knowledge and ability. The golden space-rats were aware of it and made no comment. As agreed, Zack placed his watch on a small round table at which they were all seated.

"Rudy", said Ratfink, "would you lead off and explain how this little time-experiment works?"

"Well, it may come as a surprise to you," Rudy stated with a smile, "that what we are proposing requires little, or preferably, no conscious effort on your part. I'll give you the overall picture of what we have in mind. It's necessary for the sake of safety that we establish which of us can control our modes of consciousness. It's actually about how we think.

There are extraterrestrial rabbits 'out there'," said Rudy gesturing, "and we've met some of them, who call this whole thing 'bio-feedback'. Its name doesn't matter, but how we go about developing it does! It really means that to achieve success in this experiment, you need to have acquired or already possess a high level of control over your own levels of consciousness. One of these super-space rabbits explained to us that their entire planet runs on the accepted belief that 'consciousness creates reality', and that a rabbit's expectations decisively influence all outcomes of his thoughts." He paused and scratched an ear.

"There is much truth in this. For any one of you, it may become a project that opens doors to other worlds; or you might wish to leave it as a dormant concept. It's a very different reality, and one that carries huge responsibilities. You may want to pause a moment or two to think about that," said Rudy his low melodious wind-chime voice.

When there appeared to general assent he nodded and continued, "First off, you each need to enter a deeply meditative state while observing the sweep-second-hand on the watch. At first you may experience difficulty in achieving this relaxed state of mind, don't let this concern you, we can tackle details on this later. When you do attain it, one or two of you will be surprised to find that as you observe the face of the watch, the second-hand has come to a stop!" Rudy smiled and allowed a long pause for them to all catch up.

"Your natural reaction on seeing this will be to exclaim, 'This is impossible'. However, if you can overcome this reaction while still maintaining a deep meditative state, and with half-open eyes observe the watch face, you'll discover you can keep the second-hand from moving for as long as you wish! What has occurred is that you have left 'Time', as we know it, and have gone 'elsewhere'." Again Rudy smiled and paused to allow the enormity of this fact to sink-in.

"The moment you say anything, or your physical body becomes disturbed in any way, the second-hand will accelerate and resume its normal rate. This means that you have now 'returned'. It means you've come back from somespace outside of 'Time', having left your body on 'auto-pilot' so to speak." Rudy stopped, smiled and looked at their reactions.

"Wow," and "Far out!" exclaimed a couple of rabbits as their eyes widened in understanding.

"This has nothing to do with the Rolex," continued Rudy, "it is a flawless mechanical instrument. Nor does this have anything to do with projecting mental power to stop that sweep-second-hand. It is also possible to recall where you have been when you were absent from your body. Remember, that whole period when the second-hand was stopped—you were 'away'."

Several of the rabbits were quite perplexed at this point and complained of becoming dizzy, and Rudy said it was okay for them to opt out, as there were ways around these phenomena that would occur later. He smiled his assurance.

Zack appeared to be delighted. His face was alight with comprehension, but most of the rabbits looked a little dizzy. Rudy summed up what he'd said in his wonderfully relaxing voice. It helped them in their attempts to grasp the concepts in a non-threatening way, so that even if they failed, it was okay. Rudy concluded with, "Just bear in mind that any untoward external danger will immediately return you to your body. Have no fear. You have lots of time, let's see what happens".

The small group discovered that relaxing into a deeply meditative state was not too difficult. Then after some two hours had passed, Rudy made a fearsome squeaking sound which caused the rabbits who had 'left', to return by involuntarily re-entering Time. Several rabbits had observed the Rolex stop, and also had seen the second-hand leap ahead when Rudy had squeaked. All had become 'normal' again. Zack and the Clan members who had 'stopped time', looked at each other in amazement.

"Wow!" exclaimed Tooky. "Zoweee," said Timken. "Unbelievable!" exclaimed Snickets. Other unofficially invited rabbits looked at Rudy in bewildered uncomprehending innocence, as was expected.

It was only Tesla, Kotar and Zack who looked vibrant with purpose and meaning. They looked at Ratfink and Rudy who had pleased expressions on their faces. "Let's take a long break," said Ratfink, "I think it is time we all had a good feed.

By the way, relax; it really doesn't matter if you didn't get to first base with all this bio-feedback stuff. After all, it did come from extraterrestrial rabbits, and you are not they! At tomorrow's morning meeting we'll discuss your findings. Be honest with yourselves, the truth will be inescapable!"

Zack strapped on his Rolex and without discussing their experiences the group split up, all of them engrossed by their own thought processes.

The rabbits fled in all directions to their favorite feeding places. Kotar and Tesla decided to lunch together side by side, and Zack needed a refreshing dip in the creek. He lay in the clover to dry off and partook of a light lunch via mega-frequency. He had also carefully scanned the hills and meadows as far as he could see in case his 'caretakers' should be out looking for him. All was clear.

Before Zack went to the wild strawberry patch, he visited his den to check on Snuffy, but he was nowhere to be seen, so he went on his mission alone. Stripping off his scant clothing to allow the sun to deepen his tan, he then crawled around in delightful freedom, seeking and eating all the strawberries he could find. After awhile he lay under a birch tree, gazing dreamily up through the green canopy of leaves. He heard the distant cawing of crows and nearby a red squirrel scolded. A little brown field-mouse skittered over him with delightful tickles, and Chickadees called.

Zack yielded to luxurious stretching. His mind roamed his current reality with the golden furred Space-Rats and his new rabbit companions. He loved to carress their soft fur. He also scanned his fresh experience of venturing, 'outside' of Time.

Zack unconsciously monitored the warning calls and behavior of all the local birds and animals. He felt safe. The sounds and scents of the friendly woodland touched him deeply with a wild kind of magic he could not define—and slowly he became lulled into the gentle sweetness of sleep. Later—as he lay dreaming among the summer flowers, an Elephant Hawk Moth caterpillar dropped on to his face. He gently picked it off from where it had straddled his left eye, and examined the beautiful spots that ran along each side of its body. Zack called them port-holes, and admiring its erect tail, he replaced it on a strong twig to continue feeding. For several years he'd raised these types of caterpillars as pets—all the way to moth-maturity. His greatest thrill was the finality of seeing them slowly take wing into the summer twilight.

Zack's reverie was suddenly interrupted by the loud clap of wood-pigeon wings, a prime warning to all the creatures. He fully awakened—and wariness was replaced by terror when the bark of a large dog further split the afternoon serenity. He quickly grabbed his clothes, backed under a birch tree and dressed. His heart was pounding, and a terrible fear gripped him. Those sounds announced the intrusion of man, his enemy.

He checked his sheath-knife and tightened his belt and shoe laces. Instinct told him to deviate around the disturbed area to the creek. A dog could track him on land, but would lose his scent in the water. Many times he'd seen hunted animals escape their enemies in this way.

There was not a single rabbit in sight. They had wisely gone underground. Zack saw the man and the dog in the lower meadow, and recognized him as his prime enemy 'care-taker' from home. Then he calmed down, the wind was in his favor, so the dog would not 'give tongue' to his scent. Leaving his runners on, he entered the fast-flowing water, following it upstream to a look-out he had discovered earlier. It was two hours before the man and his dog finally descended to the lower trails to disappear into the village.

While Zack waited for him to leave, he thought of how the men of the village would react if he told them of his experiences with Ratfink and Rudy. He laughed softly as he lightly skipped down to his lair under the ancient Oak. Twilight descended and peace fell on the countryside. Zack was joined in his den a short while later by about ten or twelve rabbits from the Clan. They decided to stay with him for the night; it was a furry welcome like no other could ever be. He was also surprised at the sudden appearance of Snuffy. It seems the baby hedgehog had dug a little short-cut tunnel into Zack's lair. Now they were all one happy family.

As Zack relaxed into the night darkness, he scanned his experiences of the day and slowly realized that he was discovering genuine peace within himself. He realized he no longer had to fearfully await the oft-nightly forceful attentions of his care-giver. Just a young teen—he'd wept in mute obedience to the brutal intrusions. The more Zack's sanctity was violated—the more frequently he achieved the ability to become unreachable. More tragically—he succumbed to the loss of himself—including his ability to feel. Love became a shadowed concept of painful reality.

The village far below was illuminated by dim street lights, and most of the night-life judging from the merriment, emanated from the local 'pub'. It was here in the smoke, under façades of happiness that a loud-mouth villager shouted to Zack's caregiver, "Did you find that little bastard? I know if I was you, an' I got 'old of 'im, I'd beat the livin' Jesus out of 'im!"

"No," a deep voice replied, "he prolly buggered off to find that snotty brother of his. But you can keep an eye open 'case he's still around. I'll buy you a couple of beers or so if you find 'im".

Someone else shouted, "Maybe them flyin' rats we heard of done got 'im. Serves 'im right, turning 'is back on a good 'ome, an' it don't make you look no good none to the 'thorities. Wonder what that little swine done tole 'em." There followed an argument over the existence of flying rats, problem wives, and other generally weird things;

and the whole group then further drowned their smoky realities in crude laughter and lashings of cool beer.

Next day at the regular morning meeting of the Clan, those who had actually 'stopped time', met separately to discuss what they had experienced. Ratfink and Rudy listened attentively. Kotar said that when he heard Rudy's squeak, it seemed that he had come back into himself. He'd seen the watch second-hand freeze in position, and also witnessed it jump ahead when he became fully at home in himself. Zack had a very similar experience, but neither of them could recall where they had been, while away from their bodies. Rudy confirmed this was normal in the early days of experimentation.

Tesla, however, had quite a different story, in that he had excellent recall. Ratfink and Rudy drew closer. Tesla had been quite disturbed to find that he'd suddenly found himself in the middle of a large gathering of black rabbits. He had startled them by suddenly appearing out of nowhere, and they had all drawn back from him in consternation. Tesla said they were all glossy, short furred, jet black, and had amazingly dark penetrating eyes that flashed different colors. Most outstanding, was that the insides of their erect tall black ears were a bright gold, and seemed to emanate light as they moved or flipped their ears in any way. Tesla could not estimate in terms of time how long he was with them. He had heard a loud squeak, and instantly returned to his body. The black rabbits must have been equally amazed by his miraculous disappearance.

Ratfink and Rudy exchanged knowing glances, but did not question Tesla farther. On his part, Tesla had a growing desire to meet the black rabbits again. It appeared that only about five rabbits had the necessary qualifications for space travel. It was another matter entirely as to whether the Clan found this to be desirable. Rudy and Ratfink declared the Time-Experiment a great success.

The aspiring Star Travelers agreed in principle for the time being, to just live like ordinary, sensible rabbits. Rudy asked each one of them to speak with him if anything else came to light, and on that note the meeting disbanded.

Zack however, being the owner of the Rolex watch had already decided to do further experiments. He was aware that he must be under no pressures or anxiety of any type, in order to enter the required deep meditative state of mind. Zack also recognized that being a hunted creature, did not in any way help him to attain a fully quieted, relaxed mind.

Meantime Captain Ratto had recalled Ratfink to the main base at Rat-Star, explaining that Rudy could stay as long as he wished. There was a farewell meeting and Ratfink took off. At departure he briefly warned them to look away from him for about seven seconds, and in a blinding flash of light reduced himself to a mere dot fading into the stratosphere. Rudy was delighted to have permission to stay with the Clan. In celebration, he spread his wings and flew all around the Hill-Clan meadows—much to their delight.

Snickets was still not in obedience to the intuition-training the Clan had adopted. Generally he thought that he was better off by just using plain old logic; after all, it was scientifically proven, and the 'logical thing to do'.

It was mid-afternoon when the loud scream of a terrified rabbit rent the air of the Hill Clan. It froze every rabbit in its tracks. It was twice repeated—long drawn-out death-screams. It signified the rabbit was deathly scared and greatly suffering. A small Kestrel Hawk had swooped in to pick off Snickets, who recently had become fully grown. As the hawk tried to take off with its prey, it struggled with Snickets' weight, who in turn still struggled to be free. Once again the Kestrel had to slash its sharply-hooked beak into the base of Snickets' skull, before he hung limply to become a rabbit that '*is not*'. Poor Snickets had made a gallant struggle for survival. Later, the Clan again warily left their burrows to feed. The sun's heat still warmed the meadows, buttercups and cowslips nodded their yellow heads, and skylarks still trilled the azure sky. Nothing had changed. All was '*Now*'—except for Snickets.

Tooky shed a few tears, for he loved Snickets, and that led him to thoughts about death. "Timken," he said, "Death can't be all that bad, you know, we live through a 'little death' every time we go to sleep. What is so amazing is that we don't know about it till we wake up! It's like being born. Before we 'were', we were 'not'. Then consciousness comes to us, and we find we're alive!

So Timken, dying—really dying—is losing the awareness of 'being', like when we sleep."

"I suppose you're right Tooky, but I still like 'being', more than I like sleeping." Timken sighed.

Tooky flipped his ears and smiled at Timken "We're living in 'Now' Timken—let's enjoy it." They both headed for the Cowslip patch.

Snickets — A sharp-eyed highly logical young rabbit—
the only rabbit with a jet black tail!

Chapter Five

Zack was the most affected by the loss of Snickets. He was more than sad. He hurt through and through. It seemed that Snickets' screams were his screams. They were part of the pain-continuum Zack knew so well. It had a life of its own. He and it were driven by tensions born out of rejection and love-hunger. Tears flowed down his cheeks. He longed for his brother Brett. In the late afternoon of that same day, Zack slowly walked through the bird songs in the woodland. He kicked at the odd stick on the trail, and coming to an area carpeted with blue forget-me-nots, he curled up into a foetal ball among the flowers. He shook and wept in his hurt; but despite his emotional vent, there was no let-up. The screams of poor Snickets echoed through him again, and again, and yet again.

Much later, Zack was awakened by the familiar tickle of rabbit whiskers. Timken, Tooky and Tesla were sniffing his face. They had missed him and tracked him down. Zack smiled and came to his feet, "Rabbits just are", he murmured. Then they all scampered home through the early twilight. Zack felt good at seeing the ancient Oak again. Rudy was awaiting his return with news of a special Clan meeting planned for the next morning. Everyone wanted to know why Snickets had come to such an untimely end.

First Zack had supper, and today this was supervised by Rudy who was concerned that Zack had been so deeply affected by Snickets' passing. After their meal, he and Rudy chatted and walked until the first stars twinkled. Then they all turned in for much needed rest. Eleven rabbits slept with Zack that night, and as usual, Snuffy had his snuggling session. But tonight he also latched onto Zack's left ear lobe. He noisily sucked on it while blowing into his ear. Zack just murmured, "Ease up there Snuffykin," and with a slippery wet ear, he drifted off into a deep sleep—surrounded by a mass of warm rabbit fur.

Next day at the morning meeting, Kotar and Tesla saw the Snickets tragedy as an opportunity for the Clan to learn. In addition they had some special messages for the gathering to consider, and called upon Bifflets to lead the discussion. Bifflets felt at ease. He was one of the smaller rabbits. His eyes sparkled with intelligence, and his over all competent appearance held their attention.

"First," said Bifflets, "let's examine the death of our friend Snickets. If you become all 'choked-up', don't mind. We all loved him very much. Unfortunately, Snickets never became a 'rabbit of light'. Nor did he develop the power to bring his fears under control, as most of you have in the 'No Fear' program.

But we all owe a lot to Snickets for his super-special eyesight, and we're most grateful for his early warnings of danger. However, he had a mind of his own, and was a remarkably clever and logical rabbit. But—he was given to observing the facts of a situation only. Obeying intuition rather than logic was too abstract and difficult for him, so he rejected it. We can all learn from this tragedy. Thank you Snickets, dear friend, you did not die in vain. We'll never forget you!"

Bifflets continued, "Let's be absolutely sure to continue our practice of the 'No Fear' and our 'Intuition First' programs. They will save many of our lives. Kotar and Simbala have asked me speak on the new program coming up. We're calling it, 'Sowing and Reaping'. For short, we'll call it the SAR Program! But first we'll take a snack break and also refresh our minds. In fact, let's not do any more training type stuff today in memory of Snickets." Bifflets dismissed the gathering and most of them scattered to feed in the clover. The day was heating up, and Zack headed for the creek.

Zack left his knife on the creek bank with his scant clothing, and also his Rolex for fear of scratching it on the rocks. It was a day for relaxing into deep thought if one wished, or to leave one's mind perfectly blank. After a quiet, slow, luxurious dip, Zack sat on a smooth rock by the deeper pool and watched the sun-dappled waters play with the shadows. He was surprised to be joined by Rudy. They exchanged warm smiles and Rudy took to the water where he swam silently with a lot of power. Zack smiled, he didn't think the golden space-rats could swim! Minutes later, Rudy shook off the water, and opening his wings he flew low over the meadows to dry off. He returned to sit with Zack, and watched an otter nose its way up the creek. It disturbed a heron which took off in low-winged flight with a harsh call.

By then it was time for Rudy to return to his base at the Birch. This he achieved with a graceful dip of his scarlet-tipped wings as he flashed out of sight among the willows. Zack stretched and sauntered into the cool green shadows of the woods to look for wild strawberries. Primarily he needed to 'find' himself; which presented difficulties beyond his understanding.

He rediscovered the forget-me-nots, and lay among the patches of dappled sunlight. For him, soaking up the beauty of the day by watching squirrels, birds, grasshoppers and field mice was a timeless delight. He also glimpsed the flowing tail of a red fox, and a sentry hornet casually checked him out. This was Zack's world. The wilding was immersed in the peace and security of the woodland. Vaguely, almost with apprehension, he sensed that this too would not last.

Zack checked the time by his Rolex—although time had no real meaning in his present situation. However, it did confirm for him that he and his body were flesh and blood reality. For several years now, there were days when Zack needed to prick his wrist with his knife to see if he were really 'here'. Pain gave him identity. Too frequently he felt that he lived only as a type of 'thought-form'.

When Zack's psychic pain levels escalated too sharply—he, as the real Zack, escaped to far within himself where he was safe and inaccessible—while his 'other self' ran the affairs of the day. It was strange, difficult and confusing. He never knew what triggered these two different states of mind—but it enabled him to handle life. Today, in brilliant sunlight, he exclaimed, "If my Rolex is strapped to my wrist, and I can see it and feel it, it must mean that I am here too!" In all innocence, Zack assumed that what he was experiencing was normal for any Human. Little did he realize that his very survival—necessitated his dual state of mind. Lost in thought, he explored the hills and woodland until twilight, when he returned to his furry friends beneath the Oak.

The next morning Kotar and Simbala chatted with Zack and the rabbits about the SAR principle. Tooky and Timken quickly piped up to ask Simbala what was meant by 'sowing'. However, it was Boofy who handled the question in his usual competent manner that carried authority. "Here, we are trying to observe a principle in action," he stated.

"What's a principle?" asked Tooky.

Boofy smiled, "Tooky, a principle is a kind of basic law. Planting and harvesting are basic laws. They affect the life of every rabbit in how he thinks and what he does; and also the lives of everyone around him! Lack of knowledge in the workings of this principle can change a rabbit from an '*is*' to an '*is not*', and that is sad and unnecessary. So let's check it out.

By sowing we mean planting, just like the farmers do all around us. As we already know from the farm garden below, they sow carrot seeds and up come carrots!"

"When are we next going to raid the carrot patch?" asked Timken.

"Certainly not right now!" exclaimed Boofy. "Let me continue! The type of planting and harvesting we want to examine are all about the way we think. It's about our thoughts, our words and our actions. For example, Snickets planted logic, and ignored intuition. The result was death! We sow fear, and we harvest fear along with its problems. We plant anger, and reap a fight. Let's have some more examples!"

"Plant watchfulness," said Tooky, "and you may see a weasel or a fox nearby; or plant neglect and become a meal for a hawk."

"That's exactly it. Thanks Tooky," exclaimed Boofy, "we need to consciously sow the seed of what we need. If we want carrots, we don't sow lettuce seeds. If we want respect—we plant respect!"

The rabbits milled around. They all agreed that the morning session was quite a lot for a rabbit to get his mind around. On the other hand they reasoned, it was merely a matter of observing what they were already doing—and change it. Finally, they all went their various ways. Zack picked up Snuffy and headed for the woodland.

Tesla however, had taken off and headed for the far side of the clover field. He had only one thing in mind, and that was the black rabbit tribe he'd met in the Time-Experiment. He just could not get them out of his mind no matter how he tried. The reason for this would become apparent a short while later.

Zack whistled happily as he strode the woodland. The distant clouds forecast the whole area could be in for a rainy spell, with high winds and generally unseasonable coolness. Zack was cold at times, having only his navy blue shorts and a shirt that once was white. He longed for a warm jacket. His shock of golden hair overhung his ears which lay close against his head. Zack decided that if it turned wet and cold, he'd stay at the ancient Oak and hole up with some of the rabbits until it warmed up again. Somehow, he had to try to meet up with his brother Brett. He knew he would also feel the severe loss of his rabbit companions. Rudy of course would have to go back to his base sometime, but that didn't seem to be immediately in the offing.

Suddenly, Zack's intuition triggered him into obedience. It called for him to quickly return to the Hill-Clan burrows. Holding Snuffy, he skipped lightly away before breaking into a powerful run. Upon arrival he joined Tesla and sat on a grassy hummock.

When one considers that things in Rabbit Land generally '*are*' or 'are not'; it should have been no surprise for Tesla to hear it first. It was a faint low-pitched whirring sound that seemed to be a part of the hillside scenery as natural as the cowslips bending in the breeze, or the call of Chickadees in the rose bushes. It was present in an unobtrusive way, but emanated powerful forces which could not be interpreted. The sound reached an almost musical pitch, but was different in a way that defied description. There was also a feeling of overriding alien thoughts that somehow occupied the Hillside; but not of the dangerous kind, and nothing that could be attributed to any visible phenomena.

True to their intuitive training there was not a rabbit in sight, that is, except for Tesla. That glossy black-eared rabbit sat next to Zack overlooking the clearing just below the Clan's main hill burrows. It was clear that he was unperturbed. The space immediately in front of him had captured his attention. He was apparently looking at nothing! Rudy joined Zack and Tesla. Zack was intrigued with what might happen and closely snuggled Snuffy on his lap. Rudy just smiled—a knowing smile.

Suddenly the clearing became absolutely silent. Tesla, Rudy, Zack and those rabbits that were peering cautiously out of their burrows, saw to their amazement a massive space-craft come into appearance. Not that any of them knew what it was, as no one apart from Rudy had ever seen a space-craft. Zack instinctively knew what it was, and almost breathless with excitement exclaimed, "What a space-craft! Look at those huge crystal rings that revolve within each other in opposite directions, and, look at the height! Those circles of colored lights are gradually switching off! Tesla! Rudy! I can see creatures moving inside!" It was no surprise to Rudy that seven Black-Rabbits with black and gold ears should exit the space-craft. Zack blinked but once and there're they were. On their part, the Black-Rabbits saw a scruffy half-wild human boy holding a tiny prickly animal; a smiling golden-furred space-rat, and there beside them was the strange black rabbit known as Tesla. It was he who had 'appeared' among them on their remote planet, and then shocked them with his almost immediate departure. Recognizing the need for a common mode of communication, the space visitors chose sound and 'imaging'. As the Black- Rabbits spoke, their eyes flashed in vibrant colors; which the Clan learned later was linked to their imaging system. Zack studied the scene as if he were in a trance.

All seven Black-Rabbits gathered around the welcoming creatures, and as they touched each other, the ears of the visitors seemed to light up. The outcome was that they learned that Tesla had been easily tracked from the day of the Time-Experiment. The reason that Tesla could not get them off his mind, is that the Black-Rabbits, or 'Keylons' as they were known, had locked on to him with their thought-processes, and used his mind as a dimensional-beacon. The Keylons from the planet Ektar had come to investigate Tesla's ability to transcend 'Time'. This was a mode of space-travel they did not use, and they wondered how a backward Earth-group had achieved such heights of consciousness-control.

The Keylons were already aware of Rudy's world on Rat-Star as it was where their Lexcraft space machine was manufactured. As a result, they interacted with the golden space-rats on a regular basis. The wilding however surprised them, he being quite at home with the flying rats and the rabbits. Snuffy was seen as a non-entity of no consequence whatsoever.

The Keylons had already scanned Zack's intelligence and memory-banks. They had found him to be an animal of a different level of consciousness to what they had at first anticipated. Compared to the rabbits, he was definitly a different level of 'Being'. Zack's mode of thinking was not founded on normal human educational values, that is, beyond the basics of language and numbers. As a result, apart from Zack's emotional 'separation' between him and the rest of his human-kind, they found his mind to be neither contaminated, nor damaged by the artificial value-systems by which most human Earth-lives were governed.

The Keylons saw Zack as a rarity, imprinted with a unique freedom in that he believed all things were possible. In his loneliness and desparate struggles to survive his world of pain and abuse; Zack had already reached beyond himself to meet his Creator, and was under His direction. However, the concept of Man and God was a reality beyond the scope and comprehension of the Keylons.

By this time most of the other members of the Hill-Clan had surrounded the space-craft and gazed at the Keylons. They all interacted well, but it became quite evident to the Keylons, as they intimated later, that apart from Rudy, Zack, Tesla, Kotar, Timken, Tooky, Boofy, Bifflets, and KeKe; the balance of the entire Hill-Clan could be classed as rabbits with no particular 'space' affinities whatsoever.

The Keylons invited Zack, Rudy, Tesla and the other space-rabbits aboard their craft for lunch. It was a strange experience. The interior of the space-craft was unlike anything they could even have imagined. The instrumentation and controls gave no clue as to their purpose and operation. It was a luxurious craft from a bodily comfort viewpoint. When they sat down, almost magical sensations overtook them and they felt energized and happy. Any lingering body aches or pains they may have had, disappeared.

The food they selected was of their own choice and nothing remotely to do with menus. Whatever they imaged appeared before them in its finest form. Zack was particularly pleased with the change; he would be processing real food via his mouth for the first time since the golden-rats had met up with him! It was a memorable feast for all of them, including Rudy-Rat.

Each Keylon was different, and it was interesting to watch the light occasionally beam from the insides of their ears. They were a very friendly bunch, and everyone felt quite at ease.

None of the guests were invited to see the 'engine room' in the space-craft; if it could be called that. The center portion of the craft contained the control-center, surrounded by living accommodation, and various cabins for storage or other purposes. They were all amazed to learn that the propulsion system gave the space-craft the same maneuverability as a humming bird. Rudy broke Zack's trance by whispering to him, "This is a Lexcraft. They are made by our people on Rat-Star—my home planet!"

"Wow!" exclaimed Zack. "I'd love to visit that Lexcraft plant sometime!" Whereupon he fell back into his 'trance'; his brain being somewhat overtaxed with the inputs he was receiving.

Zack correctly surmised that the space-craft did not use fuel in the Earth sense of the word. There was no evidence of energy generated by explosive force.

Indeed, the Keylons hinted that the propulsion-power was produced by power-modules energized by the crew-members as a group. Zack's intuition referred him to an abstract concept involving Bose-Einstein Condensates, but he knew he was out of his depth. He did not explore the matter further, especially with all the excitement. He was already feeling as dizzy as a rabbit that had been 'thinking' too much! In the face of this, he had a sudden urge to be lying in the forget-me-not patch. He felt a longing for the music of the creek, the scent of the woodland, and the furry touch of the rabbits.

Zack had yet to realize that consciousness-expansion involving the Keylons and space-travel would be gradual. Suddenly he returned to 'now' and recalled where he was. He'd not left the space-ship and was still visiting with the group. He had the distinct feeling his thoughts were being monitored.

The Keylons suggested they go back outside, and Kotar offered to give them a guided tour of the area to see the beautiful countryside and other forms of wild life, and suggested pointedly, they would not want to encounter Man. Three of Keylons elected to have a discussion with Tesla and Kotar, and the others requested they do some touring on their own. Meanwhile the Hill-Clan fed.

Zack headed for the woodland, if for no other reason than to separate his new reality from the former one. The Lexcraft dominated his thinking, but after a few minutes he followed his usual quest. It always seemed as though he was searching for something, and had no idea as to what it was. He almost expected to see the 'unknown whatever' to appear, but it only led to further introspection, that is, of exploring different levels of consciousness. Zack was always fully aware that he had a body, but in reality 'he' was not his body. Kotar had said this too. It formed the foundation for his awareness in life.

Lost in thought, Zack was suddenly shocked into current reality by the loud report of two shotgun blasts. Momentarily it stunned him. He had failed to see the local gamekeeper and two strange men in the adjacent meadow on which he was now focused. It was fortunate that he'd not been seen by them. As the hunters ran toward the death scene, one of them with a loud shout held up two black rabbits.

Even at that distance Zack could see a flash of golden ears as the man held up his prize.

"Keylons!" Zack exclaimed. "Here Snuffy—we have to go!" Snatching up Snuffy from his worm-feeding, Zack kept a low profile, his head and shoulders below the level of the Hawthorn bushes that divided the fields. He moved swiftly like a red fox over the considerable distance to where the Hill-Clan burrows were located. There, he dropped off Snuffy at the Oak. Once again the sight of the massive space-craft filled Zack with excitement. It was stunning and absolutely awesome. On his somewhat breathless arrival, the five remaining Keylons quickly gathered round him to hear what he had to report with such urgency. They were almost overcome with grief and disbelief at the news. They immediately boarded their space-craft.

Simultaneously, that craft appeared not to be there, although they all felt its presence. The Keylons apparently had the engineering ability to cause their space-craft to become invisible. Zack was impressed and amazed. He also envisioned a device that could change the frequency of light-waves to enable Earth beings to see all bands in the light-spectrum, and at some point, also switch to invisibility by shifting to another frequency inaccessible to Earth beings.

Rudy was disturbed, as was Kotar, and could not understand how the Keylons had failed to pick up images of Man in the area. The Keylons onboard the space-craft were asking the same questions. In an on-board analysis session, it was determined from the records that the two young Keylons who had been killed, had skipped three critical input-sessions on, 'The Weapons of Man'. This failure was attributed to youthful arrogance and inflated egos. They felt invincible and were quite sure they and their technology could handle anything that could possibly arise. It had proved to be a false assumption.

Kotar and the Clan's upper echelon had immediately run a check on records of their own Clan members to see who had 'skipped classes'. In doing so they observed the names of Katrix and Snickets. Once again Kotar noted that 'infallibility' did not exist. Here were the Keylons, every one of them a highly trained space-rabbit, yet they were still trying to come to grips with individual ego and arrogance problems. True, Kotar would no doubt turn the tragedy into a 'There is a lesson we can learn from this', type of session, but it was not a good enough solution to a recurring problem.

It was Rudy who suggested a conference be arranged between the Keylons and the Hill-Clan space-crew rabbits. Zack would join them as a cosmic entity, and Rudy as an ambassador for Rat-Star. The Keylons had picked up evidence that Zack possessed certain powers, latent as yet, that could be of great value on a space trip. He was regarded as being 'unique and useful'. It was finally decided that this special conference was to be held on Ektar, the Keylons's home planet. In any case the whole round trip would afford much needed space-experience. It would also reveal any negative character flaws in each individual, and expose them to the reality of seeing themselves differently; perhaps even not as inter-planetary travelers at all.

The Keylons offered the use of their space-ship for the trip. It was the only one available anyway, and this generosity was accepted by all; if for nothing else, the novelty of actual space-travel and the unprecedented luxury it provided. Kotar, Rudy and Zack planned for a separate meeting while in transit to Ektar, in which they would develop conference materials. Their common purpose was to tackle the problems that were killing the Keylons, the Clan, and no doubt many others. All parties selected for the Ektar trip were scheduled for departure the following day. They planned for 'take-off' at dawn.

That evening there were little farewell parties and the space-travelers promised to return at a cosmic time that could not to be determined by them. It was presumed by all to be in the 'very near future'; whatever that was. Zack intuitively knew they would be somehow encompassed by the relativity of Time, and matters of aging would depend on their speed of travel. He felt a little apprehensive in this regard as he knew that on the cosmic time-scale; one cosmic day equaled one thousand Earth years. Time being relative, translating Earth days into cosmic time would not be possible. It really came down to, 'what will be, will be'. Zack found little comfort in this as he could not bear the hurt of deserting his brother Brett. Indeed he had lingering doubts about the expedition and was not even sure that he really wanted to be a part of the Ektar trip. The Keylons had subtly hinted that he was needed, but had not elaborated on the nature of the need. However, it all seemed to add up, and intuition did not surface with instructions to the contrary. Zack obeyed his intuition.

Lost in whimsical thought, Zack took a last stroll through the woodland, and for a short while he lay on the moist mossy earth among the daisies and for-get-me-nots. He gazed heavenward at the early evening sky through the boughs of the birch trees, and slowly floated on the song-notes of a nightingale as it ushered in the twinkle of the first stars. The song never varied by one note, and he played with the idea of what he might find if a note were missing, and he were to explore the dimension within the gap created by the missing note. To Zack—life was an infinite state of eternity awaiting discovery. Life lay hidden within dimensions, octaves, frequencies and celestial harmonics that encompassed the cosmos.

He also wondered how the Keylons had so quickly determined which of the Hill-Clan rabbits possessed 'space-affinities' and those who did not. He posed the problem to his intuitive-self and left it there. This mode of thinking for him was conscious and habitual. About an hour later as he jumped across a narrow creek tributary, the answer came to him in a flash.

It was the sudden realization that Rudy, Kotar, Tesla, KeKe, Boofy, Bifflets, Timken, Tooky and himself, had the ability to '*see*', that is, to see with *other* than their physical eyes. Zack was already keenly aware that the majority of creatures experienced the world *only* through their five senses. For them, if they could not see it, hear it, taste it, smell it, feel or 'prove' it, 'it' simply did not exist. He regarded this type of 'blindness' as an affliction common to Man. Zack saw the difference as being similar to a human reading the Bible with the physical eyes of his soul, rather than 'seeing' the text with the spiritual eyes of his spirit, wherein the underlying meaning of every passage leapt into the light of comprehension. "Different levels of consciousness," he murmured.

Loudly addressing a red squirrel in a towering Chestnut tree, Zack almost shouted, "You know, that's their problem—not mine. Who am I to impose my understanding on their self-imposed limitations?" The squirrel was not impressed with Zack's soliloquy, and showered him with leaves, twigs and unripe chestnuts in addition to a sound scolding. However, Zack felt a weight leave his shoulders.

Just then, to his complete surprise, a red fox cub came trotting up the trail toward him. Its nose was low to the earth, and because Zack stood as still as a tree, it apparently didn't see him. Zack slowly went into a sitting position hugging his knees. Still the fuzzy little fox cub approached, and momentarily he thought about rabies. However, he dismissed this thought when the cub stopped, looked him directly in the eyes, and then of all things—tugged at his shirt collar. It occurred to Zack that he smelt very strongly of rabbits, which may have accounted for the foxykin being so fearless. But, when the 'big rabbit' stood up, with only a fleeting glance, the fox cub continued up the trail. That chance meeting made Zack's day, and once again a nightingale's lilting notes brought him back to thinking of 'other dimensions'. However, intuition—that remarkable power of 'knowing', said that, missing 'song-notes' to one side; there was not only a 'gap' between every note in the nightingale's song, but also between each of his own thoughts. He stretched tall and smiled. Life could never be boring; was he not about to explore a 'gap' in his own reality anyway?

Zack returned to his lair and prepared for sleep. He was joined by the warm snuggle of live rabbit fur. Snuffy had not come home. He would miss his snuffling and the way he sucked on his ear lobe before settling down. Zack fell asleep thinking of the little red fox cub. Tooky snuggled up under his chin.

Dawn broke with the sound of heavy boots, man voices, the stink of smoke and the barking of dogs. The Hill-Clan knew these were the sounds of a general clean-up raid by the two-legged creatures. The Clan would be faced by ferrets; nets would be staked over the burrows to capture the terrified rabbits, and then would come the repeated roar of shotguns as escaping rabbits were shot. Before the men left, snares would be set for the unwary. The hole under the ancient oak was ignored as it was more befitting a badger than any rabbits. Never would the humans suspect that a wilding—a half-wild boy lived in a den below the Oak—and was actually home!

A huge black dog thrust its nose in the entrance way to Zack's lair. It sniffed, barked and began scrabbling with its paws. Zack had already dressed, and now fearing for his discovery and capture, unsheathed his knife and lay in wait for a few more seconds till the heavy black muzzle would again appear. It came in, blocking the daylight with an explosive bark that filled his den with terror. Zack viciously struck up at the dark face with his blade. The blow, powered by fear, carried a terrible force. The blade penetrated from the lower jaw to the roof of the beast's slavering mouth. Blood poured over Zack's hand, and the animal withdrew with howls and yipes of pain. The men yelled at the dog, someone cursed badgers, and Zack's enemy was hauled away by its collar. It did not return. Zack was alone except for Snuffy who had hidden underneath the hay in a tight prickly ball. At the main burrows, the ferrets had been loosed and were heading underground, and what with shouting, yelling, and dogs barking in the general melee, it was a morning of horror that Rabbit Land would long remember.

Although the Ektar space-craft was still shielded by its cloak of invisibility, the Keylons could clearly see the entire picture. Their captain, a Keylon by the name of Betaka, quickly decided on a course of action. From the ship he released a dense bank of fog that rolled toward the burrows. It slowly enveloped the whole area and became thicker. In a short while the men could not even see their own hands in front of their faces.

This caused yells of surprise, consternation, loud swearing and huge confusion. But in a matter of minutes the men left by feeling their way down toward the creek. It was here that they gathered to discuss the phenomena. They all agreed the ferrets would have to be left behind and go wild. Then, with much head-shaking they and the dogs made their way home.

Terror had struck at the Clan burrows when the ferrets entered, for they were as fierce as any weasel. The rabbits fled the burrows and were surprised at the zero visibility created by the unusual fog, but it helped them escape. A little later when the dense fog had dispersed, the Clan discovered they had not suffered a single casualty.

It was Zack—the mere stripling, who had defeated the huge black dog who became the hero of the day. Zack dashed down to the creek to wash up, but the blood stains on his shirt faded only a little. He gave the Clan the whole picture of his dog escapade blow by blow. The rabbits were elated and filled with admiration at his courage; but Zack knew his actions were born not out of bravery, but out of desperation and fear.

Captain Betaka came over to ascertain the whole situation. He was disturbed to see Zack's blood-stained clothing, and was delighted that Zack was not wounded in any way.

It was while the rabbits were sniffing at cigarette butts that Zack's attention was drawn to a shiny piece of metal in the brush by the burrows. Pulling the bushes to one side he saw a double barrel 12 gauge shotgun. Zack picked it up. It was heavy and awkward to hold, and clicking it open, found it loaded with two shells. This find was dangerous because the men would come back to locate the gun. Just then Captain Betaka had an idea; he was thinking of the two ferrets still below ground. Zack!" exclaimed Betaka, "I will cause the ferrets to come out and look around, and then you can use the shotgun on them. Zack's face lit up, "Great idea! Let's do it."

The wilding held the gun to his shoulder as he had seen men do, and suddenly both ferrets emerged from a close-by burrow. Twice Zack fired at the ferrets and simultaneously he fell backwards with the roaring blasts. The shotgun fell on top of him with the hot barrel against his cheek.

Captain Betaka then realized that Zack knew nothing of the 'kick-back' from a powerful gun. Zack's right shoulder was a searing hot mess of pain and started to turn blue. So great was the pain that tears started in his eyes. He lifted the gun off himself and sat up. At such close range both ferrets had been practically blown to pieces.

Zack got up, gathered the remains of the ferrets, picked up the shotgun and took to the trail leading to the lower meadow. It was here that he disposed of the ferrets in the rose bushes. It was here also that he laid the shotgun down on the pathway. If the men came looking, he hoped they would not have to come any further.

On his return trip Zack cried bitterly in his pain. He cried also for the ferrets and the dog he had so badly wounded in the morning battle. The ferrets had such cute faces; they were innocent but were used by men as tools of death for his rabbit friends. They had come to an untimely end, and he wondered why things had to be so. Shedding tears made him feel better, but the pain in his mind could not be assuaged. Back at the burrows, Zack observed the invisibility shields had again eliminated any sign of the Ektar space-craft, and the Clan burrows had again taken on their look of normalcy.

Captain Betaka suggested they delay their departure till the morrow when everyone would be fully recovered. Betaka asked Zack aboard their craft. He specifically asked him to sit in a special reclining chair, to lean back and totally relax. Zack did as he was instructed and felt waves of healing energy pulsate through him. In disbelief he slipped his left hand under his stained shirt to feel his right shoulder. Not only was the pain gone, but when he looked there was no evidence of bruising.

It gave Captain Betaka a lot of happiness to see Zack's face light up with the discovery. Both Betaka and he partook of breakfast and then they returned to the Clan burrow area. All the rabbits had returned safely.

Later that day two men checked all around the burrows, one was holding a gun, probably the one Zack had left below on the trail. The men smoked and talked for a while, then slowly strolled down in the direction of the village.

The day passed without further mishap. Some of the baby bunnies had stories to tell of how their mothers had struck at the ferrets with their hind legs, and other stories circulated about the underground bravery of Simbala against the ferrets.

Zack rewashed his bloody clothing in the creek and the hot morning sun dried his stained attire by noon. Never before had he looked so like a wilding. It was not just his mop of sun bleached hair hanging shaggily over his ears; it was more in the defiant and defensive look that flashed blue light from his eyes.

Timken and Tooky were watching Zack, who said, "Hey Guys! We're going to have some adventures! Do you realize that tomorrow we'll be on a different planet?" Both rabbits said they did, but Zack somehow sensed they didn't have the remotest idea of what he envisioned. No pictures formed in their imagination. He caressed their silky little ears, and leaving them went to visit a wild raspberry patch he had discovered. He hoped to find some ripe berries. He was not disappointed.

That night was clear and magical with undeclared mystery. Moonlight cast shadows across field and meadow. Owls hooted and a fox barked from afar. A gentle warm breeze slowly swayed the trees. Zack and the rabbits wondered why they were leaving for Ektar at dawn. The truth was that they were really quite happy where they were. These wonderful hills and valleys reflected the beauty of the seasons and life to be lived. Zack treasured the gift of life and consciousness that was uniquely him—even his dual personalities. In wonder, he surveyed the world from his hill and slowly merged with the starlit night to 'become' the universe. He was fully alive to all that *'IS'*. It was total awareness. "What would exist if there were nothing?" He questioned aloud.

Then, breathing deeply, he wriggled below the ancient Oak to snuggle amongst the rabbits for the night. Snuffy was out night-foraging. Zack lay back, experiencing an uneasy feeling about their mission to an unknown planet.

Shortly after he settled in, Rudy dropped in to have a discussion with him. It had the effect of an exploding land-mine on Zack—when Rudy stated that he needed to talk about Zack's dual mental-states. He explained that Rat-Star needed assurance that on such a dangerous mission to which they were all committed, that there be no unknown elements to interfere with the space-trip objectives. Zack presented an 'X' factor in their plans. They needed him on this venture, and his uncontaminated inputs were required to ensure their success.

Zack sat up in the hay. He couldn't see Rudy, but rather he sensed his presence in the darkness, and he could feel his yellow fur. It took several hours for Zack to answer all of Rudy's questions, many of which found him sobbing in pain as he revealed his life history—more to himself—than to Rudy; who with Ratfink, had early in their association scanned Zack's memory banks. Unbeknownst to Zack, top Rat-Star personnel were privy to their discussion and every detail of his most intimate thoughts. They were delighted with his innocent and forthright answers. Rudy hugged Zack and wept with him in warm closeness as they struggled through the realities of Zack's life in microscopic review.

Slowly at first and increasing in its intensity—Zack felt a warmth that in some way illuminated his mind. Although he was open and accepting of change, the Star Rats had discovered they were not able to program Zack, but they were able to effectively influence his modes of thinking. Zack's mental integrity was not compromised in any way; but he saw that his hurtful life experiences were no longer in the forefront. He also saw that previously he'd approached problems by applying the 'wrong' instrument—namely—his 'then' level of consciousness—which could only ask the 'wrong' questions, with negative results. In the future, he'd find he was now equipped to question things differently—from a cosmic perspective. It was like switching keys to open an unknown, but different room that had always been there. Eventually Rudy quietly departed, but he left Zack in psychic turmoil—deep in no mans' land—where retreat did not exist.

Zack restlessly tossed and turned. However, he relaxed when he felt Snuffy return. The baby hedgehog, smelling earthy and damp, brought Zack back to local reality. He scrabbled onto Zack's thigh with little wet claws, and began to snuffle and tickle his way across Zack's tummy and chest to his head. There, with a tiny squeak he latched onto an ear lobe and sucked noisily until he fell asleep. At this point Zack was past caring—he'd already entered the twilight of cosmic dream.

Snuffy — The baby orphan hedgehog who adopted Zack as his father and mother!

Chapter Six

Dawn arrived and according to plan, Simbala and Squibby were placed in charge of the Hill-Clan until the space-crew returned. Snuffy was nowhere in sight, and Zack assumed correctly that his life would carry on without him. The explorers gathered by the space-craft, and were directed to enter through an open doorway below the fiery crystal rings.

It was here that everyone interacted. In the rabbit count were Kotar, Tesla, Tooky, Timken, Boofy, Bifflets, and KeKe. Then there was the golden space-rat Rudy, along with Captain Betaka and the five remaining Keylons. Zack was the last to come aboard. He looked well rested, and his eyes glittered with excitement. Today—even the animals perceived that Zack's facial features shone with a subtle radiance that gave him a presence of being they'd not previously sensed. They covertly peeked at him whenever they could. What they saw lent emphasis to Zack's newly found cosmic perspective. He sat in the large control-room—Tooky climbed on to his shoulder. Zack smiled as he carressed the soft little super-rabbit who nuzzled into his shaggy gold hair. Rudy smiled in greeting—he knew that Zack had courageously crossed the 'great divide', and had not looked back.

Breakfast time arrived in the luxurious dining room, and each creature ordered what they wished. Zack felt good about eating in the normal way, and even Rudy-Rat fell in with the Keylon's eating system. Immediately after breakfast all the passengers were strapped down in the main cabin. A few complained, and the Keylons told them that no one was permitted to float around cabin in transit. None of the rabbits had experienced weightless travel.

In almost complete silence, the Ektar space-craft rose to a great height. The huge crystal rings rotated counter-clockwise to each other, and apart from morning sunlight there was nothing else to see. All five of the Keylon crew could be seen in the control room. Not a word was spoken, but it was evident from their relaxed concentration that they were all of one mind. They were energizing the craft from whatever type of power it was that emanated from within each of them. Apparently it was providing enough energy to run the entire space-craft. Earlier, Captain Betaka had explained to Zack that the new time factors they would encounter would have no relevance to his Rolex as they would be converting time into space as they traveled. They were hardly underway when a confused and scared Tooky floated by Zack's face, and Zack had to grab him and thrust him under his belt. But after a while they were free to slowly move about. Most of the Hill-Clan rabbits looked somewhat uneasy, and three of them complained of being quite dizzy. But after a short period in their assigned cabins, the whole group came together again and settled in with no further problems.

Kotar, Rudy and Zack were assigned a small meeting room to formulate a program for the Ektar conference. It also had a couple of book-shelves. Zack eagerly scanned a few books, but it was Rudy-Rat who interpreted the titles for him with an amused smile and announced, "'Practical Anatomy of the Rabbit' by a guy named Bensley, and this one is entitled, 'Sex and the Rabbit', Oh! And in case you didn't know Zack, here is, 'How to Make Rabbit Pie'." This last one was published in the U.K. back on Earth, and Zack wasn't sure what relevance this book had on a space-ship run by Black-Rabbits; but on opening it he discovered it was in English. He doubted the Black-Rabbits were aware of its contents! Rudy chuckled. He said the best of the bunch was, 'Sex for Rabbits in Space–a Handy Guide', and passed it to Zack. He opened this last one, and saw that the text was wholly in Black-Rabbit hieroglyphics, but the illustrations left little to a rabbit's imagination. Kotar looked disgusted. The other volumes were Lexcraft Manuals on maintenance and repairs.

The three key leaders got down to business. They sat and looked at each other wondering how one could get a handle on overcoming ego-based ignorance coupled with arrogance. After some discussion, they concluded that the root of the problem was that most individuals were seen to be filled with self-importance and devoid of humility. Rudy said that these types sat upon a throne of 'self' which caused them to become impervious to teaching or instruction. They 'knew best'. Kotar pointed out that is was the younger teen-age creatures who considered themselves to be death-defying and invincible; plainly an ego problem. But Zack was quick to submit that some of the most atrocious crimes against his human kind were committed by egocentric humans of mature age, so in effect the problem affected all ages and sexes.

Zack's comments caused them to reconsider the whole question, and they decided to leave the matter till they arrived at their destination. Zack said as an afterthought, that he felt mature individuals had no need of an inflated ego, but were driven by high self-esteem and humility in the achiement of their objectives. These persons were quite devoid of self-importance. It simply had no relevance. He suggested that the key to the whole matter was being obedient to an 'accepted higher power'. Zack's words were pure wisdom, and he wondered from where they had originated. He felt good about what they brought to the forefront for consideration—or had he opened Pandora's Box? Action could possibly follow. Time alone would tell.

Ektar was a small blue planet on the edge of the solar system, orbited by two moons with a major star functioning like the Sun on Earth. It was mainly populated with the Keylons, a species of Black-Rabbits with extraordinarily high mental powers and intelligence.

Onboard the space-craft everyone rested except for the Keylon crew. Zack noticed how frequently the Keylons' ears seemed to beam light from their gold interiors. They made no contact with the passengers. Rudy-Rat and the space-rabbits stayed close to Zack. They passed time chatting with each other. This left the Keylons alone to concentrate on navigation as they maneuvered around strange planets and through unfamiliar star systems.

Tooky piped up, "Why can't we see anything?" To which Timken replied, "Because there is nothing to see!" Tooky accepted this with an apprehensive look and several flips of his ears. Zack smiled. He looked around him, and for the first time he realized how large an animal he was in relation to his companions. True to Captain Betaka's generalization in regard to time and space, what could be termed 'a short while later' actually worked out to a number of days based on Zack's Rolex. Finally, to everyone's relief Betaka announced that their space-craft was only Earth hours away from landing.

Their touch-down was uneventful, and Captain Betaka warned them to stay close together. He assured them this was not due to potential danger, but rather in relation to what each of them would see as they first stepped on to

Ektar. This was a disconcerting statement that made them all look at each other, but Rudy space-rat who had visited Ektar before, gave them a confident smile.

The Keylons were the first to exit, then Rudy, Zack and the Earth-rabbits. As Zack stepped onto Ektar soil, he saw unlimited miles of green woodland, clear creeks and flowers of gorgeous colors as far as the eye could see. He was delighted. Kotar and the rest of the rabbits saw acres of carrots, cabbages and lettuce as well as fields of clover. They were thrilled.

But the Keylons and golden-rat Rudy from Ratstar had disciplined themselves to stay in the same space-dimension that contained their space-craft. They saw a modern city of Black-Rabbits doing whatever it is that Black-Rabbits do; and beyond the city were huge blue lakes surrounded by forests.

The Hill-Clan rabbits were comfortable with Captain Betaka and sat to listen to what he had to say. "I know you'll find this hard to believe, but none of you are seeing the true molecular reality that you think you see." He smiled warmly.

Again he asked Zack to describe what he was seeing, and then got the pictures of what the rabbits were experiencing. He also asked the Keylons. The differences were so bizarre that the rabbits held on to each other. Zack's intuition revealed to him exactly what was occurring.

Captain Betaka explained that what each group had seen was a space-dimension that occupied the same space as numerous other dimensions, and was a construct of their personal thoughts. They learned they would have to quickly discipline their minds to stay in one dimension only; and it was necessary that they stay in the same space-dimension as the Ektar craft and Black-Rabbit City. They were also informed that the space-craft was their headquarters and they would be sleeping there.

Zack said, "It's like back on Earth, the two-legged creatures have access to numberless unknown dimensions. They all occupy the same space as the ones with which they are familiar, like radio, TV, and all manner of electronics operating on countless frequencies. They all exist as possibilities at the same time, and await our selection!"

Boofy said, "I see that our exploring of Ektar can come later. Our immediate need is to recognize our Ektar space-craft dimension which is the same as Black-Rabbit City. In that way we can stay together. It will require some mental discipline!"

"How do we stay in one dimension when we might think of something else?" asked Tooky.

"Good question Tooky," cut in Captain Betaka. "As Boofy stated, ours is the 'space-craft' dimension, which is the same as Black-Rabbit City where we'll be holding our meeting. If you allow your mind to wander away and you get lost, remember to image the one thing you are familiar with, that is, the space-craft. You cannot get lost. Just Image the craft and you'll also be back in the city."

Bifflets undertook the task of going over what Captain Betaka had said and handled a number of questions that arose. Everyone was then fully prepared for Captain Betaka's next instructions

"Practice this right now before we go further," Betaka said. "Okay? Image carrots or whatever, and then image the spacecraft. Go back and forth between any dimensions you want." All the rabbits practiced this new idea, but they kept disappearing and reappearing.

"Oh! I forget to tell you", continued Betaka, "the interesting part is that when you're visiting some other space-dimension, accidentally or not, you will disappear from this one! We will not see you! By accidental I mean when you have failed to discipline your mind to stay in this dimension!"

Tesla said, "It should be easy for us to stay together as we'll be interacting with each other at the conference. That should prevent us from going elsewhere."

Kotar said, "These mind-discipline factors are essential for any creature who thinks about space-travel."

Without any relevancy whatsoever, Tooky suddenly exclaimed, "I want a big fresh carrot!" He instantly disappeared.

"I rest my case!" said Kotar smiling to all those around him. He had certainly made his point.

Timken asked, "What would happen if a rabbit got lost in a dimension on Ektar and had disappeared from his companions? How could we find him?"

"Simple," said Captain Betaka. "He would be tracked by his brain-frequency on a Black-Rabbit scanner. Your wave-lengths are different from ours. The missing rabbit would be located in seconds. I'm not sure about you Zack! We already know your brain-frequencies do not parallel the rabbits'. Just imaging the space-craft will be sufficient." He smiled.

Except for Tooky, all the expedition members then headed for the Black-Rabbit City Conference Centre, easily identified by its huge black dome, on top of which, revolving with the wind was a large golden rabbit with black ears. None of the hundreds of Keylons that hopped around the streets took particular notice of the space-travellers. They were expected, and upon arrival within minutes were luxuriously seated. Suddenly a carrot or what remained of one dropped on to the table, and there, peeking from a chair was Tooky. Their group was complete!

The meeting included quite a number of Keylons who headed up the Ektar Federation; a management group whose concerns were also those of the visitors. It was a heavy first day at the conference center, but the group was able to isolate and focus their attention on their primary performance problem. It involved the 'mind-set' of management at any level that had become directly or indirectly responsible for the deaths of so many of those whom they supervised. It was also agreed that this was a universal problem and not limited to Ektar.

The question was simple, namely, why did any rabbit in a supervisory position need to develop such huge powers of self-importance, and then become controlled by that mind-set to the point where they were blinded by their actions? The results they achieved by this ego-dominant stance, were certainly detrimental to their agreed-upon performance objectives. Indeed, they were tragic.

Bifflets said, "I've seen many rabbits operating from their ego-thrones, so to speak. Their pride is powered from 'lording it over others', often with unfounded authority which is rarely challenged. They are at their happiest when they can inflict discomfort on those with whom they interact. Despite its negativity, it seems to boost their 'pride-power'. Each time they, 'put someone down', they also grow bigger in self-importance! It's a form of control that is evil in its origin."

A high-ranking Keylon said, "Yes, I agree. This type of rabbit is a weak-minded creature. Often they ingratiate their way into high places where they find others of their kind. They try to make themselves into 'something', out of the 'nothing' that they really are. Thereby they weaken their organization by blocking progress. Due to their very lack of effectiveness—we should identify them as 'zero-rabbits'."

"That's a good name for them," said Boofy, "too frequently these 'zero-rabbit' types possess authority, and exert power from a foundation of ignorance and incompetence. We need to question how they acquired their position in the first place." His observation brought a rustling of papers and flopping of ears. Some of the Keylons sighed with insight and frustration. However, upon breaking up for the day, they all agreed to meet on the morrow to discuss solutions and future plans. Tooky commented to no one in particular, "I believe we're making progress. Tomorrow we'll experience some real break-thoughs."

Zack returned to his room on the space-craft, which was also assigned to those rabbits who wished to sleep with him. After some minutes in reflective thought, Zack's next move was to image his dimension of green woodland, creeks and beautiful flowers. He immediately stepped into that scene.

He ran joyfully through the flowers, shed his clothes and slowly luxuriated in the creek where the water was cool. It had none of the icy edge to which he was accustomed. He felt utterly refreshed. As he left the creek to step into the Flower-Meadow to dry off, he was met by a friendly Keylon who expressed the wish to take his clothes away for the balance of the day, and without further ado he simply picked them up and disappeared.

Unperturbed, Zack wandered around in the sunshine, explored some woodland and lay beneath a group of trees to watch some unusual and brightly colored birds. Zack's dimension was still located on Ektar, but way beyond the city and the distant lakes they had seen. He knew that at any time he wished to return to base, he just had to concentrate on the image of the space-craft and relax. It was really a simple pivotal-shift between realities and he enjoyed the reflex thought-action. Suddenly he thought of his clothing, and instantly saw it was engulfed by flames although he knew not where. He watched his runners and clothing burning until nothing remained. He could not help but chuckle aloud.

He returned to the creek bank and fell asleep in the soft grass. Life was wonderful! Later, a persistent shrill but musical squeaking opened his eyes, and on fully awakening he saw two of the most different mice he'd ever seen. Big black rounded ears, gold faces and bodies with blue fuzzy tails. They had black eyes and whiskers. When Zack sat up, they fled backwards. They had never before seen a wild human boy. But when he smiled and gently held out his hand, they scampered on to it, He drew them nearer for closer inspection. They were incredibly beautiful little animals. He was speaking to them and stroking their soft fur, when something suddenly caught the eyes of the mice. Turning to see what they were looking at, he saw a Keylon just disappearing. But there on the grass, to his amazement, was a brand new clean white shirt, along with dark navy blue shorts, socks and runners. Zack laid the mice down and in one effortless motion came to his feet, while the mice scampered out of the way.

Slowly Zack inspected his gift of new clothing. Equally slowly he dressed. The fit and feel were perfect, and the soft material was unlike anything he'd ever encountered. The new leather belt was strong and flexible, and with pride he strapped on his sheath-knife and laced up his new blue runners. Zack was unaware as yet that his new clothing could be quite warm, or cool at all times according to his need. In pure delight he jumped up and down, and picking up the mice he said, "What do you think?" Their shrill musical squeaks applauded his new good looks. Zack's face was one big smile.

Feeling hungry he imaged the space-craft and was immediately back onboard. In fact they had now all returned. Rudy Rat and the earth-rabbits all looked upon Zack's new appearance with admiring glances. Captain Betaka winked at Zack and asked if his new attire was to his liking. It was very obvious that Zack was reveling in his new clean appearance and he expressed his gratefulness to the Keylon crew. Supper became available, and Zack did justice to his meal.

It was while he was eating that he felt a strange movement in the right-hand pocket of his new shorts, and feeling there was surprised to find the two mice. He must have just popped them in there before imaging the space-craft. Now he remembered! The Ektar mice wiggled and squeaked with shrill musical notes, and everyone gathered around to examine them. Zack placed the mice on the table where they looked happily up at him. He noticed they could flex their ears to lock on to sound. Surrounded by such approving glances, the tiny animals held each other's paws and danced in circles squeaking loudly in their elation.

The expedition members all felt very tired at this point and decided to turn in. Zack popped the mice into his shirt pocket and headed for his room which was also assigned to those rabbits who wished to join him. There was no trace of hay, just a large foam-filled mattress with green corduroy covering, and a heap of soft down-filled cushions. Zack placed the mice by his pillow, and following his usual bedtime procedure, carefully hung his new attire on a rack designed for that purpose. He was quickly surrounded by down cushions, mice and rabbits. It was even more snuggly than usual. There was the usual rabbit chit-chat that covered the events of the day, then, seeing the sleepy eyes all round him, Zack killed the lights. They all slept.

KeKe did some flipping and squeaking in the early hours of the morning, and Timken had to remind him of the 'No Fear' procedure. This was followed by silence, until the sun-star bathed the craft in its warm morning rays. Zack proudly dressed in his new attire, and with the mice in his shirt pocket, they all went down a short flight of stairs to join the others at breakfast. When Zack asked Captain Betaka about the two mice joining them on return to Earth, he said it was optional with that size of creature, but to ensure that both mice were of one sex or the other. To this Zack agreed and then asked each mouse what he would like to eat, and thusly they too had food appear exactly as they had imaged.

Immediately after breakfast Zack took the mice back to their meadow and assured them he would pick them up in time for the return Earth journey.

At the conference center, their second day, they were all warmly greeted by the Keylons. None of the participants had formulated any solutions to the problems they had discussed the day before; and to worsen matters, four of the Ektar Federation team had been identified as prime examples of the 'zero-rabbit' mentality they had previously discussed. Confronted with this, their arrogance and anger caused the whole group to be somewhat uncomfortable, and that was an understatement. One of the 'ego-freaks' was not only a senior Ektar consultant, but also Chairman of the Ektar Federation and Board of Directors. Additionally, entitlement—that scourge of organizations—was being challenged, and high levels of apathy had also been exposed. The full impact of these horrors almost overcame the entire group. They were stunned.

"I don't belong in this meeting," complained Tooky, and instantly he disappeared. He was too highly sensitive to the hurts of negativity and conflict.

Then Zack stood, and this gained their immediate attention due to his height. His presence in size alone demanded respect. He quietly stated that no problems existed among any of the participants, despite appearances to the contrary; inasmuch that each individual was never static, and ever in a learning process. None of the members were perfect, he explained, including him. Zack sensed a general relaxation and saw that the situation was somewhat defused. "May I suggest," he smiled, "that we focus not on, 'WHO' is right, but rather on 'WHAT' is right." The way their faces lit up with comprehension was equal to switching on a bank of lights.

In one fell swoop Zack had disposed of all personality and ego nonsense. One could almost hear and feel the thrones of self-importance collapsing into a heap. He continued smiling; his blue eyes flashed penetrating glances at the Keylons. "What we have here is an opportunity to establish guidelines not only for Ektar, but also for Earth and Rat-Star. We're presented with an honor that calls for decisive action! No individual or group can escape the hurtful steps we all need in order to gain maturity." Zack then concluded, "It calls for greater control of our selves and expansion of our levels of consciousness. However, we are all equal to the task before us. I suggest a small break, and then let's approach these problems as a team and formulate some plans!" Zack sat and faced the incredible silence before him. Then there were shouts, squeaks, and a terrific thumping of back legs as the Keylons all stood in applause. It was truly a standing ovation. Zack blushed and led the way with Rudy-Rat to the refreshment center for their morning break. Captain Betaka smiled approvingly at Zack, and he was encircled by many Black-Rabbits as he led the way.

On reconvening, Tooky brought up the concept of humility for discussion. Boofy added his comments by saying, "Humility would dispose of arrogance and assertiveness. But this can only be attained by each rabbit being accountable to a higher-power. That power would have to be God, the ultra-super-rabbit who created the whole universe—He who knows the past, present and future." Boofy's statements were met with a lengthy and thoughtful period of silence. It lasted several minutes with ear flipping and nose twitching. The meeting took a further couple of hours, after which the conference group decided to break for the day. Some Black-Rabbits heaved sighs of relief.

Being free, Zack joined Tooky and Timken at their table and respectfully listened in to Tooky who was about to address some personal concerns. Tooky looked at them both and said, "I'm still trying to figure out what Kotar said some time ago, because I too can't remember all of my *PAST*, nor do I know the *FUTURE*. My problem is that I can never examine my *PRESENT*—which is my *NOW*—because even as I perceive '*NOW*', it has already become my immediate *PAST*! I'm never in '*NOW*'. It doesn't exist for me. Is it because I'm not really here? So where am I, when the "I" of 'me', watches the stream of Time flow by like a river? Only from *within* Eternity could I be simultaneously both inside and outside the river of Time! Maybe that means my body is in Time—but I'm in Eternity?" Tooky flipped his ears and paused for breath.

Timken looked like he was grasping for comprehension. He shook his head and replied, "Wow, Tooky! You always were a little weird. I mean that in a nice way! You are of course a brilliant little rabbit in your own right. It's not your problem that we're not equal to your thinking Tooky. Though sometimes I wonder what really makes you tick!" He smiled and looked at Tooky appreciatively.

Zack said, "You're really talking about 'stopping time' Tooky, and the nearest we ever came to that was in the Time-Experiment back home. We have a lot to learn, and I'm not really sure of where you're going with this. But it seems to me that if you want to analyze your 'current' moment for some reason—you could do so quite easily by scanning the past few moments you just went through!"

Tooky took a long breath. "It's a lot more than that Zack. Maybe there's a tiny *'space'* between the 'now' of this instant and the 'now' of the next—before it becomes my *'past'*. I'm stationary within this 'space-gap', which is like a doorway into *Eternity*. I see myself looking 'out' upon 'Time-in-Motion'. My body is aging within Time, but "I" am not—if 'I' am also the 'observer'. The only thing we can be certain of is that Eternity contains 'was', 'is', and 'will be'. They already exist in multi-dimensions of 'possibilities' waiting to be called into creation within Time." Tooky stretched and flipped his ears. "Can you image that Zack? What about you Timken? Does it make sense? I hope so, because I want to know where I am if I'm not here—when maybe I really am! Is this the exact point where we convert Time into Space or Space into Time?" Tooky quivered with suppressed excitement.

"I'm trying to follow you Tooky, but I have a lot of 'blanks'." Timken looked and sounded somewhat apologetic. Zack just looked at him in thoughtful silence. "Whoa there Tooky!" he exclaimed, "You're even losing me!"

"When I get going," Tooky explained, "I have to grab every thought as it comes, and sometimes they come in too fast." Tooky looked a little disoriented, and ignoring his pending dizziness he continued, "On the other hand, were I flowing *WITH* the river—and watching the riverbank—would I not be getting flashes of Eternity from within the 'gaps' in my reality?"

"Tooky," said Zack, "You're at the frontier of rabbit-consciousness—because you're a different kind of rabbit!" Tooky's eyes rolled around and his shallow breathing became quite fast.

It appeared that Timken's warning had come too late for Tooky to disengage himself from intellectual chaos. He collapsed onto his back, thrashing his legs around. His ears quivered in a strange way as though they were vibrating.

Timken called softly, "Tooky! Tooky! You're going to be okay—just stop thinking for awhile. We can always catch up on things later. So relax Tooky! Relax!" Zack picked Tooky up, and gripping him firmly, commenced to slowly stroke him from ears to tail. He always delighted in this and maybe it would bring him round.

Two of the Black-Rabbit medical staff came over. Zack assured them that Tooky had just had a functional brain reaction; inasmuch that he'd vastly over-taxed his brain's current neuron capacity. "He's an advanced type of deep-thinking rabbit," said Zack, "and this is not an uncommon experience when brilliant rabbits of this type try to comprehend that for which their brains were not originally designed."

"This is of very real interest to us" said one of the Meds named Sedgewick. "We have a research project currently underway known as the 'Braktor Project'. 'Braktor' is the Black-Rabbit who launched the program. We've discovered that certain rabbits can expand not only their neuron-capacity, but also are able to go far beyond neuron expansion—even to the reshaping of their brains—it's known as neuroplasticity." His associate, Starko, cut in excitedly, "On top of that we are beginning to believe from research data that the individual can change his own DNA by 'being' what he is thinking—but we're not so sure that this is a good thing."

"Wow," exclaimed Zack. "That's amazing! We'd be honored to become part of your research project. We would of course not limit our study to rabbits. We'd be including Golden Space-Rats were they agreeable; and my type of being, known as Humans."

"Braktor is of course highly confidential and we'd extend you the same courtesy," said Sedgewick. "Maybe we'll chat about this after the meeting."

Tooky, who had been passively listening to all of this, pretended to show signs of physical recovery as he sat up and blinked his eyes. "Yes! It was an ear-flipping brain-failure fiasco," he said, as he struggled to his feet. "I must learn to ease up when thinking gets so totally abstract. It goes way beyond dizziness, into unknown levels of consciousness, where I'm a stranger even to myself.

Sometimes I need to find out where I am—when I'm not here. Thanks Zack, I think I'll go back to the space-craft, rest up, and nibble on some carrots." Tooky sighed and disappeared.

Sedgewick and Starko looked meaningfully at each other and returned to their stations at the conference. The break was over. Addressing the group, Zack quietly stated, "There is no one higher than He who made the worlds, the stars and the whole universe. He even caused us to *'BE'*. It is a humbling experience to recognize and accept God as the highest power. Most rabbits and my kind simply don't believe in any 'higher-power'. They believe only in themselves. Is this the crux of our problem? Is it that humility can only exist in the presence of an 'acknowledged' and 'accepted' higher power?" Zack smiled as sat back in his chair.

Most of the Keylons had that 'dizzy rabbit' look about them, indicating they had been thinking too much. It was the Chairman and senior consultant of the Ektar Federation that stood to get their attention. His eyes were bright with inspiration.

He suggested that any individual responsible for decisions that could affect life and death on Ektar; have extra heavy-duty screening-tests before being appointed to the position in question. The test was one for transparency in all matters relating to humility in serving others. There would be high self-esteem and humility—with zero self-importance.

On that note he shocked everyone by resigning from his position. He stated he would re-apply for the appointment when he had passed the new screening tests. The entire Federation Board was aghast, but not to be left out, they also resigned under the same conditions. It was an open display of the Keylons attaining a new level of maturity.

A team was then appointed to develop the new system containing 'Transparency Documentation'. The Keylons of Ektar, Rudy-Rat of Rat-Star and Kotar of the Hill-Clan along with Zack from Earth would put their signatures to the agreement when it was completed. There was tremendous applause. The formal meeting was officially closed; but there remained numerous factors that required delegation for achievement. Upon completion of these assignments, they all left for lunch.

On the way back to the Ektar space-craft, Zack quietly asked to get together with the Hill-Clan members and Rudy-Rat. It was to be a top-secret type of meeting with no Keylons. They agreed that after lunch they would all meet in Zack's meadow by the creek.

Exactly as planned, they arrived in Zack's dimension and sat in a circle on the grass by what was also becoming known as 'Zack's Creek'. They all wondered what the meeting was about as things had gone so well.

Zack spoke. "I'm concerned. I feel cold prickles running up and down my spine! Something on Ektar does not add up! It seems that everyone is very nice, and yet I feel tension. Something is out, or is about to happen! Surely there cannot be a planet that is one hundred percent safe and devoid of all dangers? It's too good to be true. What are we missing?"

All the space-rabbits looked apprehensive. Only Rudy-Rat appeared to be thinking. A soft breeze gently swayed a myriad of enchanting flower blossoms. As usual the creek softly burbled and murmured beneath the trees, and apart from the faint rustling of leaves, there was silence.

Zack voiced further concern. "We *have* to be missing something! Intuition can never mislead us—so let us all submit this apprehension individually to our intuition. We're in the hands of the Keylons and their Ektar space-craft, and we're depending on them to return us to Earth. I don't want to be trapped here on Ektar!"

Just then a shrill musical squeaking registered with the group. "My mice!" exclaimed Zack. "I named them 'Jibby' and 'Jubby'." He smiled, reached down, and pick up the little animals. They nestled comfortably in his hand.

Zack brought them to eye-level, and said in suppressed excitement, "They want to tell us something! Everyone remain silent. Jibby! What is it?" he asked, broadly smiling.

There followed a stark, bone-chilling revelation. "We have to tell you why we want to leave Ektar," sobbed Jibby. "We should have told you before, but it's the deadly animals the Keylons call 'wolves'. They're coming! It's when the second moon is in its third phase that they invade Ektar.

We don't know how, but when that moon reaches certain brightness, they come! There are hundreds of them, and their main target is Black-Rabbit City. In the forests and countryside no creature is safe, even us, tiny as we are."

Jubby cut in, "They always attack Rabbitville first, on the edge of Black-Rabbit City which is close by. The sound of terrified rabbits screaming as they are chomped and swallowed is sickening to hear. I have also seen the streets of Black-Rabbit City run red with Keylon blood. The wolves kill for the sheer joy of killing! Some rabbits have only one small bite taken out of them."

"Nothing can stop them!" exclaimed Jibby.

Rudy flashed his golden eyes. "Jibby! Tell us when that second moon will come into its special brightness phase!"

Jubby cut in, "Three nights from now, including tonight, and then it all happens!"

Rudy, Zack and the others profusely thanked the little field mice, whilst Zack placed them in their hole. Jibby and Jubby disappeared with happy squeaks.

"Well, now we know!" Zack exclaimed. Everyone expressed their disbelief that such an occurrence could be known and tolerated by the Keylons. It mystified them as to why they allowed such a disaster to be repeated on a routine basis with such astounding losses. It might also explain the air of hopeless resignation that the Black-Rabbits unwittingly expressed in their movements as they carried out their daily functions. The Earth crew all agreed not to discuss the matter back on the space-craft with any of the Black-Rabbits unless Rudy, Zack or Kotar authorized such a discussion.

The group kept turning things over in their minds. Some made comments, and others remained silent. Zack felt they could trust Betaka, the Ektar space-ship commander, and it was agreed they should approach him on the matter.

Further, they had to determine if they were in a position to fight and help the Keylons, or should they bring their departure date and time forward? If it came to fight or defense, what weapons might be available? The entire group felt deep concern for their own safety which almost turned to fear. Zack said, "We can handle this emergency—for that is what it is! It just needs step by step planning. We'll need to run our 'No Fear' program in the background while we do this, or we'll become victims. Let's go!"

They returned to their base. Captain Betaka greeted them cordially and smiled. When Zack asked for a confidential meeting between him and the space-travelers, his face became shadowed, but he did grudgingly agree to have an immediate meeting. It was Rudy-Rat who came right to the point and explained what they had discovered. Every one watched Betaka's response with bated breath.

Slowly he sat down. "The truth will both surprise and disgust you! Not too long ago the inhabitants of 'Moon-Two' reached an agreement with the Ektar Federation that unless they allowed the Moon-Two wolves the free run of Ektar to forage for feed from time to time, they would use their secret weapons and eliminate the Keylons from Ektar. No mention was made at that time as to what 'foraging' really involved. Certainly they did not expect Black-Rabbits to be the target or they would never have agreed, and of course being under the threat of annihilation the Keylons had no recourse but to allow entry to the wolves. It was 'every rabbit for himself', and has remained that way up to this present day."

When the enormity of this information sank in, the group just sat in silence. Kotar took command by saying, "We have to decide if we take the offensive, or plan a type of defence, and we don't have much time." The group shifted about uneasily. Tesla suggested they relax in silence, try not to think, and put forward whatever came to mind, however far-out it might seem. An almost eirie silence took over. Some rabbits looked at each other with far-off searching stares.

Then Tooky piped up, "What about Kotar's secret weapon, the one that the Rat-Star space-crew said he must never use again, something about committing 'atrocities' in space?" Tooky looked about him, almost expecting to be trounced and thrown out of the meeting. But his idea was greeted by everyone with such exclamations of delight and approval that Tooky was quite abashed. He closed his eyes and shrank into his seat.

"Good input Tooky!" exclaimed Rudy, looking at him proudly.

"Apologies to you Captain Betaka," said Zack. "But let us fill you in on the whole Kotar affair. We are referring to Kotar's proven ability to capture bad 'realities' and send them to another planet. He is quite unique in this talent." The entire group led by Zack then presented Kotar's history and extraordinary abilities. Captain Betaka was highly impressed. His face lit up with anticipation.

"I do believe you may have hit on the solution," he said thoughtfully. "And, if we were able to multiply Kotar's powers through us and my whole crew, it's possible we might eliminate this problem for all time. As fast as the Moon-Two wolves are beaming in, we would simply transmit them to another planet."

Kotar!" exclaimed Zack looking apologetic. "You are the center of this discussion and no one has said a word to you! We're sorry, but we all just got carried away! Please forgive us!"

Kotar smiled. "That's okay! I believe we're on to something. We can't consult with the Ektar Federation as they all fired themselves from their positions! But with the aid of the Ektar space-craft crew and our Rat-Star friend Rudy, I believe we can pull this off. We'll call it 'Operation-Moon-Wolf'. First we need to select the planet to which the Moon-Two wolves will be transmitted. Secondly we need to clearly identify the precise wavelengths and frequencies on which we'll be operating. Thirdly, most important of all, will be our need to operate as *ONE* power.

That is me, multiplied by all of us in a simultaneous operation. We have no time to lose! Tooky, if you feel this is beyond your capabilities, simply say so and you'll be excused. No problem!"

Tooky claimed he was small but powerful in his own way, and pledged his full support. Captain Betaka went to call his space-crew together, while the rabbits had further discussion. Zack headed back to Black-Rabbit City to contact the former Ektar Federation Board members. He felt they should know exactly what was going on and why. His reception was excellent and the entire Board were astounded and overjoyed that an attempt of such magnitude was already underway. It appeared that Operation-Moon-Wolf had the ear-marks of success.

Every Black-Rabbit was either openly or secretly terrified of what might happen in just two more days. In fact Zack had witnessed three Keylons lying on a side-walk foaming at the mouth. They were paralyzed with fear just from thinking about the upcoming disaster. It loomed as a large-scale tragedy that had to be averted. Zack had a momentary vision of Man's machine guns, and wondered what type of weapons the Black-Rabbits had developed. It seemed concepts of fighting back in an organized manner did not exist.

Next morning, the Ektar space crew along with Kotar's Earth group worked out their plans. The primary question as to which planet the Moon-Two Wolves should be sent was finalized with Captain Betaka and Rudy. They had selected the little known planet named Xenar, to which Kotar's bad realities had previously been transmitted. Everyone was pleased that Xenar was a closed one-way destination from which it was impossible to exit. This afforded safety and protection from any reprisals or repercussions of any type.

Zack's personal mission that morning was to be alone in order to think things through, so he returned to his Flower-Meadow and following a slow dip in the creek, he lay in the sun to dry off. Somehow, he had to explain in simple language to all the members of Operation-Moon-Wolf that Kotar needed them to all operate as *ONE* mind.

It was a 'pivotal-shift-reality' they all needed to fully understand. He recalled it was related to Bose-Einstein Condensates, but he failed to envision the total thought-linkage. There must be no break in continuity of Kotar's power until the mission was complete. Late that afternoon following a squeaky session with Jibby and Jubby, Zack returned to base.

On the way back he wondered how a kid coming on fifteen within the next week, far from his own planet, was involved in an inter-planetary war between the Black-Rabbits of Ektar and the Moon-Wolves of Moon-Two. He had to chuckle at the whole picture. What would Brett say!

It was agreed that on the night of the Wolf-Moon, the Ektar space-craft would be based just South of Rabbitville. The hill they chose overlooked a vast area of grassy plains upon which the wolves had previously arrived. It could handle the roughly estimated seven hundred wolves they'd been led to expect.

The Keylons said the evil creatures 'beamed down', and used the powerful moon-rays like a real highway. It was a concept based on principles of matter and light that were unknown to any of them. No one could mentally bridge the fact that light at certain wavelengths, combined with the harmonics of vibration could be molecular in nature. The 'wolves' seemed to 'pour' down in numbers that appeared to be almost countless. The Keylons had told Zack, that the sheer horror at the sight of these packs of slavering animals with their flaming eyes pouring down from Moon-Two—caused many Black-Rabbits to die instantly.

They also spoke of the real tragedy. It was simply that the wolves did not want dead rabbits; they wanted live rabbits—screaming in terror. The panic-stricken creatures were usually seized in bloody jaws, flipped, crunched and swallowed. The Moon-Wolves even dragged them out of their homes. The desperate screams that split the air gave impetus to the wolve's blood lust. Blood spurted in all directions. It was usually a free-for-all with rabbits being torn apart. They squeaked piteously as everywhere they struggled in futile attempts to escape.

The sheer scale of the mayhem was an unbelievable spectacle in itself. When the terrible creatures could eat no more, they just ran wild, killing any rabbit in sight and even biting each other. Sometimes vicious fights broke out. It was only when the 'Highway of Light' to Moon-Two began to weaken, that the wolves were forced to return to that highway to reach their home base.

Kotar expressed doubt as to whether the wolf leaders really had any weapons of mass destruction. Zack and Rudy agreed with him and shocked Captain Betaka, a quite senior Keylon, by pointing out that weapons of mass destruction were already being used, namely, the Moon-Two wolves themselves.

For the first time the Keylons saw their enemy in a different light, and it was at this point that Tesla brought the time factor to their attention.

"Friends of Operation Moon-Wolf," he spoke with an arresting style that almost ran shivers up one's back. "We have but two more nights before we see action, let's hear what Zack has to say about us increasing our power to ensure Kotar's success." He flipped his glossy black ears in Zack's direction. Zack arose and looked at them all in complete silence for about one whole minute. Then he spoke.

"We are confronting a task that will require 'relaxed-concentration'. It is imperative that we all become as *ONE* mind—and *ONE* power. We need to merge our force with that of Kotar! None of us can deviate from that intent! We shall not even look at each other, but concentrate on the task at hand. Each of us will focus like a laser beam on our objectives." Zack brushed the sweat off his upper lip, and looked at each member of the crew to detect any doubt that might exist at this point. It appeared they were all of one mind. "Kotar, where do we direct our focus at that time?" he asked, "We need to be totally coordinated."

"I've never handled groups of the size we'll be facing!" exclaimed Kotar. "But I will not start operating until the wolf-groups that first touchdown are within sight, and are in close proximity to our ship before we act. We need to ensure they have all landed, otherwise if the ones at the rear see the leading groups disappear; they'll flee back to the safety of Moon-Two. We will of course have previously activated the space-craft invisibility shields so they will not see us."

"We wait for Kotar's left ear to drop," said Tesla. "It's the signal that power is flowing and Operation-Moon-Wolf in underway! At the same time no one is to look at Kotar's eyes! Kotar will be looking straight ahead, but be warned, the glow of immutable intent that his eyes emit is inescapable! At that point each individual will merge his power with Kotar's. We might not get up to full strength, but our effectiveness will be a minimum of ten times that of Kotar alone, and that will be more than we need." Boofy and Bifflets both said they liked the idea of the wide safety margin.

"Now!" said Kotar. "We envision capturing groups of Moon-Wolves, twenty five or more in each pack. We image dropping a net over them; this is the 'capture', and then immediately image Xenar, their new home. There is what I call a one-piece critical 'pivotal-shift-reality' that comes into play at this point. That which you have just done is DONE! You image—you transfer—you leave it alone!

Don't question the reality of your success for a split-second or you will undo what you have already achieved. It's called 'Faith-in-Action'. Immediately you go onto the next group and so forth. We might even see major packs of one hundred wolves at a time get caught up in the transfer to Xenar! Just remember the sequence. One is Kotar! Two is Wolves! Three is Capture! And four is Xenar! Keep rotating these four images, preferably in unison. They'll never know what hit them!"

Tooky shook his furry little head in abject wonder. It was almost beyond him. He gave a typical young rabbit sigh. "This whole thing is ear-flipping space-magic!" he exclaimed. "I don't understand how those wolves bridge Moon-Two with Ektar on what seems like a highway constructed from 'solid' light!"

"Don't even try Tooky," said Zack, "or you'll have a 'short' in your brain neurons, and I can't help you right now. If you figure 'Operation-Moon-Wolf' is beyond you, just go to your quarters till it's over. Okay?"

"Yes! Thanks Zack!" Tooky was relieved and grateful for the input. As the meeting broke up they all went their separate ways to think over what had been planned. Zack went to talk with Jibby and Jubby. They were so colorful, so squeaky, and so happy, that interacting with them allowed his mind to solve other problems and expose them to his intuition.

Supper at the Ektar space-craft was a lot of fun. One could never have imagined they were preparing for a frightening battle on the following night. Afterwards they almost involuntarily began to chant in unison, "Kotar! Wolves! Capture! Xenar! Kotar! Wolves! Capture! Xenar!" Suddenly—Zack recognized what they had accidentally run in to.

"This chant," he said, "will enable us to synchronize our thinking so that we act as *ONE* force. Chanting is the key to synchronizing our power!" He was grinning from ear to ear.

Kotar was so delighted with the scheme that he confirmed the entire Operation- Moon-Wolf crew should immediately adopt the chant, Kotar! Wolves! Capture! Xenar! You're right Zack! That's the whole key," said Kotar. "I'll coordinate my images with yours—I dare not attempt to estimate the power of such unity. On top of all of that you'll be having so much fun; the greatest danger is that you might laugh yourselves silly before the operation is complete!"

"I believe the horror and potential terror of what we see will remove any excessive laughing," said Zack. "We must also remember that we can see them, but they can't see us. We must not let their blood curdling voices and fierce appearances interrupt the rhythm of our chants and imaging."

The acknowledgement of such negative possibilities put them all on alert. Each of them made internal notes about their reactions and the controlling of those reactions. It was truly an exercise of their mental faculties brought on by absolute necessity.

Operation-Moon-Wolf personnel disbanded for the night, and agreed to meet after lunch on the morrow to handle any questions and last minute matters. Everyone wanted to be well rested for the following night, including Zack, who on leaving the meeting went for a stroll in his Flower-Meadow before turning in. As usual he retreated into his world of introspection.

He derived a lot of satisfaction from studying internal questions involving problems to which he had no immediate solution. One was the matter of 'Time'. Time, the immutable force, was always the most fascinating subject for Zack. He was intrigued by little Tooky's comments on 'Time' when he had passed-out. It brought to mind the Black-Rabbits 'Braktor' project. As for Tooky, Zack smiled to himself; strange little rabbit he thought, so young, but so wise beyond his years.

In any case, Zack was convinced that an expansion into high quality consciousness must lead to an expansion into 'space', and therefore created a higher frequency response range for his entire system of thought. That in turn, meant that the broader his frequency response, the more he could function in a larger number of realities. It basically involved converting Time into Space and vise versa, as yet a concept difficult for him to fully grasp and practice.

Zack occasionally mused on the whole world that operated on a horizontal axis, which gave the illusion of time and eternity as one straight line stretching into infinity. To live in horizontal thought-mode was really a crippling type of blindness the humans mistook for sight! The huge vortex of activity, turmoil and five-sense realities they created, kept them so busy, they never gave serious thought as to why they lived, or where they were going. From birth to death they worked, struggled, played, bought homes, raised kids and tried to save enough money so they would not have to work in old age. If they succeeded in winning the 'money game', they were usually too broken down in body and mind to enjoy it anyway! Many died prematurely; fewer yet, experienced a spiritual or any other dimension.

Zack voiced his thoughts out loud, "Why do most Humans appear to dwell in an unreal world? They're like pebbles in the stream of Time—dreaming and sleeping in a world of illusion—which to them *IS* reality! But something prevents them from awakening—and until they awake—they'll never know that they were asleep! So why and how am I different? Maybe it's because I can access dimensions vertical to Time—which is my 'Now-Reality'."

Zack was convinced that sometime, he would eventually meet up with other humans at his level of questing, and they would join forces and challenge the frontiers of consciousness together. Zack was also aware that to locate such a friend would be a daunting task, probably fraught with misunderstanding.

Logic, he agreed was an undeniable necessity, but it appeared to Zack that those who were limited to logic-based thinking only, unconsciously lacked wholeness. He felt that maybe solving problems without 'conscious' application of intuitive-thinking could be an erroneous way of thinking.

Zack recalled incidents where scientists and logicians by pure-accident came up with a correct solution to a problem by obeying intuition; whereupon they ruefully apologized almost in shame for having done so. Thereafter they were forever acclaimed to be brilliant scientists, even though they gave recognition to a wholly unscientific mode of thought.

"Tooky!" Zack exclaimed aloud as though he were there, "I believe the basis for applying this 'logic only' mode of thinking is ego. Same old problem; logic and ego go hand in hand because it is 'I' who do the thinking. 'I' rely on *ME*. Everything comes from *ME*; and that Tooky—is pure egocentricity. Intuitive thinkers are not slaves to self-importance. You know, I sometimes think a simple rabbit has more common sense than many an 'educated' man, because rabbits combine logic and intuition as a team!" Zack sighed. "What do I know?" he exclaimed. Night fell suddenly. He imaged the space-craft and returned to base.

These days more than ever before, Zack's newly developed sexual maturity overcame him to the point of mind-numbing distraction. Although it was inherent in the design of young men, the motivation for release was largely misinterpreted. Alone, he attained exquisite relief among the fragrant blossoms in the Flower Meadow. By starlight he dissolved his tensions into relaxation that enabled a restful sleep. The aftermath of his satiation always ensured the return of his normal competent self, and on Ektar this was a necessity of survival. Already though, Zack discovered that he longed for the proximity of Earth, Brett and human friends—even a young woman.

However, he did wonder sometimes if he thought more like a rabbit than he should—but certainly, Zack no longer had any need to fear man, or what man might do to him; and perhaps that too was part of growing-up. But, until the Ektar-owned Lexcraft space-ship touched down back on Earth, he had fully committed his entire being to achieving the objectives they had planned.

Bifflets — Boofy's young brother; a quiet, competent young rabbit with exceptional abilities.

Chapter Seven

The fateful day had arrived. The inhabitants of Black Rabbit City would need no urging to hide out of sight as Moon-Two came into view in the evening sky. Zack and the Hill-Clan rabbits along with Rudy quietly passed the day in contemplation and rest. No further questions had come up. All they had to do was to position the Ektar space-craft at dusk and lie low.

However, late in the mid-afternoon Captains Betaka and Ratto called for a meeting to discuss their imaging of Xenar. "If we can't image Xenar effectively," said Betaka, "We might transmit Moon Wolves to places they should never be. I have pictures of Xenar." Whereupon Kotar and the entire Operation-Wolf-Moon group were able to concentrate solely on Xenar's bleak moonlit expanse of rocky terrain. For two whole hours they imaged Xenar in its location and could almost recall every rock in the picture. At the conclusion of the session they tested each other and found it impossible to think of Xenar without its desolate images. "Mission accomplished," said Captain Betaka with a big smile. "One final word, we'll all meet here for supper and then stay with the ship."

Zack intuitively felt the mission was already successfully completed, and spent an hour before supper walking the Flower-Meadow with Jibby and Jubby in his shirt pocket. Their musical squeaking delighted Zack as they settled in on the greatest adventure of their entire lives. Zack and the mice returned to the Ektar-craft.

Dusk was falling and the first stars twinkled as the space-craft touched down on the huge flat hill overlooking the plains. In silence, Captain Betaka and the Keylon crew activated the invisibility shields, while the Operation-Moon-Wolf crew moved in small groups to their locations with Kotar at the front. Zack had left Jibby and Jubby in his cabin as they would have been a distraction. Everyone waited.

Those who wait need to wait patiently. There are a thousand reasons to be impatient, any one of which could bring disaster upon the operation. It was always a matter of individual self-control. Time dragged by. But slowly, very slowly, Moon-Two arose with unsurpassed golden brilliance. Never had the members of Operation-Moon-Wolf seen such awe-inspiring splendor.

For some reason that the crew failed to establish, the entire scene disturbed their thinking. Captain Betaka commented that it felt as though 'confusion thoughts' were being transmitted to Ektar. They were probably projected at Black-Rabbit City, but the space-crew was also receiving them. He immediately alerted the group to 'deflect' or not to acknowledge what they were receiving. "To acknowledge a power is the same as accepting it, whereby we then empower it to work against us." he stated. "We must reject all alien thoughts that seek to gain entry to our minds." Betaka's remarks sounded like pure Kotar wisdom.

"It would seem by this," said Zack, "That we are up against a more sophisticated force than we had anticipated, but we still have the upper-hand with 'Kotar-power'. This moment, our greatest danger to the operation is that we keep thinking about our proposed actions against the Moon-Wolves and accidentally transmit our plans to them. Right now! This instant! Let's all just concentrate on the scene before us on the plains. That and moonlight—but nothing else!" Everyone was in perfect accord with Zack's idea. Kotar briefly stated he could immediately feel the switch in thought-power from this move.

As Moon-Two rose higher above Ektar, everyone saw the first powerful shafts of light reach the plains. The beams increased in their intensity to a degree that made them seem to be almost solid, in fact, unless it were an optical illusion, it now appeared that a brilliant highway of light had been constructed between Moon-Two and Ektar.

"Be sure and monitor your thoughts!" exclaimed Zack. "They may be able to pick up some slight variation in Ektar normalcy and our whole operation could be sabotaged. We don't know the full range of their power!"

In the next moment, a little reminiscent of Earth Husky teams competing in a race, the dreaded Moon-Wolves raced down the Highway of Light. They were headed down to the vast plains that were under surveillance by the Ektar space-craft. Everyone on board could feel huge tension. Zack felt a calmness he had not expected, and Tooky excused himself with an alarmed squeak and headed back to Zack's room to be with the mice. This had been expected and there was not a single ripple of concern. Just how many Moon-Wolves had reached the plains could not be estimated. Shortly after, it became apparent that the 'Highway of Light' was clear of the invading wolves. Half an hour had gone by when Captain Betaka said he sensed the force of the enemy approaching. He was not mistaken.

The Moon-Two wolves were generally running in groups of about fifty, and could be tracked in the moonlight from the space-craft for several miles. There were untold hundreds of the ravening creatures.

An unusual silence and calm had descended upon the entire crew, and as the two lead packs surged up the slopes, Kotar's left ear flopped sideways, and his eyes took on the appearance of blue death-rays. With incredible smoothness Zack softly said, "Kotar!" and paused. Then without a tremor, slowly his voice stated, "Wolves! Capture!" and immediately the eyes of the crew captured the first two groups of about fifty wolves each. "Xenar!" Zack's voice crisply stated. An empty space confronted them.

"The next groups are arriving," said Zack, hardly able to contain the excitement in his voice. "We may have a mob of hundreds here! Kotar! Wolves! Capture!" his voice rang out. "Xenar!" He exclaimed. A vast empty space appeared. At that point Zack warned the crew; "Do not bring the past to mind! Don't go back! Don't recall! Just think of the next batch. Wait for the rest of them!"

But no more wolves came into view. Captain Betaka's scoping instrument revealed that the final group of about possibly two hundred wolves had turned round and were heading back.

"They are on to us!" exclaimed Captain Betaka. "They don't know what, but they know something is wrong!"

Kotar calmly interjected, "There is no change in what we are doing. Direct your attention to the 'Highway of Light'. Same procedure, we'll transfer them from there! Just—do not doubt!"

All the preparation and practice of the Operation-Moon-Wolf crew had come into play perfectly. It was a one-time operation to capture and transmit the returning escapee wolves from the 'Highway of Light'. As Zack's voice gave the final cry of, "Xenar!" the highway was clear and the operation complete.

Everyone assembled in the main cabin amidst smiles, sighs of relief and numerous congratulations. It was Boofy who interrupted their triumph by saying "May I have your attention please! So far, so good, but right now instead of celebrating we should we ultra-alert to activities or anything untoward from the direction of Moon-Two. It's always a possibility that they *DO* have an unknown weapon of mass destruction they can activate against all of Ektar's inhabitants."

Betaka and Zack sat down for a conference while everyone listened. They agreed that Boofy was right on track, and a general seriousness overtook the group. Kotar was quite jubilant, although somewhat exhausted. Captain Betaka thanked him of behalf of all of Ektar, and said that 'thanks' was a tepid term in view of what had been achieved. "It will go down in the history of Ektar. It shall be called, 'The Saga of Kotar and the Moon-Wolves'." He announced this with considerable pride. The 'Highway of Light' beams were slowly fading and finally disappeared. As was to be expected, celebrations resounded throughout Black-Rabbit City and Rabbitville till dawn. Meantime the space-ship returned to base.

Zack's intuition gave him feelings of impending danger, nothing specific, but something evil, lurking or pending. He voiced his concern to the group, and it was little Tooky who piped up and who shamefacedly said, "I've been picking up Moon-Wolf thoughts. They are really scary." He looked up and saw nothing but encouraging looks so he continued, "I keep seeing a little glass container the length of a Kotar whisker and about the width of one of my ears. There is something bad inside and I can't see what it is. I know that it is so scary that even the Moon-Wolves are scared."

"Why, that's just great!" said Rudy. "But can you tell us of its whereabouts? Is it on Ektar?"

"Yes!" said Tooky, trembling from ears to tail. "It fell into a huge flower meadow, but the Moon-Wolves don't know where it is, that's why they are so scared. They have an eerie feeling that a wolf accidentally dropped it somewhere back on Moon-Two."

"The only really big flower meadow I know of is the one where I found Jibby and Jubby," said Zack. Captain Betaka confirmed that this was the only one of that size on Ektar, and profusely thanked Tooky for contributing his thoughts. The whole group looked at each other wondering what to do. Zack said, "Let me have a chat with Jibby and Jubby, after all, it's their home!"

The two colorful little field mice said if Zack dropped them back home, they would ask via the 'Flower-Meadow-telegraph', that all the other field mice go in search for the strange object, but not to touch it. Just locate it.

When morning fully arrived, everyone went about their duties. Captain Betaka made off for Black-Rabbit City to relay news of what had occurred the previous night, and the dilemma that may now confront them. Rudy accompanied Betaka, and the Hill-Clan rabbits rested up from the Moon-Wolf terror.

Zack and the mice went to the Flower-Meadow, where Jibby and Jubby were released to spread the word. It took off with the rapidity of a prairie grass fire in a high wind.

Zack however, just had to rest up; the whole affair had drained him of more energy than he had anticipated. He needed to relax in the hot sun and flower-scented breezes. He lay deep in the grass with flower pollen falling on him like golden dust and fell into a sound sleep.

In Black-Rabbit City the Ektar Federation Board had re-appointed themselves to their former positions in order that the planet may have direction and decision- making abilities. Each had promised to subject themselves to the 'Transparency Test' when it was available; and agreed that if any one of them failed he would be permitted to resign in honor.

The Ektar Board was apprehensive in regard to the existence of a terrible mass destruction weapon that may have been 'lost' in their midst, and Captain Bataka promised a progress search report each day.

Zack awoke to a chorus of loud musical squeaking in his left ear! Fully refreshed, he sat up and smiled. "Well Jibby and Jubby, what's all the noise about?" he queried.

"A relative on the far side of the plain has found a strange object and thinks it may be what we are looking for," explained Jibby.

"Do you know where he is?" asked Zack.

"Yes! We know, but it's a very, very long way from here," said Jubby.

"Okay!" said Zack quickly dressing,"we'll take the Ektar-craft and be there in a matter of seconds."

"Wow!" exclaimed Jibby and Jubby. In minutes after arrival back at base they had outlined the matter to

Captain Betaka who immediately placed the musical field mice in the control room, and asked for approximate directions. Almost right after lift-off they arrived at a massive Redwood type tree. On landing, Jibby and Jubby saw their cousin Buddy Boy waiting at the base of the tree which was the tallest around for many miles.

Buddy Boy had not touched the object, a small glass tube to which he now led them. They all stood back and peered as Rudy picked it up in his gloved hand. The tube was sealed and appeared to be empty.

"In germ and gas warfare," said Zack, "This is typical of what you might see. This vial may contain enough deadly bacteria to wipe out all living creatures on Ektar. Do not drop it, we have to figure some way of disposing of it safely." Buddy Boy was the hero of the day and secretly happy to be alive. He had planned to open it up and maybe store seeds in it. The Ektar space-craft returned to base, and a conference was called with the whole Operation-Moon-Wolf team.

"How can we get rid of it?" said Zack. "We really don't want it on Ektar at all! So let Kotar give it the 'bad reality' treatment!" he gleefully exclaimed as the idea suddenly occurred to him. There was a chorus of cheers, but not from Kotar.

"This is not a 'living reality'," Kotar said. "It's a deadly inanimate object. I've never sent a dead object, always a bad live one. It should follow the same rules though, but just in case, let's do a joint-transfer operation at full power plus!"

"There is only one place for that vial to go!" exclaimed Zack, "To Xenar!" They all laughed. "It's one-way only. Nothing can escape Xenar, let's do it!"

The deadly vial was placed on the turf a short way from the Ektar-craft. The whole group waited till Kotar's left ear flopped sideways, at which point they all stared at the vial and thought Xenar! It disappeared.

They all found the day to be exhausting. Maybe it was the terrible dangers they had been exposed to and all the efforts of concentration, but they were all tired. Even Zack who had been feeling refreshed was now flaggy. The crew had a wonderful supper and retired early. Tooky snuggled under Zack's chin and the two field mice buried themselves in Zack's sun-bleached mop of golden hair.

Everyone arose at dawn filled with excitement as to what the day would bring. All Zack and the Hill-Clan had in mind was returning to Earth. Jibby and Jubby still wanted to stay with Zack even though the Moon-Wolf threats were gone forever. It was Captain Betaka of the Keylons who said they should first all meet with the Ektar Federation Board for a closure meeting. Probably the group would be in a position to take-off on the return trip to Earth the following day.

The Ektar Federation Board had received questions from the Moon-Two leaders, but the Keylons did not release any information regarding the whereabouts of the missing marauders who came to attack Black-Rabbit City. Nor was there any discussion on the glass vial suspected of carrying deadly bacteria. It had been a decisive victory for Ektar. The Ektar Board did disclose that if the remaining Moon-Wolves ever attempted to resume their old ways, the Keylons had the capability to access the Moon-Wolves on Moon-Two and remove them. Thusly it appeared that a long-lasting peace had been established.

Zack conferred with his group and asked if it were possible to check in and see what was occurring on Xenar.

Kotar, Captain Betaka and Rudy said it would not be a wise move, and to let well alone.

It was Tooky who stated, "The Moon-Wolves banished themselves to Xenar! It's a good example of the sowing and reaping principle in action, you know, the 'SAR' program. What the Moon-Wolves planted, they harvested. Now they'll have to live with what they created. They have no one to blame but themselves!" Everyone applauded Tooky's long statement. It also clearly re-focused 'SAR' into their group-consciousness as a 'priority-filter' inserted before every thought, word and deed. Easier said than done, but they all agreed to try.

The Keylons were not fully aware of the Hill-Clan's special training in the programs known as 'Fear Not', 'Intuition', '*SAR*', 'Humility over Ego', and the newest program that Kotar had mentioned involving 'Faith'. Zack was not sure of the time frame for such extended training or if it were feasible. His main concern was the aging factor due to their expedition to Ektar. How much time may have really passed on Earth since they had left?

Zack's thoughts were loudly interrupted by an Ektar messenger. He was a very scared Black-Rabbit and looked as though he might foam at the mouth at any moment. The poor little animal collapsed on to the floor of the spacecraft and started to kick his legs like he was having a 'fit'. Only little rabbits were used as messengers because of their high speed.

"Moon-Two wolves!" he gasped. "They attacked Rabbitville last night, the carnage there is terrible. Most of the remaining rabbits fled to Black-Rabbit City and arrived this morning. Many are still bleeding with big chunks of fur missing. No one knows how many were eaten."

The entire Operation-Moon-Wolf crew surrounded the stricken Keylon. Boofy and Bifflets stroked him and assured him that he was safe, whereupon the pathetic little creature sat up and even smiled. "I'm to tell you," he stated quietly, "That about twenty five Moon-wolves are involved, and the Ektar Federation needs an immediate meeting if possible."

The messenger rabbit was dispatched back to Black-Rabbit City without delay, with the reply that the Crew would be there within the hour. After he'd left, they looked at each other in amazement. The big question being, how could this have happened?

As Tooky said shamefacedly, "What situation did we plant to reap this catastrophe? We can see the results of what we did, but just where did we go wrong?"

Kotar said, "Thanks Tooky! Good input! It's possible that a couple of small wolf-packs may have escaped at the point where the plains join the woodlands. It's likely they had seen masses of their friends disappear into thin air and then fled to hide out in the woods. This was the generally accepted explanation, as no attack could have possibly been launched from Moon-Two. Without further delay they left for Black-Rabbit City and the Ektar Board.

The meeting progressed pretty much as they thought, but it was Rudy the young golden space-rat that came up with the answer to the major question as to how and where the Moon-Wolves were to be located.

"I will fly south of Rabbitville tonight and search the woodland. I doubt the wolves will attack again tonight; their bellies must be bursting, so they'll be resting up. They will not expect to be located by a 'flying rat'", he chuckled, "And I'll be very careful once I've discovered them. I will return immediately and we'll set up a plan of action."

The Ektar Board and the Moon-Wolf crew went about their duties, and Rudy said he'd lay low till dusk. Zack went with Jibby and Jubby to the Flower-Meadow and were accompanied by Tooky who wanted to just sit and rest by the creek. The field mice told Zack about their life in the meadow and how they had learned to survive. They recounted many harrowing experiences.

"Now," said Jibby in a voice filled with fear, "We have to tell you about another strange and frightening creature! It's the giant Praying Mantis that lives with us in the Flower-Meadow. They are so big; this place should really be called the 'Mantis Meadows!'" Zack smiled at what he assumed to be their imagination running somewhat wild.

"It's so big," said Jubby, "It can pick up mice and small rabbits if they're not careful. Buddy Boy's friend was eaten by one, they'll never forget it. The Praying Mantis was lurking in the shadow of a bush. It lunged at Bobby Joe so quickly, he thought at first it was a friend playing a joke. Bobby squeaked long and loudly when he saw what had picked him up. We're talking of a Mantis at least a foot and a half tall!" squeaked Jibby.

"Bobby Joe struggled, but it was futile," carried on Jubby. "All this this thing did was to coldly inspect him with its big triangular green head moving from side to side. Bobby couldn't escape the spiny claw that held him, and as casually as we might lick an ice-cream cone, that Mantis took a big bite out of him. Bobby Joe's limp body spurted blood, the Mantis started eating, and that was that. We ran away. It was just too evil! Tooky! You must watch out, I've seen Mantis even grab and eat small rabbits!" Tooky instinctively moved closer to Zack.

"Jibby and Jubby! You just about scare the living daylights out of us!" chortled Zack, but it did seem like they all looked around them with renewed caution. Zack went for a skinny dip in the creek as was his custom on Ektar, and while the breezes were drying him off in the warm grass, he got comfortable for an afternoon nap. It was idyllic to relax in the sun-dappled shadows.

It was not until sometime later that he became aware of a tentative probing of his thighs like someone was poking at him with a small sharp stick. He stirred and then relaxed. But when the probing continued to move higher and prickled his lower stomach he awoke with a start. Zack felt a bolt of terror surge through his ear-splitting yell. He was face to face and only two feet away from a bright shiny green face with large black eyes. It looked at him intently, but what hit Zack with such force was the calm, fearless and incredible intelligence with which the creature appeared to study him. Neither had met the likes of each other before. In an almost reflex reaction, Zack gripped his knife which lay alongside him and slashed at the Mantis with the seven inch blade. In two more quick slashes he severed the Mantis into three or four pieces. He was amazed at its size, and even more surprised that it would check him out as a possible food source.

Zack wondered if the arrival of the Mantis was the result of all four of them imaging the Mantis, which would have the equivalent thought-power of being multiplied by four! He decided then and there never to think about a Mantis again. However, this was almost impossible because in the future one would always be on one's guard against them and therefore imaging them. This worked in the Mantis' favor because their victims projected their thoughts like a beacon to their enemy, and all the creature had to do was to home in on the target! On the other hand it worked in the victim's favor too! If it was decided to launch an all-out war against the Mantis, they were able to bring them in to be killed merely by thinking of them!

Tooky and the field mice who had been around a curve in the creek quickly came to see what caused Zack to yell in such a bizarre manner. In shock, they all inspected the dead Mantis. If one is a field mouse, even a dead Mantis is terrifying. Zack proceeded to slice off its head as he asked Jibby and Jubby if there were any more possibly dangerous creatures of any type lurking in the grass. He planned to show the Mantis' evil looking head to the crew back at base. They assured him that apart from a seven foot long snake, blue with brown arrow-like markings, the Flower-Meadow was a great place in which to live. Zack thought he would ask Captain Betaka about the snake when he told him of the Mantis incident, and late afternoon saw the foursome return to the Ektar space-craft. Zack was quite subdued, and could not conceive of any reason why they had not been warned of such deadly creatures beforehand.

Rudy, the happy golden space-rat set out on his mission to locate the Moon- Wolves which had struck at Rabbitville. He flew close to the ground and then on reaching the woodland, shadowed the trees in his explorations. Rudy was enjoying himself, He was gifted with the power to fly silently and observe without being seen or heard, and made full use of his abilities.

Zack asked Captain Betaka about the Praying Mantis and showed him the head. He looked quite surprised as Zack recounted what had occurred, and told him that on Ektar this particular creature was different in that it had the ability to paralyze larger animals with a single bite, and that one should be as watchful for Mantis on Ektar as one would be with snakes back on Earth. This warning also covered the danger of even touching the creature with one's bare hands. Betaka explained that when larger prey like 'Zacks', became paralyzed, the Mantis' would come together in a group to feed on the live victim. It was a bad scene. He directed Zack to dispose of the Mantis head in Compartment Three and to decontaminate himself. Regarding the blue snake, he said it was quite harmless, except to mice. Zack did not delay in obeying Betaka's directions. In fact he thought he had gotten off lightly inasmuch that although he had the size and strength, the Mantis had the power of a single deadly bite.

Meantime, Rudy had seen movement in the dusk of the woodland, and alighting in a large tree, saw that the wolves were mostly sprawled out in a clearing, either resting or sleeping. The wolf number estimate seemed to be in the region of about twenty five. Without delay Rudy flew swiftly back to the Ektar space-craft for a conference. He rightly felt proud of his accomplishment.

The Operation-Moon-Wolf crew knew their best bet for a Xenar transfer would be when the beasts became hungry in the early morning, and they planned to meet them south of Rabbitville. Even if they were going to Black-Rabbit City, they would still go through Rabbitville. A messenger rabbit was dispatched to keep the Ektar group up-to-date, and again Operation-Moon-Wolf was launched.

The procedure was almost identical to the one they had used previously. With their invisibility shields fully activated, they selected a position that gave them a broad view of the Moon-Wolf invasion. Kotar warned the crew not to project thoughts accidentally by even thinking about wolves, but for the time being just to concentrate on the empty plain before them.

"Remember," said Kotar, "Wait till the entire group is in full view. Then it's Kotar! Wolves! Capture! Xenar! That's our sequence. Do not be affected by what you see; by daylight these animals present a fearsome sight!"

The Operation Moon-Wolf crew did not have long to wait. From out of the distant woodland the small pack of about twenty five wolves streamed forth at an incredible speed. The lead animal, a magnificent creature, was probably the Alpha male being larger than any of those that followed him. His flowing movements and rippling muscle power were absolutely awesome.

The operation was to be easier than the one they had performed originally. They had a clear cut view with no stragglers. Kotar's eyes took on their formidable glow, and when his left ear dropped, the entire crew chanted in unison, "Kotar! Wolves! Capture! Xenar!" They began to smile.

But nothing happened! The wolves just surged forward like an inexorable force. The Moon-Wolf crew was flabbergasted! It was unbelievable! Like being struck by lightning! They looked at each other as the Moon-Wolves came hurtling in their direction. Captain Betaka, highly competent and ever alert, instantly instructed his crew to take the offensive with 'fog action'. Zack said loudly, "After this, we all have to meet and discuss what went wrong!" Their minds were filled with explanations that did not make sense.

Zack remembered the blinding fog from the Hill-Clan days. The invisible Ektar-craft rose vertically, then it dipped while spewing a thick bank of rolling black 'fog' which they learned later was acrid and foul smelling. It had the power to kill any creature that inhaled even the smallest whisp of vapor. The Moon-Wolves had to breathe.

Captain Betaka explained later that it was a last resort emergency measure that had to be employed for the safety of every Ektar inhabitant. "There were no options. Desperate needs required desperate measures," he said.

"There is however, just one unpleasant task that we have to undertake before operation 'fog mission' is complete." said Betaka. "The wolf carcasses have to be eliminated as they are a hazard to any living thing within a five mile radius. We will issue protective suits and gear to achieve this. Only our Keylon crew will be involved as this has been part of their special training."

Zack and the Hill-Clan rabbits along with the golden space-rat Rudy, were invited into the observation tower, where they were told to stay and under no circumstance was anyone to leave the tower until Captain Betaka issued an all-clear statement.

When the fog lifted and dissipated, there before them, strewn over a wide area were twenty six moon-wolves including the handsome Alpha male. Tooky cried. His ears flopped and his whiskers twitched. "It's just not fair, even though they were our enemies, I feel so sad that it had to be this way." Rudy-Rat comforted him and said, "Tooky, it's the way things are. As they sowed, so they reaped."

"I suppose so," sniffed Tooky. "I mean, Zack could have been paralyzed by the Mantis. Zack had to kill it. After all, it was probing him to check out his edibility." Ratfink sat beside him as they watched the Keylon crew go forth with what looked like little spray-cans. Each Keylon divided the dead wolves in approximate groups of five and began to spray them. Zack said, "Look! Amazing! Each wolf sort of sizzles and bubbles after being sprayed and then disappears! Even the grass is gone from where they lay!"

When the Ektar-craft returned to base, the entire crew assembled to pin-point why the original mission as planned had failed so completely. Kotar had nothing to contribute. He had performed flawlessly. After a two hour discussion it was deemed they had underestimated the intelligence and mental power of the Moon-Wolves. They suspected the massive Alpha male had intuitively become aware as to why their main force had disappeared without a trace. His group had not been idly resting up in the woodland, but had been practicing their offensive tactics.

The advantage had lain with the Keylons because the Moon-Wolves were not aware of the Ektar-craft. In fact, that space-craft was the only one on Ektar and was a prototype of a design made by the golden space-rats of Rat-Star.

The meeting came to a satisfactory conclusion. As Boofy stated, "We reaped the results of underestimating our enemy, but we did follow our plan." He thanked Captain Betaka for taking control during the 'emergency'. Everyone wanted a break, and they dispersed to do whatever they wanted for the rest of the day.

Zack opted for the Flower-Meadow, and this time the space-rabbits went with him. Bifflets said, "The more eyes we have watching for danger, the safer we'll all be." Rudy-Rat stayed with the space-craft to do some research.

"Yes!" said Zack, "I'm going skinny-dipping and I'm also going to wash up my clothing this afternoon, but no napping! Everyone remember, it takes only one bite from a Mantis to seal your fate! Oh! And Tooky! Your size of rabbit is fair game for the blue snakes, so watch out!" Zack proceeded with his laundry and was amazed how the strange material became clean almost as soon as it was immersed in the water.

Meanwhile Jibby and Jubby squeaked, "Stay with us Tooky, we'll show you the sights!" By that comment, Zack wondered what else the field mice had not as yet revealed. The Hill-Clan crew followed the mice around the creek-curve and out of sight. After a minute or two he wondered how and why they had become separated after all agreeing to watch out for each other. If anything, as the larger of the creatures, he'd considered himself as their guardian. Maybe he was at fault.

The departing group followed the meandering water round a bend till it revealed a small valley with a very large meadow. Flowers stretched out as far as the eye could see. The flowers were so intensely colored they were brilliant to the point of being overwhelming. As the gentle breezes swayed the blossoms back and forth, it appeared to have a sort of hypnotic effect on the animals. In only a matter of moments, Jibby, Jubby and all the rabbits with the exception of Bifflets hopped forward in the peculiar gait of rabbits that are spellbound, and moved as though controlled by an unseen power. Not one mouse or rabbit was aware of any danger, or of what invisible force had descended upon them.

Zack, who was laying out his clothes to dry, had a sudden shocking intuitive input which focused on the rabbits. His first thought was for the safety of the animals. Slipping on his shorts, he welcomed the firm feel and security of the wide leather belt around his waist. The seven inch blade in its sheath at his side added further comfort. Grabbing the sharp-pointed five foot long staff he'd acquired, he streaked along the creek bank until he too saw the Valley-of-Flowers. Instantly, Zack leapt forward to catch up with the group. He saw Bifflets in the midst of them trying to make the rabbits halt—and of all things—he was trying to wake them up! Zack was both alarmed and shocked. His heart hammered in total support of whatever he might need to do.

Bifflets yelled, "Zack! Something has mesmerized them, and seems to be directing them up that little rise to . . . .Oh! What is that thing looking out at us from that hole just above that steep bank?"

"Stay back Bifflets, I see it—it's lurking in the shadows!"

Zack perceived that Kotar, Boofy, Tesla and KeKe had come out of their trance state and had stopped. They were now trying to help Bifflets rescue Tooky and Timken. Jibby and Jubby were among the first to 'wake up' and had no explanation beyond giving a guided tour.

"A guided tour?" yelled Zack. "Have you ever been here before? Look at what is happening to everyone!"

Kotar said, "Now we're all here, let's find out what that thing is. It seems to me that these animals use the brilliant flowers around here, in the same way as an Earth spider uses a web to catch prey. It seems that on Ektar there are a lot of creatures using mind-power in order to eat!"

"From now on, for our short time remaining on Ektar, let's question what it is we're doing and why!" said Zack.

Kotar, Tesla and Zack ascended the slope to the cave-like hole. Zack was in the lead, he could see nothing in the dark entrance but with considerable force, he jabbed his staff inside the hole. The response from within was a vicious growling type of snarl. This was followed by a stream of thick yellow stinking fluid which shot forth; a small splash caught Kotar's flank where is sizzled and burnt a hole in his fur and skin. Kotar gave a very loud squeak and flopped over in extreme pain. Every breath he released thereafter was accompanied by an even more pathetic squeak. It brought tears to Zack's eyes.

Zack, seeing the enemy's form of defense, again thrust the point of his staff full-force deep in the hole while he jumped to one side, but immediately their attention was diverted by warning screams from below. They turned to see the approach of three gross spider-like animals. Each creature had six hairy legs and eight eyes which were mounted high on their heads like control towers. They were three feet tall. "A type of super-arachnid!" shouted Tesla.

More revolting yellow fluid spewed out of the hole. Things then moved even faster when suddenly their group below, along with the field mice disappeared. Tesla said, "They've imaged home base!" Slowly the monster arachnids moved up the slope. They were familiar with rabbits having trapped and eaten all kinds of them before. But Zack, at five foot nine presented a different challenge. He was an unusual kind of animal, and he handled his weapon in an unpredictable manner, having already killed one of their tribe. Zack and Tesla felt sure the creature's hesitation was due to them being unsure of what he was, or where he came from. Nor had they yet estimated the degree of risk they would encounter in taking this prize chunk of meat.

No other creature had ever looked at the 'Spider-Animals' as did Zack. He had only two eyes, but the powerful fiery blue glitter they emitted stopped them in their tracks. It was a type of blue light that no creature could approach without being destroyed. The arachnids were intelligent enough to recognize such power when so confronted, and stopped moving.

Kotar was lying on his side gasping in pain. His missing fur-patch was becoming wider. The creature had ejected a deadly substance and it was slowly eating into him. If help could not be obtained soon, Kotar would be nothing but a wet patch of yucky fluid. For once Tesla was at a loss as to what to do. It looked like the end. It was Zack who disengaged his mental processes from the conflict long enough to say, "Kotar! Tesla! Let's image the Ektar-craft and get out of here!"

"Tesla said, "Kotar is in bad shape, I'll not leave him. He doesn't have the power to image. He'd be alone. No! If we die together, so be it!"

The decision was never his to make, or Zack's. From out of the West in full view, the Ektar space-craft swept in with incredible speed at almost zero tolerance altitude in total silence. It smashed into the bodies of the three 'Spider-Animals'.

Apart from a pulpy vile-smelling mess of mashed intertwined legs, and a big pool of foaming yellow fluid, no threat remained. There was not a mark on the diamond-hard crystal rings of the space-craft. Captain Betaka was first on the scene after landing, and Zack saw the rest of the Hill-Clan along with Jibby and Jubby waving at them from the observation tower. Once Kotar was onboard he was hurried to creature-surgery for immediate attention.

Tesla quickly recovered his presence and stepped on board the Ektar-craft looking assured and as calm as if he were returning from an afternoon picnic. Even his very black ears looked extra glossy. He smiled at everyone in self-possessed splendor. Zack, the half-naked wilding with the imperious blue eyes, smiled in relief as he stepped aboard.

The crew dragged the 'Spider-Animal' from its lair. It was already dead having been twice pierced by Zack's pointed staff. The Keylons did not need if for research purposes and left the mess to fully disintegrate in the heat. The Ektar-craft stopped briefly at the creek, and it was Zack who stepped out to retrieve his shirt, socks and runners which by now were quite dry. In a matter of mere moments they had returned to base.

It was certainly time to eat, and during their festive meal, animated discussions of the whole series of events were interspersed with the laughter of relief. Rudy-Rat had already received the afternoon adventures through his monitoring system. There were also some involuntary tears for it had been an emotional rescue performed at the highest point on any danger scale. While the animals nibbled, Jibby and Jubby in a lame explanation, revealed that what they had known as the 'Valley-of-Flowers' was also called the 'Valley-of-No-Return'. No one knew why, because no one had ever came back to tell them. Had they been aware of the dangers they would never gone exploring that way. This fact was cold comfort for those who had been rescued.

When Captain Betaka came in, he announced that Kotar was out of danger, and was a lot stronger, but when his fur grew back in it would be of a different color, maybe white or black and white. This was uplifting news of the best kind and cheered up all of them. As they completed their evening meals, they could not help living and reliving the dangers they had unwittingly encountered. They all felt older and much wiser. Tooky however was still disturbed.

He kept looking at Zack until Zack finally asked him what was on his mind. "I kept picking up terrifying pictures from the 'Spider-Animals'," Tooky said in a hushed voice. "All three of them were choosing places on your body in which to inject venom which would paralyze you. They were going to dissolve you from the inside and suck you up alive, or at least until you died! All three of them wanted to make the blue light in your eyes disappear. It frightened them."

"Well! Thanks Tooky, that really makes my day, not being sucked up alive by giant arachnids!" He chortled. "Seriously though Tooky—thanks for telling me. You have amazing powers of perception, even when it involves non-rabbit creatures. By the way, I want to have a chat with you soon about your observation of where you are at that point in 'Now', when you see your 'Present' become your 'Past'. I'm not sure as to why you feel it robs you of ever being 'here'; after all if you're not here, where are you?" Zack's open friendly smile filled Tooky with nice warm feelings he could not describe. It reminded him of being snuggled in his soft, cozy nest of long ago.

At the close of the eating session, Tesla requested a general meeting for tomorrow morning of the Hill-Clan crew along with Zack, if any of the Keylon crew wished to show up so much the better. The agenda called for them to recall and identify 'life principles in action'. Their discussions would be recorded for training materials for the Clan back home, so they could also benefit. It would create horrifying realism of the first magnitude, and would be an electrifying learning session.

Captain Betaka tactfully suggested the wisdom of staying close-by and out of trouble. "Need I inform you of yet another Ektar danger to keep you in the locale of the space-craft?" he said with a broad grin. "No? Okay then, see you tomorrow. Oh! And I think Kotar will be in fine shape to contribute to the meeting as well."

When Captain Betaka so casually alluded to other possible Ektar dangers, no one gave it a second thought, but Tooky was suddenly stricken with a violent tremor. He was reacting to a series of weird and highly dangerous images that flooded his mind. Even worse, he could not make sense out of his premonition. He felt he had perceived death in its most beguiling form of enchantment.

Zack decided to stay at their base. The weird things that Tooky was picking-up made Zack uneasy. Both he and Tooky knew it was only a matter of time, before they all became involved in handling some new terror. Zack trimmed the pointed end of his stave, and then touched-up his blade with great care and precision. He'd sharpened it on the assumption that he may have to fight and stab his way into an unsure future. The blue light in his eyes glinted with intent and satisfaction. He was ready to face whatever might appear on the scene. Tooky relaxed. Zack was his ultimate guardian.

However, after a while Zack, Tooky, Timken and Bifflets became restless, and Zack decided on the spur of the moment on a plan to visit one of the distant Blue Lakes they'd seen. "We'll never again have another chance like this," exclaimed Zack. "We'll just image ourselves there, stay and explore for a while. It's light until quite late—then just image-back in time for our evening meal."

"Haven't you had enough stress for one day?" enquired Tesla who overheard them. Caught up in excitement, the group made light of what he said and immediately made preparations to leave. But then, one of Captain Betaka's senior crew-members introduced himself. He was hesitant in his approach, and obviously was experiencing some difficulty in figuring out how to say what had to be said to the group.

Zack and Tooky picked up on this right away and sitting down they assured him of their complete attention. The Black-Rabbit thanked them. His name was Kratak, and he addressed them in a low clear voice that carried an ominous warning tone—so much so—that Zack felt the very hairs on his shaggy neck rising.

"On Ektar," Kratak explained,"You need to know what I call the 'unknowable'. There are laws and principles operating here that are unstable and quite unpredictable in nature. I heard you speak of 'simply imaging yourselves to some place and returning'. You'll be startled to know, for example—that visiting the Blue-Lakes allows your arrival—but does not guarantee your return. Many travel frequencies are sabotaged by unseen alien powers that live here on Ektar. We Black-Rabbits run our affairs, and they run theirs. But when we violate an unwritten travel rule—to use your terms—we reap what we sow." For emphasis Kratak shrugged in typical Black-Rabbit fashion, then, looking intently at each one of the group, he explained.

"We discovered long ago that the Blue-Lake Country is a deadly trap of no-return. However, this has not prevented hundreds of immature young Black-Rabbits—filled with a sense of adventure—from exploring the facination it presented to them. None have ever come back." Kratak paused, and saw that his message had been fully understood. "Even worse than that," Kratak continued, "we are slowly discovering other dangers of a similar deadly nature that get triggered from unknown causes. Sometimes Black-Rabbits just disappear—and those who look for them also vanish. So I'll leave this with you to assist in your plans." The little space-rabbit crew expressed wide eyed wonder. They were filled with apprehension and fear.

Even Zack began to see the folly of what he'd proposed. Silently he wondered why he'd not thought it through. Kratak replied to his unspoken question. "Your thoughts and ours are always monitored by alien powers. It is their intent that you should take a one-way trip to the

Blue-Lakes—and never understand why you made the decision to go there in the first place!" Zack thanked Kratak profusely. They all looked at each other in amazement, as Kratak went on his way up to the control tower. Everyone went with Zack to his quarters onboard the space-craft for the balance of the day. There was safety and warm companionship in staying together. Tooky also needed an intimate snuggling session with Zack.

Betaka — Captain of the Planet Ektar Space-ship.

Chapter Eight

The Ektar owned space-craft could meet any departure time within the next two days, so with some time to spare while affairs were wrapped up with the Ektar Federation; Zack decided he would still occupy his favorite 'thinking place' which was the Flower-Meadow by the creek despite the dangers of alien creatures. He had visited it so often that he was now familiar with almost every element is his selected area. He could cool down in the creek or lie in the sun. He was very conscious of the fact that napping could be an open invitation to predators, and he was certain he'd had his fair share of involvement and escaping them so far!

Tooky and KeKe asked if they could come along and Zack welcomed the company as well as the additional eyes, both were highly intelligent deep-thinking little rabbits, and they could nibble close by.

Zack pondered a question that had stayed in his mind and demanded an answer. He couldn't shake it. It was the indirect comment by the Keylons, perhaps only intimation in the course of conversation, but the gist of it was they knew of certain powers he possessed of which they thought he didn't recognize. But to what powers did they allude?

He knew it was not his problem and handed it over to his higher-power to provide the answer. He would occupy himself with doing anything but thinking about the question! Since he'd left the village, the one thing he missed most was access to reading material. This had had driven him to introspection more frequently, and he enjoyed discovering new levels of understanding.

He laughed at Tooky and KeKe as they chased around close by him, flipping, leaping, frisking and squeaking in exuberance, but not to the exclusion of being alert. Zack also knew their intuition input channels were fine-tuned for reception and were subjected to unconscious continual monitoring. Now, Zack was thinking, if only human kind . . . . His internal screen illuminated with an incoming message.

It seemed to say that maybe the power of which the Keylons had become aware, either by astuteness or their 'Cosmic-Creature Scanners' was his spiritual-power; but why would they think he was not aware of this power?

Over a year ago Zack had committed his life to Christianity, and had already developed personal relationships with his heavenly Father, His Son Jesus, and the Holy Spirit. Although being in what could be called a 'rabbit-immersion' program, he relied on his slowly developing 'faith-power'. Faith was a term that man generally did not understand, as most of them could not perceive anything beyond their five physical senses. Maybe this was the reason the Keylons thought he lacked awareness. Zack decided not to elaborate on his secret source of reserve power with any of the Black Rabbits or his own crew.

The sun rose ever higher in the Ektar sky. It was a perfect day when almost anything could happen and probably would. It seemed to Zack that all his days were filled with infinite possibilities, all of which occupied the same space-time dimension. Today the very air was charged with anticipation. Only choices were forthcoming.

KeKe had wandered away from Tooky and was unaware that he'd had become a vulnerable 'loner'. In fact, he thought Tooky was trailing along behind him, when all the time Tooky was taking a nap alongside Zack for safety.

Suddenly, KeKe heard a strangely beautiful bird-song and quickly hopped ahead to check it out. The bird was high in a tree and floated sweet liquid symphonic notes through the green leaf canopy over the creek. Fascinated, KeKe looked up to see the musician—but the sun was in his eyes. The bird's intent was precisely that this be so. KeKe was only aware of a soft fluttering sound which came and went without apparent incident. Were it not for the sharp little stab of pain he felt on his left side as the fluttering disappeared, he would have ignored the bird.

KeKe flipped his ears and felt sort of strange and immediately hopped back up the trail to find Tooky who was beside Zack. KeKe explained the whole sequence to Zack who probed KeKe's fur but could find nothing but a small lump where the pain had hit. Zack's intuition told him this was something strange and dangerous. He instructed the two rabbits to image the Ektar-craft with him as he felt they should return immediately. They left.

It was one of the Ektar Keylon crew along with Rudy-Rat that heard the entire story from KeKe. The Keylons knew exactly what the problem was. KeKe had not been listening to a bird at all! He'd been enchanted by the siren-like song of a freshly-mated insect known as an Ektapod. This was a very large flying insect about the size of a songbird, and right after its irresistibly beautiful love-song and mating, it sought a warm-blooded creature within which it could lay an egg via its ovipositor. It laid a total of about twenty five eggs each season.

This was KeKe's experience. The Ektapod female knowing KeKe could not see because he was facing the sun, had swooped down and in a fraction of time had inserted its ovipositor deep into KeKe depositing one egg. It was a smooth almost non-stop performance. When hatched the larvae would eat KeKe from the inside out, until he died from simply not being there. KeKe would become an *'is not'*. There would be the usual cocoon creation, followed by the hatching of a new Ektapod, which in turn would also go off to sing songs of enchantment in the woodland.

KeKe fainted. The somewhat routine procedure for the removal of an Ektapod egg proceeded without delay. It was a common operation and the wound usually took about four days to heal. The Black-Rabbits who heard the song of the Ektapod said it was a song of death. When KeKe came-to, he said he thought that death had never sounded so alluring and so beautiful. Captain Betaka had smiled when he heard of KeKe's mishap, he'd told him that this was the 'Ektar incentive' to which he had alluded in order to keep everyone one board! This time Zack and the rabbits were less than impressed. Was it not said that forewarned is forearmed? They discovered that most Keylons fled from the 'death-song', but many succumbed. They inevitably became unwitting hosts for the Ektapod and just faded away to mere skeletons. That which remained after the hatching, was eventually carried away by the winds and time.

Zack stayed aboard the Ektar-craft, he'd had enough excitement for one day and spent time preparing for the regular morning meeting. He and Tesla planned to just hit a few highlights, the fine details could be studied later. It also appeared that both Kotar and KeKe would be fit to travel in the next day or so, and everyone wanted to be underway back to Earth in that same time-frame. Zack imaged to the Flower-Meadow and chatted with the field mice, and they too were delighted with the idea of leaving. Zack promised to pick them up in plenty of time. He returned to the Ektar-craft.

When dawn broke the next day, following breakfast, Zack along with Kotar, Tesla, Boofy, Bifflets, Tooky, Timken and KeKe assembled in the meeting room on board the Ektar-craft. They were joined by golden space-rat Rudy, Captain Betaka and a few of his crew; but two Keylon crew members were not in attendance.

It was Zack who suggested to Betaka that *ALL* the Keylon crew be required to attend the meeting. He suspected the missing crew members to be unwitting victims of their own ignorance and ego. Undoubtedly they felt supremely capable and felt no need to join those who apparently did require help. Much was already known about the self-importance problem. It was an evil, insidious belief in one's self to the exclusion of internal or external inputs. It exercised invalid authority from a foundation of ignorance, and it currently extended from the level of the Ektar Federation Board right down to the deceased Hill-Clan members. Captain Betaka concurred with Zack's thinking and instantly commanded the absentee crew-member's presence.

The missing Keylons shuffled into the meeting with typical expressions of superiority and condescension, which confirmed Zack's take on their previous absence. Zack arose and softly said to the group, "I believe that certain facts we have identified, common to all of us, have contributed to some of our and your rabbits to become '*are not*' realities. The discoveries and the actions we have taken in this regard so far have had permanent life-saving effects. These we're going to briefly touch on. Any course of action you adopt will be decided upon by Captain Betaka.

Zack smiled at the entire group and addressing the newcomers who'd just joined them, he recapped for the benefit of all, what they had previously discussed in the matter of *'ego versus humility'*.

As a result of this, it was interesting to see the Keylon crew gradually open-up and take on a marked attitude of respect. Indeed, for the first time the entire group took on the appearance of becoming a joint, effective team.

Tooky whispered to Zack, "From now on, the penalty for those who insist on being 'ego-freaks' is to send them out to listen to Ektapod songs!"

"Not a bad idea Tooky," said Zack aloud as he repeated Tooky's suggestion. "But let us also be aware that we do not fall in the victim-state of, 'Do as I say, but not as I do!'. That can occur all too easily." There was a general chuckle and Zack sat back in his chair as he continued.

"We'll first of all look at what we've achieved through the 'No Fear!' and 'Intuition over Logic' programs. We'll touch on the 'Ego and Humility' facts and cover the 'SAR', the Sowing and Reaping principle. That will likely be enough for any one day!" he smiled again. One or two of the rabbits looked baffled, while the rest were ready to take hold of the challenge. Tooky and Timken had already disappeared, but Zack was not too much concerned as they had previously led their own training groups.

Following an in-depth discussion, the group agreed to reconvene in the afternoon. The meeting broke up with ear-flipping sighs of relief and much twitching of whiskers.

The entire Keylon crew under Captain Betaka remained diligent and respectful—even impressed.

Rudy went outside to fly around. He'd been complaining of wing-muscle weakness due to lack of use, and apologized in advance for seeming to take off in a superior manner that was not intended. In admiration they all watched Rudy's scarlet-tipped wings display their natural beauty in flight. His flashing turquoise eyes smiled as he disappeared over the trees into the nearby woodland. Every rabbit set to and nibbled on the natural vegetation. Zack felt he needed a good feed of grilled white fish and fresh salad, and this was supplied in the usual manner onboard. Zack was enjoying 'real food'.

Meanwhile Rudy reveled in his flight-freedom. He flew right over Black-Rabbit City, the big town of Rabbitville and way out to the Flower-Meadow and the lakes beyond. Out of curiosity he cautiously flew around the edge of the Valley-of-No-Return to check on 'Spider-Animal' activity. There, to his horror he saw a group of five arachnid creatures each with its sucking tube inserted into an animal that looked like a large deer. Its eyes were open wide in terror. Though it was paralyzed, it was not yet dead. It was being slowly dissolved from within. Equally slowly it was being sucked-up. There was nothing he could do. Rudy murmured to himself, "It's the way things are."

He flew up over to the Flower-Meadow and landed by Zack's Creek, as it was now called. Almost immediately he heard the never to be forgotten siren-song of an Ektapod.

He became alert and did not yield to the musical enchantment, but at the same time, out of curiosity or devilment, he was not sure which, he had an urge to catch one of the creatures. After all, he could fly, and it would be interesting for the whole expeditionary crew to study a live Ektapod.

Rudy observed the Ektapods liked to be close to water, and wondered whether Zack had been 'egg-zapped' and simply wasn't aware of it. It could easily have happened while he was napping. He would be a natural victim. Zack had said on several occasions that he ignored minor pains he encountered while out exploring, and they simply went away. Rudy made a mental note to speak to Zack on the matter and have him checked out.

Whereupon he flew high above the wooded creek until he heard the 'Song of Death'. He located the Ektapod and in amazement watched rainbow colors flash all over its body as it burst into song. Its beak had sharp serrated edges like teeth, and the eyes were large and black. Other than that it looked much like a regular bird. But no bird ever sang as exquisitely as an Ektapod. Its voice was released to full volume immediately before mating, and reached its peak of beauty over a two week period.

At least, that's what the Keylons said, and they seemed to know the creature well. He'd also heard that if one of them were attacked, its song turned into a super-sonic scream and hordes of other Ektapods flew directly to its rescue and implanted eggs left right and center in the attacker. It was far too risky, but Rudy succumbed to the temptation to see what might happen. He flew swiftly and low over the Ektapod sticking a short thin shaft of wood into the Ektapod's back. He then watched quietly from a safe distance. Before he could even safely perch in a tree, the terrible sonic-scream pierced the air behind him. Even Rudy-Rat was intimidated. It seemed that from a dozen directions local Ektapods came to the rescue of the one that was calling, and finding no apparent enemy or cause for alarm immediately attacked the sonic-caller with unprecedented ferocity. More than a dozen ovipositors were instantly inserted into the victim who fell from the banch into the creek below. Once more Rudy had a reason to warn Zack of possible Ektapod eggs in the water—mutating to enter a warm body.

On his return Rudy contacted Zack immediately and filled him in on his adventure and what he'd been thinking. Zack was quite taken aback, but admitted that Rudy may well be right. He immediately contacted Captain Betaka and was assigned to medical attention in Black-Rabbit City in a matter of minutes. Zack requested that Rudy be with him at all times and Rudy-Rat willingly acquiesced to his request.

The Keylon Medical Team had never seen or examined a 'Zack' before. They were delighted to have the opportunity and his permission to render a minute examination of his body. The wilding lay relaxed is his naked state on the cushioned table. They started with his head and peeked into his ears and mouth, but at no time did they meet the powerful blue sparkle of his eyes. It was not until they had completed their examination front to back, and from head to toe that their attention was again redirected to an unexplained almost inconspicuous red lump on his left thigh. It did not cause Zack any pain.

Directing their attention back to his thigh, their experienced eyes and touch quickly confirmed what they had seen many times before. Zack had been 'egg-zapped', and from the appearance, it had occurred sometime in the past twelve hours. They questioned Zack, but he could not recall any specific incident, and this again confirmed a typical scenario.

They noted for his interest that upon hatching inside a limb like a thigh, the Ektapod larva was programmed to enter the blood stream to locate a richer vital organ before commencing to feed.

Zack was alarmed, surprised and also very grateful to Rudy and the competent Keylons. His life was on the line and he was being rescued. The surgery was considered to be minor as no delicate organs were involved. Zack's thigh was prepared and a tool-mechanism of special design was employed in the egg retrieval—apparently a common surgical procedure.

There was some blood loss as they had to penetrate to a depth of four inches to remove the Ektapod egg, which was still several days away from hatching. Afterwards they invited him to see the egg under a microscope—which caused Zack to recoil in horror. Immediately after the viewing, the egg was cremated by high-intensity laser-beam.

But the matter was not over with yet. It was while the Keylon medical crew were examining the inside joint of Zack's left forearm that their attention was drawn to a small bubble slowly oozing yellow foam from a tiny jagged hole. Zack gasped with fear before spluttering, "It must be from the 'Spider-Animal' saliva, same as got Kotar! A droplet must have splashed upon me while I jumped to one side after stabbing the creature! This saliva stuff eats away at the point of contact making the hole larger each day. That yellow fluid eats through clothing, hide or fur—it's like a living thing!"

"We'll have to remove that small infected section," the surgeon stated. "I think you're right—the saliva is a live self-generating substance in itself. Luckily it didn't hit you in a dangerous place—it could have been a lot worse." Zack and Rudy were transferred from the Emergency Room to a fully equipped and staffed major operating room. This time he was administered an anesthetic almost identical to the scent of Lavender blossoms. Zack smiled at the Keylons' surgical competence and was grateful for Rudy-Rat standing by to monitor things while he was 'under'.

The operation was performed flawlessly, but the surgeon did warn him that he might experience slight pain for a short while, and gave detailed instructions on exercising the joint. Zack thanked the Keylons profusely, and carefully hugged Rudy. He felt the episode was a somewhat minor inconvenience which might delay their Earth departure schedule by about four days, or remain on schedule provided Zack's surgical sites were still in first class shape. He retired with the Hill-Clan rabbits to their quarters quite early.

All of the rabbits stayed close to the Ektar-Craft. It was if as they had become paranoid in regard to Ektapods, especially as Zack had been unwittingly 'egg-zapped'. Most of the Hill-Clan including Zack could hardly wait to return to the relative safety of Earth with its better known and less insidious dangers. The entire group had already paid tribute to the Keylon Federation Board, the medical crew, and to a number of high-speed messenger-rabbits. This still put them in a position for take-off at dawn if Zack's condition was all okay.

In extreme caution, almost against his better judgement, Zack imaged himself to the Flower-Meadow for a final review of plans with Jibby and Jubby. He questioned whether they should really go home with him.

He went over the dangers of weasels, stoats, ferrets, foxes, hawks and owls—deadly mouse enemies; and explained in detail the manner in which these Earth predators took their prey, laying exphasis that mice were high on the victim list. Another key factor was that this move was a one-way, one-time move as the Hill-Clan had no thoughts of ever visiting the planet Ektar again. So there was no possibility of returning if things didn't work out.

Zack also reminded the proposed emigrants that although there were Earth field mice, it would be doubtful indeed whether they could join up with them due to Jibby and Jubby's bright coloring. The Earth mice would be scared—and life could be very lonely.

Jibby and Jubby decided after a short conference that they would stay on Ektar where the only real predators were the giant Mantis and the long blue snakes. Also they had numerous relatives nearby whom they visited on a regular basis.

Zack gave each of the field mice a tiny kiss on their soft yellow fur, "Live well Jibby and Jubby. It's been fun being with you!" He smiled through a sob that escaped him, and found a few tears on his cheeks when he placed them down by their home. At that moment he imaged himself back to the Ektar-craft where he turned in for his final night's sleep on the planet Ektar.

Upon waking at dawn everyone enquired of Zack, Kotar and KeKe regarding their state of health and how they felt. The 'egg-zap' survivors KeKe and Zack reported that all was well, and Zack looked particularly refreshed and invigorated. Kotar's skin had healed with the special Ektar treatments he'd been receiving and was showing a faint fuzz of black and white fur on his wound site. Rudy-Rat was of course in fine shape and his wings were feeling up to par after his flight from the day before. He was in excellent form and this was confirmed by his laughing turquoise eyes.

Right after breakfast, Captain Betaka made a brief announcement in which he warned Zack and the space-rabbits that the 'imaging faculty' they had used on Ektar would not work onboard the Ektar-craft or back on Earth. "In other words," he said, "if one were confronted with a predator back on Earth, one could not 'weasel' out of it so to speak." He smiled at the Earth rabbits. "Let's all get ready for the launch—I have no idea of Earth time arrival."

"Tooky—let's buckle down for 'take-off'", said Zack. "You may as well get strapped inside my belt with me!" Tooky got comfortable. But they did not take off.

Zack was suddenly called to the outside. There he was confronted with the Black-Rabbits Sedgewick and Starko of the Braktor Research Project. With them was also a strange rabbit—strange, because of his grey and white face and ears. He had a black tail. He was the most different rabbit they had yet met on Ektar, and Zack wondered if he were a true Black Ektar rabbit.

Sedgewick introduced the black and white stranger. His name was Scruffykin, and he certainly did justice to his name. Although his eyes and face exuded good will and intelligence, all of his fur looked ruffled like he'd just been in a first class rabbit fight.

Scruffykin smiled, "It's the way I always look!" he said, answering Zack's unspoken question. Starko then explained to Zack that Scruffy had volunteered to accompany them on their return to Earth mission, and would assist them in every phase of the Braktor Project, either on Earth or Rat-Star if they too became involved.

"How do you feel about this?" asked Sedgewick.

"Great," said Zack, but I'll first have to clear this with Captain Betaka." As Zack turned to reenter the space-ship,

Tooky met him half way with an exclamation of, "It's okay Zack, I've already cleared it with Captain Betaka."

"Yes! I know," said Scruffykin, catching up with Zack. "Hello Tooky!" No explanations were necessary. Scruffykin and Tooky were on the same 'wave-length', and they both smiled in mutual appreciation. Back onboard the space-craft, almost immediately the red lights showed they had imperceptibly lifted off.

It seemed that Zack, Rudy and the space-rabbits all heaved a sigh of relief that they were now underway to Earth. None of them wanted to return to Ektar. Zack wondered how long they had been 'away' in Earth-time. His Rolex was not designed to record 'space-time', at least, not as yet! So it came down to a question of waiting for Earth-time to officially reveal itself.

When they were free to move around the space-craft, Zack called them into the meeting room, where they were all introduced to Scruffykin and his reason for being there. The group was restless with excitement when the Braktor Research Project was revealed. It was greeted with enthusiasm and it took time for them all to settle down.

"I thought we might fill in some time with an idea to improve our mental stability." said Zack. "We still have problems we need to face. They assail all of us rabbits at one time or another. I'd like to address that one where we allow ourselves to dwell on situations in which things went horribly wrong—either today or in the past. I do not mean that we should not at the appropriate time review what errors may have occurred. I'm speaking of repetitiously reliving our mistakes and traumata over and over and over again. Many of us do this.

The Chief Medical Rabbits say that these situations where we survive life and death traumata—cause Post Traumatic Stress Syndrome—or *P-T-S-S.* This may occur when a rabbit escapes from a hawk or weasel with extensive wounding, involving torn ears, fur and loss of blood. It can also arise from having a narrow escape by being in the proximity of such trauma whilst it is played out.

There is a proven principle that will help us stay in control." Zack smiled. "It's known as 'Stay-In-Now' or the *S-I-N* Principle. Tooky and I have practiced this a lot. Here's how it works. We found that when trauma strikes us, it is because we have allowed ourselves to go *BACK* in time. We need to control this—so when a negative thought appears—instantly focus on *'NOW'*, which is our 'present'." Facing the group squarely he said, "I repeat—the solution is to stay in '*NOW*'." This will not happen overnight. We need to practice it every day, all day long, until it becomes habitual—a sort of reflex response.

The rabbits hung on to every word that Zack spoke. Not a single ear flipped. Not a whisker moved. They loved the intense blue sparkle of his eyes. It mesmerized them. On his part—Scruff was in perfect tune and agreement with what they were attempting to achieve.

"*Stay in NOW* and leave the past alone" said Boofy. "It makes sense. How many of us need to practice the *S-I-N* solution?" Every rabbit waved a paw, and Rudy was pleased to see that Scruff also waved his. They noticed it was white.

Tooky could contain himself no longer. His eyes were bright with excitement. "Zack! I recall there was one ancient rabbit-scribe who recorded a very powerful statement. He said that we need to capture every thought that comes to us, regardless of its nature, and subject it to obedience to our 'Super-Rabbit' or higher-power—and that's exactly what we do when we stay in '*Now*'."

"Good input Tooky," said Zack with enthusiasm. "Once we have established the concept, the details of developing it into habit-form can follow. So firstly, each rabbit needs to ask, 'Who or what runs me? Who is in charge of me? Is it just my 'past' and my fears? Or, am 'I' running me?' Eventually, being in control of one's self becomes a habit requiring no thought! Self-control takes time to achieve and the time to start is '*Now*'. This '*Now*' is our current time-point', so let's all stay in '*Now*'."

Timken interjected. "Some have said, 'Today is the first day of the rest of our lives', and there's a lot of truth in that."

Zack noticed that Scruff had quietly and thoughtfully listened to the whole presentation. He acted in intelligent good taste in everything he did. But—he did present a lot of mystery as yet.

"Anyway! That's it for today!" exclaimed Zack. "So before we all get sort of dizzy, let's quit while we're ahead!"

"I'm going to practice self-discipline," said KeKe. "I survived being 'egg-zapped' by an Ektapod, so I'm ready for anything including mental discipline!"

Boofy and Bifflets as usual took a lot in, but didn't say much. Wisdom would come forth in due course. It was the way they were, and also why they held such respect with the senior rabbits. Tesla was just silent intelligence and wisdom in repose. Timken was silent and intermittently kept scratching one of his ears. It was the one with the yellow tag. Tooky's eyes sparkled and he flipped his ears around in simple good spirits. Again Timken scratched his ear with his head to one side, and it caught Zack's attention.

"Timken, why do you keep scratching your ear?" he asked enquiringly.

"I don't know, maybe it's the tag, although it never bothered me before." replied Timken.

Tooky's intuition suddenly kicked-in, "Timken! I'll bet you got 'egg-zapped' by an Ektapod and are not aware of it! After all—this is the peak of the Ektapod mating season." Scruffykin concurred with Tooky's statement and mentally relayed this fact to him. Scruff had been 'egg-zapped' when he was quite young, and spoke from real live field experience as well as research.

In alarm they all surrounded Timken. Zack gently picked him up, placed him on a table, and called in Captain Betaka who procured a razor, and Zack shaved Timken's left ear. At the same time with difficulty he removed the ear tag. Poor Timken's eyes were wide with horror bordering on terror. He squeaked pitifully. Zack gently probed Timken's ear and then studied it under the magnifying glass that Betaka had called for. The ear being so thin yielded its secrets quickly.

"Oh!" gasped Zack in unintended horror "Here it is! It's a tiny larvae creature. It has hatched and is slowly wiggling toward the base of the ear. That's where it will enter the skull and eat into the outer layer of the brain. From there it can go anywhere! That was the tickling feeling that Timken had. From here on it will move quickly to gain internal access. I would think even sometime in the next hour. We have no time to waste!"

Timken was engulfed in horror. He fainted. Captain Betaka had an emergency surgery kit which contained a scalpel and passed it to Zack. But unexpectedly, Rudy-Rat came forward and explained that he had special surgical training and that his eyes were designed to focus microscopically with the power of laser-light intensity when necessary. This came as a complete surprise to everyone. Captain Betaka wondered why he had not run an inventory on the space-explorers' special training and abilities before this time. He was now determined it should be a Standard Procedure.

Rudy picked up the scalpel with quiet competence and authority. His eyes suddenly changed from their beautiful turquoise blue to a bright white laser-like brilliance. Scruffykin watched with approval. He'd seen hundreds of these same surgical procedures. He admired Rudy's approach and his every move.

It seemed that they all held their breath when Rudy poised his scalpel over the entry point. Timken's ear had been previously cleaned but he had not received anesthetic. However, having 'passed-out' he would feel nothing anyway.

Rudy penetrated Timken's ear with gentle concentration, and in a few moments the small shiny gray larvae wiggled in a receptacle on the table. There was little blood, and Rudy cleaned up the area. The operation was complete.

But, to their surprise and amazement, they saw the Ektapod larvae slowly rise and move in a spiral motion, while at the same time it seemed to acquire molecules out of thin-air. It grew larger by the moment—and then larger still!

As it did so, its color changed from dull grey to brilliant yellow. Rudy, having previously encountered bizarre situations of a similar nature took no chances. He quickly took the magnifying glass and in perfect aim lined it up with the larvae and a powerful laser-beam. Immediately upon contact the Ektapod larvae was cremated, but not before it had given a tiny high-pitched squeak. It was a horror none would soon forget. All that remained were a few granules of smoking black ash. Rudy was almost excessively careful in disposing of these too. He'd seen supposedly 'dead' creatures re-form and come to life fighting for survival by spitting deadly poison or by other means.

Rudy was thusly 'careful' to an extreme degree. It left the whole group wondering how the yellow Ektapod larvae was programed to survive once it was removed from its normal development cycle. No one wanted to explore the matter further as it was too horrible to imagine. Scruffykin said the entire affair had been handled with absolute professionalism. He also informed Captain Betaka that he was a highly-skilled neurosurgeon if the need arose.

Timken 'came-to', and wondered what had happened and they brought him up to date. Zack called for an immediate meeting of all persons onboard the space-craft. He stated that they should have a thorough inspection right away, and further that no one should embark or disembark the Ektar-craft after Earth landing until a detailed screening by a 'Cosmic-Creature-Scanner' had been performed. Zack did not want any Ekapods on planet Earth, nor did anyone else. This was an incredible risk factor that had to be monitored. He also stated that any inanimate objects coming on board also be scanned and analyzed.

In his consistent quest for knowledge, on several occasions Zack had also questioned Captain Betaka on the exact method of propulsion that the Ektar-craft employed. However, he had never received an answer he could understand.

If anything, Betaka was deliberately evasive. As the space-craft was designed and produced on Rat-Star especially for the Black-Rabbits of Ektar, he decided to ask Rudy about the motive-power and directional systems and get to the bottom of things.

Zack had never had a truer and more loyal, intimate friend than Rudy the young Golden Space-Rat. He loved him dearly and respected him. He loved Rudy's friendly flashing turquoise eyes, his short plush yellow fur, and his remarkable scarlet-tipped wings. Rudy in turn was somewhat entranced by Zack's piercing blue eyes, but above all he was attracted to Zack's level of consciousness and intelligence.

There were never any barriers of communication between either of the two friends, even when Zack had to overcome his curiosity regarding questions of sexuality on Rat-Star. Rudy was male and had said their sex systems were similar to those on Earth. Zack could not think of going forward in life without Rudy, and if ever there were a planet he'd like to visit, it certainly would be Rat-Star. He even toyed in his imagination with the thought of going to live there permanently.

Scruffykin became privy to the special relationship between Zack and Rudy-Rat, and at the first opportunity, Rudy-Rat and he had a very long conversation. It mainly involved matters of consciousness and the relaying of images. Scruffy was able to determine that although the Golden Space-Rats of Rat-Star were way ahead in the brain development field, they still had many unanswered questions. Rudy had said he would discuss the whole affair with Captain Ratto, his Dad, to see if they would participate in research on the Braktor Project.

Scruff congratulated Rudy-Rat on his Timken Ektapod larvae surgery, and told Rudy of an alien life form, similar in nature, where the larvae was more advanced than the one Rudy had taken out. "When it was removed," Scruff said, "It swiveled its head so that its eyes met with those of the surgeon just as he was about to destroy it with the laser-vaporizing-gun. In milliseconds of its sight reaching his, the surgeon was totally paralyzed and died a short time later.

Fortunately they had a standard back-up-procedure in place, and the second laser unit vaporized the creature. That day Rudy, I learned the importance of back-up. We lost a great surgeon, and I lost a brother. It could have been worse." Later that day, whatever 'day' meant on their return trip to Earth, Zack had an opportunity to chat with Rudy in regard to the propulsion system on the space-craft.

The time had now come to open up technical questions with Rudy about the space-craft. Rudy hesitated and then dug in, but not before Scruffykin had requested that he 'listen-in'. Rudy approved this; he had been quite impressed with what he had found in Scruffy's memory-banks. Then he began his explanation. "The company on Rat-Star that produces the space-craft is known as the Lexcraft Corporation. The machines themselves are known as Lexcraft. However, the propulsion design and computer software are customized to the type of creature that would be operating the Lexcraft. As you can imagine, there is a major difference in the computer programing software for say, Black-Rabbits and the Rats of Rat-Star."

"Fascinating!" exclaimed Zack. "But what was Captain Betaka subtly alluding to when he hinted at propulsion by 'Brain-Energy power'?"

"All Lexcraft are powered by two systems," Rudy continued. "One is the Rat-Star System which one might call the Master System because it will override any other system if necessary. The other is the CCS, Customized Creature System. For example the CCS for a Black-Rabbit Ektar-craft would have to be especially designed and programed for Black-Rabbits only, and tuned to their particular attained level of consciousness." Rudy paused. Scruffykin was impressed as he was not aware that the Ektar space-ship was manufactured on Rat-Star. He remained silent.

"Incidentally, if something ever went wrong with a Lexcraft or its crew, a rescue mission Lexcraft could control them and the space-craft—without ever approaching or accessing that space-craft. There have been rare cases where the Lexcraft people have had to 'vaporize' a Lexcraft and all living creatures onboard due to highly contagious deadly bacterial elements or alien life-forms. These of course are all pretty formidable and horrible things, but they do occur. There are some shockingly weird mutated beings existing 'out there' that we've already encountered. Their value systems in relation to life and death are very different from ours."

Zack's expressions were those of one who is wrapped in wonder with a touch of horror. "Do you have the Master Rat-Star Control for this space-craft?" asked Zack.

"No," said Rudy. "These are coded quantum encrypted systems that are unassailable by anyone in the local Universe, and are in any case only rarely called upon. I will say this however, that the propulsion and space directional system software that runs the computers has an extremely delicate 'power-control' that responds to what theoretical physicists refer to as Bose-Einstein Condensates—or BECs. In simple non-tech language it is a form of power that is 'live-generated' by a space-crew. One could call it 'unified brain-energy-power', which is engineered to produce motive-power. The energy thus produced acts as a 'faith-module' to create an 'unbroken whole'.

It means that whenever two or more people in unison join their minds to become 'one' in a mutual objective—when the desired action is achieved—the computers take over. Of course if there are five or ten people, the power would be greatly enhanced and practically infallible.

"This is almost the identical power that we use with Kotar when he transfers 'bad realities'" exclaimed Zack. "Except that it appears that BECs vary in their octaves and frequencies—as they specifically relate to a power source at its origin."

At this point Scruffykin told Rudy that certain rabbits on Ektar were now registered for BEC output. Scruffy had a BEC rating of five; which meant the equivalent of five Ektar Black-Rabbits. Rudy thanked him profusely, because the BEC ratings were standard right across—no matter what animal was rated.

He asked Scruffykin to be prepared at all times to assist in powering the space-ship on demand. Scruffy acquiesced and it was obvious that he felt good about having something highly positive to contribute apart from Braktor.

On that note it seemed that it was time for everyone to have supper. Even Timken showed up and was feeling better, though he was more severely affected psychologically than physically by the Ektapod larvae surgery. In fact several times he flipped his ears about and became just a little disoriented. This came about when he recalled the Ektapod song in his mind. He badly needed to stay in "*NOW*".

Tooky observed this and said comfortingly, "Timken, it's okay to be totally freaked-out with your Ektapod experience; you'll find it'll gradually fade into the background. Try to stay in "Now". Timken smiled, "Thanks Tooky, you're usually right!"

Scruffykin, who had now become accepted by everyone as a valid 'authority', smiled affably and approved of Tooky's statement.

But, Tooky had become preoccupied with a secret that he thought should be shared with Zack and Rudy. What he had not revealed to anyone was that when he was out exploring by Zack's Creek the day before, he had picked up a fair-sized oval-shaped green rock from under the water. Out of curiosity he'd laid it on the grass in the hot sun, and the rock being polished and dry, shone like a large emerald. Tooky was fascinated. It was the most beautiful rock he'd ever seen.

Now, onboard the space-ship he was feeling quite scared and apprehensive. He took Rudy-Rat to one side and made a full confession regarding his acquisition of the Emerald Green Rock. Rudy-Rat called in Zack right away and up-dated him. Tooky fetched the EGR from a water container and they both examined his discovery. Zack was most curious; but Rudy looked quite apprehensive, and said he thought that *IT* was studying them!

"Rudy," said Zack, "This is the very thing I was talking about the other day. We must rule that any life-forms and all inanimate objects that anyone might want to bring aboard the space-craft must first be scanned and identified!"

"I agree Zack!" Rudy exclaimed. "I thought at first this was an Ektar time-capsule, but I now feel it is something a lot more sinister."

Tooky suddenly looked strange—which caught Zack's eye immediately.

"What's up Tooky?" he asked, "is there something you haven't told us?"

"Rudy", said Tooky in a humble manner, "I think that it is a 'live rock', and it's not inanimate! When I first spied it in Zack's Creek, it seemed quite harmless. But later my attention was drawn to it by some weird musical sounds. Then there were movements in the grass surrounding it. As I watched, it seemed that the emerald green rock—I'll call it the EGR—projected colorful tiny pictures of live moving creatures—they seemed to momentarily hang in the air. I was then stricken with fear to see the same tiny three dimensional creatures—become fully dimensional—and solid—like us! Some crawled away—others flew. One was larger than Rudy, and bounded away out of sight! I was so shocked—I picked up the rock and placed it back into the creek. I thought it might again become dormant under water, the way I found it!" Tooky looked between Zack and Rudy wondering what terrible thing he had done.

"That was very good thinking Tooky, because it worked!" Rudy looked a little scared—which was very unusual. He immediately contacted the top echelon Rat-Star personnel and outlined what had occurred. All three space-crew members felt uneasy about the whole affair, but anticipated almost immediate directions.

Tooky then further explained an interesting observation he'd made—that any time he'd briefly looked away from the EGR—all activity had ceased. He'd concluded from this that he must be empowering the EGR, which was like a tiny independent world.

Scruffykin of course, had immediately received all the relevant data in a single quantum-leap of cognition. He also perceived that Tooky needed some special inputs of consciousness-reprogramming so that he would no longer have to succumb to fits of dizziness. Scruff had discovered in routine scanning of Tooky's brain, that it was in the final phase of physically changing its shape to accommodate his demand for greater neuron capacity. This was necessitated by Tooky's newest level of thinking. In fact, Tooky was a perfect example of that to which the Braktor Project aspired. Scruffykin smiled happily, "neuroplasticity", he murmured, smiling happily. He felt quite 'at home' among the crew who accorded him great respect—even though they'd nicknamed him 'Scruffy', or just plain 'Scruff'.

Just then instructions came in from the Rat-Star engineers. They stated that Tooky's EGR be kept under water in a sealed steel container, to be delivered to Rat-Star when the Lexcraft returned. The Lexcraft engineers explained to the Ektar-craft crew where to locate special steel 'sample-containers' on the lower deck. They also warned them to say nothing about the EGR to any other living being—ever, unless it was with Rat-Star senior people.

Meantime Rudy wondered whether the degree of 'brain-power' that his people had developed was equal to, or lesser than that already possessed by Scruff. Rudy intuitively knew that some 'Black-Rabbits' could be on the verge of becoming Ektar Quantum Rabbits.

If that were true—this would give them unprecedented powers. However, in view of the the Moontwo fiasco; he concluded that quantum progress would be limited only to the rabbits in the Braktor Project. Tooky and Scruff, with time to spare, met to check out Tooky's 'dizziness' problems.

Tooky explained to Scruff that his headaches had become more severe right after he'd discovered the EGR. "When I follow our usual procedure of delegating a problem to intuition—I experience what I would term 'interference'—as though another 'being' was also trying to use my brain," explained Tooky. Even as he said this, Tooky's ears flopped down and he became quite disoriented.

A few anxious moments passed before he stirred, stretched and yawned. Next he flipped his ears, and seemed pleased to find them under his control. In a few moments he looked like the Tooky of old—a smiling, brilliant little super-rabbit. He looked at Scruff and asked, "What happened?" Wriggling into an upright hopping position, "Wow!" he exclaimed, "my headache is gone too—but . . ."

"But what, Tooky?" said Zack, looking closely at Tooky with a searching glance."

"Well, I still feel a little weird—as though I'm not alone inside myself—if that makes sense."

"But the EGR is sealed in steel below the decks," contributed Tesla.

A chill seemed to envelop the whole room. Several of the group suddenly shivered. Then, with startling clarity,

Tooky began to sing a strange little tune in a low key. It was quite evident that he was not aware of what he was doing. His eyes appeared to be looking within himself, and not at them.

Zack was dumbfounded. He'd never heard a rabbit sing before! They emitted many types of squeaks—but this was unnatural and ominous—even though the notes were sweet and musical. Scruff ran his recorder and made notes. Kotar looked worried, and Rudy had an usual look on his face for a Star-Rat—bewildered and searching.

Zack suddenly smiled, and picking Tooky up, smoothed his fur in the way he loved, and leaving the room, headed for his own quarters. Rudy and Scruff ensured that security doors locked into place behind them.

Tesla said hesitatingly, "All this locked security doors business is not going to ensure our safety or the safety of the Lexcraft. Despite being in a stainless steel sealed container, immersed in icy water and locked securely away below the decks—somehow that EGR is in contact with Tooky—and this is dangerous to all of us. We're not dealing here with molecular matter; that EGR is searching Tooky for control. It needs him to activate its programming. You remember what he said about the EGR only being active when he looked at it? It needs his power! In some way Tooky has become part of 'It'." He paused. Scruffykin had a delighted look about him—like he'd just woken up in the middle of a Braktor experiment. They all returned to the main Lexcraft control centre. Rudy contacted authorities on Rat-Star, and Captain Betaka switched on the camera device in Zack's cabin. The whole space-crew were anxious to see what was happening with Tooky.

The surveillance lens revealed Zack and Tooky snuggled up, apparently fast asleep. They appeared to be perfectly normal. Rudy received permission from Captain Ratto back on Rat-Star, to run a mental scan on both Zack and Tooky. However, they pointed out that the major risk he would be undertaking was that he might become the same as Tooky. Rudy had been given a choice by Rat-Star to either proceed or hold-off. He decided to hold off for while. Supper was consumed in silence. Each of the space travelers was deeply engrossed in his own thoughts. They all avoided direct eye contact with each other—it could well create and empower a deadly team situation whereby their worst fears could become their current reality.

Zack and Tooky had their supper together in Zack's cabin. He perceived that Tooky had a fine grasp of their total situation and the problem at hand. He felt sure by morning, they would come up with a solution.

When Tooky had the urge to sing that night—he desisted. He suddenly remembered from back at Zack's Creek on Ektar, that musical tones from the strange emerald green rock had preceded the actual projection of the strange signs and pictures. That was the sequence. Musical tones, pictures, and then projections into living reality! He awoke Zack and revealed this discovery.

"Yes Tooky," said Zack. "But did you also observe that *you* still had the choice—to sing or not to sing? It seems that you're still the decision-maker—and that is critical to our analysis!"

"That's true!" exclaimed Tooky. "That must be part of what we're looking for!"

Zack kissed Tooky's silky ears, "You're on track Tooky, all we have to do now is find out why, how, and when music has to come into being to trigger the sequence. Let's just release it to our intuition, and see what arrives in the morning."

Tooky looked sleepily at him, "Yes—in some way, I think it's all going to come together and leave us in control. He snuggled up beneath Zack's chin. Even under these circunstances—it was a blissful interlude for both of them. Dreams trailed their thinking into other forms of reality—almost as real as the one they had just left.

Scruffy—who heads up neuroplasticity research on the Braktor Project.

Chapter Nine

Time really had no meaning onboard the space-craft. There was just a feeling of being present in sort of an indefinable 'Is-ness'. When Zack asked Rudy about it, he attributed the sensation as one that originated through the 'Uncertainty Principle', on which he did not enlarge apart from saying that it was neither here nor there. Scruff just smiled.

Zack and Tooky appeared for breakfast. They looked rested, quite calm and assured. The look in their eyes was infectious, and everyone suddenly had the ability to meet the eyes of everyone else. There was a huge drop in tension, and a mass of questions to be handled. Scruff was anxious for things to unfold.

Zack started in. "As we're all aware—all great truths are simple. It is we who compound their complexity. In the early hours of this morning when Tooky was possessed of the need to 'sing'; we both came together as 'one', in the way we'd planned before going to sleep. We ran the 'No Fear' program with which we're all familiar; and because the whole EGR thing is a big fear—it worked in a big way!" There were rabbit stirrings and ear flipping all round—they were all entranced with what they'd heard.

"Intuitively," Zack continued, his young face alight with insight; "it was revealed to us that we need to question why musical notes must preceed any EGR action. This really got us going with a lot of hilarious laughter! Tooky—who is able to pick things up that others can't, had an idea that although each note was heard separately by us—they may be received by the EGR force as a single sound—without gaps or spaces between the notes. It's hard for us to imagine, for example, the Rabbit National Anthem—as a brief single sound. If this is true, it means that the EGR power has removed Time from the equation—and that leaves us where no rabbit, rat or boy has explored before!"

The whole space-crew, especially the Earth rabbits, had that well known 'dizzy' look on their perplexed faces. Tooky came to the rescue, "Tell you what, Zack and I will hole up with Tesla and Scruff for a while and run some of our ideas by them. Let's see what happens. Since we ran the 'No Fear' program, no further urges to sing have come upon me!" Tooky scampered away to arrange a meeting.

No anticipated time of Earth arrival had been forecast. In the meantime all of the live creatures onboard including those who had been previously relieved of their Ektapod eggs had been minutely inspected. No further Ektapod evidence came to light or any other alien life forms either at egg stage or beyond. However one of the crew complained of a headache and of feeling 'dizzy'. He was subjected to further minute examination, but no further physical symptoms had made an appearance. Zack suggested that the Hill-Clan rabbits, along with Rudy and Scruff go to their general quarters, he would join them and keep in touch with the flight crew and Captain Betaka via the screens in their rooms. This would be a reverse form of quarantine for the healthy members, and they would wait and see if anyone else developed headaches.

Boofy and Bifflets had their own deep discussions on things. Tooky and Timken decided that frisking and leaping around made them feel good, and they were joined by KeKe. Tesla isolated himself in deep thought and was somewhat 'unreachable', a normal state of affairs. However, this was more so now with the addition of the engineering required in relation to the EGR. The latter had become so complex that Tesla was severely challenged. He had to blueprint the production of delicate ideas whose very principles had not been conceived of on Earth.

Zack and Rudy joined Kotar where they examined Kotar's new fur that was growing in. He was indeed going to wear a patch of black and white where he had been 'salivated' by the 'Spider-Creature'. Kotar said he would wear it as a medal of honor for having been part of the frightening Arachnid confrontation.

Zack said to Rudy, "That Bose-Einstein condensate business we were talking about; from a Lexcraft viewpoint it would need to be a scientific explanation, but I'd also like to view it from an unscientific angle!"

"I'm with you," said Rudy cautiously, "Carry on!"

Scruffykin, who'd just come on the scene, asked Rudy if he could quietly participate by listening, further, he requested permission to ask questions but only if they were of a highly relevant nature. To this Rudy acquiesced

"Well," said Zack. "I'm saying that the concerted type of 'power' to affect the computer running this space-craft, would have to be of a Bose-Einstein Condensate magnitude. It would need to act as a cohesive whole, because one Keylon would not have enough power. But, five Keylons and their captain acting as 'one', yes, it must work because they are then operating as a 'unified thought power' unit."

"That seems to add up," said Rudy.

"Well anyway," said Zack, "In future I'll refer to the Bose-Einstein Condensates as BECs. Now, I understand that when an individual's brain cell membranes vibrate sufficiently to pull themselves into a BEC, they are creating the most coherent form of order in Nature—the order of 'unbroken wholeness'. A valid question might be; what type of neurobiological or brain mechanism is it that lines up brain neurons in a condensed phase within an individual? By 'condensed', I mean operating as a single whole."

"Yes! That's the question I would ask," said Tooky who'd just returned from his session with Tesla. "I think it would be when his entire thought-process is concentrated on one objective excluding all others." Rudy complimented him on his input. Tooky might be somewhat little, furry and cute, and although he became dizzy at times, he had a good head on him. Scruff gave him a warm smile.

Zack smiled at Tooky and continued, "The unbroken-wholeness mechanism that is so necessary would have to be activated by either an inside power—one's self—or a 'higher-power' Of course it would be necessary that the different brain states active in each individual be identical in order to jointly act as *ONE*. Your 'ego-freaks' Tooky, do not have this connection." Scruff nodded approval in his usual affable way.

"You're probably right Zack", said Tooky. "Because as we know, it would never work with those who are filled with self-importance—they would never co-operate with each other, and most certainly not with a higher-power.

I'm just going to conclude by stating I think that BECs are 'faith-driven'. I know that 'Faith' is the opposite of 'Fear'. I also know that 'faith' is 'belief' activated by trust. Therefore faith is an immutable motive-power always available at a 'Now-Point' in Time."

"It's similar to that 'Holy Super-Rabbit' stuff you were talking about," said Tooky. "But it's falling into place, slowly!"

"Zack, you'll have to dump that 'Rabbit-Immersion' program if and when you go back among the humans," said Rudy. "They might even lynch you for calling God a Rabbit!" They both laughed.

"Sorry Tooky!" exclaimed Zack, "I just get carried away thinking of my own kind and what they believe, and of course it doesn't all apply to rabbits."

"Not necessarily" said Scruff. "At Braktor we're finding more and more that many rabbit principles apply to numerous other animals; with the exception of the Ektapods which are a breed unto themselves, and they are dangerous."

"This is getting boring," said Timken. Zack and Rudy laughed, but Scruff looked thoughtful.

Tesla and Scruffy had reviewed the mass of input from Tooky in relation to him and the EGR, and Tesla had modified his conclusions with a few quantum leaps of thought which included unheard of principles. Tesla believed these principles had to exist—because they fell into place so naturally. He achieved access to them as though he'd invented them. Indeed—the discovery of new principles was no big deal. In these mental 'escapades', Tesla left huge amounts of data to be proven, as he leapt from peak to peak among the mountains of comprehension. "Let someone else do the heavy duty labor," he smiled. "I'll just work with peak facts.

In regard to the EGR," Tesla explained, "it was relatively simple. The power-source wavelengths that the EGR uses are so entirely different from any of ours, that I've already blocked their transmission. Tooky is entirely released from any EGR influence. By the way, Tooky's concept of musical notes with the Time element eliminated—are the basis for much of my research with converting Time into Space and vice-versa. He's one very bright little rabbit. As for the EGR, once the Rat-Star authorities have taken possession, our responsibility is through anyway." Tesla looked a little worn and tired and said he was going for nap.

Suddenly Captain Betaka entered the conference room. His face expressed deep concern. "Zack, Rudy," he said in somber tones, "We have a severe problem. Three of the other crew members have come down with terrible headaches and complain also of their vision becoming limited. In reality we have 'lost' four of our crew, and this limits our power sustainability, I may even have to ask you, Rudy, to contact Lexcraft and Captain Ratto for a course of action in order to be prepared for whatever may occur."

"Leave it with me Captain Betaka," said Rudy. "I believe we need action now rather than later. Zack! Scruff! Standby! We'll probably need your power as we proceed." Rudy, ever cool and calculating in an emergency situation went to his quarters alone. There he contacted his father Captain Ratto and detailed the situation. It was understood the Rat-Star group would be back in contact shortly.

Two hours later the instructions came in loud and clear. It confirmed what they had been thinking but had not discussed.

Captain Ratto stated that Zack, Kotar, Boofy, bifflets, Tesla and Tooky would be the new crew with Rudy-Rat as their new Captain. Scruffykin would replace Rudy if he became incapacitated. Captain Ratto instructed that the remaining Keylons should immediately go into quarantine. Captain Betaka was not surprised and implicitly followed their directions.

The large screen above the Lexcraft space-ship central control module became illuminated, and Rudy knew they had been switched over to Lexcraft master-control. Both the Rat-Star Rats at Lexcraft and the space-crew could see and hear each other with astounding clarity. Rudy and the new crew were introduced to Chief Engineer Ekona—who would take over operations. All the Ektar-craft personnel had to do was to simply follow instructions. Everyone was delighted.

"We'll perform your take-over of the space-craft in several steps." Announced Ekona. "The screen will be split into one third Lexcraft control staff, and two thirds, your solar map. You can clearly see, as can we, precisely where you are." Ekona's voice portrayed the very essence of competence and authority, but also included the warmth of common understanding of their joint dilemma.

"Secondly," said Ekona. "I understand from Rudy that you've all been discussing modes of generating propulsion-power, and have been exploring the formation of Bose-Einstein Condensates that you now call BECs. Rudy has acquainted us with Scruff's BEC power, and this will serve as reserve back-up. This is great, and totally unexpected, because we need the BEC concept. It is the core-essence of what powers this ship. It allows you to direct the controls through the software, which in turn instructs the computers to perform certain tasks. At the Lexcrafts' normal speed of travel, no physical brains could operate fast enough to effect control. We can discuss details later!" Ekona chuckled.

"Now, we are not going to bring your minds into the 'unbroken wholeness' of unified-thought that we need, either through 'positive thinking' or 'Holy Rabbit' methodology. Both are far too complicated to be effective in a situation like this. I want you to think of one thing only, and that is the word 'Lexcraft'. Let that word Lexcraft and the image of this craft become imbued in your consciousness. This is far less complex than involving philosophies and spiritual beliefs, even if they are correct.

So your immediate singular task is to think 'Lexcraft' as individuals to the exclusion of all other thoughts. Then overlap with each other's Lexcraft thoughts. You may find it too distracting to meet one another's eyes. Okay? So first image Lexcraft and exclude all other thoughts—and then overlap and merge with the each other's thinking. Lexcraft! Lexcraft! Lexcraft! Go ahead and try it!" Momentarily all seven members hesitated and looked at each other.

Kotar said, "This is the same method we used when we transferred the Moon- Wolves! We know exactly what to do!"

Tooky was the first to squeak, "I'm no longer a rabbit, I'm a Lexcraft!" he snickered. This caused Scruff to ermit a delighted chuckle.

"Excellent!" exclaimed Ekona. "That even goes one better than I had in mind!" They could see on the screen how excited he really was. They could even see his fuzzy golden tail flipping from one side to the other.

"Me too!" said Kotar. "I'm a Lexcraft also!" Before long the whole crew had diverted to Tooky's method of actually 'being' the Lexcraft.

"Ekona declared he had never stepped into an emergency situation where 'brain motive-power' propulsion-energy, had been comprehended so quickly.

"Now!" said Ekona. "I'm going to expose your 'Lexcraft-power' to a tiny portion of the software, so that no damage can be incurred, and at the same time we'll take a reading on the Lexometer of your total power output. So watch. When I drop my hand, think Lexcraft! And become Lexcraft as one unbroken whole! Ready?" The eyes of the crew were shining with excitement. "Yes!" they exclaimed in unison. The experiment lasted for one full minute, at which point Ekona raised his eyes from the instrument and looking at the crew he exclaimed, "Fabulous! We're in business. Congratulations!

Thanks Tooky for taking the whole experiment on step further ahead in effectiveness. The proof is that it works! I have only one small problem—the input was so powerful that it disrupted the circuits on the Lexometer. I'll have to replace the unit. The performance was far above our expectations."

The new crew was instructed to take a break, get something to eat, walk around and relax. KeKe and Timken felt left out and deeply hurt, especially as they had been excluded from being 'crew'. Zack returned to the control screen and explained the potential problem to Ekona who said, "No problem, put them both through the 'Tooky System' and they can be part of the crew. We are way ahead of where I thought we might be anyway. Thanks a lot also to you Zack for opening up the whole matter of BECs. You may have saved the whole ship!"

Everyone relaxed their bodies and minds and nothing further took place. Zack returned to the control room screen and was told that the space-craft was in no danger, and it was a unanimous decision at the Rat-Star base they get a good night's rest and take over full control the next morning. They planned a minor full-scale navigational experiment for next morning, and then to proceed with their journey.

In checking up on the sick Keylon crew in quarantine including Captain Betaka, it was discovered that they had passed out into some kind of stupor. Two of the Keylons were also bleeding from the mouth and ears. Zack and Rudy decided in the late afternoon to discuss the status of the Keylons with Rat-Star base. The control room screen was monitored and continuously active, so help was always available without delay.

It was the opinion of the medical staff on Rat-Star that the Keylons were suffering from Black-Rabbit Fever. It was peculiar to Black-Rabbits and connected in some unexplained way to their color gene. It was not transmittable to other members of the rabbit family. However, in many cases it was terminal. Rudy and Zack thanked the base staff and turned in for the night.

Dawn announced itself by waking up the crew via internal timing, there was no sun. Onboard the Lexcraft some weird things were being felt without being seen. Zack, Rudy and Tooky were super-sensitive to such things, with Tooky often received images he'd rather not see. Two of the Keylon Black-Rabbit ex-crew members had deceased overnight.

Regrettably, Captain Betaka had also succumbed to the fever. He and the others were in a coma. It did not look good. Zack wondered what they would do with the highly infectious remains of last night's victims. Rudy checked in on-screen with the Rat-Star base while Zack stood by.

They were instructed to wear gloves when removing the dead Black-Rabbits, and to deposit them into 'cubicle three' below the main deck. They located the cubicle which was clearly marked. A button had to pushed, and instructions appeared on a direction-screen. It was Zack who quietly and sadly pressed the button on cubicle three. A door slid open and an impersonal voice requested he deposit his cargo and gloves on the stainless steel tray, which he did. The door closed automatically, and that was that. Zack wondered how they would handle critters of his size, but quickly dismissed the thought from his mind.

The strangely persistant intuitive feelings that Zack, Rudy and Tooky had felt a little earlier began to get their attention. Over breakfast they lightly touched on their concerns, but it was little Tooky who kept picking up images of Jibby and Jubby. Initially, Tooky almost dismissed them from his mind, but his 'No Fear' and 'Intuition' training kicked in with such force that it surprised him. He looked up at Zack, who immediately responded with, "What is it Tooky?"

"I'm not sure," said Tooky, "But why do I keep seeing Jibby and Jubby, we left them in the Flower-Meadow back on Ektar! You did, did you not Zack? You were the last to see them."

"Yes! That's true Tooky," said Zack becoming somewhat mystified. But his feelings of mystery were replaced with utter disbelief. If what Tooky had said was true, and he was usually right in his assessments; why and how did Jibby and Jubby get onboard?

"Tooky! If they're onboard, do you know where they are?" asked Zack.

"I checked that," said Tooky, "But I couldn't find them." Rudy was quite concerned. "Keep on top of it Tooky, and report to us immediately if something comes in. They did not have long to wait. When Zack went to his quarters which were now separate from the Hill-Clan rabbits, the first thing he saw was Jibby and Jubby laying on the floor. They were both bloated and obviously dead. But, they were slowly moving in a weird, uncanny and disjointed manner unlike anything alive. Frozen in his tracks, Zack watched them for a moment or two in horrified fascination as two yellow heads burst through the distorted mouse skins. Zack had witnessed the hatching of two unknown mutated aliens.

Terrified, Zack slammed the door and rushed to Rudy who was in the control room. As he burst in, Chief Engineer Ekona immediately saw the expression of terror and alarm on Zack's face—his eyes were filled with incredulous disbelief and horror.

Rudy took command of the situation. "Hold on Zack!" He exclaimed. "First, run the 'No Fear' program from within you. Without realizing it you have become a model of 'fear' in action!" He smiled. "Now, that's better Zack, tell us what happened."

Zack explained his findings and reactions. Rudy then highlighted the Jibby and Jubby scenario to Ekona. He then elaborated on the Ektapod fiasco in which they had become deeply involved, even though the 'egg-zapping' season only lasted each year for approximately a three week period.

"But," explained Zack; "these are not Ektapods. These are a lot smaller with large yellow heads."

Ekona now had two major problems that demanded his full intention. The critical one was that the Lexcraft BEC propulsion system had been sabotaged. The crew members' minds were in a disarray fear and horror at Zack's discovery. They were all, except for Rudy, in an automatic individualized survival-mode, and were far from being in a BEC state.

The Lexcraft had been invaded by two small field mice which had undoubtedly been 'egg zapped' by some insidious alien life-form. It appeared the larvae had hatched, and the alien creatures had already eaten Jibby and Jubby alive from the inside out. As to what might appear next, Rudy was not sure.

Strange life-forms had life cycles and unknown powers, including the incredible ability to 'mutate on demand' in order to handle any situation they might encounter. The dangers were beyond imagination.

If the Lexcraft should become a mutated alien habitat, it was possible that it might have to be vaporized. Any life-forms on board would cease to exist regardless of whom or what they were. The space-craft occupants would have no say in the matter, nor would they be consulted. Fortunately, this could only be triggered by Lexcraft controls on Rat-Star. In a millisecond it would happen.

Zack sat down, covering his face with his hands. But even with his eyes closed he could not dismiss the utter horror of what he had encountered. He was so overcome by the reality of the situation, he became frozen into immobility.

It was Scruffykin who came over to Zack and gently touched him on the shoulder. Zack looked up and found he was looking into eyes that held such serenity that he immediately calmed down. Scruff smiled, which relaxed Zack even more; whereupon Scruff placed his paws on Zack's head and hummed a little tune. To Zack, it was very similar to Rudy-Rat's 'green-light' treatment. In a matter of moments Zack was free of depression and bubbling with energy. He profusely thanked Scruff and made a mental note to investigate the whole 'healing' phenomena. Scruff just smiled in an unperturbed manner as though it was as normal a routine as getting out of bed.

Meantime in the main navigation cabin, Rudy immediately enquired of Ekona if there were any high-intensity laser-beam type weapons onboard. He replied in the affirmative but did not know where they could be located. The crew was informed of the situation, but they could not recall seeing any weapons. Rudy also reported to Ekona that the remainder of the Black-Rabbits who'd gone into a coma had not survived, and that they and Captain Betak had been taken to Cubicle Three for disposal. These cold hard facts sent a chill throughout the ship.

"This is the creepiest and most horrible thing I've ever heard of!" exclaimed Tooky. He looked as though he'd like to hide until the whole threat was over. Boofy and Bifflets as usual were quietly confident and standing by to obey instructions. Rat-Star base had no suggestions other than exercising extreme caution when they next opened the door to Zack's room to confront what might be there. Rudy volunteered to investigate and said he would transmit his images to the control-room screen for all to see. When Rudy had arrived at Zack's door, he signaled the crew to activate a type of fire or hazard-proof door behind him so that nothing could escape past him. They all returned to the control center, while Rudy opened the door. What he saw, they all saw, including those at Rat-Star. At this point no weapons had been located.

Reposing on the table were two creatures of a type no one had ever seen before. They were each about five inches long with large yellow heads, the rest of their bodies were a bright blue, except for a bright red line running down their backs from head to tail. They had black legs, ears, and tails.

They were winged, and this maneuverability factor gave cause for alarm. Everyone in the control room and at Rat-Star was 'knocked for a loop'. No one had ever seen life-forms that relaxed with such an unperturbed attitude as did these. It was as though they were in total control. It had a definite unsettling effect on the entire crew that made their hearts pound in apprehension. Rudy suspected they were mutations. They coolly studied him with an intelligence that even he found to be quite disturbing. Upsetting, because he perceived they had access to his thoughts and the ability to react to those thoughts.

The creatures came to their feet with wings vibrating. When Rudy revealed to controls-base that the aliens could receive and follow their thought-processes no one felt safe. On the other hand the colorful critters could not monitor everyone's thoughts simultaneously, so there was some room in which to move.

There was little doubt that the creatures had never seen a golden-winged space-rat before, and Rudy picked up that they were somewhat intimidated by his size, especially as he had wings too. "What do you want to do and how can we help you?" asked Rudy. He noticed their eyes brightened when his question yielded its interpretation. However they did not reply.

Rudy knew from experience the greatest danger with most mutations was their automatic programing to mutate to meet any threat; the key was to avoid causing them to feel threatened. So Rudy relaxed completely. The little misfits began to flit around the room. Rudy thought they were getting restless for some action. His intuition kept prompting him, Xenar! Xenar! So he quietly transmitted images of BECs, Aliens and Xenar to the crew on board, as well as to Rat-Star. Rudy did not believe the strange animals could interpret the special meanings of those words. However, Captain Ratto and the onboard crew immediately picked up on his suggestion and knew what had to be done. They rapidly brought Ekona and his engineering staff into the picture. BECs were nothing new to them, but Xenar was.

While watching the creatures flit around, and explore, Rudy imaged BECs! Aliens! Xenar! And *NOW!* It took about five more minutes for the crew to get Ekona and his engineers into synchronicity with those on the Lexcraft. Even In that small time-lapse, the mutated aliens had acquired the ability of projecting a new 'unity of intent'. It was powerful. They met Rudy's eyes with dangerous intensity. He looked away.

Rudy sensed ruthless control-power emanating from their eyes. Moment by moment he felt that their intelligence was exponentially increasing to a terrifying control-level. He experienced their repeated attempts to transfer his total 'cognizance of being' to their own. They had not yet achieved perfect 'unison of attempt' in their control efforts; if they did, it could be deadly and irreversible. Never had Rudy been so alarmed as at his recognition of this fact.

Rudy sensed the 'transfer' moment coming up. He imaged BECs! Aliens! Xenar! BECs! Aliens! Xenar! He projected this thought sequence about seven times until synchronicity of intent and power became as 'one' with the onboard crew and Ratstar. Unbeknown to them all, Scruff was completely in tune with them and was thankful for the Xenar images he'd received from the crew. Now they really were, all 'as one'.

Almost in disbelief, Rudy saw the little blue and yellow aliens suddenly disappear. It was like magic! Scruff's secret input had given the operation huge impetus. He was indeed a rabbit of considerable talent and ability. Rudy sighed with relief. The eyes of the alien creatures had begun to penetrate his entire mind to the point where in a matter of a few minutes more, they would have been able control him, and even take over the whole space-craft. Thank heaven that Lexcraft had ultimate control through space-ship 'vaporization'.

Rudy returned to the main control-room. He never wanted to see such scary types of animals again; and wondered, but only briefly, how the Moon-Wolves would react to the aliens' arrival on Xenar.

Rudy was laughing as he met with the rest of the crew. They were joined by the Lexcraft staff and Chiefs at Rat-Star. It was the laughter of relief. They had survived an awesome dilemma and lived to tell about it!

On discussing how Jibby and Jubby came to be onboard, Zack thought that at the last moment, as he imaged the space-craft for his return to base, they had jumped onto his runners and disembarked in his room.

Or, were they caused to jump? Zack felt sad at the loss of two such good little friends, and wondered what type of creature had used them its reproductive cycle. He shuddered.

Rudy had now turned his attention to cosmic time factors; and although they were not travelling anywhere near the speed of light; he kept recalling a fabled Earth limerick. He hoped that it did not apply to speeds lower than that of light! He recited the limerick out loud to himself:

> "There was a young lady of Wight,
> Who traveled much faster than light,
> She departed one day,
> In a relative way,
> And arrived on the previous night!"

Scruff couldn't help hearing him, and joined in on the last two lines. They both laughed. Everyone had different versions in regard to how much time had passed on Earth while they were away. Scruff had nothing definitive to contribute either. It then took only about seven minutes to regain BEC propulsion-power, and once again everything quietly hummed along normally.

Everyone was now in high spirits. They had discovered that it was highly beneficial to dwell in the '*NOW*' element of Time. It had taken a lot of conscious self-discipline to develop this state of mind. But they had yet to achieve this as an habitual state. Previously they had primarily used the 'sowing and reaping' principle negatively by dwelling in the 'past'. The fruit of which was pain, remorse, and regret, in addition to personal condemnation. Scruff privately cataloged every crew-member in relation to their '*NOW*' status and abilities; it was prime Braktor research material.

Zack lay on his bed. He found it hard to believe that he was hurtling through the cosmos to the only place he really knew—his own planet Earth. Before Zack fell asleep, brilliant little Tooky joined him. He quickly hopped up on to Zack's downy mattress and snuggled down. They both fell asleep. Tooky's silky ears trailed over Zack's cheek, and Zack sighed in a sleepy state of euphoria. '*NOW*' was a beautiful living reality!

Tesla — A brilliant rabbit—a genius who lives a different reality in a world of his own!

Chapter Ten

Tooky awoke first. He was not sure why or what had awakened him. He wriggled out of Zack's grasp and this caused Zack to waken also.

"Hi Tooky! What's happening?" he asked, his sharply penetrating blue eyes studying the little rabbit.

"Something's not right. Something has happened!" exclaimed Tooky. "It's in the control room!" Without further ado Zack pulled on his clothes and they both went to see what had disturbed Tooky. There was supposed to be a skeleton on-duty night crew of Kotar, Boofy, Bifflets, and KeKe; but they were shocked by what they now saw.

Kotar, Boofy and Bifflets were dazed and trance-like, while little KeKe had 'passed out'. The main control-room screen was black, which meant that communication with Lexcraft and Rat-Star was non-existent. It also meant that power-flow to the computers had been interrupted. However, the Lexcraft was at least on some form of auto-pilot power.

"What gives?" squeaked Tooky.

"Wow!" exclaimed Zack. "Tooky, get Rudy-Rat, Scruff and the others in here immediately, I'm going to check a few things out."

Tooky fled for help, and although Boofy and Bifflets were conscious with their eyes wide open, they were not 'here', and just gazed straight ahead, nor could they be roused. It seemed that KeKe was just in a more advanced state of whatever it was that overtaken them.

Rudy was first on the scene with Scruff, followed by Tesla, Timken and the almost breathless Tooky. Rudy's beautiful eyes flashed various colors while Zack explained what they had found. Next, it was Rudy who instructed that the four night crew comprising Kotar, Boofy, Bifflets and KeKe be taken to their quarters for recovery. This was executed without delay. But, something of a sinister nature was making all of them apprehensive. They sensed that an overpowering thought process was at work which interfered with crew members' thinking.

Rudy and Zack realized that the Lexcraft was powerless and drifting someplace in the solar system without direction or control. Powerless because those in charge of maintaining unified power-flow via the Bose-Einstein Condensate of unbroken wholeness were now incapacitated.

Zack made a mental note that a cosmically encrypted generic form of BEC power should be built into every Lexcraft. Tesla thought it to be a mere matter of finely tuned oscillations on an assigned protected frequency. Kotar just shook his head, and mostly everyone wondered what to do next.

Zack and Rudy decided it was necessary to first reactivate the communication systems with their screens. But BEC unified-power was unavailable with the crew being in utter disarray. It was Scruffykin who spoke up, saying "Rudy, Zack, I can produce more than enough BEC power by myself—to get the entire communications system running.

Let me sit by that control there. Tell me what you want done. You handle the computer controls—I'll do the rest"

Both Zack and Rudy looked at Scruff in incredulity. They couldn't quite believe what they were hearing from this lone 'Geeky' Ektar rabbit. "But," said Rudy, you're only rated at five BECs and this may take even more!"

"Rudy, I actually max out at about seventeen BECs, but no one as yet has officially recognized that I have this capacity. I even have research underway that confirms that I can also double that output capacity!"

"That's good enough for me," said Rudy. "Sit here, I'll do the rest. Oh! And by the way—you were participating in that alien-transfer operation weren't you? I wondered where that massive surge of power had come from!" Scruff looked a little sheepish. "Thanks anyway Scruff," said Rudy in an admiring tone. "You're a fine crew team-member."

Meantime, when Tooky checked up on Kotar, Boofy, Bifflets and KeKe, to their surprise all four had recovered, but did not know to what they had succumbed. Apparently they'd been watching the Rat-Star-Lexcraft screen and whatever they'd received from it had caused the state in which they had been found. The group briefly conferred and decided to assign one particular member of their group to monitor the screen and communicate. In that way they might isolate a cause or get a clue on what had happened. It was Kotar who volunteered for this duty and this was endorsed by all.

Scruffykin went into his 'generating mode' with his usual affable smile, and Rudy's heart quickened to hear the quiet hum of all the major electronics flashing into life.

Shortly after, the big screen became active and Ekona beamed his warm smile of welcome to Kotar only, as the screen had been rotated for him alone to monitor. Interestingly, Ekona said that it was the Ektar Lexcraft that cut off communications with them, and not the other way round. When Kotar released this information it became of grave concern for the whole crew. Kotar explained to Ekona the reason for him seeing only Kotar and no other crew members.

When Kotar asked Ekona for the Solar Chart to see where they were in relation to planet Earth, he became alarmed because despite what Ekona said about distance and timing, the solar system that the Ektar space-craft was receiving on their screen was quite different to that which Lexcraft on Rat-Star was sending to them. Kotar could not identify any of the planets, moons or stars he was viewing. Kotar excused himself from Ekona and briefly conferred with Rudy and Zack.

Tooky who was standing by, suddenly flipped his ears and startled everyone by squeaking loudly, "It's a beetle! It's a beetle!" He looked stricken with terror.

"Hold on Tooky," commanded Rudy. "First run your 'No Fear' program Tooky. What is a beetle?" Tooky's eyes were still wide with fear. "A big beetle is running this ship Zack, and it's in the room that Betaka had. I can see it! It's about five inches long and three inches wide. It's all jet black except for a yellow cross on its back! Its eyes are horrible!"

Poor Tooky fainted. Zack picked him up and gently stroked him. In a few moments Tooky 'came to' and was much less frightened. What scared Tooky most was that he could 'see' the beetle so closely and in so much detail, he thought it might really be inside his head!

"It's okay Tooky," said Zack. "We've already overcome some pretty horrific situations, so let's just take this in our stride one step at a time!" Tooky wriggled. He loved being held by Zack.

Now that the crew was up to full force, Rudy reassigned BEC power-outputs to other crew members, which released Scruffykin from this chore as he could be more valuable elsewhere in their current emergency. Rudy was pleased with Scruffy's technical abilities. He also admired his low-key approach in the way he handled specialized knowledge. Scruff was an unexpected asset.

"I have a picture of a black beetle with a yellow cross in my Cosmic Rattopedia," said Rudy. "It's about the size that Tooky described. It has a seven year life cycle. At the end of the seventh year these beetles seem to appear out of nowhere in vast numbers. They breed and then disappear for another seven years. I'll bet that was why it was not in Captain Betaka's field of experience, it also being such a rural life-form."

Zack looked at the group, "We have a similar insect breeding cycle on Earth with the Cicada, and it has a seventeen year cycle. However, it's harmless and millions of them breed and also provide a feast for birds and other predators. Anyway," he concluded, "when this 'Beetle' has been located it has to be killed instantly. Timken, you search every storage compartment or place that could possibly hold a laser-type weapon. Captain Betaka was no fool, he knew he had them on board and I believe him. The only foolish thing was that he did not know where they were located! Timken, report back on anything that you cannot name that looks like a weapon. Of course, do not go into Betaka's old quarters."

Timken flipped his ears and hopped rapidly away. Boofy reminded the group of the Beetle's unknown powers which had to be extensive if it was running the ship, and warned everyone about guarding their thoughts, especially if a laser weapon was found.

"We have to assume it has thought-reading powers," said Bifflets. "It's a fairly safe solar assumption, so let's not think about beetles and weapons. We know this Beetle-thing can drop trance-like spells on other creatures, and well may do so in self-defense. That Yellow-Cross Beetle obviously has propulsion capabilities in the BEC class, even as an individual, unless it is being additionally powered from a base

KeKe said, "I'm never going to want space-travel explorations again! I've seen first-hand the deadly situations one can run into. I'm staying on Earth where I belong! I only hope we get back safely! I can just see our old meadow with yellow cowslips everywhere; and no Ektapods!"

Kotar was instructed not to reveal what was occurring onboard to Ekona at Rat-Star base because the Y-C-Beetle was almost sure to pick it up and take some action—maybe even of a violent and decisive nature.

Scruffykin captured the attention of everyone by revealing some bizarre facts he'd picked up from the Y-C-Beatle. He'd had some difficulty in picking up its brain-frequency, but had finally succeeded. Now he smiled in satisfaction.

"In reality," he stated, "Our whole crew of living creatures is being viewed by the Y-C- Beetle as mere 'egg-zapping' material for his females. His ability to provide 'ovipositor receptacles' for his mates; makes him a prime designated 'breeder' of consequence. He is reveling at this most pleasurable attribute, and smiling at the sheer quantity of 'live meat' he has captured." The stunned crew members looked at each other almost in disbelief, as they went about their duties.

Scruff was resting up from his BEC outputs. He just sat sat quietly off to one side in the main cabin. His mind was operating like that of a champion Earth chess-player. He saw every living being on the space-craft as though the Lexcraft were a big chess-board; and, he had the incredible advantage of being both players at the same time. Scruff was ready for action, regardless of what might show up. Being thusly equipped, it placed Scruff unofficially in the highest management position onboard the Lexcraft. He was devoid of ego; and every increment of increased power that came to him, he merely offset it with an equal commitment to greater humility. His mission was to serve their objectives. For him, self-importancwe did not exist.

A half-hour had passed on Zack's Rolex before Timken returned. He looked a little confused, but said he had found some strange 'things' in Cubicle Four.

"Let's go," said Rudy, and let's think of wild roses—nothing but wild roses. The Y-C-Beetle won't have a clue as to what is going on!" Zack, Rudy and Tesla went on the mission to Cubicle Four. In a matter of minutes the 'strange things' were determined to be three laser-vaporizing-units of unprecedented portable power.

"As we look at these weapons remember they are wild flowers." said Zack. Their scent and color are exquisite!" Rudy quickly confirmed how to operate the 'flowers' and all three of them headed for Betaka's old quarters. They closed the guard door behind them before they opened Betaka's door. All three projected identical thoughts.

At first they did not see the Yellow-Cross-Beetle, but he saw them, and revved up his wings for flight if need be. The three focused directly on the sound he'd created. Without a second thought, on eye contact, Zack, Rudy and Tesla simultaneously fired their lasers. The Yellow-Cross-Beetle was probably seeing pictures of colorful plant-life and was probably wondering what it was all about. He was reduced to a tiny puff of foggy vapor. Again the three fired at the vapor, and then nothing remained. However, a lot of damage was inflicted on the wall behind where the Beetle was standing; in fact; the metal was still glowing red when they left.

Zack almost collapsed with excitement, fright, effort and relief. Rudy's eyes flashed gorgeous colors, and Tesla, mimicking an Earth movie western, blew into the end of his laser-gun and with dignified mien stuffed it into his belt. Zack just looked in wonder at the whole scene. Alert Tooky brought in a 'Cosmic-Creature-Scanner' and located nothing but the laser crew. The threat had been eliminated. Scruff silently applauded.

It was at this point that Tesla requested of Rudy-Rat the uninterrupted use of the space-craft's small 'lab-workshop' for about five hours. "It's an idea I've been working on," he explained. "I've designed a BEC frequency-modulator device to replace our 'live' BEC generating units! Be patient Rudy. It will work!"

Rudy-Rat was both surprised and pleased, "Go ahead Tesla. It sounds great, especially as it will release all those who had to commit BEC power to run things. You might even be able to patent the device and sell it to Lexcraft!"

"First things first," said Tesla, and mumbling to himself he disappeared inside the 'lab'.

In the central control room they turned the communication screen round again and brought Ekona at Rat-Star up to date, along with the balance of their own crew members. Now the Solar Map revealed a need of considerable correction in relation to the local galaxies. Ekona estimated that an additional 'day' would be required to enter the Earth's immediate Solar system.

The entire crew could only surmise that Captain Betaka had unwittingly brought the Yellow-Cross-Beetle onboard when he violated the rule—that anyone who re-entered the space-craft must be checked with the 'Cosmic-Creature-Scanner' [CCS].

After this latest episode Tooky spent a lot of time with the CCS, wherein he minutely checked every section of the Ektar-Craft until he was completely satisfied that no foreign life-forms existed among them.

"Well," said Rudy to the group, "Something else we have to consider is that this Lexcraft belongs to the Black-Rabbits of Ektar, and there is only one surviving Ektar Rabbit on board, namely Scruff, so we'll have to consult with him on how and when to return it."

"As I see it," said Zack, "Firstly we return to Earth and drop off the Hill-Clan rabbit tribe along with me. That will leave Scruff and Rudy to take the ship back to Lexcraft at Rat-Star. On the other hand Scruff might elect to stay on Earth for a spell. I do think though that Captain Ratto and young Ratfink should come over to Earth as they did in the past, and then return on the Ektar-craft to Rat-Star as a group, even if just for safety reasons.

"That is what I had in mind," replied Rudy. "What will you do Zack? You do have a brother, Brett, you want to look up. And life does go on." He smiled. Zack did not look up and remained silent. He feared that if he looked at Rudy he would burst into tears. How could two 'beings' become so close? It was just too emotional. He still toyed with the idea of going to live with Rudy on Rat-Star, that is, if such were permissible.

The truth was that a dilemma was coming into focus for the whole crew. It was simply that none of the group wanted to break-up and go their separate ways; they had been in such close life and death types of adventures. It seemed unthinkable that they could separate! They were now a 'cosmic-family'.

"I shall miss sleeping with you Zack," said Tooky allowing his eyes to go moist with tears.

Zack gently picked up Tooky and nuzzled him. "I will miss you too Tooky," said Zack, "Upon our Earth landing, we must first determine what happened to our version of 'Time'. We must get into the reality of Earth-time, and I'm sure I'll have to reset my Rolex. We'll also have to reset our own thinking. For example, suppose none of the Hill-Clan we once knew are still alive? Then, how will we think and what will we do?"

Quietly Tooky stated, "It matters little! We are all in 'NOW', regardless of 'Time'." Then flipping an ear and looking thoughtful, Tooky said, "The other day Kotar said something about 'power' that I found to be interesting, but at the time I didn't quite grasp it. Maybe it's something to talk about and it'll help pass the time". He looked across at Boofy, who smiled. "I recall that Tooky, but I got lost too! Zack can you handle this? I remember you were quite thrilled with Kotar's message.

"Yes," said Zack, "I remember it well, Kotar was expounding on the fact that 'power' is always conceived of as the application of 'force' in some way. But, in talking at one time with senior 'time' research rabbits; he discovered they had an entirely different concept. One of their 'Tesla types' who also seemed to dwell mostly in a world of his own, said that the concept of 'true power' has nothing to do with 'applying force'; which he called a low-level state of ego-consciousness—shadowed by insanity."

"Yes! I remember that," said Tooky. "It's coming back to me! His concept of 'No-Power' is the authority contained within what he called the, *'ISness of Being'*; whatever that is."

Zack interjected with, "Back on Earth—some ancient scribes call it the 'All-Power' of '*I AM*' and reference it to the Creator. Rudy also touched on this at one time. He described it as a power, not force, that simply *'IS'*. I suggest however, there are few creatures who will ever achieve this state of 'being'.

"Sounds like that Super-Rabbit stuff to me." said Timken.

Kotar had quietly joined the group, almost unnoticed. "Okay you space explorers" he cut in. "The way you're going, you'll be dizzy beyond any state you ever had before—apart from the fact it's a boring discussion, even if you are just trying to pass time. In reality that whole concept belongs among Zack's kind—definitely not rabbits! So why don't we talk about getting mates, and raising baby bunnies? At least that's real!"

Everyone applauded Kotar's input. Even Zack in his innocence and vulnerability hinted at similar aspirations, and ended up looking a little confused. For him to find a mate would firstly entail the monumental step of learning for the first time, how to trust his own kind. This would be 'breaking-ground' right from square one. He suspected that it would be a difficult, hurtful and traumatic task.

But apprehension fell heavily upon the group. No matter what they discussed, it was not enough of a distraction to divert their thoughts from their almost imminent landing back on Earth. Several of the crew members sighed and looked at each other. The apprehension they felt was almost palpable, and time seemed to 'speed-up'. Finally they became resigned to whatever reality might confront them.

Suddenly, Scruff stood up and announced to the group that Tesla was about to join them. Knowing Tesla had secreted himself in the lab for some hours, a ripple of excitement seemed to surge through the crew. Sure enough, the lab door opened and Tesla appeared. He carried a small oddly shaped piece of electronic equipment, and they could tell from the look on his face that he was quite elated with his invention. With his tall jet-black ears erect, Tesla proudly announced, "In simple terms, this is a self-energizing, multiple-frequency Bose-Einstein-Condensate generator. The core of the unit is a series of the one quarter wavelength coils I designed—they, yielding the greatest amplitude of vibration.

It will respond selectively to the particular wavelength emitted by the oscillator, while the other wavelengths remain inert. This idea came to me originally while I was experimenting with an altogether higher range of octaves. At that time I was trying to identify the source of some incredible 'celestial music' to which I had become attuned." Tesla laughed. "The result being that the electrical coils I've designed, being of quarter wavelengths, have the same properties as a tuned musical string. They can vibrate not only to the fundamental note, but also a wide range of upper and lower harmonics. This unit can be set to match the brain-frequency of whatever group wishes to acquire a Lexcraft. It then bridges that frequency, say for Black-Rabbits, to match up with the BEC drive system. It opens up a whole new solar-market for Lexcraft." The curious crew all studied the highly complex chip-sets and circuitry without any remote comprehension. They just shook their heads in amazement. "Shall we try it?" asked Tesla in his assured manner.

Rudy-Rat said he would contact Lexcraft on Rat-Star and Captain Ratto. There followed a discussion which also involved Tesla, but there was little enthusiasm for what Tesla had invented. It was simply beyond the Lexcraft Rat's levels of comprehension. Scruffykin gently interrupted the personnel at Rat-Star base, and said he partially knew how the new BEC unit worked, as he was very much aware of the oscillations available in the higher ranges of octaves, and he felt sure that it was among these frequencies that Tesla had harnessed and directed the energy-flow. After a few more minutes of conversation, Lexcraft somewhat hesitantly gave permission to the space-craft crew to proceed—with what Zack suspected were 'crossed fingers'.

Zack clapped his hands. Rudy jumped up and down, and all the rabbits cheered. Tesla looked serious. He, Rudy, Zack and Scruff all surrounded Tesla as he removed the titanium plates that sheltered the master controls. This operation would not have been possible without Lexcraft's permission. The engineers had to release control-signals from Rat-Star to allow access to the propulsion unit and inintialize the installation. However, Tesla's addition was located dangerously close to the space-craft's 'Self-Vaporization' unit. It caused some apprehension among the Rat-Star engineers and the crew. In reality, Tesla's addition was a far more delicate operation than any one had anticipated.

It took three Earth-hours on Zack's Rolex, to achieve installation and link-up with what they called the 'Tesla-Power-Unit' or TPU. Now came the critical part. Lexcraft had to send an encrypted radio signal to cut current power and switch to Tesla-Power. Zack studied the serious concern on the face of every engineer at the Lexcraft Plant. There was just a remote chance that the proximity of the TPU to the Vaporization-Activator chip-set might be affected by stray frequencies escaping from the Tesla unit. The possibility existed that these could be 'leaking out of sequence' with the finely-tuned harmonics in the main drive.

If this were true, the net result would be one of total annihilation. Captain Ratto came 'on-screen'. He said he was relying on the data that Tesla and Scruff had supplied, and he needed to make everyone on the space-craft aware of the massive risk-factor they were undertaking in the event they switched power. "Are you really ready for this?" He asked.

The whole crew looked at each other with the sudden realization that their lives were on the line. Tooky said, "It really comes down to how much faith we have in Tesla and his engineering." They all looked from Tooky to Tesla. Both he and Scruff were beaming with confidence. The space-crew were about to discover how much they really trusted these two somewhat mysterious rabbits. Boofy shouted, "Let's go for it!" Then, meeting the eyes of the others for agreement—he clapped his paws over his face and yelled, "SWITCH!"

There was a momentary pause as all lights, motors and computers were stopped. Total silence and darkness enveloped the space-craft. They all held their breath—bracing for the possible split-second lag before they were evaporated into Eternity. Seconds ticked by.

Softly at first, but with increasing intensity, the crew heard a faint highly-pitched whining sound. Then the beautiful hum of live electronics softly clicking in to action met their ears. It was time to breathe again. When the lights powered up, they all blinked at each other, and glanced at the control screen as it activated.

"Hey!" shouted Captain Ratto, "You're still there!" They all laughed in relief. Some had tears in their eyes. The engineers at Lexcraft were overcome in their admiration for Tesla's advancement of Lexcraft engineering. They shook their heads, and had difficulty in conceiving of how an unknown Hill-Clan rabbit from several galaxies away could be so brilliant. Lexcraft engineers were full of excitement, and impatient to see Tesla's TPU in action. They would have to wait.

"Well, intelligence is found throughout the Universe," said the smiling Scruffykin. Then, dropping into his crude lingo he said, "They ain't seen nothin'yet! We might just be ordinary rabbits, but by the same token—they is just common space-rats!" Tesla, Zack and Rudy had a good laugh. They could hardly believe the changes that had come about, and once again turned their attention to Earth arrival.

To pass some time, Timken was about to reopen a discussion on mates and mating, when KeKe, who had been unusually quiet for the past few hours complained of 'falling darkness'. The whole crew upon hearing this curious statement looked at him; whereupon KeKe just doubled up and collapsed onto his side. He lay very still. Everyone was immediately shocked. What possible reason could there be for KeKe to keel over as though he were dead? Perhaps he was. Then, before their horror-stricken eyes, KeKe's sides began to slowly heave as though he were moving around inside his furry coat. It was a bizarre and unnatural sight.

Tooky's cute face was a mask of fright, and all the rabbits drew back, while Rudy and Zack, equally horrified, also waited to see what would happen next. It was revolting to see KeKe's chest protrude as though being pushed out from within by a sharp object. Several of the rabbits gasped in surprise as slowly the blood-stained tip of a serrated Ektapod beak began to appear.

Then, a vile odor suddenly permeated the whole cabin and noses twitched. Zack held his nose. The space-crew watched in hypnotic fascination as the alien life-form split KeKe's chest in two, and emerging, it wriggled itself upright on the level surface. For an insect the size of a song bird, its appearance was beautiful, yet most assuredly it was an alien angel of death.

Rudy yelled, "Hold your breath! Don't breathe that stench! Get masks!" He opened a cabin storage bin close by, and threw handful after handful of the devices among the crew, who quickly strapped them over their faces. "Make sure the straps go over your ears," he shouted. Zack fitted his mask and watched as all the rabbits' tall ears flipped to the vertical position.

"That smell is being emitted by the Ektapod." Rudy explained, "It's a gas that attacks the central nervous system. Be careful of every move you make!"

The alien apparition was now fully emerged. It uttered piercing, raucous screaming sounds and stood up; aggressively spreading its two three-clawed feet.

Most gripping of all was when it moved is head and focused its jet black eyes on the rabbits. The all-knowing, commanding intelligence those eyes projected was almost tangible. It froze the rabbits into motionless terror.

"Don't look at its eyes," yelled Rudy, "and if you got even a small whiff of the gas, you'll be under its control!"

It was quite evident the creature had total awareness of its position, and had reason to assume it was in control of the situation with which it was confronted. The sheer arrogance and boldness of its presence brought every second of passing time closer to the proximity of death for every crew member. It was Rudy who reached for Tesla's laser-vaporizing-gun. Within three seconds of grasping the laser, Rudy aimed and fired the weapon. The Ektapod was reduced to vapor, and even after this, Rudy fired at the vapor with two additional blasts. Nothing remained.

"Now!" said Rudy, "Do not remove your masks. We have to immediately replace them with oxygen units. Then we can open the air cleaning valves." He beckoned to Zack, "Let's find that oxygen stuff. The rest of you, stay exactly where you are." Despite his youth, Rudy-Rat made a fine commander.

The balance of the space-crew collapsed into the cabin chairs, gasping through their masks with relief. In a matter of minutes Zack and Rudy returned with a small trolley on which were piled oxygen cylinders and masks. The change of masks was completed and Zack, who was standing by the clearly marked air valve controls, turned them on when Rudy gave him a nod. Within seven minutes on Zack's Rolex, the flashing green lights came on and all was clear. Rudy said to the crew, "Okay! We can now breathe normally." He gave them all a huge smile.

"Expect the unexpected," exclaimed Rudy, "Poor KeKe! Who'd have thought that he'd been 'double egg-zapped'? More importantly—why was this question not raised earlier? You were the last Ektapod victim Zack, monitor yourself carefully! We'll also have you under observation; though I believe the surgeons performed their task flawlessly based on vast experience with Ektapods." Zack confirmed that he felt first-class.

"Now," said Rudy, "does anyone here feel he is not in charge of his limbs, or his mind? Stretch each leg, flip your ears, twitch your noses, and then ask each other some simple questions. This will reveal whether or not you may have inhaled some tiny gas particles. If so, we'll have to handle this problem with some urgency." Everyone responded positively. Great relief was experienced by all.

"You are probably wondering how I know so much about the Ektapods," said Rudy. "It all came back to me from a lecture I attended back on Rat-Star. The creature they were explaining was not an Ektapod, but very similar in its design and capabilities. Apparently they inhabit a number of planets; so I drew on that knowledge source.

I was right on the nerve-gas; and that razor-sharp serrated beak is what the creature uses on its paralyzed victims. That beak is a weapon too. Regardless of the victim's state, whether partly or fully incapacitated, the Ektapods slash their eyes out first—swallowing them whole, it can then proceed at its leisure depending on where it is. It may even share its food source with others of its kind if they are in the vicinity. I can still vividly recall the photos of some sightless Star-Rats who were rescued—too late to save their sight."

"I can't believe that this whole thing happened," exclaimed Zack. "How?" he questioned while shaking his head. The rabbit crew needed refreshments, and this would help them recover from the horror of their shock. Zack, who was familiar with 'disposal procedure', took on the task of attending to KeKe.

Shaking with tears, he pulled on latex gloves to pick up the pathetic remains of that handsome, much loved little rabbit. Zack stumbled on his way to access 'Compartment Three', his eyes blurred with tears. With reverence he carefully placed KeKe on the stainless steel tray along with the gloves, and pushed the button. "Bye Bye KeKe, I'll never forget you," he whispered. Only a faint whirring sound replied.

Zack returned to his cabin and cried uncontrollably. Every time he envisioned KeKe's bright-eyed, furry little face and relived the softness of his silky ears, it brought on fresh paroxysms of sadness, pain and tears. It was Rudy, who understanding what was occurring, came to Zack's rescue this time. He placed a firm hand on Zack's shoulder and asked him to sit on the edge of his bunk. He looked fully into Zack's tear-filled eyes.

"I've never before had occasion to use my 'Green-Light' powers," Rudy stated, "so now's as good a time to experiment as any. Healthy Star-Rats routinely expose themselves to 'Green-Light'." He smiled.

"Whatever is that?" sniffed Zack as he completed the mopping up of tears.

"Before we discovered you, Zack, Captain Ratto, Dad, used his 'Green-Light' powers to revive Kotar and Tesla after a bad weasel attack! Now, I need you to just relax and pretend you're star-gazing—or, you may if you wish, watch my eyes. It's up to you."

Zack did as was bidden and elected to watch Rudy's eyes. Slowly a soft green light appeared and then became brighter by the second. It seemed to illuminate the whole of Rudy's body, and simultaneously Zack felt the pains of his physical and mental trauma disappearing. In amazement he felt warm pulsations of energy flow through him, and saw that his own body was also fully illuminated with green light. Pulses of exuberant energy continued to surge through him until they seemed to ripple him to his feet.

"Finished!" exclaimed Rudy. Zack was delighted, and thanked Rudy with a huge smile and a warm hug. Rudy also smiled in appreciation. "Hey! It's a first for me too! It works! Thank you Zack! By the way, it's okay to think of KeKe as a loving memory; it'll never affect you again in the way you've just experienced."

"Now!" continued Rudy. "We are just about to have an analysis meeting. Top echelon Rat-Star executives will be contributing and asking questions via our TV link-up screens. Other galactic powers who are members of the Star Alliance will also be watching with more than casual interest."

"Yes! This'll be really interesting—what they conclude with, that is," said Zack. "Maybe we can't land on Earth until certain things have been proven; like who else was 'double-egg zapped' by their Ektapod. Me, for example or Timken! Those other galactic powers will certainly be viewing our conclusions and courses of action."

The analysis-meeting took all of five hours. It was determined that Zack and Timken were the primary threats to planet Earth, but scientists had calculated from the data that if either Zack or Timken were 'double-egg zapped', the Ektapods would already show signs of their presence. However, in their private circle, all the space-crew members including Scruff confidentially decided not to use 'logic'; but to rely on their intuition in the way they all normally lived. It was better to 'know' by intuition, than to 'theorize' by logic.

Zack and Timken both agreed to absolute transparency in the whole matter, even if their 'hunch' turned out to be incorrect. Scruffykin nodded his approval to all that had occurred, including their current thinking. He smiled.

Tooky was quite concerned and alarmed when he exclaimed, "I scanned KeKe thoroughly with the Cosmic Creature Scanner and he came up negative. So is that unit faulty, outdated, or are we dealing with other insidious unknown factors?"

Rudy-Rat promised a full investigation by Rat-Star engineers and everyone wanted to know how and why the Creature-Scanner had failed them.

They were all snuggling down preparing for a well-deserved nap, when Tooky perked right up and said, "Tesla, I want to know more about the 'celestial music' you heard, you know, when you were trying to track down its source!"

Tesla looked up attentively. Few rabbits had ever asked him questions on this, as he had only referred to it in an inconsequential side comment. For a moment or two he studied Tooky. He wondered why Tooky's ears were so long for such a small rabbit; but when he looked into Tooky's bright intelligent eyes, he realized that here was a rather special—somewhat different rabbit—who might be able to comprehend the musical mystery that seemed to emanate from the stars. Zack, Rudy, and Scruff also looked at Tesla for an explanation. All four were silent with anticipation.

Tesla relaxed. It was pleasurable to be in the presence of humble intelligence that was also coupled to the wisdom of 'other-worldly' dimensions. "When I speak of hearing 'celestial-music . . ." he paused, "I'm really speaking of a type of conscious awareness of that which is not contained in 'Time'. I do not hear it with my ears", he paused again.

"Yes! Yes!" exclaimed Tooky, "I'm with you, carry on."

Tesla's face appeared to be glowing as he thought about the music. "In the still of a star-ridden night, when the world connected with my body is silent, the music comes to me. When I'm lying on top of a hill gazing into the cosmos—a silent level of consciousness comes to me. I do not think—for there is no need to. I do not interrupt it. I allow *'IT'* to become 'me'. I then have a feeling of oneness that I call the *'I AM'* awareness."

Tesla shifted his position, his black ears very erect, and glancing at the four eager faces before him, he continued with, "Music—being notes and sounds that you're familiar with, and which I've also referred to in the making of the TPU, is not always comprised of 'music' as we know it. Celestial music is an indefinable orchestral input of awareness that bridges worlds, stars and beyond. In the crudest of terms—it's a cosmic love concert—and that's difficult to grasp! One has to relax internally and expand one's consciousness of being in order to remotely apprehend even its smallest part. Are you with me?" he asked, looking from one to another.

"Yes," said Zack, although he sounded a little foggy.

"I'm with you," said Rudy-Rat. Scruff just smiled, and Tooky looked exhuberant with understanding.

Tesla said, "Words, words, words, they mean nothing unless linked to specific comprehension," he sighed. "Anyway, our world of words whether it be of Rabbits, Rats or Men, cannot remotely touch that which we wish to describe or explore." Tesla flipped his ears down and looked sleepy.

"Thank you Tesla". They all seemed to chorus their gratitude at the same time. Tooky looked especially pleased. He hopped over to where Zack lay and snuggled up to him. Meantime the night-crew took over, and a general feeling of 'normalcy' took over the entire space-ship. They slept—restlessly.

In the 'morning'—whatever that was—everyone had awakened and had breakfast when Bifflets, who was sitting in the 'observation' deck, called out, "Look at these planets we're just passing, they sure look 'Earth-like'. I'm speaking of the coloration, that bluish tone, and we're not even in our home galaxy as yet! Do you suppose they are inhabited?" he asked the others who'd joined him.

"I don't see why not," said Tooky. "Common sense tells us there is no reason as to why Earth should be the only populated planet in the entire Universe. That concept of limitation must have originated with men who can't believe that anything of importance could exist outside of their own limited understanding. Of course everything has to be scientifically proven anyway—or it doesn't exist. Also that which is 'proven' is always changing in the light of new-found knowledge. Is that right Zack?"

"Yes, it's sad Tooky," said Zack. "Because the most important elements of life cannot be scientifically proven. They are simply intangible like thoughts, Time and Space. When we speak of what science and logic have contributed—their value is beyond our comprehension. This

Lexcraft is an example of it; but, we also have to keep in mind the design of the new Tesla propulsion system. It was NOT based on logic or any scientificallly proven principles; and as you know, it really rattled the scientists and engineers at Rat-Star. Tesla does not invent things; he discovers and applies as yet unknown principles! If we get Tesla going on this—we'll all get dizzy!"

In typical rabbit excitement Tooky chortled in delight. "But first I'll quadruple my brain neurons and wait for my brain to finish its 'new-design' thing, and complete its change of shape." Zack smiled at Tooky in complete agreement.

Rudy-Rat quietly said, "Zack, you were saying the other day that you felt sure that humans exist on other planets. Where did that come from?"

"That's true," Zack said, "but most Humans would call it speculation, and maybe they'd be right! But where it says in the Bible that Jesus will send his angels, and shall gather together His elect from the four winds, from the farthest bounds of the earth to the farthest bounds of heaven—it sort of sounds like Jesus is not just speaking of those on our planet. I remember in another place, He said He'd gather His elect from the four winds—even from one end of the Universe to the other—not just from one end of the earth to the other—the Universe!" Zack met Rudy's eyes in recall; "Oh! And how about when Jesus said, 'And other sheep I have, which are not of this fold; them also I must BRING'. Note Rudy, they have to be brought. If they are already here—how could you possibly bring them? Further if you're going to 'bring them', the question arises—from where?"

Silence reigned for a full minute before Zack exclaimed, "Hey! Rudy! Look! We're in familiar galactic territory!"

Further discussion ceased as they quickly brought dawn with them on the final approach to Earth. The little blue home-planet filled the whole crew with awe and excitement. Their waiting came down to a mere matter of minutes, then moments; and quite suddenly the massive space-ship silently touched down in Hill-Clan territory. Tooky had climbed up on Zack's shoulder and nuzzled his ear. The crew looked at each other, and finally after several minutes of hesitation Rudy said, "Okay, let's venture out." They collected up their gear and stepped onto the soft turf among the daisies, cowslips and buttercups. Immediately, all the rabbits joyously hopped, leapt and frisked around in their old familiar meadow. Scruff however, stayed by the space-craft and just surveyed the scene.

Zack strolled down to the same crystal clear waters of the creek, and glanced across at the ancient Oak where he had once lived. He walked up to it and perceived that the hole which was the entrance to his former home was very small. Or, had Zack grown bigger?

Kotar, Tesla, Boofy, Bifflets, Timken and Tooky checked out the burrows. There was no sign of Simbala. All they saw was a strange rabbit tribe. It was evident that neither of the groups knew each other. The new owners of the old burrows appeared to be quite scared of the Space-Crew and especially of the massive space-craft. They found Rudy—the golden Space-Rat—to be even scarier.

It was little Tooky who 'broke the ice'. He being the smallest among the rabbits, they were not fearful of him. Tooky approached an Elder Rabbit and introduced himself and the crew. Other senior rabbits gathered around, and as they discussed things generally; it became evident that the Space-Rabbits were creatures of legend. It seemed that some years had passed since their departure, but the story of the Space-Rabbits had been passed down from one generation to another right up until today.

The new Hill-Clan rabbits were at first very apprehensive of Zack and Rudy-Rat. They were so much larger than they and totally different. Rudy spoke to them soothingly in his magical 'wind-chimes' voice. They saw his wonderful eyes flash in different colors as he addressed them, and became more enthralled than fearful.

To further break the ice, Rudy asked one of the smaller rabbits to jump up, and he would take him for a flight, a ride to the creek and back. It was Trixie, a cute little female rabbit that took Rudy up on his offer. All the Clan gathered round as Rudy took off. Trixie squeaked with both fear and delight, and when she returned, it was Tooky who helped her down. He loved the feel of her fur, and the look in her soft eyes. When she looked directly at him, he dropped his head bashfully. Poor Tooky's heart pounded and he was overcome with strange feelings—but they were feelings he liked. Zack and Rudy winked at each other as Tooky and Trixie hopped over to her burrow to meet with her family. In the meantime, Rudy took a few more of the smaller rabbits for a round trip to the creek and back.

By this time the whole tribe had joined in the strange reunion. It was a celebration of a type never seen before. Rudy got in touch with his Dad, Captain Ratto, and Ratfink his brother. It was arranged that they both join them on the Lexcraft to make further plans.

Tesla had gone into a big patch of cowslips and was busy feeding in a little clearing to one side of the celebrations, when a weasel showed up like a flitting shadow along the hedgerow. Tesla had become so fearless with what he had been through on Ektar, that he sort of dismissed the weasel from his mind. Then he recalled Captain Betaka's words about not being able to 'weasel out' of certain situations. To the weasel's surprise, Tesla did not freeze in terror whilst the weasel killed him with a deep bite behind an ear—Tesla merely looked at him almost in curiosity.

He waited till the weasel was directly in front of him; then merely pulled out his laser-gun which was still strapped to him from the Beetle and the Ektapod encounter—and vaporized the weasel! The weasel's mate hidden in the grass fled in terror. A rabbit had the audacity and ability to make a weasel disappear! The incredible news spread like a wild grass-fire through the kingdom of the weasels, and far beyond. What if a new world-order had been established?

Tesla went back to feeding, but was surrounded by the Hill-Clan rabbits who wanted to know how he had made the weasel 'disappear'. Rudy stepped in to explain. Rudy also announced he was going to drop the Ektar-craft invisibility shields, but warned the Clan of its location so they'd not run into it accidentally.

Zack went back to the creek and did his usual skinny-dipping and drying off in the sun. He lay under the birches thinking of the giant Praying Mantis, the Ektapods, Beetles and the terrible Spider-Animals. Zack relaxed completely. He had no enemies here except those of his own kind; Man, who lived below in the village of Woodbury which he planned to visit.

Meantime Scruff remained with the Ektar space-craft. He needed an in-depth discussion with Zack on his spiritual beliefs. Zack's origin and brain design, spoke of immense but latent powers awaiting activation. Scruff decided to stay on Earth for a while and to make Zack his primary Braktor research project.

Zack was mentally readying himself for the Woodbury mission, and outlined his plan to Rudy, who agreed to hide out not too far away in case Zack was subjected to some man-made calamity and needed to be rescued.

Zack had decided to sell his seven-inch blade knife and pay for a haircut and shave. He had never shaved before. He thought that his long-haired unshaven appearance would attract too much attention in the village. He did not realize that haircut or not, eyes would follow him wherever he went. It was in his lithe buoyant stride and the way he confidently carried himself; as if he were able to handle almost any challenge that might arise. He also needed to adjust to being surrounded by humans. What strange animals! What did they think about? Why did they live the way they did?

Zack had difficulty in focusing on men as humans. They were quite different from rabbits, or mice, or the golden-furred flying Space-Rats from Rat-Star. He smiled to himself, and murmured, "Remember—men do not think like rabbits!"

Slowly, Zack ambled in to a local newspaper and magazine store, primarily to get the date and time for his Rolex. He reached for the daily paper and tears came to his eyes as well as shock, when he realized that a number of Earth years had passed since the Lexcraft had taken off, but he had only aged about seven years, making him about twenty years old. But according to the papers, about thirty-five years had gone by. No wonder the Hill-Clan they once knew were no longer in existence.

When his walk brought a barbershop into view, Zack entered and asked the young hairdresser if he knew where he might sell his knife to get a shave and a haircut. The young barber was struck by the mystery that Zack presented. His shaggy sun-bleached hair and direct blue-eyed stare aroused his curiosity. Where did he come from? He'd never been seen in Woodbury before. On that note, he agreed to both the shave and the haircut in exchange for the knife. Another thing that captured the barber's attention was Zack's beautiful and rather expensive Rolex Submariner. His shorts and shirt also appeared to be of a weave and type of material he'd never encountered before. Zack was somewhat evasive when it came to specific details of where he'd come from, apart from saying he'd worked on a farm for a long while and was here in the village to explore and locate an old friend. When the haircut and shave was completed and Zack looked in the mirror, he blushed at what he saw. It was a total transformation. He was most pleased and thanked the young barber profusely, who in turn refused to accept his knife as payment and said, "It's on the house."

Outside on the street, Zack blinked in the bright sun as he looked at the Village stores and older homes. He glanced into the store windows at merchandise in addition to his own reflection. He smiled. What he saw was what the villagers saw; a tall, good looking young man, slim, with muscular build and a shock of beautifully groomed sun-bleached golden hair. His eyes were startlingly blue and spoke of experiences beyond his years.

He strode with strength and purpose. In the village park Zack sat on a bench for a while to watch the ducks and the little humans feeding them. He kept seeing the Flower-Meadow and Ektar, and only slowly did he adjust to the reality of where he was in the Universe. Finally he resumed his mission and hurried back to where he had left Rudy behind a haystack.

"Wow!" exclaimed Rudy, "What a change, now I can see what you really look like!"

"I feel so good too, Rudy, and I didn't have to sell my knife. The young barber said it was on the house! I guess now we're back I have to find money and buy food or I'll starve!"

"Something like that," Rudy agreed. "Anyway, let's go back and see what is happening. By the way, I don't think Tesla should go around zapping weasels with his laser gun! Hey! Did you see little Tooky fall like a ton of bricks for that cute Trixie rabbit?"

"I sure did Rudy, I hope he's happy and settles down. They'll have cute little bunnies and a raft of Space-Rabbit stories to tell them! I think he'll survive very well with his training and also his natural intuitive abilities. As we know, he can pick up thought images from those around him. That is quite an asset and adds to his maturity."

When Zack and Rudy returned to the Hill-Clan location, they found a number of celebrations underway. Boofy, Bifflets, and Timken had quickly followed Tooky's lead and found mates. Scruff did not have mating on his mind. He was already immersed in understanding planet Earth, and if anything had become more 'Tesla-like' in many ways. Everyone else was ecstatically happy; after all, it's not every day that Hill-Clan bunnies marry real Space-Rabbits!

Kotar, Tesla and Scruff preferred to stay alone, pretty much as they had done previously, mainly acting as Elder Advisor Rabbits. All the young rabbits looked with awe at Kotar's patch of black and white stripes caused by the terrible yellow acid-saliva from the 'Spider-Animals'. It was a special honor just to touch Kotar's patch and to hear of the battle with the Arachnids. All during the long winter nights coming up, Space-Rabbit stories would be told and retold. They would also be passed down from generation to generation.

"I have to find my brother," said Zack to Rudy. "I really don't know as yet what I can do, or want to do. I keep thinking of going back to Rat-Star with you Rudy."

Rudy thought for a moment or two, "It would not work out Zack. I know you'd love to see how we live and what we do, but we have to face the inevitable, which is sex. You're at an age now as a young man when you'll think of nothing but sex! It's the way young men and Space-Rats are designed!

We have the same situation on Rat-Star. But no one on Earth or Rat-Star will approve a relationship between a Man, and a Flying Yellow-Furred female Space-Rat!" Rudy laughed, as did Zack.

"But I know what you mean. You need to continue the friendship we've developed and the brotherly love that has sprung up between us. I feel it too. We enjoy each other's company. We can still have adventures by arranging visits. I'm sure you'll land up on Rat-Star sometime! Rudy looked fondly at Zack. "I love you Zack, for all that you were—and what you have become."

"Thanks Rudy, it's exactly as it is between us. We're very good friends. We could hardly be otherwise with all that we've been through together. I need to hug you Rudy, and ruffle your yellow fur!" Rudy laughed as they embraced, and Zack shed involuntary tears.

"Who would have thought that since you discovered me crawling around eating wild strawberries that we would land up as fellow space-travelers," said Zack.

Just then, little Tooky and his bride Trixie met up with Zack and Rudy. They had much the same question, namely, when would they see each other again. In theend all the

Space-Rabbits along with Rudy and Zack agreed on regular meetings once or twice a year, and this would include visits to Rat-Star.

Early next morning Captain Ratto and Ratfink arrived and joined Rudy in a long session of 'catching-up'. It was such pleasure for the Space-Rabbits and Zack to interact with Ratto and Ratfink again. Zack wondered why life could not always be friendly. Here on Earth this small group had interacted in interstellar relationships involving Rat-Star and Ektar. No one thought of war and killing and taking unfair advantage of each other. All was peaceful and respectful, except for the problems they'd encountered on Ektar.

Although the three Space-Rats were readying for departure to Rat-Star, they had not forgotten the weird EGR sealed and awaiting analysis by Rat-Star engineers. Despite this, they were insistent on holding off until Zack had located and contacted his brother Brett.

Rudy said he had recorded Zack's brain frequency and would tune in during the course of each day. In the event that Zack needed help or rescuing, Rudy assured him they would bring the Lexcraft over to pick him up.

Zack slept under the birches that night and Tooky came to see him and stay over. Both of the space-travelers were softly 'leaf-whispered' to sleep. Life was as perfect as it could be.

In the morning Tooky dashed off to keep company with Trixie; and Zack, after saying Good Bye to the Rats and several of their Space-Rabbit crew, set off for the village. He planned to make enquiries of several sources that may have been connected to his brother's transfer to yet another foster home. It did not take long for the word to get around the village, and they assumed he must be a grandson looking for Brett.

Zack was able to sell his knife and round up enough money in order to eat, and that first night on his village expedition, he slept under a haystack in a nearby meadow. He bought food supplies rather than eat in cafes, although the wonderful smell of home cooking nearly changed his mind on two occasions.

Early next morning found Zack walking up the nearly deserted village main street, and he was captured by the smell of hot ham, eggs and hash browns. The aroma of fresh coffee finally forced him to capitulate and he consumed a big breakfast. Funds were very low.

As Zack got up from his table and was sliding his chair back, a sun-tanned older fellow walked slowly over to him. He looked Zack over from head to toe, and said, "If it were not for your youth, I could swear that you were a younger version of a good friend I had some years ago, a fellow by the name of Brett.

We chummed around for a while when he was in his late teens, and then one day he sort of disappeared. Of course I could be wrong, but there was something about his eyes that you have too! Sorry to get so personal, but are you connected to Brett in any way?

"Yes, we are connected," said Zack, his eyes widening in surprise, "But it's a long story. Matter of fact I came here to start tracking him down. That will be quite a job after a thirty-odd year lapse!"

What did you say your name was?" the man queried.

"Zack," said Zack.

"Yes! It's coming back to me now, he had a brother named Zack who was also in a foster home and later on I heard he'd run away and was never seen again.

Of course you're too young to be him, but I'll give you a hand anyway." He looked Zack over from head to toe. "My name's Will, William actually, but Brett always called me Willie! You can too if you wish!"

"Thanks Willie," said Zack smiling. When Zack smiled, his face lit up in a way that is rarely seen. It was a little like a powerful light beam that emanated from his startlingly blue eyes, and encompassed his whole face in a projection of love and good will.

Zack had not interacted with humans, especially of his age group for what had turned out to be about seven years. He was devoid of facades and uncontaminated with the devious and convoluted thinking of the average man. He was, in a manner of speaking, 'brand new'!

Zack felt like he was in a dream as he followed Willie out of the café. "Where do we start?" he asked.

"Let's try the Government offices first. Of course they might have destroyed all the old records from that far back." And so started the long, tiring search from office to office and by the end of the day, they were both quite tired. "By the way, where are you staying?" Willie asked, glancing up at him.

"I'm not," replied Zack, "I'll probably find shelter close to a haystack someplace!"

"I won't hear of it! You'll stay with me. It's not much of a place but it's better than a haystack!" So Zack accompanied his new friend Willie home, which turned out to be a quaint little cottage with a thatched roof. The name 'Honeysuckle Cottage' was carved on an ornate wooden sign. Zack smiled in anticipation. Cool air greeted them when the door was opened, and Zack also breathed the fragrance of roses by the front door. The ceilings were low, and everything was spotlessly clean and meticulously laid out, in fact everything had a 'cared for' touch.

Willie smiled at Zack. He had nice white even teeth. "There's no place like home!" he exclaimed. Zack immediately went over to investigate the bookshelves while Willie said something about making a good pot of tea.

Truly, Zack had not read a book for several years. It seemed that he needed to lick up words like they were raindrops in the desert. There were many volumes he discovered that he'd like to dig into, but in the end he selected one that seemed to match-up with his current thoughts.

Slipping off his runners, Zack lay out full length and sank into the soft old sofa. He relaxed with a book he'd chosen entitled, 'Walden', by Thoreau, but in a matter of moments the little volume slipped from his fingers and he fell fast asleep.

Willie shuffled in with Zack's tea, and took in the whole situation. Picking up the book, he studied the youthful form before him. It always seemed to him that when people slept they left their fears and troubles behind which caused them to look much younger. Willie allowed his eyes to trespass on Zack's boyish young face. He felt the innocence, purity and vulnerability of this questing youth, and dared to even think of him as angelic of countenance. Willie placed a light blanket over Zack and returned to the kitchen to sip thoughtfully at his tea.

The first stars plotted their course in the early evening sky and a bright moon appeared. Willie listened to the bats squeaking, while an owl hooted from deep within the adjacent woodland. Before he turned in for the night, he took a final peek at Zack who was lying in peaceful repose sound asleep. "Thank you Lord," said Willie, "For gifting me with Zack's visit."

Slowly the moonbeams illuminated the old cottage, furniture creaked, mice skittered around, the stars revolved as they had for eons, and night magic bid farewell to yet another day as it vanished into eternity.

KeKe — A sensitive fun loving rabbit. KeKe brings a touch of 'home' wherever he is!

Chapter Eleven

Zack awoke with a start; he'd forgotten where he was. Then he felt the warmth and softness of the old sofa and remembered Willie. He smiled. The enticing smells of fresh coffee and bacon wafted from the kitchen. He sprang to his feet and found Willie flipping blueberry pancakes. Zack's mouth watered at the thought of pancakes, syrup and bacon. He found it hard to believe that everything to do with eating from now on would be handled in an entirely different way!

Willie gave Zack a delighted grin. "Good morning young Sir!" he exclaimed. "First I'll let you visit the bathroom where you can take a nice hot bath. Throw your clothes outside the door and I'll pop them in the washing machine!"

"Good morning to you Willie!" enthused Zack. "Boy! Did I sleep well!" His smile seemed to illuminate the whole room. It had a quality of being both expressive and expansive.

"Tell you what Zack, breakfast is just about ready to serve, why don't you just do minor ablutions and we'll eat first!" suggested Willie.

Zack scampered away. He had a wonderful 'home' type feeling. No threats, no dangers, no alien creatures, just a good friend and the 'chore' of gobbling up piles of luscious food. He returned in a few minutes to find Willie filling their mugs with scalding hot coffee. He watched the rising steam in fascination.

They both dug in without delay. Zack liked the way Willie looked. He was slim, trim, clean, neat, and he spoke in a manner that suggested he'd been exposed to a good education. The man and the cottage both had 'character', and his cooking skills topped everything off in style.

After a few breaks in the task of making blueberry pancakes disappear like magic, Zack asked Willie whether he'd care to enlarge on his connection with Brett.

Zack then discovered that Willie had never married or had kids and was sort of a 'loner'. He felt drawn to a special something about Willie. It invited trust and loyalty. It epitomized the man known as Willie, and Zack thought that if Brett had chummed around with him—then he must be quite a first class type of being.

As Willie refilled their coffee mugs, he smiled and looked across at Zack with warm expectancy. "I want to hear all about your adventures Zack. When our eyes meet, I can feel you searching. You need to get a lot off your mind! I hope you'll find that I'm worthy of that trust."

"I do," said Zack. "But it'll take a lot of time."

"Take all the time you need Zack, I've nothing planned. Take the whole day or the whole week!" he smiled warmly at Zack.

Of all things, at the precise moment that Zack looked across at Willie to start his Space-Rabbit saga, he burst into tears. He did not know why. He shook and cried uncontrollably and staggered into the living room with hoarse cries of psychic hurt and pain, where he collapsed onto the sofa. He pounded the cushions again and again, but he could not regain control.

Willie was quite taken aback at the turn of events, and tears escaped his eyes as he followed Zack. He felt emotionally afloat with him like they were both in a raging, violent storm at sea. He longed to reach out and to hold the kid, and soothe him; but his maturity and experience in dealing with life's situations forbade him to do so until the storm had somewhat subsided.

Gradually Zack ceased his heaving and shaking and though still sobbing pushed himself into a sitting position on the sofa. Somewhat shamefacedly he turned to Willie, who passed him a clean, folded blue and white handkerchief.

"I'm sorry Willie! I just can't help it," spluttered Zack as he unfolded the hanky. "Thanks Willie. The saga is so great, the terrible abuse at the foster home, my hiding out in the woods, the rabbits, the yellow-furred flying space-rats, the Black-Rabbits of Ektar, the alien creatures, the Lexcraft space-ship!" Zack cried helplessly, waving his arms around almost in desperation. Willie's eyes opened wider in both horror and amazement, but he quickly brought his facial expressions under control.

"Tears are the gift of healing Zack, whether we're twenty, fifty or seventy. They're natural and human," said Willie in a soothing low key voice.

It seemed that Zack's expressive blue eyes held Willie's in mute appeal to bridge a gap into intimacy of understanding. He was in all innocence appealing for love to fill the vast void that he'd experienced for so long.

Zack needed human-bonding rather than rabbit-bonding to move forward in life. He did not understand why he was so tearful, other than that another human's loving concern for him had caused his emotional collapse. It was devastating to him that an unknown fear should strip him down to total vulnerability born out of some hidden need.

Slowly Willie sat beside Zack and put his arm around him allowing Zack's slim form to fall into his arms where he clung and wept in abject surrender. He wept at sadness, to loneliness, but most of all for the warmth, touching, and love he'd never known till now. It was new, warm and strangely beautiful. Willie held Zack silently, closely and firmly. He also struggled to withhold his own tears.

After a while, Zack calmed down and sat up heaving a huge sigh. He had founded a fragile foundation of intimacy and trust. It felt very good. When Willie had released his 'adopted son', he knew his own needs had also been met. He had established a family. On Zack's part he had to almost convince himself that he was not a rabbit, and he no longer wished to be a yellow-furred flying space-rat. He just wanted to be what he was; Zack, a twenty year old kid with his life stretching out before him.

"I think I'll take that bath now," said Zack smiling almost apologetically.

"Welcome home Zack," said Willie. "I hope you'll stay for a while, I want to hear the whole Space-Rabbit saga!"

Willie was surprised that Zack only had socks, shorts and a shirt, all of which were woven and formed out of a material he'd never come across before. He dropped them in the washing machine. Zack luxuriated in a hot bath with bubble soap and a short time later stepped out squeaky-clean. He wrapped a bath towel around him and emerged to find that Willie had this clothing in the dryer.

"My clothes will take only one to two minutes to dry," he told Willie. "It's a fabric they create on the planet Ektar. It comes clean almost instantly on contact with water whether hot or cold. It's amazing stuff." Willie immediately stopped the dryer and retrieved Zack's clothes; and passing them to him exclaimed, "These clothes came from another planet?" Willie was awe stricken.

Zack showed Willie the unusual weave and feeling of the material. Oh! I almost forget. This clothing also automatically compensates for changes in temperature. If it gets cold it warms up and vice versa!"

"Astounding," exclaimed Willie as he led the way to the back door. "I'm going to put on some tea and we'll sit in the back yard and hear your full story. We'll track Brett down tomorrow. I have a hunch he's not more than about sixty miles away."

"Oh! Fantastic," said Zack.

What Willie called the 'back yard' was a very private site comprising some five acres of land. The cottage stood by itself well off the roadway and was accessed by a short winding pathway all bordered with tall trees back and front. The grassy area was white with wild clover, and a short way from the back door was a huge clump of honeysuckle in full bloom. Oaks, Beeches and Silver Birches dominated the area. Toward the rear of the huge garden with its vegetable patch, ran a clear little creek. It burbled its course through the lilac bushes and disappeared into the woodland beyond.

Zack and Willie relaxed into comfortable outside chairs, and when Willie brought out the tea, he looked expectantly at Zack.

"Yes!" said Zack. "It's time to tell quite a story, though it's mainly about rabbits, Space-Rabbits that is!" He smiled one of his delightful smiles that seemed to bestow life-giving properties on those who received them. Willie thrived on Zack's smiles. He found Zack's youth to be reminiscent of his own and yearned to help him more. Indeed, his own youth was as of yesterday it seemed, and he wondered what had happened to all the in-between years.

Over the entire day and well into the evening Zack told Willie of his adventures. Willie was enthralled. Sometimes they took a short walk along the woodland trails while Zack's tales unfolded, and when they came to a small lake it seemed quite natural for them to go for a swim.

Already Zack had become to Willie the son he'd never had and often wished for, and found that he loved him without reserve. Willie was also wise enough to know that love does not hold or restrict, it releases and does not imprison. Love grows when it is free to come and to go.

Zack and Willie walked slowly in the twilight back to the cottage. Pheasants called, and the first bats flitted low in the evening sky to start their nightly onslaught on the insect population. Just as they reached the cottage, a nightingale burst into full song, and Zack was filled with joy as he scented the honeysuckle while stepping up to the Cottage door.

Willie showed Zack to the bedroom he'd assigned him. "This is your own private domain Zack. It's also your den, retreat, or whatever you want to make it." He paused and smiled at Zack who in turn gave Willie a quick hug.

"Thanks Willie," said Zack gratefully. "It's just beautiful!" He stepped to the lead-paned window and gently opening it discovered it was the window to the right of the front door. The fragrance of honeysuckle reached Zack and as always he closed his eyes in bliss.

A short while later they both sat down to a good supper of steak and ale pies, with garlic mashed potatoes and broccoli. Zack was also offered his first ever beer or ale, his choice. Zack then learnt the basics of handling liquor. He had much to learn as yet, both in matters of alcohol and sex, not having been in touch with other youths of his age group for several years. Willie felt like a father to Zack, and Zack responded accordingly.

After supper Zack relaxed with Willie and discussed how he might meet up with a young woman who wouldn't reduce him to tearful vulnerability. Whereas love and intimacy should cause him to open like a summer flower, Zack discovered that he 'froze' on contact with other humans. Male closeness invoked a special type of terror that went beyond 'freezing'. It was trauma-survival that had to be lived. Willie assured Zack that with females he simply had to be him; a good looking young man of some twenty summers. Zack almost smiled in relief.

Wille assured him that when the right young woman came along; her sensitivity would heal him and meet their every need. It would be the foundation for a wonderful future. This, Zack accepted, and thanked Willie for his input.

Willie and Zack retired for the night. Willie, feeling highly emotional over Zack's relationship problems withheld his tears; they never seemed to be far away. He was experiencing the unaccustomed joy of being a 'father' and loved every moment of it. His whole life had taken on new meaning and purpose.

Zack gazed through his window into the night sky while breathing deeply of the cool flower-scented air. He felt secure and could hardly contain his happiness at being back on Earth. There was his familiar Moon and the Big Dipper, and owls hooted in the woodland. Within his bedroom walls behind the wainscotting, Zack was delighted to hear the skittering and pattering of mice as they explored the cottage for their nightly feed. Zack heaved a sigh of relief; there were no threats, no insidious alien creatures waiting to discover him. A sense of absolute peace descended on Zack as he fell asleep.

Rudy had picked up on how well Zack was adapting to his new situation, and explained to Zack via mental relay that the space-craft would be leaving in a couple of days for Rat-Star. Zack then asked Rudy if it would be okay for Willie to meet him as well as the Space-Rabbit crew. Rudy had already scanned Willie's entire history, intent, purpose and life style, and was extremely pleased with the father-son relationship. He had no hesitation on agreeing with Zack's proposal.

Early next morning when Willie and Zack greeted the sunrise, Willie suggested that it was a day for shopping.

"I beg to disagree," said Zack firmly, "We have more important things to do!" He smiled.

"Such as?" questioned Willie.

"Well, some things are more important than other things on certain days for certain reasons," said Zack trying to be mysterious.

"I ask again, such as?" said Willie with just the faintest hint of challenge.

Zack smiled boldly at Willie with a mischievous blue eyed twinkle. "Well," he said, "It will happen today that one known as Willie, is to meet Rudy the yellow-furred flying space-rat, his father Captain Ratto and his brother Ratfink.

He will also meet the space-rabbits Kotar, Tesla, Scruff, Tooky, Timken, Boofy and Bifflets; and some wives of said rabbits whom I have not met as yet, although I've met Tooky's Trixie." Willie gasped in surprise.

"You'll also see the Lexcraft space-ship which belongs to the Black-Rabbits of Ektar. As you know, the original Black-Rabbit crew all died on the way back to Earth. It was a sad affair! The Lexcraft people on Rat-Star will be returning the space-ship to Ektar. That is being arranged."

"You really mean that?" said Willie in delighted disbelief, "really?"

"Yes! Really! The Rat-Star group is returning to home base in two days, and they agreed that it's okay for you to come and visit before they leave. By the way, you'll recall the Space-Rats have access to our entire brain memory-content, even from Rat-Star, their home planet. You've already been scanned and our relationship has been approved!" Zack chuckled. "However, you realize we must never tell another living soul about this except for Brett.

I also have news of Brett! Rudy-Rat has found Brett and has already scanned him! Brett is a lot older than *I am,* probably about your age as you were both young teenagers together. My age will be a shock to Brett, especially as he thinks I'm dead! He feels that if I were alive I would have found him and arranged to get together sometime. So we'll have to be careful how we handle this. We must also remember to take along some extra handkerchiefs!"

Willie flopped onto the sofa. It was almost more than he could handle. "Tell me Zack, where is he?" he asked quietly.

"He's in a little town called Sooketon; it's about seventy-seven miles from here!"

"Oh! My God! I've been through that little place a number of times! Wow! I'll see Brett again, and we'll all be together! How can life be so good?"

"Only God is good," replied Zack.

Immediately after breakfast, Willie and Zack took a shortcut around the end of the village, mainly to avoid raised eyebrows and questions. It was quite a trek, and Rudy was aware of their progress. Willie kept looking at Zack as though to say 'I don't believe it, show me!' But as they approached the meeting place, they saw that the whole Hill-Clan had turned out for the occasion.

Right at the front were the Rat-Star Rats, followed by the Space-Rabbit crew including Scruff; then the new wives of the space-rabbits, then the Elders and the rest of the Hill-Clan.

Before they got introductions going Willie just stared, because behind the groups, there, looming up in awesome proportions out of the remaining early morning mist was the magnificent Lexcraft space-ship! It was indeed massive and 'other-worldly' in its whole design and presence. Willie was totally stunned by its huge slowly revolving crystal 'rings of fire'. It seemed to span galaxies by appearance alone.

Zack broke the spell, introductions were made, and the whole group intermingled. Willie had more evidence of Zack's adventures than he could comfortably contain. The whole scene left him in a trance of believability, but he survived. It was the highlight of his entire life.

Ratfink and Rudy took Zack for a brief walk on a woodland trail in order to talk privately. Although the space-rats were current with Zack's experiences, they needed to check out his current plans. They were however, highly concerned with Zack's contribution to Scruffy's Braktor 'Brain' Project. Both of the golden-rats requested to be kept 'in the loop' while discoveries were made.

To this Zack agreed. He said that for Scruff to gain true analysis of Zack's supposed 'latent-powers'—Scruff himself would have to become a Faith-filled Christian. Of course, if he were already involved with a counterfeit power that believed that all power originated with 'self' and not God—that would develop into an interesting situation. "You'll recall" said Zack, "That my Faith is founded on the belief that, 'everything comes from God—nothing comes from me'." After several more minutes of discussion, the three friends rejoined the main celebration group.

It was a perfect day—not a sign of a weasel, and they learned later that Tooky had laser-gunned a hawk that was about to snatch Bifflets just the day before. So the whole Clan gathering affair was in an uproar with little bunnies frisking everywhere, pretending they were space-rabbits. Celebrations continued throughout the day. Never had there been so much squeaking, frisking, leaping and hopping around. But like all good things—they do come to an end.

Eventually, Zack and Willie had to head down the trail toward home, but not before Tooky had a super snuggling and nuzzling session with Zack, who promised they would have other meetings. In the meantime he explained that Tooky could hardly be lonely with little Trixie by his side; especially as a bunch of baby bunnykins could well show up in the near future.

Before they all went their various ways, Rudy ordered that the laser guns be returned to the space-ship as they were the property of the Black-Rabbits of Ektar. Having retrieved the weapons, Rudy stored them onboard and performed his regular duties. Everything that Zack had told Willie as he had replayed his adventures in outer-space were validated. So great was his excitement that at times Willie forgot to breathe! It was now okay to do so.

Willie shook hands with the three Space-Rats and felt as good about them as did Zack. He especially was attracted to Rudy-Rat and felt deep satisfaction in knowing that Zack had such true and loyal friends—despite their quite different appearance as compared to Humans. Little Tooky just left him speechless with amazement; he'd never sensed such close understanding with an 'animal'.

Willie and Zack then headed home down the trail to the village of Woodbury. Rudy once again dropped the invisibility shields, and all the Hill-Clan turned in for the night.

Willie and Zack were mostly silent all the way home to the Cottage. They just fell into reviewing what had happened all day. Just before they disappeared into the privacy of their bedrooms, Zack turned to Willie and thanked him most profusely for all he had done, and Willie with tears in his eyes embraced the youngster with a surging love he'd never felt before. The feelings were mutual, and Willie was left reeling from a type of joy he could hardly comprehend.

In his own room, Willie murmured "Heavenly Father I thank you for Zack in the name of the Lord Jesus Christ." He lay awake for a while counting his blessings and good fortune, and fell asleep thinking of Brett's face on seeing the two of them tomorrow.

Even after he was in bed Zack could not think of sleep, so he slipped on his navy shorts, fastened on his runners and quietly left the Cottage. He walked slowly into the night toward the woodland. The pathway was deeply shadowed but moonlight illuminated the trees.

The air smelled of damp earth and was richly scented with the smell of ferns and other vegetation. A soft warm breeze ruffled his hair. He breathed deeply. "Life is good!" he exclaimed.

On the edge of the woods a hay field was also bathed in magical moonlight. A haystack was forming and would be completed and thatched in a few days. He saw rabbits in the lower part of the meadow. Zack delighted in the smell of new hay, and climbing up on the stack, he lay in a little hollow to watch the stars and listen to the night birds. He felt as one with the whole wild world. It caused him to surge with elation.

As he relaxed and became a little sleepy, a small rustling sound came to his attention with several small movements in the hay. He raised himself, and as he did so—it was Tooky who jumped on him, followed by Timken and Bifflets. Zack laughed aloud and snuggled all three.

They explained they had followed him home so they would know where he lived and could come to visit him.

Tooky had seen Zack leave the house and joined by Timken and Bifflets they had followed him to the haystack. Zack felt wonderfully 'at home'. He was still living as a 'wild boy' surrounded by somewhat remote woodland, and with three of his best friends. He pulled some hay over him and fell into a deep sleep. As usual Tooky's ears rested on his cheek, and Zack smiled sleepily as they all snuggled down for the night. An aura of great happiness fell upon the haystack. Even the stars seemed to smile in cosmic joy.

Morning came almost too quickly. Zack snuggled and kissed the bunnies and saw them on their way back to Hill-Clan country. He told Tooky that as soon as he was settled in his plans he would be in touch with him and the others at their home base.

He did not want them exposed to predators unnecessarily. It was also his final warning as they parted. "Be predator aware!" Zack smiled as they scampered away.

He returned to the Cottage and Willie saw him arrive. He greeted Zack with a cheery "Good Morning," as Zack headed for the bathroom to shower for the day ahead. Willie did not comment on the rabbit fur and hay clinging to him.

As they had breakfast, looking fondly at Zack, Willie said, "Before we get our bus tickets to Sooketon and go looking for Brett, let's first shop in the village and get clothing for you. We don't have to come back to the Cottage and you may change in the store if you so wish."

"Sounds great!" replied Zack. He had feelings of tension and excitement for what he would face as the day unfolded its adventures among humankind.

In the village they quietly entered a mens' clothing store. Willie said that if questions arose as to whom he was, just to explain that he was a visiting grandson, and give no more details. This was Zack's first shopping expedition. Not that they 'shopped' anyway, it just being one store. But it was Zack's first experience of its type.

Zack selected undershorts, socks, and four shirts. Next came two pairs of long pants, a wind-breaker and a rain jacket. He also picked up two more pairs of navy blue shorts, and settled on extra footwear with New Balance runners, and a pair of light hiking boots that gave excellent ankle support.

When he was through, Willie threw on the pile a dozen handkerchiefs and met Zack's eyes with a smile. The store owner was very pleased with the large order, and asked Zack to select anything he liked that caught his fancy. "It's on the house!" he exclaimed as he admired Zack's physique.

Zack was surprised and looked at Willie, who nodded his approval with a huge smile. Zack had forgotten belts, so he selected two high quality cowhide belts to complete his order. However, he decided not to change, but just wear his usual Ektar attire; he wanted to be very comfortable without 'breaking-in' new clothing, especially footwear. When Willie had shaken hands with the store owner, he asked him if they could leave their packages for pick-up in a day or two as they were not returning home right away.

So Zack's new attire was put into safe storage until he would call for it. They then left to acquire tickets for Sooketon, and while they were waiting at the Bus Depot Willie slipped Zack a handful of paper money notes and having time to spare, explained to Zack the vagaries of money and cash-flow. This was difficult for Zack to grasp, but realizing the value of what he'd been given, he sealed it safely in a pocket.

They only had to wait for half an hour, and Zack used this time to study the 'Humans', as he called them. They were all different in a way he could not as yet categorize. Then, once on board, the bus flowed smoothly and swiftly through the lush green hills to locate Brett.

Both Willie and Zack read a magazine and a newspaper that had been left by a previous traveler, and in a couple of hours they stepped off the bus. Both felt apprehension as Willie headed for a phone booth to search for Brett in the local directory.

'I'd almost forgotten that you're both Michaelsons," said Willie. "How does that sound, Zack Michaelson and Brett Michaelson? Did you also almost forget your real name?"

"Yes!" said Zack." It has a nice sound to it. I'm Zack Michaelson!" he laughed.

"Ah!" exclaimed Willie. "I think we have him. Take this address down. We won't call him, we'll just show up. It's Saturday and he'll likely be home!"

Next they dropped into a Chamber of Commerce office to pick a local map of the area, and in no time at all had located Brett's place of residence. It was within a half hour walking distance, and after a quick coffee they set out to complete their mission.

Brett's home was a small detached house with loads of hollyhocks in the front flower beds. It was Zack who released the large brass door knocker and stepped back.

Footsteps sounded from within. When the door was opened, there to Willie, was an older version of what Zack would probably look like in the years ahead. The same bright penetrating blue eyes and open honest smile of welcome, even to apparent strangers.

"Good morning," said Brett looking at them both inquisitively, "What can I do for you gentlemen?" Zack and Willie looked at him appraisingly.

Just a moment," exclaimed Brett, "Don't I know you?" he said looking at Willie.

'You sure do Brett! It's me! Willie from long ago! And this is a young friend of mine I want you to meet. He's actually more than a friend!"

"Oh! My God! Come in! Come in!" exclaimed Brett. No sooner were they in the living room when Brett hugged Willie real hard, and this found them in tears. They both asked the same question, "How many years has it been?"

Brett then turned to Zack, looking at him curiously. Willie held Brett's arm. "Now hang in there Brett, this'll knock your socks off! You'll probably collapse because it will take a lot of explaining! This kid IS your young brother, but don't try to make the age fit! We'll come to that later! This really is Zack, your young brother!"

Brett flumped onto the sofa in tears while holding his head and burying his face. "You are Zack?" he almost screamed. "I can't believe it! I thought you were dead long ago. How come you look like you're only eighteen or nineteen?"

"Actually I'm twenty," Zack spluttered. "But I am your young brother," He sat beside Brett who immediately embraced him in profound hysterical joy. Willie produced handkerchiefs all round. He'd come well prepared for this emotional upheaval.

"Oh! Brett!" exclaimed Zack, "it'll take some long explanations between Willie and me, but it's all true! I'm Zack Michaelson your kid brother!"

In the meantime Willie had observed a small liquor cabinet from which he hefted a large bottle of Grand Marnier, and grabbing some glasses from the kitchen he placed everything on the coffee table in front of the sofa. "I think we all need just a little snifter to settle us down," said Willie quietly.

Brett clung to Zack as though he might never let go, kissing his tanned wet salty cheeks, while at the same time trying to mop up his own face.

"You know Zack, I never married. I'm on my own. I have a little newsstand on the street that leads to the downtown area. I never thought I'd ever see you again. The years went by and I kept hoping. I believe your foster home background is similar to mine, we'll compare notes later!

Willie poured the fine liquor, and they sipped it slowly and gently while they all looked at each other.

"This must be one of the greatest days in my whole life," said Brett.

"But," said Willie, "We'll have to start the story from the beginning, so let us warn you right now, you'll hear some pretty astounding stuff, a lot of which is quite frankly, unbelievable! But since meeting Zack, and you'll hear all about that, I've been able to validate by personal experience everything you're going to hear!"

God! It can't be too soon for me!" exclaimed Brett. "But tell you what, why don't we all sit in the garden under the trees where it's very private and cool. By the way, that is the bathroom if anyone needs it," he said, pointing to a door to one side.

Zack headed for the little room. "Morning coffee disposal," he grinned. Willie and Brett went into the garden with their drinks and settled into easy chairs overhung by giant oaks. Red squirrels chased around among the branches.

"Willie, you old hound! How and where did you discover that handsome young kid whom you say is my brother?" said Brett. "Not 'say', he IS your brother, you'll only have to ask him a few questions before he relates his far-out adventures to prove beyond a shadow of doubt the truth of who he is! Who else would know of what you both went through before you were separated into different foster homes?" He lowered his voice, "Here he comes now."

Zack strode toward them carrying his drink. He moved with the easy lithe grace of youth whereby the earth seemed to rise to take his steps. His blond hair shone in the sunlight, his tanned well-muscled legs and slim build were a pleasure to see in motion. But it was Zack's all-encompassing smile and blue eyes which were the most arresting.

"Grab a seat Zack! Get yourself comfortable. I'll get us all some glasses of cold water first. Zack will want to wet his whistle as his adventures unfold!" Brett then fetched the water, and they both looked expectantly at Zack. The sky was a cloudless blue and a sense of serenity pervaded the whole garden and Zack inhaled some fragrance from nearby red roses.

"Brett," said Zack in his youthful resonance, "What you hear today must never be mentioned or alluded to in any way at any time! I will also tell you right now that your very thoughts are being monitored at this moment, as are Willie's and mine too!"

Brett's mouth dropped, "Okay, whatever you say Zack, I'm ready."

Willie turned to Brett, "It's a long story with many incredible adventures, so we might want to walk around a little too.

We'll take a lunch or other breaks as necessary and continue at any pace you like Brett. It's going to take the rest of today. If it's okay with you we'd like to stay over tonight, then tomorrow we can all make plans and so forth."

"No problem Willie, I see you have toiletry bags with you but little else, no matter, everything with go smoothly! Let's go Zack!"

The Space-Rabbit Saga commenced. It was of course interrupted throughout with questions from both Brett and Willie. A dramatic highlight was the battle with the Arachnids in the Flower Meadow, and Zack displayed his scarred left forearm and the tiny scar on his thigh. After lunch, they continued to move through the day as though they were in some kind of dream. It was a once-only experience.

Brett realized and accepted Zack as his brother, including his age which had come about as he became enmeshed in Einstein's relativity of time theory. Brett recognized he had much to learn about inter-planetary travel. It was a difficult concept to immediately comprehend.

"Were you away a little longer Zack, I would not be here. It's such an amazing universe," said Brett.

"Yes!" said Zack. "It's like little Squibby. I sort of expected to see him with Simbala, but they had long since been taken by 'Earth time' It's not easy to grasp!

The Bible says, and I think it refers to the cosmic time scale, that a thousand Earth years are the same as one cosmic day! That takes a lot to get one's brain around. It means that a man who's lived for sixty two and a half years on Earth has only existed for an hour and a half in 'cosmic time'. I worked it out!"

"What I find so wonderful Zack is that Tooky, Timken and Bifflets actually slept with you again last night!" said Brett, and Willie nodded.

The evening meal was slow roasted chicken, mashed potatoes and fresh garden peas. It was sumptuous. After supper Zack said he was pretty tired, especially after reliving the adventures he had experienced. Brett showed him to a small guest room, and equipped him with towels for the bathroom.

Willie and Brett settled into a discussion born out of a long-trusted relationship and agreed to meet on a regular basis. Willie explained that Zack had already expressed his wish to remain in the area of the Hill-Clan for the next few years or longer.

Willie confided in Brett that he wished to provide a home, like a father for Zack, if that were okay with Brett.

He then went on to explain how in the next couple of months he wanted to meet with Brett and his legal counsel to arrange upon his, Willie's death, for Zack to inherit the Honeysuckle Cottage property and what remained of his bank account. Both Brett and Willie were mature men of the world and perceived this to be an excellent plan as Willie had no immediate or close relatives of which he knew. It was also clearly evident that Willie had acquired a family; with which Brett was in complete agreement.

"In fact," stated Willie, "I don't think I should wait for months to do this, why don't we arrange for this in the next two weeks. You set up the appointment up with your law firm Brett. I also have to change my will around a bit in view of what has occurred."

Zack came out of the bathroom and bid Brett and Willie a good night and disappeared into his room. "Where am I going to sleep?" asked Willie.

"On the couch of course!" said Brett with a chuckle. The two friends stood looking at one another. "By God!" said Brett, "We're lucky to have each other and Zack."

Night fell with all three retiring with their private thoughts and feelings. Zack missed Tooky's silky ears and was surprised at how much he missed their nightly snuggling session.

Morning and the smell of bacon frying roused both Zack and Willie, and after morning ablutions, they joined Brett to slowly sip on his special strong coffee. It coursed through them and again raised their excitement level as they scanned in their minds what was taking place in their lives.

Breakfast was quite a satisfying spread; but more importantly, there was such a feeling of intimate camaraderie; it seemed to connect them in an unbreakablebond. The legal discussion of the night before was never referred to, but was firmly established in the minds of Brett and Willie.

Before they left for the bus-stop Willie had an opportunity to take Brett aside for a few moments. "Brett, we must never lose sight of the fact that Zack recognizes himself as a 'spiritual being'. He's young, but already his whole approach to God is not in 'religion', but in personal relationships with all three members of the Trinity. I was amazed! That's more than I can say about me! I only pick up my Bible a few times a year!"

Brett asked, "Which version of the Bible is Zack using Willie? There are so many these days."

"I think it's a new version with the old King James and the Amplified running side by side," replied Willie. "Boy! He's reading everything he can lay his hands on! He's not had a book to read since he was about thirteen! Poor kid! That's like being thirsty for seven years! Don't worry Brett, we'll nurture him, but it's probable that he'll teach us!"

"Thank God it's you Willie," said Brett. "Tell you what, I'm thinking of selling all my stuff and moving up closer to you. No need to be seventy miles away. We all have so much to share! Zack's an inter-planetary traveler too! I can hardly believe it!"

"Brett! Let's talk about this later. I have enough land at my place in Woodbury, and you could put up a small cottage in any one of several locations," Willie enthused.

Just then Zack joined them, and amid farewell hugs they parted. There were tears of happiness in the eyes of all three. The bus sped on its way. Zack and Willie returned to Honeysuckle Cottage after picking up Zack's clothes at the store.

When they arrived at the little thatched-roof cottage, Zack ran ahead and scampered up the pathway to drop off his packages. Willie saw the joy in Zack's face and felt a surging pang of love-pain for the wilding that almost split his chest in two. His life had been lonely for far too long. Although the Cottage was a base, Willie knew that Zack was really a wild creature who would never be tamed to the habits and practices of men. Money would be the least of his concerns and would not be an objective.

Zack ran down to the little creek, and as he passed the honeysuckle bushes he stopped to embrace them and deeply scented their fragrance. He sat on the creek bank thinking of the Hill-Clan bunnies, and became lost in thought.

On returning to the Cottage, he found Willie busy at making a good pot of tea. While the kettle was boiling, he hung his new clothing in the closet and before joining Willie for tea he put on undershorts for the first time in years. It seemed strange.

Then he decided to wear a pair of the new navy blue shorts and a soft rayon shirt; and although he'd not planned to go anywhere, he fitted on his new hiking boots to break them in comfortably. They were a perfect fit and he welcomed the support they gave his feet and ankles. After licking his comb through his golden locks a few times, he sauntered forth to join Willie for some tea.

He was mainly seeking approval from Willie, and certainly received it as Willie eyed him up and down. "Zack," he exclaimed, "you look super. If any girls see you, you'll be sunk!"

Zack blushed with confused thoughts of sex and its complications. Maybe it would happen to him like it had occurred with Tooky and Trixie. He hoped so. At this stage of course, Zack totally lacked experience in developing relationships. The whole matter was embarrassingly new to him. It would take time.

Until he'd met Willie, Zack had experienced little interaction with 'normal' humans. His fellow-beings had acted out their inhumanity to man and to youngsters like him, in a grossly abusive manner. They seemed to be driven to inflict pain upon others. Just bringing this to mind gave Zack a cold shiver and momentarily made him feel quite unsure of himself. However, now he was a man, things would be different! He'd experienced inter-planetary travel with other Beings of the Universe, and this made him a unique Earth being. He'd faced the dangers of Ektar, and survived. He now also possessed knowledge that placed him far above those who would appear as threats. In addition he had his 'spiritual' strength that went far beyond the crude concepts of what the humans knew as 'power'. He was a part of *'I AM'*

He looked up to meet Willie's eyes with innocent, mute-appeal. "Thanks Willie," he said gratefully in a low voice. "Thanks for the clothes, the money, this wonderful room, the beautiful garden, and of course you Willie for being you! Is it okay if I stay?" He queried earnestly.

"Yes Zack! You may stay as long as you wish, my home is now our home!" said Willie. Tears had started in Willie's eyes as he responded to the almost pathetic and plaintive tone that had possessed Zack's voice in his asking. He walked over to Zack, warmly hugged him and said, "We're also going to have regular visits with Brett. In fact it appears that he'll be living very close by!"

Zack's face shone with a unique happiness, and for him, his feelings were indescribable. He looked at Willie searchingly.

"Do you know of any older, perhaps deserted rabbit warrens in this immediate area Willie? I was thinking that if there were, I'd ask the Space-Rabbits to join me with their wives and live close by. I would also enlarge the vegetable garden considerably!"

Willie laughed. "Yes! I knew you'd be lonely for the rabbits and them for you too! And yes, there are some older rabbit burrows on the west side of the property under the Hawthorn bushes."

"Oh! Great!" said Zack, I'll have to tell Tooky when I next see him and get the ball rolling. I fear for them in that long journey from the Hill-Clan territory to the Cottage. There are just too many predators."

"Anyway, let's have tea and a snack. What would you like for supper?"

"Anything you cook up," said Zack, "As long as it's not rabbit pie!" he added ruefully.

"You and your rabbits!" exclaimed Willie. "By the way, I really like your new outfits. How do the boots feel now?"

"Oh! Very good, I hardly know that I have them on, and I understand that is how they should be."

"Well, for supper Zack, how do you feel about a prime rib roast with Yorkshire pudding, asparagus and garlic mashed potatoes?"

"Oh that again," said Zack gloomily in jest. "I guess someone has to eat it up!" he smiled and patted Willie on the shoulder. "You know Willie, you're quite a chef! Your grub beats anything we had on the space-craft. I'm pretty well free, how can I help?" So Zack went to get some asparagus from the garden and proceeded to peel the potatoes.

"Why am I so happy Willie?" he asked. "It just feels that I belong here, although I'm really an intruder into your privacy and way of life."

Willie stopped what he was doing and came over to Zack. He gripped him by the shoulders and looking directly into Zack's blue eyes said, "Zack, never again think of yourself as an intruder, you are my family, Brett is like a brother and one cannot get much closer than that. This is your home!"

Willie had become so intense it was almost like a declaration of undying love. It brought tears to his eyes as he released Zack. Neither the feelings nor the intent were lost to Zack. He knew he was really 'home'. He'd also found a real father.

"Thank you Willie. Just thank you," said Zack humbly. "But I am a bit weird you know. I'm really sort of a wild creature, like I don't belong to the humans, except to you and Brett, and a lot of the time I prefer to run around like I did on Ektar, except I should perhaps wear a loin cloth. I didn't see any in the clothing store. Who sells them round here?"

Willie chuckled. "No one sells them here because no one wears them! But we'll figure something out. Why don't you just wear your regular shorts and forget the underwear, it's then much the same thing. You don't have to look like Tarzan you know!"

"You're right Willie, that's what I'll do, but I do need a good stave, like the one I killed the giant Arachnid with, I can put a sharp point on it. No I can't, I forgot, I sold my good knife to get pocket money so I could eat! Darn!"

"The best wood for a stave is Ash. It's remarkably good in many ways; we'll go and cut one with my small axe. As for a knife, there's a good store in the village, we'll check out what they have."

"Wow!" said Zack. "You're the greatest, but I do have one concern though, it's all money, your money; I've never asked you if you're retired or what. I know money doesn't grow on trees!"

"I'm somewhat fortunate Zack. I inherited Honeysuckle Cottage from an uncle along with a small guaranteed income which started at age fifty five. I'm okay but not wealthy. I need to grow my own vegetables and scrounge a bit here and there to make things meet. You'll have noticed I don't have a phone for example and I keep things to a minimum."

"I'll try not to be expensive," said Zack. Willie laughed as he ran this statement through his mind.

The next morning Zack started out early for the Hill-Clan territory, complete with Ash stave sharpened to a point on one end with Willie's axe. It being a warm morning already, he wore only his Ektar shorts and runners.

In an hour the Hill-Clan warrens came into sight, but as he came closer, it was Kotar and Scruff who first spotted him and gave the all clear signal to the others. The Space-Rabbits were first to greet Zack.

He sat in the clover with Tooky on his lap, and waited for the Elder Rabbits to come on the scene; and upon their arrival he put forward his proposal for the new rabbit warrens just west of the Cottage.

The Chief of the Elder Rabbits said it was up to the individuals involved. But no other Hill-Can rabbits were interested in the move except the Space-Rabbits and their wives, which was what Zack had expected. Within an hour, all those who were going to leave, assembled with Zack and they started their trek south to Woodbury. Scruff came with them in order to be close to Zack for the Braktor Project. In two hours they arrived at the Honeysuckle Warrens as Zack had named them. Some rabbits were thirsty and drank at Little Creek, while others viewed the vegetable garden, and of course Honeysuckle Cottage itself along with Willie.

When Zack opened the door, Willie was sipping on some tea one moment, and the next moment was surrounded by twelve rabbits. Willie only recognized Tooky due to his small size and extra-long ears. After introductions had been completed, all the rabbits left to open up their new homes, do repairs and all the usual things that have to be done.

After supper Zack and Willie studied the vegetable garden to see how it might be expanded and lay plans accordingly. There was plenty of water available from Little Creek to water the gardens. Zack would have his hands full. One thing he had not counted on was Tooky leaving the burrows every night to sleep with him. In fact, Trixie had a few things to say about that! Problem solved!

Next day Willie and Zack went to the sporting goods store to look at knives. Zack missed his old seven inch blade knife. He had used it to kill a giant Praying Mantis on an alien planet, and that in it self had deep significance for him.

Zack wanted a really impressive length of sharp steel. He finally found it in a gorgeous Gerber with a ten inch blade complete with sheath. It was expensive and Zack paid for it out of the cash Willie had given him. "I have another knife you might like to see, it has a seven inch blade, good steel too!" the store owner said. "Just came in the other day, fellow was short of money."

Zack gave an exclamation of surprise on seeing it. "That's my old knife," he said to Willie. "I had to sell it in order to eat last week!" The store owner smiled, "You can have it for the same price as I paid him! What do you think?"

"It's a deal," said Zack. He was glowing with happiness. When they were outside of the store Zack said, "If he knew this knife killed a giant Praying Mantis on the planet Ektar a few weeks ago, this knife would be priceless and head for a museum!"

"You're right there Zack, you made a good deal!" Willie was so proud to be seen with Zack. Everywhere eyes were drawn to him, but Zack just smiled. They returned to the Cottage with his treasured knives, and Zack knew he'd strap on his new Gerber every time he went exploring.

Two weeks from Honeysuckle Burrows opening up, Willie and Zack went to visit Brett at Sooketon.

It was here that for the first time Zack realized that the affairs of men are subject to laws, rules and regulations for the common good of all. It also came as a shock to him when they visited Brett's legal counsel that he was asked to sign some very legal looking documents.

Brett and Willie explained to Zack for the first time about the disposition of their property and assets upon the death of either one of them. He had difficulty with this input, and it sort of stunned him; but in humility and respect he obeyed their instructions Zack was a little dazed as well as grateful at the outcome of the meeting. He discovered that he really liked the young legal partner Michael Redmond, who assured him that if he were ever in any sort of trouble regardless of its nature, Zack was to contact him and he would handle the matter. He gave his card to him, and glancing at Brett and Willie saw that it had their absolute approval.

Everyone seemed vastly relieved after the legal mission, and Brett treated them all to a wonderful supper. Zack was introduced to wine for the first time. He was silent on the bus trip home. Gradually he realized that he possessed the elements of being 'well to do', but he also felt guilty because he had really done nothing to deserve such consideration.

Zack did not realize that he was regarded as a survivor of a remarkable interplanetary expedition, and had unwittingly acted as ambassador to the Ektar Federation on Ektar, as well as having similar relationships with key personnel on the planet Rat-Star including intimate friendships. Zack was a celebrity in the eyes of Brett and Willie; although he did not feel like one. Indeed, he could never reveal what had occurred to a living soul on Earth!

All Zack wanted to do for the time being was to sort of 'find himself', live semi-wild with the birds and animals, including daily interaction with the Space-Rabbits, their wives and babies. He also realized that the time would come quite soon, when all of the space-rabbit crew would join those who are 'Are Not'. The inevitable must occur sometime anyway, and his meetings with the bunnies would then have to come to a halt. The Space-Clan would eventually be just natural wild rabbits, and neither he nor they would know each other. Zack felt he would miss Tooky most of all.

Zack steadily studied his Bible which confirmed a lot of his thinking. It left multilayers of insights to be discovered. These could only be keyed by wisdom and maturity as he grew in spiritual strength over a long period of time. He mainly devoted his attention to the New Testament, which in turn often referred him to the Old Testament. He committed a huge amount of time to reading them and to scanning numerous other unrelated volumes.

But the mainstream activity that took Zack's and Willie's time each day was the research they quietly conducted in regard to Zack's clothing from Ektar. Brett was also committed to this project. They discovered there were no fabrics on Earth comparable to Zack's shorts, shirt, socks and runners. They had the fibers analyzed in various laboratories in both North America and Europe. Zack had given his shirt, socks and runners to research, but not his shorts.

He'd found that not only would the fabric compensate for heat and cold, but also seemed to form and fit to his body as he grew. The shorts were silky-smooth and the fine weave was both strong and stretchy. It was discovered that the fabric fibers could be produced synthetically with great effectiveness. Some of the final tests were conducted locally on their leased premises in the village of Woodbury.

The research into fibers and fabrics was a long, time-consuming job, but within a year it was completed. However, it left them heavily in debt with mortgages and bank overruns of several thousands in Pounds Sterling. They met with Brett's law firm and formed a company to be known as the Ektar Fabric Corporation. It was set up under the control of the young law firm partner Michael Redmond.

Michael was able to conduct confidential negotiations for Ektar Fabrics with venture capitalists, investors and major fabric producing corporations world-wide. Zack, Willie and Brett had neither the experience nor the ability to handle such a massive project, nor did they wish their simple lives to become complicated by endless and boring technicalities. They really wanted to live as simply as rabbits, especially Zack. He just wanted to greet the dawn each day by breathing deeply of the early morning scents from the gardens and woodland that surrounded them, and generally merge with life as it unfolded.

His music would be bird song and creek chatter. Above all, he wanted to walk through life each day as though he were wandering through the Garden of Eden with his Creator.

Meantime, Rudy-Rat still communicated with Zack in line with their previously established Star Alliance agreement which included the Hill-Clan. It was always evident that Zack and Rudy missed being together on some adventure, but Rudy felt sure that a meeting opportunity would present itself in the very near future.

About a year later, a total buy-out surfaced for the Ektar Fabric Corporation. It came in the form of an offer in the amount of fifty-five million dollars from a conglomerate of fabric manufacturers. A goodwill preliminary draft in the amount of ten million dollars was attached. The purchasers wished to acquire all the patents, fabric formulae and research data. Nowhere in the proposed contract was there a mention of the planet Ektar. The contract also contained a clause that paid the partners a tiny percentage of gross sales in perpetuity.

Willie, Brett and Zack sat in the law office in Sooketon looking at a piece of paper worth US.55,000,000.00. Michael Redmond was elated, and rightly so. He had performed his mission and task flawlessly. They agreed to pay him five million cash when all corporate matters had been concluded.

Michael's next assignment was to locate a major investment wealth management firm for the partnership. When this was achieved, all Willie, Zack and Brett had to do was to arrange their lives in any way they so wished. Willie thought that maybe Zack would meet a loving young woman and start a family.

On returning to Woodbury, Zack called for a meeting of the Honeysuckle Warren. He wanted to explain the wonder of that which had occurred. He also began to realize that they were after all, just rabbits!

There was nothing they really needed except for possible additional protection from predators. The rabbits were not remotely tuned to the values of man. They would have paid fifty-five million dollars for a single carrot. Money values were beyond their comprehension. Zack, Brett and Willie had a three day meeting at Honeysuckle Cottage. They relaxed and planned. The world lay at their feet.

Zack could not sleep that night, and after the others had bedded down, he got up and slipped on his Ektar shorts. Next he laced up his hiking boots, strapped on his Gerber blade, and then slowly as though drifting in a dream. In deep thought he walked the moonlit woodland pathways beyond the Cottage.

As he emerged from the trees where they joined the big meadow, there was a flash of golden light and a not so alien whirring sound. When silence and a lone nightingale provided the only night sounds, Rudy-Rat appeared it seemed out of nowhere.

"Why, Rudy! You yellow-furred flying space-rat!" Zack exclaimed in joyous voice. "I've been thinking of you. I really miss you!"

Rudy joined him also with a joyful greeting. Zack looked down on Rudy to meet his flashing gold eyes. They both embraced and danced around. Of course there was almost nothing that Rudy did not know already, so there was no catching up on the news on his part. He told Zack of his recent second trip to Ektar with two Lexcraft space-ships, one of which was owned by the Black-Rabbits and had to be returned. They had stayed for almost two weeks, training crews and getting them used to the new Tesla-Power Unit. A number of new Standard Security Procedures were introduced and had been agreed upon.

Zack again thanked Rudy and explained how dazed he felt at the recent turn of events in his life and the huge implications of unprecedented wealth. Rudy took in Zack's concern and his lack of direction in what to do next. He immediately determined that what Zack needed was a complete break to get much needed perspective.

"I have an idea," said Rudy looking fondly up at him. His eyes flashed beautiful blue and gold colors. "Why don't you go back to the Cottage, grab a shirt and a light jacket, at the same time leave a brief note for Willie and Brett. Just say, 'Gone to Rat-Star with Rudy for a few days. Don't worry! It won't affect our age differences, see you soon!'" he smiled.

Zack gasped in delight and hugged Rudy. "Oh! Rudy, yes I'll be right back!" He skipped lightly away and almost 'floated' to the Cottage door. As he opened it Tooky showed up. "I know all about it Zack, I just got a picture from Rudy! I'm here to say Good Bye!" Zack picked up little Tooky and snuggled and nuzzled him as he usually did, which sent Tooky into a sort of blissful trance. Then he scribbled the note for Willie and Brett, picked up his gear and left silently. Tooky scampered away to be with Trixie.

Meantime Rudy flew around and rounded up Scruff as he was not aware of their almost immediate departure for Rat-Star. Scruff needed to be with Zack for his Project; and Rudy also believed that Scruff would be of value in contributing his unique talents and abilities to what they might encounter on returning to Rat-Star. On the road to high inter-planetary adventure, Zack realized he was so rich in so many ways apart from money. Who else had a Tooky? And who else had a flying Space-Rat as an intimate and personal friend—and from another planet?

Clouds passed over the moon leaving the woodland in darkness, but Zack had taken the pathway many times before and knew his way. Next there came the big hay meadow, and there lying a short way off was a magnificent Lexcraft! Its fiery crystal rings slowly revolving while lights appeared on the upper deck enabling Zack to see other golden Space-Rats onboard. Rudy joined him from where he'd been standing in the tree shadows, and told him of Scruffykin's imminent arrival to accompany them.

Zack! I'm so very pleased you could come; I missed you more that you may realize! But, there's something else I have to tell you." He paused, wondering how Zack would react to what he was going to say. "You'll recall the EGR we were to deliver to the Rat-Star engineers?"

"Yes," replied Zack, "what about it?"

"Well, the area of Rat-Star assigned to such projects is similar to your Silicon Valley, but way larger. It's called Ratekra and is purposely isolated in a valley the other side of the Rotax Mountain range due to the extreme danger of the experiments they conduct there. I'll tell you Zack, the news is not good; in fact it is somewhat catastrophic!" Rudy hesitated.

"What happened?" asked Zack. He looked at Rudy incredulously, hardly believing what he heard.

"No one really knows the exact details," said Rudy, "but it appears that the Chief Engineer is as much of an ego-freak as the Chairman of the Ektar Federation was. He acted on his own as an ultimate authority; and when the staff obeyed his instructions against their better judgment and opened up the EGR container with no forethought—all Hell broke out.

They thought they were to simply check out a strange rock, but this was not the case. When we left for Earth with this Lexcraft, all communications on Rat-Star had officially ceased to exist."

"My God!" exclaimed Zack, "weren't they warned of the possible dangers?"

"Yes! But you know the type. You can't tell them anything. I don't know what we'll find when we land back on Rat-Star. Seeing Zack's concerned face, Rudy said, "No! We're not going to land in Ratekra! We'll actually put down at the Lexcraft Plant as we need a routine check-up." He smiled, and Zack relaxed.

As they entered the Lexcraft space-ship they were met by Captain Ratto and Ratfink. Just then Scruff joined them, and he and Zack were introduced to the other crew members and sat in the roomy main control-room with Rudy. Zack's head was awhirl with confusion at what Rudy had revealed.

Zack leaned back, and was strapped into the luxurious seating by a couple of quietly competent young Space-Rats. They were scheduled to depart almost immediately, but there was a minor delay. One of the golden Space-Rat engineers had to attach what he a called a 'Tooky Kit' to Zack's shoulder straps.

Zack then discovered what Tooky had not told him, namely, that he had previously arranged and received permission from Captain Ratto, that if the opportunity should ever arise he could accompany Zack on a Rat-Star trip.

Trixie had also agreed it would be good for him otherwise he would be sad-faced until Zack's return and they'd all be unhappy.

Tooky came aboard and the door silently closed. He raced across to Zack and got snuggled, nuzzled and 'blissed' before being strapped into his custom 'Tooky Kit'. The crew-members were all delighted with Tooky, and almost instantly realized that his 'imaging-abilities' were nearly the same as theirs. Tooky's eyes sparkled with intelligence and acquired wisdom.

There was a faint humming sound, and in a matter of moments Zack's blue planet Earth receded from view. He lovingly thought of Willie and Brett and their wonderful home, and of their reactions to his note. He smiled. He thought briefly of Kotar and the other space-rabbits, and then they too disappeared from mind.

Zack had become an inter-planetary traveler. He was truly a cosmic being. It seemed that at a precise moment, the perspective of his entire mind had irreversibly changed forever. The humility he felt, increased with the immenseness of the power he experienced. God alone remained. Zack smiled

"In my Father's house are many mansions," Zack quoted; as he witnessed unnamed heavenly solar systems appear one after another to vanish into Eternity. "And other sheep I have which are not of this fold, them also I must bring. Thank you Father!" Zack said in a hushed voice. "Whatever may happen, Father, You are in charge. I will obey your instructions as they are relayed to me through the Holy Spirit."

Zack's lonely thoughts were of innumerable dimensions occupying the whole of Space. It filled him with joy to have the love of his inseparable little 'Tooky' rabbit, and also of his loyal friends Rudy and Scruff. All were contained in God. "In Him we move and have our being," he whispered.

Silently, with silky-smoothness and imperceptible power, the awesome Lexcraft space-ship effortlessly hurtled at unimaginable speeds through the star-ridden universe toward Rat-Star. Zack snuggled little Tooky 'fur-ball' into his embrace, and as usual, that blissful rabbit's furry ears nestled warmly against his cheek. With an almost angelic smile, Zack yielded to sleep murmuring, "Night-night Tooky."

THE END!

Afterword

As Space Rabbits came into being, each of the bunnies revealed individual and unique personalities. They and I became more than friends; we became family! The more I got to know them—the more I loved each rabbit for what we had become, including Zack and the golden Space-Rats. We shared a close and endearing relationship.

I also discovered that rabbits have similar problems to which Humans and other Creatures are subjected—whether here on Earth or some other planet! I experienced elation at the Rabbits' success in learning and applying new life principles. Equally, I was moved to tears when certain bunnies lost their lives.

Zack's abusive life history to which I allude are reflections of my own upbringing and eventual escape from a toxic, highly dysfunctional family situation. Zack dissociated from an early age—which is the equivalent of being absent from reality for varying periods of time. As we leave him onboard the Lexcraft space-ship at twenty years of age—he still regards Humans primarily as enemies to be avoided. We trust that Brett and Willy's advice for Zack regarding a Human mate will hold true. For Zack, safety has always been associated with isolation and solitude. Rabbits immerse him in a state of euphoria. They do not exist on Rat-Star.

Throughout our Cosmic Space-Family adventures, we experienced a sharp learning-curve in adjusting to different states of consciousness. Our newly discovered levels of comprehension, once attained, could never be lost or negated. Thusly we became a new-order of Beings. Each of us advanced in his own sphere. Whether Rabbit, Rat or Human—we can never again return to being what we once were. Perchance—sometime, somewhere, among the celestial music of the stars—we may meet again!

Edwards Brothers Malloy
Oxnard, CA USA
September 4, 2014